MYRINA HOLMES

DEMONS AND WONDERS

I

MYRINA HOLMES
DEMONS AND WONDERS

ANNA TRISS

WARM PUBLISHING

WARM PUBLISHING
El Paso, Texas
www.warmpublishing.com

Original title: *Myrina Holmes: démons et merveilles*
published by Black Ink Édition
La Jarne, France

Interior design by Warm Publishing
Cover design by Scarlett
Translated from French by Iris Clark

ISBN: 978-1-958447-33-8

To Marie and Farah, my Sinful friends…

"The only way to banish a demon is sometimes to yield to it." Paule Saint-Onge

PROLOGUE

MYRINA

A beautiful night to die.

As raging flames consume the small farm lost in the middle of nowhere, I settle my butt on the seat of my motorcycle, and cross my ankles. Then I lift my head toward the Milky Way. I'm feeling rather poetic tonight. Not a single cloud obscures the twinkling lights that dot the celestial expanse like diamonds scattered on a cloak of dark velvet. Although I remain a city girl at heart, I concede to the countryside this considerable advantage: when the sky is clear, a veritable starry enchantment unfolds before the amazed eyes of the beholder.

I may not look like it with my unabashed bitch persona, but I'm a sensitive woman. Sometimes, the little girl hidden inside me makes an appearance, like right now.

Usually, she doesn't stick around for long, that little brat.

I lower my head thoughtfully toward the furnace that bathes the surrounding fields in an amber and gold glow. A blackish column stretches above the farm. That, too, is fascinating. The swirls of smoke seem to form strange, distorted silhouettes that spread their shredded wings in an attempt to escape the fire. Like demons of mist.

But it's not through fire that you overcome a demon of this kind. Trust me on that.

I pull a pack of menthol cigarettes from the pocket of my jeans and light one up. A dirty habit for my health—I agree. My life expectancy is already shortened because of my particular nature, but I further reduce it by poisoning my lungs. On the other hand, I always smoke a cigarette after a mission. For me, the smoke is inseparable from the delicious feeling of self-satisfaction over a job well done. But I should try to cut down. Ondine, my half-sister, keeps telling me that. A nicotine patch might help solve this problem, maybe.

Or not.

A shrill but fierce scream cuts through the night, interrupting my health considerations. Removing my cigarette from my mouth, I frown toward the farm.

Well, looks like one of them is still alive.

Job done, my ass!

With a flick, I toss the half-smoked cigarette to the ground, exhaling a puff of smoke, and then grip my faithful crossbow engraved with runes. I could take my gun, but I'm a purist. With a swift motion, I notch a silver-tipped bolt, cock the lever to tighten the string, and aim it toward the building, positioning my dominant eye in front of the sight. I carefully watch the open doorway, expecting to spot a huge dark mass among the flames any second now.

Hurry up, tough guy.

Time ticks away. The fire continues to do its job. A section of the roof collapses to the right with a thunderous *crash*. But nothing comes from the entrance side.

It must have just been a cry of agony. He's dead.

I slowly lower my crossbow.

Suddenly, something shatters the windowpanes.

Something big.

Something burning.

Something charging toward me at full speed, screaming in pain and fury.

Without losing my composure, I raise my crossbow, inhaling.

The giant fireball is only thirty feet away from me now. He runs as if his ass is on fire. Which is literally the case.

I press the trigger, exhaling.

My whistling bolt embeds itself in the creature's head and cuts it down in its tracks.

The demon collapses on its back, its flaming body jerking… before coming to a stop. The smell of grilled chicken fills my nostrils and awakens my barbecue craving to the point where my stomach grumbles. Too bad our apartment building doesn't allow us to have grills on the balcony.

After resting my crossbow on the bike, I approach the creature, drawing my sword with its gold handle and silver blade. Its affectionate nickname? Feather. Partly because my sword is incredibly light, and partly because I found it funny to have such a whimsical name for its function. It always surprises people the first time I reveal the name to them. They must expect something super badass like Steel Fang, Executioner's Blade, or Demon's Bane. Well, they're wrong. It's Feather, end of story.

I know—I'm an original.

Anyway.

If this were an action-horror movie, the old demon Pridefiend, with his twisted horns lying on the ground, wouldn't quite be dead. Taking me by surprise, he would spring up like a devil with claws outstretched and…

Well, you bastard! I think to myself as I see him come to life when I'm less than three feet away from him.

But he doesn't get up. He just moves his scaly arm slightly, groaning like a wounded animal. Pathetic.

Oh, poor thing.

I brandish my long Feather above him and swiftly chop off his head with a single stroke at the neck.

Well, that's one thing done, I think as the roof of the farm collapses in a cloud of smoke and embers.

The satisfaction of a job well done—nothing beats it!

As I gaze at the stars, I wipe the black blood staining my blade with a pink handkerchief embroidered with daisies that I stole from my sister.

Truly, a beautiful night to die.

The Fourteen Legions of Demons

The Sinners, Associated with the Seven Deadly Sins

The Lustspawn, demons of Lust
The Slothlings, demons of Sloth
The Greedlings, demons of Greed
The Ragebeasts, demons of Wrath
The Envyfiends, demons of Envy
The Gluttonfiends, demons of Gluttony
The Pridefiends, demons of Pride

The Virtuous, Associated with the Seven Cardinal Virtues

The Justspawn, demons of Justice
The Prudlings, demons of Prudence
The Temperlings, demons of Temperance
The Braveryfiends, demons of Courage
The Faithfiends, demons of Faith
The Hopelings, demons of Hope
The Charityfiends, demons of Charity

CHAPTER 1
HELL AND DAMNATION

"Lust is the most intoxicating of the deadly sins." ~Anonymous

MYRINA

As I open the door to my apartment, the first thing that catches my eye is unexpected.

A leather jacket sprawled across the doormat.

I let out a disappointed sigh as I step over the jacket.

Then, I stumble over a size eleven sneaker, accidentally kicking it. Just as I manage to avoid tripping over a pointed-toe stiletto lying nearby.

I spot a crumpled men's shirt, its collar stained with red, tossed haphazardly across my couch.

And there, in the middle of the living room, is a black dress adorned with rhinestones, rolled into a ball.

Following the trail of clothing, I find a faded pair of jeans on the sideboard. A torn pair of tights lays at the foot of the coffee table. Where are the socks? Ah, I spot one on top of the television. The other must have vanished into a spatiotemporal vortex.

In front of the partially open door to a bedroom, a blood-red Wonderbra catches my eye.

I start to pick up on feminine moans and male panting… tinged with pain.

It was about time I arrived.

Without hesitation, I push the door open, stepping on a thong and a pair of boxers.

The two lovers, caught up in the heat of the moment, don't hear me come in.

With her usual vigor, my older sister rides a handsome young man with blond curls on her bed. Her black curls cover her small breasts as she rolls her hips, emitting small, enthusiastic cries. Her head is thrown back, and her eyes roll back in delight. He may not notice from his perspective, but Ondine's usually sky-blue eyes have turned crimson with pleasure. I reckon he'd freak out a bit if he noticed. Though… the guy seems totally out of it. His dull eyes are locked on the ceiling. His face glistens with sweat, his limbs tremble, his cheeks are hollow… and his complexion is pallid, almost cadaverous. The imminent climax? Yes. But not only that.

With my tongue pressed against my teeth, I whistle at my half-sister. She immediately turns her head toward me, still thrusting, and gives me a smile as radiant as it is welcoming. Her lover, on the other hand, doesn't even acknowledge me.

"Myri! You're already home? I wasn't expecting you so soon!" Ondine exclaims joyfully in our native language.

"I can see that," I grumble, gesturing to her bed with a tilt of my chin.

She adopts a falsely contrite expression, shrugging her slender shoulders.

"You know the rules, though. We don't bring food into the house."

"We had nowhere else to go, Myri," she argues, tapping the young man's cheek as if he were a little dog. "He's a student; he still lives with his parents. And I didn't have any money to pay for a hotel room."

I curse as I watch the guy inhale and exhale faster and faster, his eyes wide open.

Hell and damnation, he's on the verge of a heart attack!

"Damn it, Ondine, you're going to kill him, stop!" I bark in the demon tongue. "I don't want a corpse in my house!"

"But I'm about to climax, Myri!" she protests petulantly, speeding up her hip movements.

"I'll count to three!" I exclaim threateningly. "One… Two…"

My half-sister childishly sticks her tongue out at me and moves away from her human lover with a frustrated growl.

Immediately, the young man catches his breath, and color returns to his cheeks. He blinks, disoriented, emerging from his erotic trance.

His gaze lands on Ondine, who crosses her arms over her chest, sporting a pout. My sister's eyes have returned to their normal hue.

"But why did you stop, beauty?" he asks, bewildered.

She gestures toward me, offended by my intervention.

The guy turns his head toward me, lets out a gasp of astonishment, and grabs the sheet to cover his genitals. As if I hadn't had time to see his screwdriver!

"Who are you?" he exclaims indignantly.

"Her roommate. Get out."

"What?"

I don't like to repeat myself. Maybe I should have let him die.

I grab my pistol that's tucked in my jeans and point it at him to urge him to move. The guy jumps in fear and, in a completely stupid reflex, raises a pillow to hide behind. I shake my head, casting a horrified look at Ondine. She doesn't seem particularly surprised by her lover's absurd reaction.

Where does she find these morons?

"You'd better get going, honey," she declares softly, stroking his arm.

And there you have it, a little touch of tactile hypnosis to influence him.

The guy runs off without looking back while I tuck my firearm into my waistband. The door to our apartment closes five seconds later. The idiot left naked! I hope he doesn't run into one of our neighbors on the way; we already have a bad reputation in the building, my sister and I. Mr. and Mrs. Larousse, our old neighbors on the floor, accused us of being prostitutes.

If they only knew…

"Party pooper," my sister grumbles as she heads toward her wardrobe to put on a black satin nightgown.

"Ondine, you're out of line! If I hadn't shown up before the fateful moment, he wouldn't have survived."

"Nonsense, Myri! You're always dramatizing. I have perfect control over my powers."

"Tell that to the mummified guy I found on the couch last month."

The one I had to bury in the woods in the middle of the night, on top of it all. Ondine was supposedly too tired to accompany me. I think she just didn't want to ruin the manicure she'd gotten that very morning.

"He doesn't count. He deserved it. He called me a slut while we were fucking. Just because I'm a succubus doesn't mean I can tolerate that kind of disrespect. I have my pride," she declares, shaking her long dark hair.

She shines, naturally. She has absorbed a good part of her partner's sexual energy through the sin of flesh. It's the main power of succubus and incubus. Glossy hair, peach complexion, red lips, shining irises—a bombshell. In her presence, demons drool and mortals stutter. Hence the creed of the Lustspawns: you catch more flies with honey than with vinegar. They enjoy comparing humans to insects. I don't joke about those things. It's not a joking matter.

"We. Don't. Kill. Fucking. Humans," I coldly lecture her.

"Even if they insult us?" she argues, perplexed.

"Even if they insult us." I think a legislative reminder is needed to teach her about responsibility. "You're entitled to *one* slip-up a year, Ondine. I didn't report the incident from the other night to my superiors, but I don't intend to cover for you every time. The next corpse you leave in your wake will obligate me to file an official report with the Trackers. I won't be an accomplice to another murder of a human. If you can't control yourself, feed exclusively on demons of your own kind."

"Humans taste better. You're terribly narrow-minded, Myri."

"*Justice* is terribly narrow-minded. I'm just applying it."

"You would never report me to the authorities," Ondine refutes, staring at me, a shadow of doubt in her eyes.

I deliberately remain silent. Keeping my face impassive, I simply maintain eye contact with her bewildered gaze to nurture the uncertainty within her.

She's right, of course. Although I'm threatening her like this, it's not because I like it. It's mainly to shake her up and make her realize the gravity of her mistakes. Truth be told, even if such a thing were to happen, I wouldn't betray her. I wouldn't risk her being executed by my CIT Tracker colleagues. One slip-up per demon per year—that's forgivable. The second? That's it. Three options: death, prison, or exile. I'm well aware; I regularly arrest and dispose of repeat offender demons. But Ondine is my sister, and despite the headaches she causes me, I love her with all my heart. The only thing that matters more to me than my duty is my family. I'm not one of those brainwashed soldiers who blindly obeys demonic authorities and would be willing to kill their own parents to comply with the laws. My loyalty to my superiors still has its limits.

Don't misunderstand Ondine. She's not the lovely fool she appears to be. Carefree, casual, sometimes cruel? Yes, undoubtedly. Like most Lustspawns, in fact. But she possesses the intelligence of experience. I'm twenty-four; she's a century and a half older than me.

"It's easy for you to say, Myri," she snaps bitterly. "You have the benefits of our powers without the drawbacks. You're not compelled to sleep with men to survive. You only do it to de-stress and blow off steam, but you could do without it if you had to. I can't."

I grimace. She's forgetting an important detail.

I deal with plenty of inconveniences. I'm a hybrid, part Justspawn and part Lustspawn. In other words, my dual nature is associated with both justice and lust, a virtue and a sin whose compatibility is unstable. Hence my reduced lifespan; I won't live beyond forty years. Hence also my congenital infirmity, which sometimes plagues my existence. Granted, I possess useful abilities in the context of my work that compensate—I won't deny it. Strength, speed, agility, endurance, regeneration, immunity against the powers of minor demons and others… But I would gladly trade them all for a normal human life free of handicap. I'm an outcast in the world of demons. What was originally my weakness, I turned into my strength by joining the CIT, the order of Trackers. But that doesn't mean I should rejoice in the fact that I have at most fifteen years left to live. I've resigned myself to it, that's all. I didn't have a choice.

"Let's talk about something else," I eventually say to break the tension. "Is there any meat left in the fridge? I'm starving."

"Me, too," my half-sister agrees, flashing a smile with her sharp canines.

Food is a subject that always brings us together.

***

While I fry the two XXL steaks in the skillet, Ondine, leaning on the bar, is texting one of her many demon partners. I'm addicted to cigarettes, and she's addicted to her phone. She proudly proclaims the smartphone is undoubtedly the best technological innovation of the human race. She told me when she was a young demoness in the 1880s, Bell had just invented the first telephone, and naturally, such devices were not widespread. To communicate with her lovers, she had to resort to postal services, but her passionate letters often took weeks to reach their recipients.

"How did your mission go tonight?" she inquires from behind me.

"Fine."

"How many Pridefiends were there on the farm?"

"I didn't count. Eight, maybe. Or twelve. Or fifteen. To be honest, I have no damn clue. In the heat of battle, I tend to overlook the details."

She mumbles something. With the sizzling of the cooking, I can't hear her. I ask her to speak up.

She raises her voice. "A gang of outlaws, Myri?"

"Yes. Rebels planning an attack to take down a Virtuous Magistrate. A tip-off from an informant." I open a cupboard, looking for a blue cylindrical box. "By Satan, didn't you buy salt when you went grocery shopping?"

The legend that salt is the weakness of demons? Another load of crap.

"It's your fault; you should have written it on the list," she grumbles.

Forget about the salt. I'm not going to argue with her over such a trivial matter.

"Myri, I have something to tell you."

I hate it when she introduces a topic like that. Usually, it spells trouble. I turn to her, spatula in one hand, the other hand on my hip. She puts her phone down on the bar, sending me a hesitant look from beneath her long, curled black lashes. As if her seductress act is going to work on me!

"I'm seeing someone, Myri."

"So what?"

One more, one less…

"Not just sex, Myri. Dating. He knows I sleep with others to feed, obviously. It doesn't bother him. He has affairs, too. We have an open relationship, and it's only the beginning, but… I think it could be serious."

Well, well, well… Now that's news. It's the first time Ondine has been involved with a man. I can't help but smile.

"Who's the lucky guy, sis?"

She clears her throat.

My smile fades. I have a feeling I'm not going to like what she's about to say. "Sis, reassure me. He's not human, right?"

That would be dangerous for both of them. Liaisons between demons and mortals aren't prohibited by our laws, but they're strongly discouraged. We have a big secret to preserve: our existence. Besides, humans are fragile. They die easily.

"No, no, he's a demon."

"A Virtuous demon, is that it?"

She lets out a crystalline laugh as if I had just cracked a joke. "Not at all. He has no virtue; he admits it himself."

"Ondine, what species?"

"A Hybresang."

My eyes widen like saucers. Good lord! There aren't that many Hybresangs in Infernum. I only know one by reputation. And I have no desire to meet him in person. Ever.

"Kelen Wills?" I breathe, incredulous.

She nods.

Damn it all.

I would have preferred a thousand times it was a human or a Virtuous demon.

Even Lucifer would have been a wiser choice!

"Myri, I know what you're thinking," she says, taking the lead. "But he's not like the rumors describe him. He is—"

"Worse?"

"No, different," she cautiously nuances.

So, if I rely on her evasive answer, the prejudices circulating about Kelen Wills are accurate.

"How can you be dating someone like that, Ondine?"

"Well, he's not that unbearable. His arrogant and ambitious jerk side adds to his charm. His belligerent impulsiveness makes him even more virile. His authoritative selfishness doesn't bother me that much, he's not as greedy and lazy as they say, and he's the best lover I've ever had," she lists dreamily.

I scratch my arm; her words give me hives. She's completely masochistic…

"And besides, he's super sexy, even more so than most Lustspawn males. I understand why some demonesses fight to spend a night with him, Myri."

This distressing remark makes my eardrums bleed!

"He rules the Legion of the Ragebeasts with an iron fist. As for his gluttony, it's impressive to watch, I assure you! The other night at the human restaurant, there was an all-you-can-eat buffet. Kel ate everything, Myri. It took him almost two hours. The waiters and customers were all speechless. Even when he's gorging himself, he's hot. I was getting hot flashes."

I grimace. Here is my dear older sister in all her glory! Drawn to vice in all its forms. That bastard of a Hybresang Magistrate will hurt her, that's for sure. If she gets too attached to him, he'll inevitably break her heart. And it'll be up to me to pick up the pieces.

But it's her business, after all. If I get involved, it's likely to backfire on me again. So, for once, I decide to keep my big mouth shut. I pivot toward the stove to flip my rare steaks in the pan.

All I can hope for is that their affair won't last and that I won't have to rub shoulders with the worst demon who has ever set foot in our world.

CHAPTER 2

HIS IDLE MALICE

"I prefer a comfortable vice to a virtue that bores." ~Molière, Amphitryon

Kelen

Hell is paved with good intentions.

The subconscious is paved with sins.

Mine in particular.

Especially when it's based on very pleasant memories.

I revel in lust with two, stunning, naked Lustspawns in my bed. Slender twins with golden skin and long fiery hair. One of them, pressed against my back, skillfully unbuttons my shirt while the other peppers my throat with passionate kisses, emitting hoarse moans. I run my right hand over the sculpted thigh of the succubus facing me while my left hand lingers on the silky buttocks of her sister. Girls tend to be easily jealous of each other; I always have to make sure to take care of both at the same time if I want to avoid it escalating. Fighting adds spice to the bed, of course, but today, I have no desire to stain my white sheets with black blood.

The twin behind me opens my shirt and pulls it back to strip me of it. The other takes advantage to slide her moist lips along my bare chest. I tense with pleasure as four hands unfasten the belt of my pants. The two sisters burst into laughter, complicit in debauchery. I frown as I feel a pair of fangs brush against the bulge of my abs. I seize the culprit by the chin to lift her head just as the other demon, behind me, lowers my pants.

"Do you wish for me to retract my fangs, Your Dark Eminence?" she inquires with a mischievous smile, her large cinnamon eyes locked into mine.

After a moment of consideration, I slowly shake my head.

That could be… interesting.

The Lustspawn runs the tip of her tongue over her lips and fangs, then leans forward, opening her mouth, and—

"Kelen," a familiar male voice calls near my ear.

I move my head from side to side, letting out an annoyed grunt as if trying to shoo away a mosquito pestering me during my sleep. "Leave me alone, Sam. Can't you see I'm sleeping?" I grumble under my breath.

"Kel, forgive me for insisting, but we're in the middle of an important meeting," my faithful lieutenant retorts in a tense whisper.

I open one eye. Then the other.

Damn, he's right. I was so bored that I dozed off during a council of my demonic staff. As a result, everyone is staring at me in stunned silence. Thirty pairs of eyes are fixed on my majestic self as I slouch on my throne, arms crossed over my chest.

I sit up, dignified in my chair, clearing my throat and adjusting the silk tie around my neck. My armor was too dirty from yesterday's activities—dried blood is a damn stubborn substance—so I opted for my midnight-blue bespoke suit this morning. I stand out from the other demons, but I couldn't care less. I have a thousand times more class than all of them combined, that's for sure.

Serena, my fiercest Ragebeast captain, stands before the long table, her iPad in hand. She was probably reciting the figures related to our legion's logistics and the number of pacts sealed with humans. She glares at me with carmine eyes as if I had just inflicted the worst insult upon her.

She knows me, though. She knows perfectly well that when I'm bored, I sleep. It's entirely her fault. If her report wasn't so soporific, I would have stayed awake.

"What's on the agenda?" I ask calmly, accustomed to being the center of general attention—whether it be fearful, admiring, or hateful, for that matter.

"The reproduction of otters in Hungary," Serena declares coldly.

"Which explains why I fell asleep," I retort casually as Sammael coughs to conceal his amused chuckle.

A sigh of annoyance shakes Serena's chest under her red breastplate, which is adorned with my emblem. The golden lion's head holding a dagger between its jaws is the symbol of the Enraged, the most formidable army of the fourteen demonic legions. Why is it so formidable, you might ask? Because I lead it, of course.

"Your Idle Malice, do I need to start my monthly report from the beginning?" the captain mutters through her teeth as I yawn like a tired beast.

"No, summarize. I have a crucial appointment in ten minutes," I decide, waving my hand dismissively in her direction.

I'm lying, of course. Even if I did have a real appointment, punctuality would be the least of my concerns. I'm always late. It's a principle I never deviate from.

Serena daggers me with her eyes again before resuming her presentation.

A slight approving smile forms on my lips. *Your Idle Malice…* Well, I must admit this combination of terms suits me rather well. Overall, I'm not offended by these kinds of remarks when they come from my close associates. I have a sense of self-deprecation, unlike the other six Grand Masters of the Sin Legions, who take themselves terribly seriously. Susceptible demons can't stand mockery and criticism because they lack self-confidence. Not my case. I'm fully aware of my immense worth; it's been proven for centuries. And when my enemies publicly challenge it with disrespect I can't tolerate—which doesn't happen often, thank Satan—it doesn't affect me. Simply because I kill them before losing my temper. Shedding the blood of fools is a powerful sedative.

And to think I'm portrayed as a hot-tempered being. I've never understood why I'm burdened with that reputation.

Five minutes later, as I'm on the brink of dozing off, the ringtone of my smartphone blares loudly in the meeting room. *Highway to Hell* by AC/DC. The other demons are instructed to silence their phones under the threat of having their thumbs chopped off—not a big deal, thumbs grow back for us—but this rule doesn't apply to me. I'm the boss. Might as well enjoy the privileges that come with that higher status.

Containing her fury with great effort, Serena rolls her eyes and roughly sets her tablet down as I answer my phone, earning only blasé looks from my underlings.

"His Idle Malice speaking."

"Forgive me for disturbing you during a council, Your Cruel Eminence, but we're facing a major incident," announces my succubus secretary in a sugary voice.

"The Apocalypse?"

That event isn't scheduled until the next century, or so I believe. Maybe I should check my calendar more often.

"Close. A Braveryfiend Rebel has infiltrated your mansion in an attempt to steal digital documents from your desktop computer. He was apprehended by your elite guards while trying to crack your password. Should I contact the Tracker Order for them to handle it, Mr. Wills?"

"Absolutely not. Keep those CIT bastards out of my affairs." Damn, what's her name again? This succubus has only been in my service for five decades, and I've only fucked her three times, so I haven't quite remembered her name yet. Better stick to a nickname to be safe. "Bring the prisoner here, darling."

"Yes, Your Vile Lordship."

Three minutes later, the door swings open, revealing two Ragebeast soldiers dragging in a Rebel with a swollen face and a vacant expression. Silver handcuffs bind his wrists. As I examine the Braveryfiend spy with silver scales stained with golden blood, I stroke my chin, weighing the various options for extracting information from him. I wouldn't be opposed to a little torture session to stretch my fingers and unwind my mind before indulging in my third breakfast of the morning, but… why waste unnecessary energy, after all? My telepathic powers work perfectly fine on minor demons.

So, I delve into his mind. Unsurprisingly, he doesn't remember his identity or his past. No faces or names emerge from his nebulous memory. This Braveryfiend has been hypnotized before being sent off, like most of the Rebel lackeys. I simply detect his written mission: to discreetly infiltrate my office, hack into my personal computer, and send all my confidential files to a mysterious email address, anonymous666@hellonearth.com.

I share my discovery with my staff and put the fate of the

prisoner to a vote. I present them with two options: hand him over to his former Braveryfiend legion as a goodwill gesture toward our Virtuous rivals or execute him right here and now. The Rebel doesn't react to my words; he seems completely disconnected from reality.

Unanimously, all thirty members of my council raise their hands when I mention his execution.

I wouldn't go as far as to say I've established a democratic system within my legion, but occasionally, I consult my officers before making decisions to give the impression their opinions matter to me. It's a managerial strategy, you see.

I delegate the deadly chore to Sammael, who draws his serrated executioner's sword as the two Ragebeast guards pin the prisoner face down. A precaution that's not really necessary, as he doesn't struggle. With vacant eyes, the Rebel doesn't flinch as my lieutenant's gleaming blade rises above him.

Sunk into my throne, I suppress another yawn of boredom as Sam's sword cuts the head off the spy, splattering the stone wall with a spray of golden blood.

Smooth sailing.

My lieutenant always proves himself impeccably efficient when it comes to executions.

I could have done it myself, but I wasn't going to dirty my fine suit for a pathetic Rebel lackey.

***

I consider myself a philosophical demon in my spare time.

Let's look at an example.

As I was saying before I got lost in my salacious dream, hell is paved with good intentions, and the subconscious is paved with sins.

Morality and propriety are the social barriers that obstruct the dark truth of the soul. Good and evil are general ideas designed to control some and categorize others. The saint who swears he has never thought of inflicting pain is a liar and an impostor. He deserves to burn in purifying flames or be sacrificed on the devil's altar.

The Virtuous are nothing but hypocrites who don't own up to their secret vices.

Justice is blind.

Prudence is the realm of the hesitant.

Courage is an abstraction.

Temperance is synonymous with cowardice.

Faith is the domain of the weak.

Hope belongs to the credulous.

Charity is merely a selfish means of self-valorization in the eyes of others.

They are just words. Concepts. They are never absolute, only relative. I know human nature and demonic nature.

In his work *1984*, George Orwell's character, Winston, said, *"I hate purity. I hate goodness! I don't want any virtue to exist anywhere. I want everyone to be corrupt to the bone."*

I echo his words. I have thought of them for centuries.

And if the only true virtue were truth? Then the roles would be reversed, and we Sinners would be the Virtuous ones. Because we claim our vices. We don't hide behind the masks of morality and propriety. We don't repress our desires, emotions, and impulses. We hold the key to truth. And therefore, to freedom.

My words are not fueled by my pride. They reflect the reality most people deny with such bad faith.

After this philosophical aside, let's get back to the heart of the matter.

My death threat email.

From: Kelen Wills

To: anonymous666@helloneearth.com

Subject: Displeasure.

Rebels,

Your futile attempts to hinder me are beginning to wear thin. So far, I have shown leniency toward you, but your latest provocation has momentarily irked me. If you persist in your madness of trying to harm me in the execution of my duties, I'll take great pleasure in personally tracking each of you down, one by one, and subjecting you to suffering so severe that the ancient Scandinavian practice of the blood eagle will seem infinitely merciful compared to the medieval tortures I'll reserve for you before deigning to grant you the comforting sweetness of death.

Most unfriendly regards,

Kelen Wills.

And I attach to my email a close-up photo of the severed head of the Braveryfiend Rebel to illustrate my words.

There you have it. The whole truth, only the truth, nothing but the truth. I have been transparent about my intentions.

QED.

Am I not the most virtuous of Sinners?

CHAPTER 3
THE CALL OF DUTY

"Associated with a woman, the devil himself loses the game." ~Polish Proverb

MYRINA

Since time immemorial, portals have existed between the world of humans and Infernum, the world of demons. The Arcadus connects the two parallel planes: mirrors, paintings, closets, doors, windows. A demonic rune, invisible to humans, is engraved on each Arcadus so we can identify them at a glance. According to the official census of the Trackers, there are no fewer than a million portals scattered throughout the world. Humans can't pass through them unless accompanied by one of us, and this exception requires a government visa signed by a major Tracker.

However, we demons can use the portals at will to move between universes. Each of us holds an assigned magical badge that serves as a timecard so our comings and goings are rigorously controlled by our authorities. Indeed, some demons are prohibited from passing through due to their misdeeds. If they attempt to cross an Arcadus using their personal badge, the portal doesn't open, and the demonic rune doesn't light up. To counter this problem, the Rebels have resorted to trafficking Arcadus cards in order to hide with impunity in the mortal world. Numerous stolen or counterfeit badges circulate here and there, making my job as a hunter all the more difficult.

Ondine and I have chosen to live among humans because of my special profession and the duality of my nature, but this isn't the case for all demons. Some of them despise mortals so much they hardly ever go into their world.

In any case, demons have a lifespan of several centuries, even millennia for some particularly powerful Sinners and Virtuous. As a result, it's difficult for demons to form attachments with mortals. Such things remain rare but have happened in the past. These fleeting friendships and loves generally end tragically. I learned that the hard way.

In Infernum, the laws of physics are different from those you know. Don't look for scientific, environmental, or astronomical coherence. There are two suns during the day—one red and one black—and two moons at night—one silver and one golden. There are no seasons, no rain, no tides. On the surface, there are no oceans or rivers, only pools of warm water trapped in the mountains. Otherwise, most water sources are underground. Since demons hardly need to hydrate, the lack of water isn't an issue. Furthermore, gravity is weaker in Infernum. To give you an idea, it's equivalent to that of the moon, which always requires a short time to adapt to during my stays. The ambient temperature varies between sixty-eight degrees at night and one hundred degrees during the day. Vésave, the colossal volcano that stands at the center of Infernum, erupts once a century before going back to sleep. Fourteen armored megalopolises of skyscrapers, twice as high as those of humans, housing millions of busy demons, are governed by the fourteen leaders of the demonic legions, the Magistrates.

I was born in Infernum twenty-four years ago, but I spent my childhood on Earth. My mother is a Lustspawn and my father a Justspawn. I am the *unnatural* product of a forbidden love by our laws. Indeed, Sinners and Virtuous aren't allowed to officially unite. But as you can imagine, it happens sometimes. Even demons have feelings, and as a human proverb claims, *"The heart has its reasons, which reason knows nothing of."*

Before being uncovered by the Trackers, my parents and I formed a small, almost ordinary, happy family. Then, when I was ten years old, my parents were found by demonic authorities and were judged for concealing my existence. Their punishment was exile in the Limbo, a secret parallel plane between the two worlds, because my Justspawn grandfather, a former Magistrate who still had influence over the big shots of Infernum, interceded on behalf of my parents to spare them from death. As for me, I was entrusted to the order of the Trackers, who trained me and made me one of their own. I didn't have a say in any of this, obviously. My life changed radically overnight.

These unions are strictly prohibited because the combination of genes from a Sinner demon and a Virtuous demon can result in three consequences.

The first possibility: an early miscarriage, the most common case.

Second possibility: deformed monsters, beings more akin to ferocious and stupid beasts than demons. These extremely violent and hungry creatures, whom we call the Soulless, are systematically killed by the Trackers because they can't be controlled or tamed. Once, I was confronted with the corpse of a mother devoured by her Soulless baby just after its birth. It wasn't a pretty thing to see. Yes, you need nerves of steel in my line of work.

Finally, the third possibility, the rarest: my case, a hybrid demon who possesses the genetic characteristics of both parents, specific powers stemming from her bloodline… but burdened with a physical anomaly and a reduced lifespan in return. My old Tracker master told me that I'm only the fourth half-Sinner, half-Virtuous hybrid in Infernum since our world began. The other three have been dead for ages, so I'm currently the only living mixed blood of my kind.

Anyway, purebloods are extremely rare nowadays. Mentalities and customs are changing… *About time, I'd say!* Sinners and Virtuous are less concerned with breeding within species. My sister Ondine, for example, is three-quarters Lustspawn and one-quarter Envyfiend… But she's not considered a true hybrid because she only has the blood of Sinner demons in her veins.

On the other hand, my sister's new guy, Kelen Wills, is a true Hybresang. I don't know why the Magistrates and Trackers make such a distinction between him and other mixed-blood Sinners, but apparently, he's… what absurd term did I hear on Radio Hell the other day? *The genetic future of Infernum's Sinners* or some such nonsense? In the eyes of the Sinner Magistrates, this Hybresang, over thirteen hundred years old, is a genetically perfect being, endowed with the seven demonic vices and, consequently, devoid of the weaknesses inherent in each species. Some even claim he's the most powerful demon in the world. A potential megalomaniac bastard, if you ask me!

As for the Trackers, they are made up of Sinners and Virtuous warriors. If each legion has its militia, we somehow represent the demon police. Long before I was born, they called this service the FBI, Federal Bureau of Infernum, but humans took over the acronym in the 1930s to name their own order, and my superiors renamed the bureau CIT, Central Intelligence of Trackers. When disputes or conflicts erupt between the two camps, threatening the balance of our demon society, we intervene to reconcile the heated minds. We're neutral, at least on paper—in practice, it's a bit more complex. Moreover, believing that the Virtuous are less vicious than the Sinners would be a cliché. You can't judge a book by its cover in our profession. Recently, we've also been hunting the Rebels, deserters who plot in the shadows to overthrow the government of Infernum. Our authority is supposed to be recognized by all demons. Our creed: maintain order and peace at all costs.

When I woke up, I had no idea of the extent of what was going to hit me today… or the royal mess I was about to get myself into.

✳✳✳

My phone vibrates on the bedside table so hard it makes the glass lamp shake. I open one eye to look at the name displayed on the screen. My boss. I grab my phone with a sigh, turn up the volume, answer, and press the device against my right ear as I yawn loudly into the microphone as a greeting.

"Am I waking you up, Myri?" a cavernous voice grumbles. "It's eleven AM, though."

"Rough night, boss."

"You weren't working last night."

"Tell that to the obese Gluttonfiend who decided to traffic organs in the club where I was hanging out with my sister. His damn fists were the size of a pair of anvils."

The Gluttonfiends, demons of the sin of Gluttony, have a nasty tendency toward cannibalism. The one I happened to corner, by sheer luck in the club's locker room, was carrying two pink Hello Kitty coolers containing human hearts and brains obtained from the hospital morgue. He'd planned to sell his illegal goods to three of his hungry buddies… who bolted like scared rabbits when they saw me coming.

This kind of thing always falls on me.

"Did you get him, Myrina?"

"Yeah, boss," I mumble, rubbing my still-sore sternum despite my rapid regenerative ability.

The fatso got a good beating, a century behind bars, and a fine of 10,000 Forks, but before I could snap my silver handcuffs around his chubby wrists, that bellyaching jerk managed to land a punch in my chest that sent me flying sixteen feet across the room. If I had been human, he would have fractured my ribcage, and I would have died on the spot. If I had been an ordinary demon, I would have survived, but I would have been hurting a lot more waking up today. Fortunately, as a hybrid, I'm tougher. Of course, if I had caught this Sinner in the act of devouring a human, I would have had the legal right to execute him on the spot. Such gruesome murder isn't considered a slip-up by the law, but an inexcusable crime.

In short, my night of hookups went down the drain. The only guy I brought home last night was a massive, unconscious Gluttonfiend that I had to drag by the feet to the nearest Arcadus with the intention of tossing him into the CIT prison on Infernum. The worst part was that the dealer was so bulky his body wouldn't fit through the narrow gate frame. So, I was forced to chop off one of his arms at the shoulder, but since I didn't have my sword with me— arrest and amputation weren't part of the plan, I remind you—I had to hack away at his thick flesh with whatever I had on hand: a simple knife. It took me a long time. I had to knock him out several times during my chore because he kept waking up screaming in pain every ten minutes. Those Gluttonfiend demons are real wimps. They always go overboard to look for sympathy.

"I have an unidentified Faithfiend corpse on my hands, found this morning in a human church, Myrina," my boss announces over the phone. "I thought of you."

"Why?" I hiss suspiciously.

"Because you're my best asset, you're a workaholic, and you live for challenges."

"Yea right, Zagam. You thought of me mostly because no Tracker at HQ wants the case—admit it."

"You know how the guys are… They're not too keen on stepping out of their little comfort zone."

I got it. Most of my devoted colleagues at the CIT scrupulously avoid going to Earth to carry out their duties. They prefer to stay on Infernum to slap fines on minor demons who break the aerial traffic code and participate in putrid burp contests in the offices.

"Malphas is already on scene," my superior adds. "He hypnotized the human cops to make them scram from the crime scene. The field is clear."

No, damn it! Not him!

"You know I don't work in pairs, Zagam."

Especially not with Malphas. I'm not that crazy!

"He's just there to support you today, Myrina. You'll be the one in charge of the investigation. If you need a hand with something, he'll help you," my boss asserts sharply.

"He can handle it all by himself. I don't want to see him."

"Malphas is already working on another case simultaneously. I know it's not easy between you two because of your personal history but make a little effort and suck it up for the job!" Zagam orders me imperiously.

Not easy? That's an understatement! I'd bet a gold bar that Malphas volunteered to be the scout when my boss announced to the Trackers that he was considering assigning me to the investigation. I'm not proud of myself on this one. *Once*, I made the mistake of mixing my professional and personal life by sleeping with my colleague Malphas, and ever since… well, he harasses me every chance he gets. Despite me rudely rebuffing him every time, he persists in heavy flirting against all reason. Being a Pridefiend, his inflated ego couldn't handle that I slipped away while he was sleeping and, more importantly, that I didn't call him back after our night. He texted me the other day saying he was in love with me, but I don't believe it for a second. All he wants, in my opinion, is another steamy night… so he can get back at me by pulling the same stunt the next day.

Despite his three centuries, that whore demon is a real kid at heart. He's not inherently evil, but he has the intellectual depth of a rotten clam. His only interest in life: collecting beer caps between two women. You get the picture, right? Sure, he's as handsome as a god—and he knows it; he never leaves home without his pocket mirror, mini perfume spritzer, and comb! But he's not much in the brains department and has a downright detestable macho temperament. I deeply regret the night we spent together a few months ago. Plus, it wasn't even worth it; I only had a lackluster orgasm… while Malphas boasted about giving me ten before I succumbed to his advances in an Infernum bar, my mind clouded by the demons' potent absinthe, Dragon's Bile.

By the way, I also couldn't help but notice that the huge frontal horns he takes so much pride in under his demonic form aren't proportional to the attributes he sports in his human appearance. If only he knew how to use them… I'm not talking about the horns, of course.

Anyway, Zagam leaves me no choice. I'm going to have to deal with it, unfortunately.

After jotting down the coordinates of the crime scene and hanging up with my boss, I head to take a shower, mentally preparing myself for a confrontation with Malphas today and to examine the corpse of an unnamed Faithfiend.

Yup, I sense a crappy day is looming ahead for you, Myrina Holmes.

CHAPTER 4
MAGISTRAL INTERVIEW

"There exists a sin more destructive and intoxicating than lust. It is the passion for power." ~Jean-Charles Harvey, *The Paradises of Sand*

MYRINA

After my shower, I find Ondine on the living room couch, engrossed in a pedicure, a red nail polish brush between her fingers. With her feet up on the coffee table, she occasionally glances at the television screen, which is tuned to channel 666 of Infernum. Hell TV is only available to demons; it's a magical channel inaccessible to humans. My sister is casually watching a historical documentary about the most famous Sinners in our world. Photos, anecdotes, and biographies flash across the screen.

Not really her usual style… Ondine prefers the program *Cavern or Catacombs for Sale* about real estate and the latest controversial show, *The Reality TV Demons*, where seven Sinners and seven Virtuous are locked in a huge castle for seven days with weapons and deadly traps hidden everywhere. The only rule? Survive, of course. The winner pockets a million Forks, Infernum's currency. I came across it the other night while zapping. It's the goriest, most immoral, and nauseating show I've ever seen, but my sister assured me it's breaking all the ratings records. When a demon contestant becomes too unpopular—because they're a bit too nice, generally—viewers can vote by text to have them killed by another contestant, choosing the method of execution themselves.

"Hey, sis, sleep well?" she asks cheerfully.

I grunt in response.

"I just made your coffee, it's on the countertop," Ondine says, pointing her brush toward the kitchen.

I grunt in thanks.

"The host is going to interview Kelen, live, in three minutes!" my big sister exclaims, excited as a flea on acid.

I grunt with an indifferent expression.

"Oh, Myri, come on, come watch TV with me. You don't even know what my boyfriend looks like!"

"Yep. And honestly, I couldn't care less," I mutter as I go to fetch my steaming cup of coffee.

"But it's an unprecedented event! Kel has never granted interviews to demon journalists. He's categorically refused to have photos of himself published in Infernum magazines until now. A few blurry shots leaked in the '80s, but the paparazzi suddenly disappeared after that."

That Hybresang is touchy. He doesn't like disobedience, evidently.

"He maintained the mystery surrounding him to enhance his aura of danger among his enemies. But he recently changed tactics. His new agent advised him to work on his public image more to serve his political ambitions."

"What political ambitions?" I ask, suddenly curious about this combination of words.

"They'll talk about it in the interview, if you want to know," Ondine sings with a smile, tapping the spot next to her on the couch.

Sly succubus.

With an annoyed sigh, I sit down on the couch, stirring my overly sweetened coffee. I need my daily dose of sugar to start the day on the right foot. I can feel in my gut that I'm going to need it today.

"It won't last too long, will it? I don't want to be late for work; I have a date with a fresh corpse."

"Barely five minutes," Ondine assures me, rolling her eyes.

The report on Wolfgang the Flayer ends with a photo of a demon hanging from a weeping willow by its tail. The charming and dynamic presenter, Fianèle, with his silver ponytail, continues on the set, "Now, the exclusive interview you've all been waiting for!"

Thunderous applause, whistles, and enthusiastic cheers echo in the background.

"You've all heard of Kelen Wills, the Magistrate Hybresang at the helm of the Ragebeasts for several centuries, but few demons have had the privilege of meeting him… and even fewer have had the privilege of surviving that fateful encounter!"

Laughter erupts from the audience. I grit my teeth, already irritated by this introduction. It's as ridiculous as it is theatrical.

The ass-licker presenter waits for silence to return to the set and raises a hand toward a curtain of purple velvet. "Ladies and gentlemen, I have the honor to present *the* Sinful Demon in power. I give you Keeeeelen Wills!"

A stunning brunette Lustspawn with a plunging neckline and a mini-skirt—a Megan Fox look-alike—pulls back a curtain with a Miss World smile, revealing her sharp fangs. A tall, athletic figure appears on the screen to the excited cheers and loud applause of the audience.

Kelen Wills.

The camera zooms in on his silhouette.

Of course, the detestable Hybresang doesn't wave to the spectators, nor does he deign to give them a friendly smile or a complacent look. He ignores them as he crosses the set with an assured… no, reeking of arrogance. The Virtuous presenter stands up from his desk to nervously extend his hand. Kelen Wills gives a condescending glance at his trembling fingers and gives him a *monumental* cold shoulder, which seems to disorient Fianèle. The Magistrate Sinner leisurely unfastens two buttons on his suit jacket before sitting down in his black chair like a king settling on his throne before his court. All that's missing are the trumpets and the red carpet to complete the picture.

Pathetic.

In my peripheral vision, I see Ondine giving me a sideways glance, gauging my reaction. But I don't flinch. It's not for nothing that they call me the Amazon among the Trackers. Firstly, because the name my parents chose to baptize me with is that of a fierce Amazon queen from Greek mythology. Secondly, because I'm known for being a hardened warrior who doesn't often show her emotions.

Anyway, right now, Kelen Wills only inspires one emotion in me: immeasurable contempt. I don't understand all the demons who adore him like a deity. This guy's ego is so big that a tank wouldn't be enough to contain it. Just seeing him on screen infuriates me.

If his supreme jerk character didn't revolt me so much, I might find him attractive. A little bit. In his own way. *No, stop it, Myri.* Okay, fine, this fucking demon is undoubtedly the hottest man I've ever seen in twenty-four years of life, but there's no way I'm admitting that detail to my sister. I'd rather get scabies. Or cholera, even. So, at this moment, my face doesn't show any emotion as I take in every feature of Kelen.

Dark angels don't exist, but if they did, they would undoubtedly take on the sublime appearance of that demon.

Even through the screen barrier, I can feel that he exudes Vice with a capital V through every pore. Because not only does Kelen Wills embody sin, but he also inspires it in others.

First example, the sin of gluttony.

Thick, perfectly tousled, dark chocolate hair with golden highlights under the studio lights.

Flawless caramel-colored skin.

Luscious lips of incredible sensuality that resemble forbidden fruits and make you want to sink your teeth into them.

Large, shimmering, golden-brown eyes far too bright and penetrating to be human… that invite you to break morality in all its forms.

Now, the sin of pride.

His masculine features are outrageously magnificent. Harmonious. Chiseled. Proud. His forehead is broad, his eyebrows well defined and black, his nose straight, his cheekbones prominent, his jawline square, and, above all, the bastard has *a dimple on his chin*. I'm a total sucker for dimples on the chin. In fact, it's even the first of the four things I check out in a man: dimple on the chin, eyes, hands, and butt. Stunning eyes, powerful hands, muscular butt… but no dimple on the chin? I'm not interested, move along, buddy! I don't know why I've been fixated on this absurd detail since I was a teenager. Maybe because it looks like a permanent and vertical mini smile on the chin…

Once, while I was drunk—again!—I hooked up with a guy with an unattractive face because I found his chin dimple very attractive. Well, you get the idea.

Next is the sin of wrath.

It can be summed up in two words: His gaze.

He's royally pissed off about being interviewed. I don't know if the presenter picked up on it, but my vigilant Tracker eye detected the nuance. Deep within Kelen's dark eyes burns a threatening and uncontrollable flame that could easily turn into a devastating blaze at any moment. He sends a warning message to the rest of the world: "Danger is contained for now, but not chained."

Last, but certainly not least from my point of view, the sin of lust.

An immense muscular body highlighted by his impeccable suit, overflowing with bestial sex appeal characteristic of his hot-blooded incubus lineage. No wonder the majority of women soak their lingerie over him! Ondine already knows what's hidden under his white shirt, jacket, and pants, and for a very brief moment, I feel a microscopic twinge of jealousy because of the hormones associated with my cursed succubus heritage. Yes, let's be realistic, with a hottie like that in her bed, the result must be explosive. And knowing my sister's taste in lovers, I'm sure Kelen is the mega-dominant type in bed. She likes to alternate between the two extremes by sleeping with docile blond humans and dominant dark-haired demons.

Finally, there you have it.

I scowl. Okay, I'll admit it. Her new boyfriend Hybresang is a devilishly sexy bad boy, who could tempt a nun and make her question her vow of chastity. But he's a *huge* malicious jerk, and that makes all the difference.

Hence my immeasurable contempt.

Kelen is more slouched than seated in his comfortable armchair, his right leg raised and bent, ankle resting on his left knee, forearms resting on the armrests. Ondine giggles at his casual posture, which contrasts with his stylish suit. He looks like a cheeky and lazy teenager summoned to a disciplinary hearing. I understand better what my sister meant by *working on his public image*. Kelen's agent might disapprove of the laissez-faire attitude he's displaying. I wouldn't be surprised if he yawned in the middle of the interview, honestly. The sin of sloth in all its sluggish splendor. He reminds me of a lion lounging in the shade, waiting for his lionesses to go hunting and bring back prey for him to devour. In my opinion, like the other Magistrates, he probably doesn't often dirty his hands with blood. But... I also don't forget the latent anger that haunts his gaze. Lazy perhaps, but formidable for sure. A lion is still a lion, and it can easily tear your head off with a single bite.

"Thank you for graciously taking the time to grant us this interview, Your Dark Grace," begins the smarmy host, nodding behind his desk.

"Thank you for having me," replies Kelen in a voice of indifference, indicating he couldn't care less.

A deep, charismatic voice that fits the character perfectly, by the way. As soon as he spoke, a captivated silence fell over the set... while demon spectators murmured as the host thanked the Magistrate.

Honestly, it completely escapes me how someone like him manages to command such deference solely through his physical presence. If he were a human among humans, I wouldn't be surprised, but we're demons. To earn the respect of one's peers and be credible in a world like ours, one must prove oneself and fight fiercely. Kelen Wills is exempt from this... because he was born Hybresang. This extreme favoritism isn't normal, damn it. While I've been marginalized by my mixed heritage, he's reaped all the benefits of his hybridization! This guy has had a silver spoon in his mouth for centuries, and no one has ever thought to take it out and slap him with it. Everything goes his way; nothing can stop him. A spoiled rotten brat playing war games, nothing less!

God, my sister's new boyfriend has only uttered six words, but he's already driving me crazy. I sip three mouthfuls of coffee, urging myself to keep my cool. I think Kelen is triggering an irritating crime of being too damn good-looking. In other words, if he were significantly less attractive, I might find him a tad more likable.

"Kelen... do you mind if I call you that?" the host politely inquires.

"Yes, it bothers me. I don't address you by your first name, so don't call me by mine," retorts the Hybresang with a biting tone.

A bit of applause from the audience greets his sharp comeback.

"Oh, he's off to a strong start; he's on fire," remarks Ondine with an amused smile.

"I bet your guy doesn't call Fianèle by his first name because he doesn't know it," I remark, setting my coffee cup back on the coffee table. "He's got a bone to pick with him, doesn't he?"

"Kel has a bone to pick with all the Virtuous," Ondine replies. "He can't stand them."

"A legitimate reason for his aversion?"

She shrugs while crossing her long, slender legs. "He's a very secretive demon, you know. We don't talk much, him and me. Usually, we spend more time screwing than talking."

"Surprising," I grumble as the host poses a question to his guest.

"…learned that you opened a club on Earth three months ago. It's already very successful, according to my sources. What kind of establishment is it, Your Eminence?"

"It's a swinger's club," Kelen replies in a neutral tone. "The 1001 Nights of Lust."

Many libidinous cheers erupt from the crowd, eliciting a faint smile from the Magistrate. Lord, are these demons recruited for the audience based on a low IQ?

"Have you been there already?" I ask Ondine while the Hybresang Magistrate explains the concept of the luxury club.

"Oh, yes!" she exclaims dreamily. "That place is really awesome. I've had three amazing nights there. Actually, I'm going to work there from time to time; Kel's cool with it. 3,000 Forks a month, not counting tips, according to him."

Ondine is a stripper, and she's fed up with her current club. Her human boss is an old lecher who exploits the girls to line his pockets.

"The 1001 Nights of Lust is a great place to feed the Lustspawns. All the Sinners and their human lovers are welcome. Well, as long as the newcomers show a clean slate, pay the entrance fees, and behave properly," she explains quietly.

"Humans," I repeat, frowning in discontent. "I've heard about the club, but I didn't know mortals were involved. I imagine the demons wipe their memories after these orgy nights."

And that's not legal, damn it!

"Yes, Myri, but with their written consent," she emphasizes with a hint of exasperation.

"A written consent under hypnosis is not consent *at all*."

"No, but you're paranoid! They don't use hypnosis, I swear. Human free will is strictly adhered to at the 1001 Nights of Lust. It's a principle Kel never deviates from. He's actually explaining it to the host right now. He respects demon laws, unlike other Magistrates."

"That's what he claims. I don't believe a word of it."

"You're annoying, always suspicious of everyone, Myri. Not all Sinners are bad, and not all Virtuous are faultless."

"I'm aware, idiot."

"…and your medium-term political plans, Your Eminence?" inquires Fianèle.

Kelen Wills fixes his amber eyes on the camera. His gaze is magnetic and piercing even through a screen. It feels like he's speaking directly to each viewer. He has incredible presence.

"The news was officially announced last night by the Virtuous Legion, but I'm taking advantage of this show to present it to those demons who may not yet be aware."

Like me, for example!

"In order to avoid countless wasted time, recurrent administrative overload, and the communication problems inherent in our outdated organizational system, the fourteen Magistrates have decided to appoint spokespeople. Two ambassadors, so to speak. Two Federators, one Sinner and one Virtuous. Their upcoming role is essential: the unification of the legions. Furthermore, we Magistrates believe every demon in our world has a say. Every voice is important to help us improve things and integrate them into the fast-paced train of progress. Mindsets and times are evolving, my brothers; so are governments. To this end, the election of the Federators will first be submitted to the demon population of Infernum, who'll choose two candidates per party. Two Sinners and two Virtuous will emerge at this stage. Then, the other Magistrates from each camp will decide among the four candidates. I announce to you that five Sinner Magistrates have come forward to take on these new roles. I'm obviously one of them."

And another round of hypocritical ovations from the audience!

"My four colleagues and I will start campaigning today to present our different programs to the public opinion. The first round of elections will be held in the fourteen capitals of Infernum next month. We count on each of you to express your voice and make the *right* choice."

And he throws a majestic smile at the camera, as eloquent as it is charismatic, signaling, "I am the right choice."

The right choice, my ass. If I vote, it won't be for you, that's for sure! I think bitterly.

"Two Federators," I summarize, doubtful. "A euphemism steeped in demagoguery that actually means *regents*."

"For decades, the Magistrates have been talking about implementing this reform, Myri," Ondine reminds me, playing with her gold earring. "But until recently, they kept dispersing, arguing, debating, evading… until Kel slammed his fist on the table and ordered them to break out of the procrastination maze. In the end, he prevailed." She sighs with a voice dripping with admiration that makes me feel nauseous.

I'm not fooled. Kelen Wills already thinks he's the center of the demon world, and now he wants to acquire the title legally. Becoming the Federator of Sinners would be an excellent steppingstone to achieve his goal and grab even more power. A disguised double monarchy—that's what this charade is! Most demons in Infernum won't see through it. They'll be too happy to have had the opportunity to participate in the vote the Magistrates orchestrate. Heck, the elections might even be rigged.

But it's all over my head. Politics has never been my thing. What really gets me going and excites me more than anything is hunting down Rebel demons. As long as they don't interfere with my job and it doesn't affect my personal life, I couldn't care less about government measures like this.

"We wish you good luck in your noble campaign, Your Dark Grandeur. By the way, my assistant informed me that we have received numerous calls from female viewers since the beginning of the show," Fianèle continues with a sly smile, which his famous guest doesn't reciprocate. "They all ask the same question: does the mysterious Kelen Wills have a charming demoness in his private life?"

Ondine holds her breath… just like the women in the audience, surely.

"No. No serious relationship," Kelen replies with a wintry

coldness, and without hesitation.

My sister utters a vile curse in our language, and I tap her tense thigh in a sign of feminine compassion. *That's it, sweety. Let it out. He doesn't deserve you. He can't even admit to being with you.*

I hope she didn't think he would say something on TV like, "Yes. I'm in love with Ondine, a splendid Lustspawn. By the way, if you're watching… Will you marry me, my scaled doll?"

"Sis, he's not worth it, even if he's good in bed. He's dead weight. You should drop him and— *Ondine no!*"

With a suddenness that catches me off guard, she draws my revolver from its holster. She fires a bullet right into the forehead of her *boyfriend*, and the TV screen explodes in a shower of sparks.

I snatch my firearm back from her hand, scolding her. "Damnation, you're crazy! If the neighbors heard the gunshot, the police will come!"

"I'll buy a new TV and hypnotize the cops if I have to, Myri. I'm breaking up with that asshole right now!" she roars, grabbing her phone.

"Ondine, he won't pick up; he's in the middle of a live interview."

"I know, I'm not stupid! I'm going to leave him a scathing voicemail to tell him I'm dumping him and that I never want to see him again. He's ashamed of our relationship? Well, look at me!" she shouts, gesturing furiously at her goddess-like body. "He can go back to being single and go screw himself at the bottom of the Vésave crater, that two-bit Magistrate!"

I give my sister an approving smile as she seethes with rage, her blood-red eyes matching the color of her nails.

Well said, sis.

Well, it's not as important, but I have a date with a corpse.

CHAPTER 5
THE LEAP OF FAITH

MYRINA

As I approach the church my boss indicated over the phone, I brake and park my motorcycle on the edge of the sidewalk. I turn off the engine, put down the kickstand, and dismount, taking off my metallic purple helmet.

Two demons in their human form await me in front of the steps to the building.

Malphas the Pridefiend Sinner is accompanied by a teenage Virtuous demon. From his scent, he's a Prudling, a demon of Prudence. Unknown to me. He's a chubby redhead with brown eyes and cheeks sprinkled with freckles. His eyes are round like coins, and his hands are buried in the pockets of his slightly too tight sweatshirt—which is stained with barbecue sauce—as he stares at me, blinking rapidly, while I toss my long, biochromatic hair back.

"Are you babysitting, Malphas?" I ask, eyeing the young Prudling, who looks rather wary.

"Hello, Myri," my colleague responds in a bored tone. "This is Sean. The new intern."

An aspiring Tracker who hasn't passed his exams yet, then. Malphas must have screwed up big time to end up with a newbie

Virtuous on his tail. Zagam has a history of dumping the responsibility of interns onto Trackers who mess up.

I bite my cheeks to keep from snickering at the odd duo these two make. Malphas, 180 pounds of muscle at 6.1", handsome smooth face like a football player, green-gray eyes, platinum-blond hair styled-messy with gel, dressed in hipster chic to the nines and, on his right… Sean the intern, intimidated little redhead with a bit of a gut.

"Ms. Holmes, I've heard so much about you! It's… it's a great honor to meet you, ma'am" the boy stammers as he nods in greeting.

Not mutual, brown-noser. "Cool. Thanks, kid. But let's get one thing straight: the next time you call me ma'am, I'll also have the great honor of ripping your balls off with my bare hands."

Sean pales and emits a strangled gurgle.

Without taking his eyes off me, Malphas flashes a sly smile, then leans toward his assistant to whisper, "She's particularly touchy about her age because of her reduced life expectancy. Call her by her name, avoid staring at her too long, never talk to her about parsnips, and everything will go swimmingly between you. Admire my technique and take notes. Wooing women of her caliber is quite an art. My dear Amazon, let me point out that you look radiant today!" he adds with emphasis, leering at me from head to toe. "Did you get new studded jeans?"

I shake my head, glaring at him.

"Mm, did you go to the hairdresser, perhaps?"

Missed again, idiot.

"Did you put death stars in the depths of your periwinkle pupils, maybe?"

Hell, I already want to gut him on the sidewalk, the gutter poet! "Shut it, Malphas. Where's my stiff?"

"Inside. He's eager to meet you."

"Okay, I'm coming."

"But come on, what about chivalry?" my annoying colleague whispers, making a theatrical gesture toward the church door.

With my fist, I give him a brutal shove in the side to get him moving. "Chivalry for you means 'Move aside so I can check out your ass.'"

"You've missed me, too, Myri. None of the demonesses I've

plowed these past few weeks moan my name like you do," he alleges with a knowing glance that sends a shiver of disgust down my spine.

He's delusional! I've never moaned his name. If memory serves me right, I yawned in his face in the heat of the moment before adding, "Hurry up, Malphas, I'm about to fall asleep."

I let it slide. I don't want to argue with him; I'm not here for that.

The three of us enter the empty little church.

The cops only had time to put up their yellow crime scene tape before Malphas arrived to hypnotize them all and erase their memories. Zagam told me over the phone the humans believed our demon stiff was wearing a *very* realistic costume. Meanwhile, two Trackers paid a visit to the police station to brainwash the other officers aware of the case as well as the only witness, the old priest who discovered the dead body this morning. My colleagues took the opportunity to wipe the digital records of this freshly opened case. It's quite an operation to cover our tracks. The *Men in Black* with their neuralyzer that looks like an e-cigarette can put away their glasses and black suits!

A scent of Virtuous blood assaults my nostrils.

Walking along the aisle between the pews lining the nave, I study my surroundings with a curious glance. It's a charming Gothic-style church dotted with side columns, topped by stained glass windows depicting scenes from the Old Testament.

And, right in the middle of the transept...

The body of the Faithfiend, a demon of Faith.

Well, I'll be damned, this isn't something you see every day!

Like a divine staging, he's haloed by a wide sunbeam that gleams on his silver scales and his golden blood. With arched eyebrows, I look up at the large hole in the stone vault above the stiff. Let there be light, my brothers!

Am I admiring the aesthetic aspect of such a spectacular crime scene?

Yes, but don't tell anyone. It wouldn't look good for a Tracker.

Around the Faithfiend corpse, the marble floor is cracked and downright *sunken* in some places. The collision must have been extremely violent. Like a meteorite, the demon had smashed through the church vault before crashing to the ground in a shower of debris.

"I can't even imagine the height and speed at which he must have fallen to cause such damage," I remark, placing my motorcycle helmet on a bench.

"At least six miles of free fall, I'd say," Sean evaluates with a perplexed tone. "Well, if we base it on the altitude of a commercial airplane, which is between thirty thousand and forty thousand feet. That gives us an approximate speed of 995 miles per hour. But it's just a personal hypothesis."

Oh really? I nod with interest. The intern is moving up a notch in my esteem. A scientific apprentice Tracker is always good to have.

"I bet you a hundred Forks that we'll find traces of Dragon's Bile in his body after the autopsy and blood analysis. All winged demons know they shouldn't fly when they're drunk. It's not for nothing that the CIT does aerial prevention ads on Hell TV. Look at his wings, Myri, they're broken in several places. This idiot crashed head-on into an airplane," Malphas concludes prosaically, crossing his arms over his chest.

As usual, he's totally off track. Even though I haven't examined the stiff in detail yet, I've already noted two or three elements that suggest premeditated murder. Including the staging, of course. A demon of Faith—drunk or not—who would have collided with an airplane in mid-flight and would have landed precisely on the roof of a church would be a strange coincidence. Probability—one in tens of millions.

I've seen enough corpses and atrocities in my life to stop believing in coincidences.

My colleague Malphas isn't a bad Tracker, but his preferred domain is action, not preliminary investigation. Like when he fucks, actually. He's a brute specialized in brawling. A fighter, not a tracker. He's as dumb and narrow-minded as an emu. Before we slept together, this character trait didn't bother me much. We became buddies, and I enjoyed teasing him. But since that regrettable night, I find him downright unpleasant. If he'd stop harassing me, maybe we could be buddies again. Anyway, that's not the point. *Get to work, girl, you've got your hands full!*

I slip under the police's yellow tape and approach the body of the Faithfiend, watching where I step to avoid the golden splatters and debris on the ground. I take rubber gloves out of my jeans pocket while examining my Virtuous client, who's lying face down, arms spread. Four or five flies are already buzzing around him, drawn by the stench of death. I instruct Sean to take photos with my phone. He eagerly complies while I put on my gloves. I crouch down to touch the scaly body, starting with the neck.

The absence of rigor mortis indicates death occurred less than three hours ago.

His two wings, with bloodied gray feathers, are dislocated in multiple places, forming odd angles. I cautiously feel one at the base. Small bone fragments shift under the touch. I also notice the golden blood has coagulated on the various wounds. It's not *just* the impact that caused all these fractures.

"His wings were broken before his fall," I whisper, furrowing my brow.

"Yeah, because of a plane," Malphas retorts immediately, behind me.

"No, idiot. Someone broke his wings yesterday or last night before tossing him from the heights this morning, so he'd have no chance of surviving the fall."

I lift the demon's wrists one by one. Golden burns surround his scaly skin, evidence he was captive to his torturer. And three of his claws are missing.

"Traces of silver handcuffs. Since Faithfiends have no regeneration ability, he likely suffered for several hours."

"Ouch, that must have hurt."

"Neither you nor the human cops touched anything, right?"

"Of course not, Myri," my colleague grumbles. "Don't question my professionalism."

What professionalism?

"Sean, did you snap him from every angle?"

"Yes, ma—Myrina."

"Okay, I'm going to turn him over."

I slowly roll the Faithfiend onto his back. The torture theory is confirmed: he has several fine, bloody stripes and swollen bruises on his throat as if he was strangled with a silver wire *for fun*, not to kill him.

As well as a large golden drawing engraved on his abdomen, incised into his scales with a sharp blade.

"Oh, fucking hell," Malphas swears, stepping closer to get a better look at the mark. "What the hell is this? A bird?"

"The symbol of the Faithfiend's faith—a dove."

"Are you sure it's a dove? Looks like a deformed chicken. Your so-called killer isn't good at drawing."

"Sean, photos!" I exclaim, ignoring my colleague's foolish remark.

The intern immediately raises my phone.

A flash blinds me, I blink. "Not me, you idiot Prudling! The corpse!"

"Oops, sorry," the boy mutters with a contrite smile.

Damn, these two idiots really aren't helping me!

I search the bare-chested corpse, which is only wearing ordinary black pants like you find everywhere. Nothing in the pockets. No papers, no objects, no badges. No jewelry, scars, or tattoos. Not a single distinguishing feature. Like all Faithfiends, he has gray hair, pointed ears, and a normal Virtuous scent. He must be between one and two centuries old, no more. His nose and cheekbones are broken, and his forehead is all dented from the landing. I feel his flesh for any other potential injuries. His rib cage is also fractured, but that's probably also due to the impact of the fall. In addition, he sports a black mark over his heart, the size of a palm, which piques my curiosity. *That's strange.* It resembles a superficial burn.

I plan to send a photo of this to the Faithfiends' militia on Infernum, asking if they have a missing person report that could match his profile. I'll also have to wait for the results of the autopsy from the CIT medical examiner. But even with these elements, I'm not sure I'll be able to identify him. When one of ours passes away, they permanently lose the human appearance attached to their demonic form at conception. If he's not already known to our judicial services, this corpse's DNA won't match that of criminals in our database.

I already have a plethora of questions swirling around in my head.

Could this demonicide be the work of a fanatical Rebel? An enemy Sinner? An outlaw Virtuous?

A settling of scores driven by vengeance?

A crime of passion, perhaps?

What the hell is the motive?

It wasn't a human who committed this murder. They're not strong enough to overpower us.

Was this Faithfiend pushed from an airplane? Carried away in the arms of another winged demon? Was he unconscious or hypnotized during his fall?

In any case, he was alive before the impact, I'm convinced of it. It's not a corpse that was dropped from the sky.

And damn, why go to such lengths to perfect this macabre staging? The broken wings, the torment, the dove, the dizzying fall, the choice of the church... Because usually, when one demon intends to kill another... they proceed in a gorey and trivial way. No fuss for killings! Decapitation, immolation, disembowelment, and throat-slitting are the most common methods used by demon criminals.

All in all, this new case stinks like a Gluttonfiend's liquid fart.

"Hey, that reminds me of the leap of faith," Sean comments.

I pivot toward the Prudling intern at the same time as Malphas.

"The leap of faith?" I repeat, removing my blood-soiled rubber gloves.

"In the human video game *Assassin's Creed*. The hero jumps from the top of a tower to test his worth, his courage, and his dedication to his order. He lands in a haystack or in the water. That's the leap of faith. If there weren't all these clues proving that this guy was tortured before being dropped into the void, I would have said it was a suicide to atone for his sins."

A leap of faith... Atoning for one's sins...

We might be onto something.

"Malphas, be a dear and comb the area around the crime scene for other clues. Sean, hand me my phone. I'm going to call the CIT to get a cleanup team and transport the body to Infernum." I dial the boss's number while staring into the empty, lifeless eyes of the mysterious Faithfiend without a name, with broken wings. Suddenly, I have a bad feeling. "Do you know one or two prayers, intern?" I mutter ominously as I press the phone against my ear.

"No, I'm atheist, Myrina. Why?"

"Because someone should pray that this Virtuous isn't the first in a series of really grim murders."

CHAPTER 6
SUPERMARKET CLEANER

"Desire is a naked virtue." ~Eugène Beaumont, Penséier

KELEN

The Magistrates have never needed the Arcadus. We can teleport from one world to another at our leisure. A convenient power that I couldn't do without, given the nature of my professional obligations.

After listening to Ondine's tumultuous voicemail in my earbuds, I materialize in front of the door to her apartment on Earth. I survey my new surroundings while sniffing the dusty air with a mixture of disdain and perplexity. Old yellowing wallpaper peeling in places, grimy olive linoleum, paint chipping on the doors… It's the first time I've visited her rundown building. And undoubtedly the last. Among humans, I always feel like a swan misplaced among pigeons. We don't have the same values, nor the same worth. However, unlike some Sinners, I wouldn't go so far as to say they're just insects to be trampled.

No, insect larvae would be a more appropriate term to define them.

After removing and stowing my earbuds in my suit pocket, I lightly press my finger on the doorbell button. A few seconds later, the door opens, revealing a lovely succubus with raven curls tied up in pigtails. She's wearing a green plaid miniskirt and a fitted white blouse, the open collar accentuating the delightful curves of her chest. She seems astonished to find me on her doorstep.

"Kel! B-but… what are you doing here?"

"I just listened to your message, Ondine. So, you're leaving me, little Lustspawn?" I ask calmly and smoothly, lifting her chin with my index finger to make her look up at me.

She nods weakly, unable to meet my gaze, her cheeks turning pink. She was much more vehement on my voicemail, but now that I'm facing her, she's completely defenseless. Good. I didn't appreciate her message at all. I intend to make her understand that no one has the right to address me in that manner, let alone cut ties with me. *I* make the decisions, end of story. There's no room for debate.

"Look at me," I order, adopting my most authoritative tone, the one I usually use to immediately command obedience from my demon soldiers.

And of course, she obeys immediately.

She nibbles on her pretty vermilion lips, her big clear eyes filled with desire.

"Mm, girl, are you *sure* you want to leave me?" I murmur gravely and seductively, gently trailing my finger along the curve of her graceful neck.

Her heartbeat and breathing quicken as I twirl a lock of black hair around my index finger… and she vigorously shakes her head, pleading with me through eyes saturated with remorse.

There's no need to use demonic hypnosis on Lustspawn females to get what you want from them. Incubus pheromones are enough to influence them.

A shadow of satisfaction spreads across my face as she quickly opens her door for me. Stepping inside her home, I clench my right fist, cracking my knuckles. She's going to get the spanking of her life, and I guarantee she's going to love it.

***

MYRINA

With my mind preoccupied by my new investigation and my

bladder aching, I arrive home around three PM. I immediately detect the scent of a powerful male demon in my apartment. A major Lustspawn, if I'm not mistaken. I identify his foreign sexual pheromones mixed with the familiar ones of my sister. By Cerberus's name, Ondine is hopeless! My narrowed eyes scan the living room. Phew, no clothes in sight. The guy must have left recently, hence the lingering scent in the room.

My sister, on the other hand, is still here, her faux leather handbag hanging on the coat rack in the entryway. I hang my holster on the adjacent hook.

I trot toward the bathroom to relieve myself. As I approach the slightly open door, tendrils of steam brush against my skin, and I hear the sound of water running on the tiles. I can't wait for her to finish washing up—especially since the devil spends at least half an hour in the shower each time—because I'm on the verge of wetting myself. Pulling down my zipper, I step into the bathroom, shooting a grouchy glance toward the opaque sunflower-patterned shower curtain that's pulled shut over the bathtub. After lowering my jeans and panties, I sit on the toilet seat.

"Ondine, please, sweetheart, make an effort for me! I'm fed up with you bringing poor guys home," I grumble as I relieve my bladder. "Do I bring my one-night stands here? No, never, because I make sure to keep my intimate affairs outside. It's really not rocket science to apply this little cohabitation rule. I value my privacy."

No response from the shower. The water continues to flow abundantly into the bathtub.

I furrow my brow, puzzled by her silence. Surprising. My exuberant half-sister always has something to say. Could she be upset by my reprimand? Unless she's wallowing in sorrow over her breakup with her dark Hybresang bastard… Yes, that must be why she slept with the first incubus that came her way. She wanted to forget Kelen in the arms of another demonic lover. My heart squeezes with guilt. I've been a bit harsh on her. I sigh.

"Okay, darling, I'll let it slide this time—you had a good excuse. But don't let yourself get down because of Kelen Wills; you're worth so much more than him. He's just a huge piece of crap," I say, my thoughtful gaze landing on the toilet paper holder, inspiring an idea to cheer Ondine up. "By the way, I bet you 10,000 Forks that he has a special lackey who wipes his ass when he takes a dump. Imagine his minion—he must use triple-ply luxury toilet paper with K.W. initials and wear a solid gold toilet brush on his belt. Kelen Wills's designated *Supermarket Cleaner*!"

My cynical laughter echoes oddly in the bathroom and drowns out the sound of the water jet. But Ondine doesn't join her giggles with mine. I chew on my lips, a tad anxious. Oh shit, she must be feeling really down! Normally, my cheesy humor makes her laugh heartily.

I quickly finish my business, pull up my panties and jeans, flush the toilet, wash my hands, and head toward the bathtub.

"You're not crying because of him, sweetheart?" I whisper sadly, reaching out my hand.

As I'm about to pull back the shower curtain, she grabs it on the other side at the same time and yanks it open with a strong pull, anticipating my intentions.

And I come face to face with Kelen Wills in the flesh.

Standing in my bathtub.

Drenched.

Naked.

Not happy.

I scream.

***

KELEN, THREE MINUTES EARLIER

While Ondine heads to the corner bakery to buy some bread, I take the opportunity to have a good, hot shower. Between the spankings and everything else, I've sweated a lot during our delicious romps. In a good mood, I whistle as I lather my chest with her vanilla-scented shower gel. I'd rather smell a feminine fragrance on my skin than the musky sweat that lingers after intense physical and energetic exchanges. I love the smell of sex… only during sex.

I hear the front door of her apartment slam shut. Well, well, my lovely little mistress is already back? She was quick, that minx… I wouldn't be opposed to the enticing idea of her joining me for a wash in the bathtub. Well, a little blowjob in the shower is always appreciated, especially since Ondine is the queen of blowjobs. That's her best quality. That and her enticing physique. Otherwise, I wouldn't have bothered coming back to fuck her; I can snap my fingers and have a seductive demoness jump into my bed and spread her legs for me.

I open my mouth to invite the Lustspawn to come rub my parts, but my highly developed sense of smell detects a powerful fragrance that isn't hers. Quite intoxicating, in fact. I already smelled the trail of this sweet scent when I entered the apartment. It's her half-sister's, Myrina Holmes.

A damn Tracker.

Ondine has already talked to me about her, but I knew her by reputation before. In fact, few demons in Infernum are unaware of her name because this girl is a unique half-Sinner, half-Virtuous hybrid... and apparently the best warrior in the CIT. She's nicknamed the Amazon. I've heard she handles the sword, crossbow, and revolver with exceptional skill.

I suspected I would eventually cross paths with this Tracker one day, but I absolutely didn't expect this noteworthy event to happen under these particular circumstances.

On the other hand, this could be... entertaining.

The bathroom door creaks open at that moment.

Very entertaining, indeed.

I hear hurried footsteps on the tile floor, the zip of a zipper, and the rustle of denim. The girl walks toward the toilet, six feet from the bathtub.

I had the good sense to leave all my clothes in Ondine's room. The Tracker hasn't detected my presence yet, which is ironic for a woman of her profession.

"Ondine, please sweetheart, make an effort for me!"

She continues her monologue in a clear and harmonious voice. Indeed, she believes it's her sister in the shower. A sardonic smile forms on my lips. With my customary discretion, I slightly part the hideous curtain to take an amused look at the formidable Amazon sitting on her throne, emptying her bladder like any other average demoness. Too bad I don't have my phone handy. I would love to show a picture to all the members of my staff, so we could have a good laugh at her expense during our meeting and—

I raise an eyebrow, pleasantly surprised. By Satan's forked tail, she's quite something, this Tracker! I hadn't imagined her like this at all. I've never seen a photo of her, and Ondine described her as a real tomboy. So, I'd visualized some sort of androgynous chick with a swimmer's broad shoulders, an austere face, and short hair. I was miles away from reality.

Despite the indignity of her current position on the toilet seat, this hybrid female specimen is a pure demonic marvel. I even have to concentrate to not start getting hard. Generally, I manage to control my erections, thanks to my Lustspawn blood.

I don't listen to a single word of her chatter, too occupied with ogling the strange creature fulfilling her natural needs. Her body is an ode to Lust. Even seated, I can tell she's rather tall and, above all, built like a Russian missile. Thanks to my experience and my incubus side, I have a keen eye for female measurements. *Mm, 5 foot 8 inches, 150 pounds, 37-26-38.* I'd bet my fang on it. I can make out more than half of her long, shapely thighs. They would look stunning wrapped around my hips, those thighs. And her round, generous breasts molded in her black tank top would fit perfectly in my palms. Finely muscled arms, a flat and firm stomach, a graceful long neck…

The Tracker oozes that feminine sensuality typical of succubus, with an extra something. She's both slender, statuesque, and voluptuous. As for her heart-shaped face… the engine matches the bodywork. Her delicate features bear an undeniable family resemblance to Ondine's, perhaps colder and harder. The Tracker's chin is more determined than that of my mistress, and her cheekbones higher. Yet I note three similarities between the two sisters: the golden complexion, full lips, and a slightly upturned nose. Her long, wavy hair isn't obsidian like my lover's; Myrina's unusual mane is a warm autumnal brown interspersed with thick silver streaks. Cruella de Vil but much younger and much hotter. And those eyes! In thirteen hundred years of life, I've never seen the likes. They're *purple.* Not a pale, bluish purple… a brilliant amethyst, yet full of dark mysteries. They illustrate the duality of her demonic nature. Sin and virtue incarnate in an exquisite body that exudes a femininity both wise and wild.

If I were a pathetic human starring in a pathetic movie, I'd probably have a pathetic crush on her.

But right now, all I can think about is buying a priority gold ticket to visit all the sensational attractions at the new Myrina Land Park. I've never had the chance to bed a Tracker, let alone a hybrid. Therefore, adding a hybrid Tracker to my conquest list would be a nice trophy to boast about to both my friends and enemies for a few decades.

It's not an unlikely scenario in the immediate future. I'm naked under the shower and… I'm Kelen Wills, for crying out loud. When she discovers me in the bathtub in all my virile glory, there's a high probability the Tracker will ignite like a match and pounce on me with claws out in an animalistic frenzy, excited like crazy by my dreamy body and pheromones. With a bit of luck, Ondine won't mind seeing me screwing her little sister in the bathtub and will undress to join us eagerly. The three of us will indulge in a fantastic sensory debauchery under the shower and—

"… for Kelen Wills."

My attention snaps back to Myrina instantly as she utters my name. Did she spot me fantasizing about my steamy threesome? Telepathy, perhaps.

"You're so much better than him."

My jaw tightens. Definitely not, Cruella de Vil, nobody's better than me because I'm the best at everything!

"He's just a massive piece of crap."

By all the sinners' saints, how dare she blaspheme like that?

"By the way, I bet you 10,000 Forks that he has a special lackey who wipes his ass when he takes a dump. Imagine his minion—he must use triple-ply luxury toilet paper with K.W. initials and wear a solid gold toilet brush on his belt. Kelen Wills's designated *Supermarket Cleaner!*"

This stupid demoness is laughing her ass off on her toilet.

My fist tightens on the shower curtain, veins popping under my tan skin.

I. Am. Fucking. Mad.

Supermarket Cleaner.

She just insulted my magnificent behind.

Nobody insults my perfectly proportioned ass.

Nobody.

The insolent creature straightens up, pulling up her panties and pants before I can even catch a glimpse of her little pussy. That detail might have slightly softened my murderous mood, but it doesn't.

It doesn't matter that this exotic creature is beautiful and desirable. I'm going to *slaughter* her.

"You're not crying because of him, sweetheart?" the Tracker gently inquires, approaching the bathtub.

No, sweetheart, but you'll soon be crying because of me, I promise her in thought.

I violently yank the shower curtain, glaring daggers at the fucking half-breed.

The horrified Amazon screams at the top of her lungs… And lands a monumental punch square in my face.

MYRINA

Warrior reflex when you find a guy naked in your bathtub when you thought he was your sister?

Punch him in the face with all your might.

Kelen Wills or not.

I don't catch the rest because my brain isn't as quick as my body.

Just as my fist comes away from his bloody nose, Kelen grabs my wrist with supernatural speed and violently pulls me toward him, causing me to stumble forward.

I grab the shower curtain, getting tangled in it as I thrash around, pulling it off the rings. We never hit the bottom of the bathtub because he teleports us to my living room during our fall. We collapse onto my wooden coffee table, shattering it into a thousand pieces. I try to knee him in the balls, but he quickly blocks my leg with his arm. He teleports us to the kitchen and onto the countertop. I grab a saucepan to hit him over the head, but he intercepts my wrist again, burning my skin with his Ragebeast fire power.

I whimper through gritted teeth, dropping the saucepan as I struggle. He growls, teleporting us to Ondine's bedroom and onto the bed. I bite his forearm. He roars in pain and tries to slap me, but I dodge. His hand knocks over a bedside lamp, which flies through the air. I scratch his shoulder. He curses, and he teleports us back to the living room. He roughly pins me against a wall. I elbow him in the sternum and kick him in the knee. He twists my arm behind my back, straining the ligaments in my shoulder. We roll on the floor, fiercely grappling and getting tangled in that damn shower curtain. Damn, I forgot he's naked. I feel his long thing whip against my thigh and—

"What's going on here?" my sister's stunned voice screams.

Kelen and I freeze together, me straddling him, my hands clasped around his thick throat. He grabs the shower curtain and pulls it away from our heads. Ondine stands in the doorway, wide-eyed and open-mouthed, holding a baguette. I can imagine how it looks from her point of view. Me, her sister, disheveled and unkempt, riding her naked and wet boyfriend on the living room floor. Or her ex, I'm no longer sure.

"It's not what you think, sis, I swear!" I exclaim vehemently.

"Myri, what did you do to Kel! His face is covered in blood! And there are bites and scratches all over his body!" she exclaims, pointing her baguette at us.

Wait, what? She's defending *him*?

I cast an incredulous glance at my opponent, who gives me a smug little smile that's extremely annoying. I did give him a good beating, that's true. His nose is smeared with black, liquid-like ink. His nasal septum is even deviated, but in less than an hour, the cartilage will be reset and the wound healed. Same for my wrist burn. Long live cellular regeneration, hip hip… hooray.

"That asshole provoked me."

As I pointed out in the bathroom, I value my privacy. And to think this damn pervert was right next to me while I was peeing! I console myself vaguely by thinking that he couldn't spy on my thoughts with his telepathy because I'm immune to the powers of demons and… well… damn, wait! I've never been faced with a Hybresang before, after all. He's much more powerful than the others; maybe he can read my mind…

"Ondine, your half-sister viciously attacked me. You witnessed it," Kelen intervenes, fixing me with his chestnut eyes, imbued with paternal severity. "Agent Holmes, I hope you have the number of a good lawyer."

I'm left speechless, not because of what he said, but because of his voice, precisely. It's much deeper and more cavernous than on television. It rumbles in his throat with authority and ripples in his chest like thunder. I've never heard a male voice so deep, captivating, and sexy. I now understand why the audience was so silent and attentive during the interview.

"A… a lawyer?" I ask.

"Count on me to file a complaint against you and send a report to your CIT superiors with photos of my injuries as evidence. I have several solid reasons to sue you, kid. Aggravated violence against my vulnerable self, unfounded insults toward my distinguished posterior, attempted sexual assault, and passionate attempted murder of a defenseless Magistrate."

I arch an eyebrow, stunned by his surreal accusation.

"Not only will you be fired from CIT, but you'll end your short life in prison. Abuse of power by demonic law enforcement is not acceptable, and given your disrespectful behavior, I'll make it my personal mission." His icy voice softens. "Unless you present me with your most sincere apologies properly, by prostrating yourself before me and begging for forgiveness," he suggests, raising a condescending eyebrow, finishing off my scandalization.

"What! Not in a million years, I'd rather die in a cell!" I curse vehemently.

"Very well, Agent Holmes," he growls threateningly. "Ondine, fetch my phone from the bedroom!"

"Kel, please, don't you think you're being a bit excessi—"

"Right away, Lustspawn!" he barks, making Ondine jump, who looks between us even more bewildered and torn.

"You're not allowed to talk to my sister like that, Wills!" I retort sharply. "Ondine, go fetch my gun instead! I'll put a silver bullet in his sorry ass to give him a second asshole. That'll knock some sense into his thick skull!"

"A second asshole, really now. Your arrogance is oozing more than an old Pridefiend female. I'd be curious to see that, Agent Holmes," he challenges with a slight smirk.

Oh, I'll quench his damn curiosity!

I quickly regain my footing to grab the revolver from my holster and wipe that smug grin off his face, but Ondine steps in front of the coat rack and grabs me around the waist, pulling me against her to stop me. If she wasn't my sister, I'd give her the beating of her life!

"Let go of me, Ondine!"

"Myri, just stop it, you're out of control. You're going to get us into serious trouble!" she hisses in my ear.

"Listen to your sister. You're escalating your situation by the second," Kelen confirms behind me.

I turn to glare at him. He's towering over me now, too. Our living room suddenly feels a lot smaller. With the back of his hand, he casually wipes the dark blood splattered on his face.

A human would likely have tangled their hips in the shower curtain to conceal their manhood. But demons have almost no modesty, and the Magistrate is perfectly comfortable in his perfect nudity. The water droplets and streaks of foam glistening on his bronzed muscles drip onto the floor, mirroring my liquefied will. My rigid Justspawn reason battles against my boiling Lustspawn hormones.

Don't stare at his dick, Myri.

Don't. Stare. At. His. Dick. Damn it.

DON'T STARE AT HIS DICK!!!

I stare at his dick.

By the tentacle of Greedling. They shouldn't call him Hybresang, but Cocksang.

And the worst part is, he's flaccid! I dare not imagine the size of that thing when it's—

"Ondine, would you kindly inform your half-sister that staring at a demon's dick, one whom we've just met and assaulted, is incredibly rude?" the owner of the equipment says with infuriating nonchalance.

"Myri, stop looking at Kel's junk. It makes him uncomfortable." She sighs beside me.

I lift my gaze to the upper deck. Unbelievable! Given the smug smile he's sporting, he's not uncomfortable at all. *Quickly come up with a sharp retort to put him in his place, Myri!*

"You're hardly deserving of the title Magistrate, Wills."

His smile instantly fades. His eyes, pinned to mine, redden with fury. Take that, you arrogant asshole! This time, it's my turn to smile!

"I'm going to freshen up, dry off, get dressed, and then head straight back to Infernum," Kelen declares, addressing my sister.

I second that idea, good riddance to the Hybresang!

"You start your shift at the 1001 Nights of Lust tonight at exactly ten PM, Ondine. I've reserved a dressing room in your name with your stage costumes. Agent Holmes, consider yourself lucky that I'm feeling lenient today. You have forty-eight hours to come to your senses and offer me your most sincere apologies. Otherwise, I'll ruin your career and your life. Have a nice day, ladies."

He teleports into the bathroom, the door slamming loudly behind him, propelled by a telekinetic force. A dramatic exit for the braggart!

"You're back with him," I lament, rubbing my face wearily. It's not a question, but an observation.

"Yes, Myri. Breaking up with him was a mistake."

"You're so naive… He influenced you with his incubus pheromones; the place reeks of rutting beast everywhere in the apartment."

"Perhaps. So what? I need this job at the 1001 Nights, Myri. I've already quit my other position. Kel came back to me to win me over after hearing my voicemail. I didn't expect him to put in so much effort for me."

"What kind of *effort*? Did he beg you to forgive him? Did he recite you a poem? Did he bring you gifts?"

"No, not at all. He gave me a very exciting spanking as foreplay and made me climax three times in a row."

Exorcise me!

"Then, he explained he told the host during the interview that he was single because he was following his agent's advice. It was a slight omission to enhance his image as a Federator candidate, Myri. Making people believe he's free as a bird will earn him extra votes from his demoness fans."

It's the worst justification I've ever heard.

"But once the elections are over, he'll make our relationship official."

"Yeah right, Ondine. And the day he does that, Kim Kardashian will remove her butt implants and announce to the media that she's still a virgin."

She laughs carelessly before sending a pensive glance toward the bathroom door.

"Don't worry too much about his threats. Kel is mad at you because you hit and insulted him, but he's not as vengeful as he claims to be, especially when you know how to appease him." She gives me a confident smile. "I'm sure I can persuade him not to press charges against you by giving him a good blowjob."

She's got a real sense of family devotion, my succubus of a sister!

"So, what about you? Tell me! How did your date with your stiff go?"

KELEN

I teleport directly to my office. I don't want to risk running into my servants with my face in this condition. If it were to be revealed that a demoness broke my nose with a punch, and *especially* that I spared her following this unfortunate incident, it would tarnish my reputation. For the same reason, I won't take the Tracker to court. And I have other priorities, like crushing my Magistrates rivals by winning the Federators' election.

But I intend to make her believe my threat, so she'll eat out of my hand like a submissive little bitch.

On Infernum, rarity is a coveted gastronomic delight, and the predictable difficulty of the conquest doesn't deter me. On the contrary, it adds a good pinch of red pepper to the tasting. Whatever action I undertake, I never let myself be discouraged, and I always get what I desire.

My advantage? I have no scruples.

Taming the Amazon's spirit by breaking her steel will is undeniably gratifying.

I open the drawer of my desk and pull out my antique leather-bound notebook, which literally dates back to the Middle Ages, preserved from the ravages of time by a conservation charm. Under the letter M—like the other letters, in fact—hundreds of female names are listed. More than half of the girls listed in this book are celebrities, dead or alive. A few are humans with whom I've made a pact that brought them fame and fortune in exchange for their souls. Most are ambitious demonesses posing as human personalities, thanks to their powers. I won't disclose which ones; I'm bound by professional secrecy. But I've fucked them all at least once for form's sake. Yes, this legendary notebook is none other than my prestigious trophy list, and I take great pride in it. My personal Holy Grail… I mark their names before or after sleeping with them, depending on the circumstances, but it doesn't change the result: none of them has ever resisted me.

I scan a few names at random.

Mary Boleyn. Marie-Antoinette. Mata-Hari. Marilyn Monroe. Madonna. Marie Delpech. Miranda Kerr. Margot Robbie.

Confidently, I pick up my fountain pen from a pencil holder to write another name at the bottom of the page.

Myrina Holmes.

Finally, a challenge worthy of my stature

CHAPTER 7
FIERY HEARTS

MYRINA

The large, antique mirror hanging in my room is an Arcadus. I press my magical badge on the red, eye-shaped rune with a vertical pupil adorning the top of the cherry wood frame. The demonic symbol lights up promptly, and the reflective surface begins to ripple like a pond, distorting my reflection. I step through the portal, allowing myself to be engulfed by the warm, silvery liquid.

And there I am, directly in the CIT headquarters.

With gravity much lower on Infernum, I've taken the precaution of wearing special, particularly heavy boots. I feel lighter; indeed, excluding the shoes, I weigh six times less than on Earth, about twenty-five pounds. If I were to take off my heavy boots, I could have fun executing cheetah-like leaps—and I'd surely bump my head against the ceiling. That's the cool aspect of it. But as I've been spending much more time on Earth than on Infernum in recent years, my body isn't quite used to the effects of low gravity anymore. If I were to stay here for several months, my spine would lengthen, I'd lose some muscle mass, I'd have problems with my inner ear, weakened bones, blurred vision, nausea, dizziness… As a demoness with good regeneration ability and excellent physical resilience, I'd eventually adapt to these temporary side effects, but I have no desire to do so. I enjoy my expatriate life on Earth. Humans are generally less complicated than demons. In fact, they're even a breath of fresh air in my daily life.

I tuck my badge into the pocket of my jeans. In the corridor with charcoal tapestries, two Trackers are wrestling with an Envyfiend Sinner who roars at the top of his lungs, thrashing about. They're trying to subdue the demon of Envy to lock him up, probably. The criminal—a colossus with black scales and wings of red feathers—had managed to break free from his silver handcuffs by sheer force and removed the iron mask covering his mouth. *Not good.* He spits a stream of acid into the face of one of my colleagues, who screams in pain, his flesh melting off his skull, smoking. The other Tracker then grabs his revolver and shoots the Envyfiend in the temple with a silver bullet. The idiot. The corrosive black blood of the monolith splashes him, and he too screams. He collapses on the ground, writhing next to his colleague, who groans like a baby. Sighing, I step over the corpse of the Envyfiend criminal, making sure not to step in his acidic blood that's eating away at the floor.

"Hey, hey there, beauty!" the first Tracker calls to me, despite the expression of pain contorting his face, which is as ravaged as it's unrecognizable. "Nice to see you, it's been a while since we've seen you around here! What's new with you?"

"I got assigned to the new case, the Faithfiend corpse fallen from the sky. Hey, you two should go to the infirmary."

"Oh no! In an hour, we'll be good as new," his colleague croaks with a strangled voice.

The oversized ego of male Sinners demons… They prefer to suffer horribly while their tissues regenerate on their own rather than go to our Virtuous nurse, who could speed up the process with her healing power.

"Who was that guy?" I ask.

"A Rebel we picked up in a squat. The boss wanted to grill him."

"Well, interrogation's off the table now," I comment, eyeing the sticky bits of brain scattered on the floor. "I'll pass on the message; I've been summoned to his office. Have a good day, guys. And next time, remember Envyfiends have corrosive blood!"

"See you later, Myri!" my two battered colleagues exclaim in unison.

And you wonder why I'm the best warrior in the CIT with all these dimwits who have no common sense? The acronym *Central Intelligence of Trackers* doesn't apply to everyone here. For most of them, it would be more like the *Central Idiocy of Trackers*.

Like my father and grandfather, my boss Zagam is a Justspawn, a demon of Justice. He has been the director of the CIT for about two centuries. Needless to say, Zagam commands authority, and you don't want to mess with him too much. Despite being Virtuous—meaning upright, honest, and rigorous—he has the temper of a raging Ragebeast demon.

Apparently, he eats kittens for breakfast.

I consider him somewhat like my big brother. I adore him. Well, every other day. On the days when he's in a bad mood, I abhor him.

As soon as I step through the door adorned with the CIT's overly stylish emblem—two swords atop a shield stamped with a balance—I notice he's in a foul mood today, and I deduce I'm going to loathe him. His little brown eyes turn silvery in a split second and glare at me like two gleaming daggers.

Uh-oh, I'm in for it.

"Are you kidding me, Myri?" he growls in a guttural voice. "You assaulted Magistrate Kelen Wills yesterday?"

Crap. That Hybresang jerk wasted no time.

"Self-defense," I justify, shrugging.

Behind his desk, Zagam snorts with anger. A nerve-wracking tic given the size of his nostrils. I'm sure I could fit my fist in there, but I'm not about to test it. Yes, I'm talking about nostrils because my boss is in his demonic form. Seven feet two inches tall, weighing in at 286 pounds of muscle. How can I objectively describe him… Rough and bovine features, round eyes, elongated snout, pointed teeth, ivory horns, hooves, and claws—he looks like a minotaur. Except instead of having thick brown fur like the mythological creatures invented by humans, he sports silver scales like all Virtuous demons. A scaled minotaur, if you will. Not a very friendly creature.

"That's not what Wills told me on the phone."

"He's a big liar, boss. Trust me, his version is false."

"Whether he's lying or not, it's not my problem. He sent me a selfie of his bloody face as proof. He even threatened to sue you. I had to suck up to him to buy some time, Myri, and you know I hate sucking up to anyone! You're going to go apologize to him face-to-face and pray he drops the charges."

"Zagam, listen, I'm going to be honest with you. I'd rather impale myself on a Pridefiend horn than apologize to that son of a bitch. I have nothing to apologize for!"

"The CIT's reputation is at stake, Myrina. Can you imagine the chaos it would cause on Infernum if such a scandal were made public, especially with the Federator elections approaching? The Amazon who beats up a Sinners candidate while he's taking a shower? All the journalists from Hell TV and Radio Hell would descend on us like vultures!"

"But come on, boss, it's just a bluff! Wills would never shout that from the rooftops, even to play the martyr and garner sympathy! If the demons of Infernum found out that the *evil and terrible*" — I mime air quotes with my fingers — "leader of the Ragebeast legion was struck and humiliated by a woman, it would seriously undermine him. His magisterial pride as a Magistrate couldn't handle it."

"Maybe. Or maybe not! I couldn't care less, Myri. If you don't want to apologize to him, I'll take back all your weapons, restrict your access to the Arcadus by blocking your badge, and you'll be suspended from your duties for an indefinite period."

My jaw drops. I'm shocked by his ultimatum.

"But, Zagam, I—"

"*It's an order, Myrina Holmes!*" he bellows, pounding his fist on his desk with such force that it snaps in half.

He grumbles in frustration, lowering his pearly eyes to the wreckage. It's the third desk he's replaced this quarter.

"Okay, okay, calm down, don't get on your high horse! You win, I'll apologize to Wills!" I relent, begrudgingly.

Zagam nods sharply and gestures for me to sit across from him. I slump into the chair, my jaw clenched. He retrieves the file that slid into the crevice now dividing his desk in two and tosses it to me without ceremony. I catch it midair and undo the fasteners holding it shut to examine its contents meticulously. It contains printed photos of my stiff Faithfiend taken by intern Sean and a sheet covered in Malphas's scribbles. My Pridefiend colleague has underlined *collision with an airplane* three times, the stubborn fool. He exasperates me.

"Kelen Wills has scheduled a meeting with you tonight at ten PM sharp in his office at 1001 Nights of Lust. Don't be late, he doesn't like to wait. I'm counting on you to stroke him the right way."

And I'm counting on you to drop dead, Zagam.

"As for the Faithfiend in the church, you'll handle putting the paperwork together as soon as you get the autopsy report back. I want your report on my new desk as soon as possible." He settles back into his chair. "Your first impressions?"

"A good old-fashioned demonicide."

"That's what I feared."

"How's the autopsy coming along, boss?"

He clears his throat, eyeing the large potted cactus in the corner of the room. His only decoration. Zagam doesn't like to be distracted by anything while he works.

"It's underway, Myrina. The initial blood tests, performed by Lexi upon the body's arrival, revealed nothing conclusive. This demon isn't registered in our computer records, and no suspicious substances were detected in his blood."

"He must have been hypnotized to remain docile during his detention."

"Possibly," he replies tersely.

"Faithfiends aren't easily hypnotizable, Zagam. Even the minors. Their faith protects them from mental influences, generally. The murderer is probably a major demon more powerful than average. That narrows down our list of suspects. How many majors are there in Infernum? A thousand?"

"More than ten thousand, Myrina."

"I see."

Damn it.

Needless to say, the fourteen Magistrates and all their commanders are majors. About a third of the CIT members, too. They hold the highest positions in demon society. But four species don't have the power to hypnotize their own kind: the Gluttonfiends and Envyfiend Sinners, as well as the Braveryfiends and Charityfiends Virtuous.

"I've sent his photo to the Faithfiend militia," I inform Zagam. "No missing persons reports match his profile. Nobody has reported this guy missing yet."

"Maybe he had no family, who knows. But I don't understand

why the killer carved a dove on his chest. It doesn't make sense. You could tell at first glance that he was a Faithfiend."

"I lean toward punishment, boss," I murmur as I study the photo of the symbol carved into the chest of the corpse.

"Punishment?" Zagam repeats, disappointed.

"His torturer punished him for being what he is: a demon of Faith. The murderer used the victim's emblem to make him suffer before killing him. It's a form of morbid irony, you know. He would have turned the Faithfiend's strength against him to change it into weakness, in a way. Similarly, regarding the symbolic significance of the leap of faith. Sean gave me a clue with his reference to a video game. I feel like the killer was trying *to test* the Faithfiend through this killing: *I break your wings and drop you into the void—let's see if your faith saves you!* And the answer is no, obviously."

Zagam frowns, crossing his hands on his lap.

"By Satan and Lucifer, if you're right, we're dealing with a real lunatic."

"A lunatic… but a powerful and intelligent one, boss. The worst combination possible. I think we're going to have a hard time catching this one."

"You underestimate yourself, Myri."

I give him a sly little smile. "I said we'd have a hard time, Zagam. But I never said it was impossible."

He returns my smile knowingly.

Someone knocks timidly on the door. The Justspawn allows the visitor to enter. I glance curiously over my shoulder. A Prudling demon appears, a paper in hand. Two small, red, frontal horns, a pug nose, and a bit overweight. His olfactory signature tells me it's Sean, the young intern in his natural form.

"I bring you the coroner's autopsy report, chief. Hello, Myrina."

"Hi, Sean, everything okay?"

"Yes, thank you. Would you like some coffee?"

"Yes, please, dear. Five sugars," I answer.

"I'll get that for you."

"You're a sweetheart of a demon," I compliment him with a dazzling smile that makes him swallow hard.

The silver scales on his face turn as red as a dragon's. He hands the document to Zagam before hastily making his exit… tripping over the threshold in the process. My boss chuckles as soon as his office door closes behind him.

"Quite the charmer, Myrina. Another lovesick admirer to your credit, eh?"

"It's just a crush, he's young."

"You should put your Lustspawn pheromones on standby. When you're around, it distracts half the guys in the CIT."

"My pheromones are already on standby, Zagam. Don't worry, I have no desire to deal with another pain in the neck here. Malphas annoys me enough as it is."

"Next time, show up in your demon form; it'll calm their ardor for a while. And they'll never again dare approach you within one hundred feet."

I chuckle softly. It's a tempting idea. I usually avoid reverting to my original form because it consumes a lot of energy due to my hybridization, but sometimes, I transform on missions when I have to fight one or more particularly tough major demons. My Lustspawn sadistic side relishes the sight of fear in their eyes. The weakness and exhaustion that follow when I return to my human form almost make it worth it.

Let's get back to business. Zagam reads the coroner's report, furrowing his brow before handing it to me. The multiple fractures caused by a torture instrument—a hammer, according to the expert—and the use of a silver cord around the neck are confirmed. As well as the cause of death: the fall. I curse as I read the last lines of the document.

"Damn! His heart was *carbonized* in his chest?"

Which explains the black mark on his chest.

But not the how or why.

I've never heard of anything like this, and judging by his darkened expression, neither has my boss. Setting fire to a specific organ inside a body is unprecedented! Major demons gifted with pyrokinesis can only incinerate what they touch, like the Ragebeasts, or what they see, like some Braveryfiends.

We're on a whole other level here…

Furthermore, the new information implies something else: this gesture was performed post-mortem, as the Faithfiend wouldn't have survived such treatment. So, this bastard of a murderer returned to the crime scene to make sure his victim was dead before burning his heart!

The burned heart surely has a meaning, but I don't know what it is. Something related to faith? Love? Disease? Bravery? Further research is needed.

Before heading to the 1001 Nights of Lust, I'll have to go back to the church to inspect the crime scene again, in case we missed an important clue yesterday.

Lunacy, power, and intelligence. The infernal trio.

CHAPTER 8
THE 1001 NIGHTS OF LUST

"Lust: 1+1=69." ~Raymond Queneau,
The Diary of Sally Mara

MYRINA

"You could have made an effort with your outfit, Myri." Ondine sighs, her high heels clicking on the pavement.

We cross the road under the nocturnal drizzle swirling in the pale light of the streetlamps. The air is cool, and my sister, more sensitive to the cold than I am, keeps shivering.

"I remind you I'm not here for a good time, sis."

I admit I stand out compared to her. We're different in many ways, and this reality is even more striking tonight. I'm wearing a black leather jacket that I have no intention of taking off, boyfriend jeans ripped at the knees and thighs, and studded biker boots. I didn't even bother with makeup; I was too lazy coming back from the church—where I didn't find any additional clues.

My sister, on the other hand, is dressed to the nines for her first night working at the 1001 Nights of Lust. Her light eyes are enhanced with kohl and false lashes, and her full lips are painted crimson. She's slipped into a tight, silver, satin dress that almost shows her backside and a little black fitted jacket. Her matching high heels, the same color as her outfit, add a good four inches to her height, giving her a pair of stunning, slender legs that will drive the club's clients wild.

I've never been able to walk in high heels. Three inches is already a challenge for me. When I wear shoes like that, I wobble around like a limping giraffe. Ondine, on the other hand, naturally has a sexy, swaying gait worthy of a top model. And then, I'm already three inches taller than her to begin with. With heels like my sister's, I'd reach six foot one and tower over most men. I'd hate having to tilt my head down to look my future lovers in the eye. Taller than me is better. Same height, that's fine. Below is a deal-breaker.

I might make an exception for the charming actor Zac Efron because he has a killer body and crazy blue eyes. He's supposedly five foot eight, a few inches shorter than me. But in my opinion, I'd probably scare him off with my combination of brown and silver hair and my unique violet eyes. I tend to intimidate human males easily, even when I try to be sweet and calm.

Which doesn't happen often, to be honest. Because I can't help but shut them down as soon as they say something stupid. It's a reflex. I'm a real spitfire; that's well known.

And it really annoys me to be here to apologize to the tyrant Kelen Wills! I would have much preferred to spend a peaceful evening on the couch in front of the TV; there was a documentary about Jack the Ripper tonight. Purring, Putrid would have come to curl up on my thighs, begging for lots of cuddles and scratches. Oh yes, by the way, Putrid is our alley cat. He's so chubby that he has trouble licking his own butt to clean himself, hence his name. He has black fur and a pair of golden eyes like a Machiavellian psychocat.

He's our beloved big baby. We both have fun shouting, *"Smelly Cat, smelly Cat, it's not your faault."* the cult song by Phoebe in the *Friends* series, of course! As soon as he returns from his urban escapades, he elicits indignant meows and angry hisses. But otherwise, he's a sweetheart.

The 1001 Nights of Lust is a secret club located on the outskirts of the city. The neighborhood is deserted at night. There's no name on the gray, rectangular building that resembles a windowless warehouse. Nothing indicates its function to humans who wander the streets during the day. However, a magical demonic symbol visible only to us is drawn above the reinforced steel door. It's a fawn's head with twisted horns adorned with thorns: the allegory of the sin of lust, the emblem of the Lustspawns.

Ondine takes her badge out of her glittery pouch and places it in front of a sensor. The metal door unlocks. Only employees have free access to the club. My half-sister lowers the door handle and pushes the door open. I immediately catch a whiff of various demonic pheromones while rhythmic music assaults my eardrums. "*Voulez-vous coucher avec moi, Lady Marmelade.*" Ah, it's the original song from the 70s, remixed in a modern way, not the version from the movie *Moulin Rouge!*

Well, straight into the thick of it, as Grandpa Amon would say! My lovely retired Justspawn grandfather, former Virtuous Magistrate.

Yes, I can confirm demons listen to human music without moderation. We have many talents, but except for six or seven Virtuous prodigies on Infernum, we play music like amateurs and sing like pots and pans. You can't have it all. It's one of the few things demons envy mortals for. Sinners have musical tastes specific to each species. For example, the Ragebeasts love super aggressive hard metal; the Lustspawns love sexually explicit, languorous songs; the Slothlings love classical melodies that promote sleep; the Gluttonfiends love music about food… You get the idea.

A Ragebeast bouncer welcomes us into the vestibule in his human form: a giant, bodybuilder with a shaved head and dressed in all black. Ondine gives him kisses on the cheek.

"Mm, doll, you look mega hot in that dress," the demon says, squeezing her butt, which makes her giggle. "You're going to put all the clients in a trance when you perform on stage."

"But I'm always mega hot no matter what I wear, Paymon," she retorts, giving his wandering hand a little smack. "Keep your pervy paws to yourself. You know Kel doesn't like touching the merchandise. Is there some eye candy tonight?"

"Yeah. The Virtuous Beliale arrived about twenty minutes ago with her gang of debauchees. They reserved the best room just for themselves. Too bad I'm on duty; I would've loved to watch their orgy. From the moans and screams we hear intermittently, it sounds super-hot," the guy named Paymon says with a bitter smirk.

Ondine's expression darkens with discontent. I can guess the reason. According to rumors, Beliale, the Virtuous of the Lustspawn, is Kelen Wills's former mistress. In fact, she's also a candidate in the elections for the position of Sinner Federator and is Kelen's most serious rival. Ondine isn't jealous of the other demons her boyfriend sleeps with, but Beliale is the exception that proves the rule. Why? I have no bloody clue. I don't know if Kelen and Beliale are still screwing around, but Ondine can't stand the Magistrate at the head of her legion, that's for sure.

"You're not going to introduce me to your pretty punk friend?" the bouncer murmurs, turning his lascivious attention back to me.

"She's my sister, Paymon. Myrina Holmes."

At my name, the lecherous grin on the colossus's face instantly disappears. His complexion turns pale, and he instinctively takes a step back, muttering something in our language.

I burst out laughing at the Ragebeast's reaction. "Chill out! I'm not here for work. Didn't your boss warn you I was accompanying my sister?"

"He didn't, but I knew," says a male voice to my right. "Ondine, Myrina, welcome to the 1001 Nights of Lust."

"Saaaaam!" my sister exclaims joyfully, going to warmly embrace another Ragebeast, one who opens his arms for her.

Raising an eyebrow, I see Ondine press her mouth against the newcomer's… and give him a deep French kiss, arms around his neck.

Okay…

I should clarify: some particularly close Lustspawn friends exchange this kind of saliva-filled greeting, but it's rare for succubus or incubus to do the same with a demon of another species. Ondine is very sociable and tactile, but she doesn't show affection like this to just anyone. This deep kiss proves that she holds Sammael Daniels, Kelen Wills's right hand, in high esteem. Almost as dangerous as his boss, he assumes several roles within their legion: Kelen's lieutenant, manager of this swinger club, assistant manager on Infernum, spokesperson for the Ragebeast demons, and executioner and torturer in his spare time. In short, his Hybresang boss delegates many tasks to him… because Kelen is as lazy as a constipated koala, in my opinion.

Ondine pulls away from his lips, caressing his cheek. They whisper a few words I can't hear over the background music, then Sammael turns to me, an arm wrapped around my sister's waist. A human might think they're in love. I can guarantee you that's not the case. Ondine has never felt that kind of emotion toward a man. That's why I hope with all my heart that she won't fall for Kelen. As long as their relationship remains confined to desire, admiration, and esteem, I can handle it. But if she ever fell in love with such a bastard, I can't even imagine the catastrophe that would ensue.

"Myrina Holmes, I'm delighted to finally meet you," Sammael greets me. "Ondine has had nothing but praise for you."

I offer a tender smile to my sister, who returns it with a knowing wink. There isn't much in this crappy world that manages to penetrate my stone-cold heart. Only four people have earned a place there. My sister Ondine, my grandpa Amon, my boss Zagam—on his good days, mind you!—and my cat Putrid. Although I don't often agree with my exuberant roommate and we argue every three days, we've been inseparable for a few years now.

I size up Sammael's appearance with an appreciative glance. Setting aside his warrior-like build, he's the exact opposite of Kelen Wills. However, he's also extremely attractive in his own right. With his angelic features, eyes as cerulean as Ondine's, and long honey-colored hair cascading over his shoulders, he's no less appealing than a male incubus. He sports a small dimple in his chin, less pronounced than Kelen's, but really quite nice. I wouldn't mind fucking Sam one of these days. We'll see later if there's any chemistry between us. His friendly smile is promising. Note to self: ask Ondine if she's ever slept with him and if he's any good in bed.

"Don't believe her praises, she lies like a dentist," I quip to the club manager.

Sam and Ondine burst into laughter, exchanging glances. Hmm, what exactly did she tell him about me?

"Miss Holmes, did you bring any weapons?" the bouncer inquires. "Your sister must have told you they're not allowed at the 1001 Nights of Lust and that Mr. Wills doesn't tolerate any misbehavior here."

"Absolutely, Paymon. Myri left all her toys at home," Ondine assures him. "You don't need to frisk her."

"That's right," I confirm, flashing an innocent smile at the doorman. "Anyway, I would never have let you frisk me, big guy. Unless you have a masochistic penchant for compound fractures."

He shoots a nervous, uncertain glance at his boss, who nods in agreement, signaling him not to enforce the security protocol with me. *Well done, Sam, you score a point.*

Just because I don't have my crossbow, gun, and saber doesn't mean I'm harmless. On one hand, I have my hybrid powers and my little knack for martial arts. On the other hand, I've tucked a silver knife into my boot just to be on the safe side. I wasn't going to show up empty-handed for a meeting with Satan in the heart of debauchery and vice. I'm not that crazy.

"I'll take you to Kel's office, Miss Holmes," Sam informs me. "Ondine, you can go to your dressing room and get ready. I've laid out your schoolgirl costume on the couch. Your act is scheduled for ten-thirty, okay?"

"No problem, Sam. I've been practicing it at the apartment these past few days," she says enthusiastically, planting a kiss on my cheek. She must be eager to hit the stage and fire up her audience. "See you later, Myri. I'm counting on you to be nice to Kel."

In your dreams, sis.

***

KELEN

"Was it good, Kel?" my barmaid whispers, wiping her mouth with the back of her hand as I zip up my pants.

I needed to relax before my meeting with the Tracker to ensure I'd keep my self-control. Lilas, one of my Lustspawn employees who serves as both a waitress and a dancer, volunteered by offering to give me a blowjob. I appreciate her dedication and enthusiasm, but I'm very demanding. I give her a little encouraging pat on the head before wheeling my chair back to let her leave. On all fours under my desk, the busty brunette gazes up at me adoringly, licking her lips. She's cute.

And to top it off, she swallows.

"Not bad, darling. A bit rushed at the beginning, but you made up for it in the end."

"I'll do better, Kel, I promise," she coos, straightening up. "Do you want anything else? A quick fuck?"

"No, that'll be all," I reply.

Her slender shoulders slump. She seems disappointed, but honestly, I couldn't care less.

"Go back to serving the customers at the bar."

After Lilas leaves, I stand in front of the panoramic window overlooking the main hall of the 1001 Nights of Lust club. My desk towers over the vast club. Most of the time, the window is tinted; I can observe all the demons bustling on the ground floor without being detected. There's a button on the wall to clear the glass so the Sinners can see me from the outside, but I hardly ever press it. Besides, I rarely mingle with the crowd. Sam constantly navigates among the customers, chatting with regulars, giving out friendly smiles, and maintaining our commercial image.

My new agent had advised me to be more present downstairs. I'm not interested at all. I believe I've made enough efforts by granting a television interview to announce my candidacy and kick off my campaign. He scheduled another interview with Radio Hell for me next week. I plan to cancel it. Contrary to what he claims, my dark aura of mystery appeals greatly to the voters: polls among the populace are revealing. Currently, forty-three percent of Sinners are considering voting for me in the upcoming elections. My Lustspawn competitor, Beliale, is close behind with thirty-nine percent. The other Magistrates candidates share fourteen percent, and there are only four percent of undecided Sinners left. The abstention rate will presumably be very low, as this is the first time in all of Infernum's history that a democratic vote is being organized. Most likely, Beliale and I will be the two candidates vying for the position of Federator. We will then persuade the other five Magistrates to elect one of us. I already know my former mistress will sleep with each of them to get their votes. According to my informants, that succubus slut has already won over the Gluttonfiend Magistrate.

MYRINA

The song *"Naughty Girl,"* by Beyoncé, just started playing in the room with its contemporary-chic decor. Two stunning Lustspawns in their demonic form sway on the podium to the wild cheers of the crowd. One of them is dressed as a nurse, the other as a maid. They caress each other's arms, stomachs, and breasts as they move around the dance pole with feline grace. Their black scales shimmer under the bright spotlights, and their pointed tails coil sensually around each other, tantalizing the spectators.

I'm somewhat relieved to see the clients aren't exposing themselves to everyone. Except for the two strippers, no one is naked. There must be private rooms or chambers reserved for debauchery, like in a brothel. I was afraid I'd have to navigate through a massive, frenzied orgy. It's not that I'm a prude, far from it, but there are limits. Despite having my fair share of one-night stands, I'm not as uninhibited and adventurous as my sister. Threesomes, swinging, and more hardcore practices like sadomasochism are definitely not for me. I'm less uptight than the Virtuous demons—and yet, some of them are nymphos behind their prim façades!—but I'm overall less uninhibited than the Sinners. Out of curiosity, I once made love to a woman. A beautiful blond succubus, a childhood friend of Ondine's. Oh, it wasn't unpleasant, but it confirmed to me that I'm heterosexual and not bisexual like the overwhelming majority of Lustspawn. My sex life may seem dull and conventional compared to my sister's and other Sinners. Nevertheless, I'm fully fulfilled in this aspect of my life.

My gaze falls upon a formidable Gluttonfiend male biting the neck of a human in a corner of the room. With a hand tangled in her hair, this gluttony demon presses her against the wall, rubbing frantically against her. An ecstatic expression contorts the girl's features… and a trickle of red blood runs down her neckline. A dull rage hums within me. With clenched fists, I take a step in their direction, ready to intervene. Sam grabs me roughly by the arm, furrowing his brow sternly.

"Miss Holmes, may I remind you that 1001 Nights is a neutral space governed by its own charter? You're here tonight as a guest of Kelen Wills, not as a representative of the law. Our club is not under the jurisdiction of the CIT, and you have no legal right to exercise your duties here unless you have a justified mandate from your higher-up. Like everyone else, this human signed a consent form upon arrival. If the demon were to go too far with her, we would sanction him ourselves and forcibly eject him from the building. We have cameras installed everywhere and are very vigilant about adhering to safety rules, rest assured."

I cast a frigid glance at his hand gripping my arm. "You have three seconds to let go, Daniels. Not one more."

With a disgruntled growl, he complies.

I shoot a gloomy glance at the Gluttonfiend and his human companion. He has just stopped sucking her blood, and they are staring at each other intensely. The demon whispers something in her ear, tapping her hip, then takes her hand and leads her to the bar. As she follows him, she presses a tissue against her wounded throat with a blissful smile that turns my stomach.

"Have there ever been any slip-ups since your club opened, Daniels?" I inquire imperiously.

"No, Miss Holmes. Sinners who struggle to control their impulses aren't admitted to this establishment. The regulars are all aware Kelen would personally punish them if they didn't adhere to our internal rules. And believe me, Miss Holmes… No sensible demon would want to be punished by a Magistrate Hybresang. Tempting Satan would be less risky."

Driven by a premonition, I slowly raise my head toward the tinted glass window overlooking the room. I feel like I'm being watched by someone.

A slight shiver runs down my spine.

I'd bet a million Forks that's *his* office and he's watching me.

CHAPTER 9
HUMBLEST APOLOGIES?

"The midday demon often arrives at two o'clock." ~Pierre Dac, The Thoughts

MYRINA

Sammael knocks on the door of the office to announce our arrival to his boss before opening it and gesturing for me to enter. On guard, I cautiously step into the large room with walls cluttered with shelves of ancient books and masterful paintings as Kelen's lieutenant discreetly withdraws.

I don't know much about art. A scene of a bloody battle from ancient Rome… Nymphs dancing in the woods with a satyr… The autopsy of a corpse performed by Renaissance doctors… And one of them is even more disturbing. It depicts a young female human in a bed, dressed in an ivory gown and lying on her back. Given her backward-leaning position, she appears dead. A strange, small demon resembling a gargoyle sits on her stomach. In the background, a rather eerie horse's head with bulging white eyes emerges from the shadows. I don't like this painting at all; it gives me goose bumps.

Standing in front of the bay window overlooking the main room of the 1001 Nights of Lust, Kelen Wills has his back turned to me. Apparently, he's on the phone with someone, as I can see part of his earbud among his hair.

Is my gaze magnetically drawn to his rounded, muscular ass that's accentuated by his elegant black trousers?

Unfortunately, yes, three times over.

So, I force myself to look away while listening to his conversation with one ear. I'm annoyed he doesn't end the call to greet me. It would be a small courtesy, considering I came here to present my damn apologies. Rudeness in all its unworthy glory!

"…don't care about your petty attacks on my private life in the press, Hallow," Kelen calmly states.

Hallow, the irritable leader of the Envyfiend Sinners, is one of his competitors.

"You have no proof of what you're claiming." A brief mocking laugh shakes Kelen's well-defined shoulders. "Right. You rely on the defamation of a bitter housewife who's furious about not being invited into my bed after she had the audacity to make her crude advances. You spread rumors as mediocre as they are absurd about me, but the voters won't be fooled. I won't even stoop to respond to you through the media; that would give you an importance you lack."

He turns to me without hurry. With a lazy eye, he looks me up and down without the slightest decency while his interlocutor responds to him, then he speaks again in a distant tone. "Hallow, if you feel threatened by my superiority in the polls and my popularity among the voters of Infernum, that's your problem, not mine. You conduct your political campaign with a blatant lack of subtlety. You should fire your consultants; they're notorious incompetents. Unless, of course, you wish to further ridicule yourself, I recommend that in the future, you contain your expression of envy toward me."

A malicious smile blooms on his lips for two seconds. "But if you lack the strength to do so, continue to cowardly denigrate me in that rag you call a newspaper; I encourage you to do so. I suppose you're not yet aware of this detail, but I've already gained three additional points in the polls thanks to your intervention in the press. Conversely, you've lost two points. If you didn't annoy me so much, Hallow, I'd send you a good bottle of Ambrosia Nectar to thank you."

With that, he pulls his phone out of his pocket and hangs up on the other Magistrate, looking me straight in the eyes. "Agent Holmes, you're five minutes late," he states evenly.

"Consider yourself lucky, Wills. You've gained five minutes during which I didn't tell you to go fuck yourself."

"That wasn't on tonight's agenda, but why not?" he remarks. "The place is ideal for indulging in that kind of release." He gestures lazily toward the panoramic window. "I can have the BDSM room cleared out so we can have some privacy there. Have you ever experienced the burning caress of a studded whip on your soft buttocks, my little wildcat?"

My little wildcat? Anything else?

Do I nickname him my big raging raccoon?

"No familiarity with me, Wills! And spare me your nauseating innuendos," I grumble, glancing at the bizarre painting on his wall, which *also* gives me acid reflux.

"Is it to your liking?" my interlocutor says while taking off his earbud and placing it on his desk.

"This painting?"

He nods, clearing his throat.

"Hell no, I find it hideous."

Kelen moves closer to me, admiring the artwork. I muster the strength to not step back and lose ground, which would be a demonstration of weakness. Thankfully, my sister's boyfriend freezes about nine feet away from me, hands in his trouser pockets.

"For my part, I find it quite fascinating. What bothers you about it?" he asks.

I sigh in exasperation. "It's eerie, oppressive, almost unhealthy. The shadows and lights, the hallucinating horse, the grimacing monster, the girl's corpse… Everything bothers me, really."

"She's not dead," he contradicts confidently. "She's asleep. These two creatures are from her dream. It's an oil on canvas by a great painter of the 18th century named Fuseli. *The Nightmare.*"

"Hmm, is it a copy?"

"No. I never bother with copies, Agent Holmes. It's an original. A perfect forgery is displayed at the Detroit Museum. Even human experts were deceived by the counterfeit artist I hired."

There's a certain pride in his voice. Pathetic. Conceited. Pompous. To show off, the thirteen-century-old Magistrate of the Ragebeasts flaunts his considerable culture like indigestible rhubarb jam on a toast.

I can't stand rhubarb.

"The malevolent demon crouching on the belly of this young woman is an incubus as humans perceive it," Kelen explains calmly. "Some art critics have seen it as an expression of the dreamer's sexual desire, wishing to copulate with the devil, hence her open position on the bed and her virginal robe. The horse with glassy eyes, watching her like a voyeur, would be an allegory of male libido."

"Really charming, Wills. I'm not so surprised you like this horror after all," I comment, grimacing.

"I have many other works of art in my home that you might find more to your liking. Ancient weapons, Greek sculptures, rare trinkets. I love collecting beautiful things... unconventional ones," he remarks thoughtfully, noticing my dark hair streaked with white strands.

Damn, and he's flirting with me on top of it!

"We should invent a fifteenth legion and a new sin just for you," I retort, shifting to the side on principle. "We could call these demons the Devil's Buffoons, a legion affiliated with the sin of Supreme Foolishness. You'd quickly be overstaffed; Infernum is already saturated."

Kelen lights up with a slight smile, locking his gaze with mine. He has a very... vexing dark beauty. His shiny pupils resemble two blocks of dark marble flecked with gold. Like the burn on my arm, his perfect nose is healed. Messy hair, stubble, and a midnight blue shirt with the collar open, revealing the beginnings of his sculpted chest. In short, he's hotter than the hottest of all Earth's models... and he knows it all too well. A demon version of a nuclear bomb.

That I absolutely *do not* visualize naked. No. Not at all. I swear on my sword that I have erased his silhouette from my memory. I've deleted the irritating memory of his magnificent V-shaped torso dripping with water, his athletic thighs, and his long—

"Agent Holmes, what do you think of the 1001 Nights?" he blurts out, interrupting my mental digressions.

"Your club sucks."

I've succeeded in my aim: his smile fades. He wanted my opinion, didn't he? Well, let him deal with it.

"What are your constructive arguments?" he retorts with a hint of quite satisfying annoyance.

"The main one is this: you exploit humans like cattle."

"What a narrow and skewed view, Agent Holmes. We mutually benefit from each other so that everyone gets what they want. Humans are here of their own free will to enjoy the present moment in the company of ours. Or rather, should I say mine, since you're only half a Sinner," he insinuates with a disdain he doesn't bother to sugarcoat.

"I've inherited the best halves of the Sinners and the Virtuous, Wills. While *you* accumulate all the flaws of the seven races of the Sinning demons," I accuse, stiffening like a pole.

"That's your perspective, but not everyone in Infernum shares it. Myself included. Besides, can we consider your inability to control your physical and verbal violence, your shortened lifespan, and your mysterious handicap as far more significant flaws?" He scrutinizes my face and then my silhouette intensely, certainly trying to discern the birth defect in question.

At his jab, a shiver of displeasure runs through me. God, he's detestable. His tongue is as sharp as the tip of my sword. How does Ondine tolerate a guy like him?

For the other use of his tongue, Myri, my mischievous, succubus inner voice whispers.

My sense of justice as a Justspawn takes over. I don't know when or how, but I'll make him pay for his insult. If there's one thing I don't tolerate being attacked on, it's my handicap. I hope Ondine won't divulge anything to him. I'll brief her on that.

"I could have apologized if you had been decent to me from the start, Wills. But you can still shove your golden toilet brush up your ass if I'm supposed to do it now."

He doesn't seem surprised or annoyed by my biting retort. "Given your character, I expected nothing less from you, Agent Holmes."

"We'll meet in court, then. And I'll fight!" I snap defiantly.

With calculated slowness, as if to create a suspenseful moment, the Hybresang begins unbuttoning his cufflinks to roll up his shirt sleeves to the middle of his tanned forearms.

It pains me to admit it, but this simple gesture is horribly sexy and masculine. In a parallel world, if I had encountered such an attractive man on the street or in a bar, if he hadn't been involved with my sister, and *especially* if he hadn't been the despicable Kelen Wills, I would have approached him without hesitation. When I like a guy, I go for it head-on. But in his case… I'd rather swallow rat poison than show him that he doesn't leave me indifferent. Physically speaking, that is. Because his personality disgusts me.

"After some thought, I won't be pressing charges against you, my little cat. My time is too precious to waste on ruining your promising career as a Tracker," he finally lets out.

I raise a skeptical eyebrow, struck silent. My intuition was correct: he had been bluffing! But if he suspected that I wouldn't consent to his demand, why did he pressure my boss to have me come to him tonight?

Damn, was it a trap?

"We started off on the wrong foot, you and I," the Sinful Magistrate continues, assessing me with a suspicious impassiveness. "The context of the conflict in the bathroom wasn't conducive to a good initial understanding, I agree. But we must bury the hatchet for Ondine's sake." He cracks a charming smile, igniting a tiny ball of warmth deep in my belly. "One could almost say I'm your brother-in-law, Myrina. Doesn't that prospect *excite* you as much as it does me?"

My brother-in-law—him? Good Lord, I still feel like vomiting!

"I didn't authorize you to call me by my first name, as far as I'm aware. And you're not my brother-in-law. Not now, not ever. Don't play the gentleman; you're not believable. Ondine isn't one of those mindless bimbos who swoon over you, Wills. She'll see through you sooner or later and leave you for good. You're the embodiment of evil."

And also the embodiment of male, but let's move on.

"I savor your compliment, *Myrina*. Evil is my *raison d'être*, after all. By the way, how's your new investigation going?"

I nearly bite my tongue as I grit my teeth. By the iron trident, how could he know? Would he have contacts at CIT? Unless…

Oh, no! He must have questioned Ondine about my job, and she spilled everything, that bitch! I'm going to kill her! Damn it, I won't tell her anything about my work anymore.

"Mind your own moldy scales, multi-Sinner," I retort.

"I have a long arm and unlimited means. If you showed goodwill toward me, I could give you a claw to identify this Faithfiend who seems to be giving you a hard time already," he suggests with an innocent look that doesn't suit him at all.

"And why would you grant me this favor? Don't make me believe you're disinterested!"

"Just a peace offering, my little cat. Look no further."

"No, I'll manage on my own, Wills. I don't need your claw. You're the last demon in Infernum I'd want to owe anything to."

I'd rather sell my soul to Beelzebub.

"I don't offer my help to just anyone, Myrina."

What a privilege!

"It's a golden opportunity; it would be a shame to decline it due to misplaced pride. When you change your mind, let me know through your sister."

"I won't change my mind, Wills."

"Yes, Myrina, you'll change your mind. Just as you'll change your mind about me. I'm your ally, not your adversary. A card up your sleeve."

"A pebble in my boot, more likely!"

"I'll even provide you with an ace to enrich your hand and demonstrate the extent of my goodwill. I have a hypothesis about the flaming heart of your Faithfiend corpse. Do you wish to hear it?"

Well, he's managed to pique my curiosity, the pretentious bastard! I furrow my brow, crossing my arms over my chest... but failing to conceal my interest.

"Go ahead, then," I grumble.

"The flaming heart is the emblem of the Legion of Charity demons."

"Well done, what a revelation!" I scoff, rolling my eyes. "And do you think that's not one of the first things I considered, Wills? I ruled out that idea outright. The murderer would have to be completely idiotic to signal to CIT that he's part of the Charityfiends' Legion!"

A smug smile spreads across Kelen's full lips. "Myrina Holmes, that interpretation is far too logical to apply to a twisted brain like that of the demon you're chasing. Dig deeper."

"Stop dragging out your cheap effects and spill the spicy sauce!"

A gravelly chuckle erupts from his throat. "*Spill the spicy sauce,* Myrina? What an eloquent image."

I respond with an impatient grunt.

"Very well. In my opinion, it's a hidden, yet deliberate clue. How do the young people say it these days… an easter egg, if I'm not mistaken?"

"And what else?"

"Your murderer is a nasty poker player who wants to include you in his card game, my dear. By burning the heart of his victim, he's put you on the trail of his next crime."

"What?" I murmur, eyes widening. "His next crime, you say?"

"He's a serial killer possessed by a complex of divine omnipotence. It seems obvious to me, given all the grandiose staging he arranged in that church. He wants to impress and leave a lasting impression; beyond the symbolism he conveys, he probably has a pathological need for social recognition. I've encountered many human psychopaths and demons over the centuries, and I guarantee this murderer won't stop there. This is just the beginning."

By Cerberus's castrated balls! His reasoning is frighteningly coherent. "In other words, you're suggesting that he set fire to the Faithfiend's heart to announce to the investigators his next victim: another Virtuous, a Charityfiend."

"Exactly, little cat. Care for a drink?"

I shake my head curtly.

He heads to his minibar and pours himself a splash of purplish Dragon's Bile before adding two ice cubes. "Unfortunately for you, there are millions of Charityfiends in Infernum. It's a slim clue, but it at least allows you to better understand the psychological profile of your killer. Well, I won't teach you your job."

With that statement, Kelen takes three swigs of the strong alcohol. His Adam's apple trembles in his throat. I bite my lower lip, pushing from my mind an inappropriate fantasy in which I would lick his chin dimple before biting into his enticing Adam's apple while sliding my hand determinedly into his pants… Satan be praised, he can't detect it, but the tips of my nipples have just hardened under my leather jacket, and a sneaky wetness soaks my panties beneath my jeans.

The worst part is, he hasn't touched me at any point, nor has he unleashed his incubus pheromones to seduce and arouse me. Yet, I am aroused. Against my damn will. I'm ashamed my body reacts like this over a trifle. I can't stand this guy, but deep down, I'd like to fuck him wildly to satisfy my own curiosity. I feel awful for betraying my sister in thought, flipping the bird to my moral values, and reaching the pinnacle of perversion by my standards. I don't often feel guilt, but right now, I'm swimming in it.

Regaining my composure, I argue, "No, indeed, you won't teach me my job. You're a warrior and a politician, not a CIT inspector. You're so sure of yourself, but you can't know if this is an isolated murder or the first of a series. You're not a psychic."

"Listen to your Tracker instinct, Agent Holmes. It confirms my impression; I see it in your eyes. You'll acknowledge it when the second victim is found."

"But the motive isn't—"

"It's time for you to leave, little cat. Your company has been quite pleasant and entertaining, but there are still a billion tedious tasks I must attend to before sunrise, and I can't afford any slip-ups, tempting as they may be." With a penetrating glance, he presses a button on his screen and holds it to his ear. "Sam, get your ass to my office to escort my guest to the club's door; I'm done with her."

What a first-class bastard. He summons and dismisses me as if I'm at his beck and call!

Thirty seconds later, his second comes to get me. At the threshold, I glance over my shoulder at the Hybresang sitting behind his desk, maintaining my challenging gaze with a cryptic smirk.

"Good night, Virtuous Sinner. Pleasure to see you again. And don't forget these words for your investigation: as Alessandro Morandotti pointed out, '*Patience is a virtue acquired through patience.*'"

With that quote, he remotely closes his office door with his damn telekinesis, forcing me to step back to avoid getting hit in the face. Sammael chuckles softly; I glare at him.

Number one on the list—previously nonexistent—of my suspects?

Kelen Wills.

I'll have to keep a very, very close eye on him.

CHAPTER 10
THE PURITY OF PERVERSION

*"The demon is a tempter who never tires,
thus he never lacks the opportunity for the
crime to which he invites." ~Daniel Defoe,
Moll Flanders*

KELEN

"So, Sam, what do you think?"

"I understand what you see in her. Her beauty, her temperament, her intelligence, her power. You're right, she has something extra." My lieutenant Ragebeast hesitates for a moment. "But she's a Tracker, Kel, not an ordinary demoness. I think you're playing with fire on all levels; it could backfire on you. You should at least end your affair with Ondine before making a move on her sister. That would be the minimum requirement."

"Ondine doesn't matter."

"Exactly. If she doesn't matter to you, then leave her."

"That wouldn't be a good move. She's my ticket to Myrina's life."

"So, if you hurt her along the way, it wouldn't bother you at all?"

Through the bay window of my office, I watch Ondine lazily sway around the dance pole to Beyoncé's "Baby Boy." Sensually stripping on stage, the succubus employs several flirtatious gestures: she blows little kisses, sucks on the tips of her claws, and licks the metal pole with her forked tongue. The spectators applaud and whistle enthusiastically. I made the right choice hiring her; she's going to bring in even more cash for me.

"No, Sam. Because I know you'll volunteer to console her by opening your arms and your bed so she can forget her disappointment." He lets out a skeptical grunt. "I never told Ondine that our relationship was serious, and I didn't promise her anything about the future. She's just a fleeting pastime, like the others. If she imagines something else, that's her business."

"You're a complete scumbag, Kel," he comments disapprovingly.

I glance at my second with a mocking smile. It's the first time he's reproached my libertine attitude toward women; usually, he couldn't care less. It implies that Ondine means more to him than she does to me. If I trust my intuition, he feels more than just friendly affection for her. Surprising. Especially since it's been about two or three centuries since he last slept with a woman. Lately, he's only been interested in men.

If Sammael explicitly admitted to me that he wants to pursue a relationship with her, I would gladly let him try his luck. But if he doesn't ask me the question, I don't see why I should do him that favor. I'm not here to play matchmaker for everyone. I have other things to do, and there's no "Cupid" written on my forehead. Furthermore, in my view, when you really want something, you don't wait for it to fall into your lap: you do everything you can to seize it. In human terms, that's called having balls. In our world, we tend to say that you have to take the demon by the horns.

"I'm not sure you'll get anywhere with Myrina Holmes, Kel. If she had the same life expectancy as us, I'd have a more nuanced speech, but her time is limited, and she seems very stubborn from what I've heard from your mouth and Ondine's. The other day, her sister mentioned in front of me a traumatic event that occurred in her life a few years ago. She didn't reveal more about it, but she more or less told me that Myrina withdrew into herself after that event and avoided any form of attachment to anyone, except for her close ones. And you… she simply can't stand you."

"I appreciate your input, Sam, but I have no intention of taking it into account," I retort wearily.

"The opposite would have surprised me."

I change the subject abruptly. "Any news from our informants about the Rebels?"

Silence. Downstairs, Ondine has just dropped her bra. My lieutenant swallows as he gazes at her small, scaly breasts coated in multicolored glitter, before regaining his composure.

"No, Kel. Our latest lead didn't yield anything. Yesterday, I sent a squad of Ragebeasts into a Rebel nest. Serena was leading them. Our guys were ordered to capture and torture them, one by one, to get them to spill the names of their leaders. But when our demon soldiers stormed the warehouse, it was empty. Those bastards had all fled before we arrived. I don't know how they knew we were coming. Espionage, hacking, or—"

"A major Hopeling with a gift of double vision," I interject, pensive.

"You took the words right out of my mouth," he mutters, tilting his head to the side to admire Ondine as she hangs upside down and gracefully slides along the pole.

I've inherited many powers from the Sinners, but I don't have anything in stock that resembles the gift of foresight possessed by some Virtuous Hopelings, the demons of hope. Too bad—it would be useful for crushing my enemies.

"I hope the CIT didn't hear about your intervention, Sam?"

The tedious hunt for the Rebels falls primarily under the judicial functions of the Trackers. Every demonic militia in Infernum is supposed to report to the CIT the information gathered about the rebels. Which I didn't, as you can imagine. The major Trackers scrupulously enforce the laws and lack backbone. Most of them are incompetent. I almost despise them as much as the Rebels. Except for Myrina Holmes, the pretty little standout.

"No, we were careful. If they had found out, believe me, we would have had a steep response from them," Sam emphasizes. "By the way, Magistrate Beliale asked to see you after her orgy."

"Tell her, with your most commercial smile, that I'm not available."

At least, not for her.

"She's not going to take it well, Kel," grumbles my lieutenant.

"As always, Sam. That damn diva's sensitivity hasn't improved over the centuries. If she wants me to grant her an audience, she can make an appointment through Clara."

"Ciara, Kel. Your secretary's name is Ciara."

"One letter off, you nitpick." I furrow my brow as I see an intoxicated Envyfiend grab Ondine's ankle on the stage. Furious, she delivers a swift tail whip to his face to calm him down. A tail slap, as they say among demons. "Call Paymon and tell him to kick that jerk out, pronto."

In my club, we don't touch my employees without their consent.

A pleased smile spreads across Sam's lips as he retrieves his phone from his pocket. "Should I order him to break a few bones on the way out?" he asks, a glimmer of hope in his blue eyes.

"No, my friend, we're not barbarians. Let him settle for cutting off a finger and feeding it to an Gluttonfiend."

MYRINA

What the hell am I doing here?

I'm back at the 1001 Nights of Lust. With a morbid fascination, I'm watching the unleashed clients engage in scenes of depravity around me in the main hall. Lounging on the floor, reclining on sofas, or standing against the walls, dozens of demons and humans fornicate. Lustspawn waitresses, wearing nothing but red thongs, weave through the room, their trays laden with cups of Dragon's Bile and various erotic accessories. Some offer their personal services and actively participate in the orgies.

The guests regularly change partners, and several groups of people are so intertwined that they resemble mountains of anonymous limbs, twisted bodies, and damp hair constantly moving in all directions under the multicolored beams of the spotlights. The scent that pervades the room is a blend of musk, sweat, pheromones, perfume, and body fluids. Naked and glistening flesh slaps against each other with varying degrees of speed; the moans of pleasure, the erratic gasps, and the echo of mischievous laughter create a rather unique cacophony. Techno music pulses through the speakers. I raise my eyebrows in perplexity as I see two enthusiastic young women kneeling between three well-built demons. One of them caresses the leather strap of a whip.

I need to get out of here. I don't belong in this place.

And nobody pays me any attention…

Except one man.

My troubled gaze meets two dark, shimmering pits of perversion. Kelen Wills.

He stands at the other end of the room, leaning against a wall, half in shadow. When he moves, I hold my breath. He's wearing the same outfit as during our meeting, with one difference: his shirt is open, revealing his muscular chest. With calm and determined steps, the emperor of the Sinners makes his way assuredly through the room, stepping over and around the naked bodies writhing on the floor. Women in the throes of passion cast hungry glances at him and offer him seductive smiles. Feverish hands brush against his ankles and legs as he passes, as if pleading for him to join the carnal festivities. But he ignores them. He continues on his path toward me with the smooth gait of a predator. His amber eyes never leave mine.

When he stands in front of me, a sarcastic half-smile spreads across his lips. "You seem as comfortable in this environment as a lost succubus at a Faithfiend religious conference, Agent Holmes. Nothing in this room tempts you?" he asks, his tone dripping with ambiguity.

God, there's only one thing tempting me, and it's standing right in front of me. Because Kelen staring at me while standing still amid a swirling demonic sex orgy is a damn visual torture.

He hasn't raised his voice. Yet, I hear him distinctly despite the cacophony of noises and music. Strange.

"Why am I here, Wills?"

"The delightful expression of your subconscious, my little cat."

"What? Am I dreaming?"

He doesn't answer my question.

"Let's go to my office," he suggests, extending a hand to me. "The ambient agitation isn't conducive to an intimate discussion."

I eye his long fingers warily. An intimate discussion, huh?

"You have nothing to fear with me, Myrina."

"That's precisely what the devil would say to lure me into his lair."

"But, my little cat, you're already in my lair. And you know as well as I do that the devil doesn't exist, nor does god. Come."

His command is so imperative that I instinctively slip my hand into his. It's firm and burning. My fingers tingle at his touch.

Kelen teleports us to his office on the first floor. The light is off, and we're immersed in a grim half-darkness. Only the psychedelic glows from the main room illuminates the space through the bay window. I release the Hybresang's hand and step back. If this is indeed a dream, I want to wake up, now. I don't like where this is going. I shouldn't have followed him. Bringing my arms behind my back, I painfully pinch my wrist. In vain. I'm still asleep.

"You seem even more stressed than downstairs, Myrina. I'm greatly flattered that my presence is responsible for your agitation."

"Stop it, I'm allergic to nonsense. You wanted to talk to me; you have two minutes," I retort with a polar tone.

"Oh, because you believed me?"

"Wills, I'm not here to play!"

"Of course you are, my little cat. We're here alone together because your head is cluttered with repressed desires and unconscious frustration toward me. It's your erotic dream, not mine. Don't be offended, but my fantasies are much more original and imaginative."

"My erot—you're delusional!"

With unwavering confidence, Kelen takes a step forward, nodding his head.

With nervous uncertainty, I take a step back, shaking my head.

"And even in your dreams, you refuse to let go of your desires and admit your attraction to me," he continues.

He comes closer, and I step back with all my muscles tense.

"Isn't that the height of absurdity? Morality is a barrier that separates you from truth and freedom, Myrina. Until you tear it down with your own hands, you'll never find your inner peace. I've seen through you from the start, my little one. The duality of your nature gnaws at you from within. You don't feel like a Sinner or a Virtuous one. You're constantly torn between vice and virtue, between your insatiable hunger and your unfounded guilt. Behind your armor and your shield of an Amazon, you yearn for truth and freedom that the Trackers can't offer you. You need a solid guide to lead you off the beaten path and emancipate you from your condition. And above all, someone who understands you. I could be that demon."

A cynical laugh bursts from my throat. It feels like I've swallowed sandpaper.

"What nauseating rhetoric! You're the worst hypocrite in all of Infernum! I've seen through you, too. A guide? A master, you mean! All you want is to subjugate me and make me your new submissive bitch. You've set yourself some twisted challenge to corrupt me, dominate me, and add me to your collection of trophies to feed your infinite ego. But you're wasting your time. I'm not prey. I'm a hunter and..." As I take another step back, my back hits the glass. Damn it, I'm stuck. "For god's sake, don't come any closer, or I'll rearrange your face again,

Wills!"

He places a hand beside my head on the glass. I weigh the options between breaking his arm or giving him a knee between his legs.

"Mm, it's quite interesting that you bring up the theme of domination and submission when I haven't mentioned it at all, my little cat… A revealing interpretation of your own desire. Have you ever read Freud's theories on dream interpretation, as well as the repression of libido? The life drive, Eros: love, emotion, reproduction. The death drive, Thanatos: pain, self-destruction, death. Yet another opposition that tears you apart and characterizes you. Two opposing energies you've been juggling since your teenage years. That's why you throw yourself so passionately into your work as a Tracker and indulge in meaningless flings with men. They're distractions. Deep down, you want to submit to my authority because you know I'm the only demon strong and powerful enough to fulfill all the suppressed desires. Because of your Justspawn blood, you deny this truth… for now. As for corrupting you, let me laugh… By definition, one can only corrupt purity, Myrina, and you're far from being an innocent."

Psychological pressure. This manipulative bastard trying to tempt me into giving in to carnal desires is terribly cunning.

Wake up, Myrina Holmes! Right now!

"You don't know anything about me, Wills. You don't know what I've been through."

"Then tell me."

"No."

Kelen doesn't like being told no. With his fiery gaze locked on mine, he leans in toward me. It's now or never to defend myself physically. If this is just a dream, I can very well give him a beating without any consequences! But… damn it, as unbelievable as it may seem, I have no desire to hit him. His closeness is intoxicating. I don't know if I'm wet in my bed, but in my dream… yes. My back, stomach, and thighs are on fire.

"Who hurt you, my little wildcat?" he inquires, his voice menacing, his face just an inch from mine.

"No one," I lie, my throat tight with sadness.

He scrutinizes me for a long moment, eyebrows furrowed. Then he places his hand on the collar of my jacket. My breath shortens.

"Tell me, Myrina," he demands in a softer, more suave tone.

I shake my head.

He slowly lowers the zipper of my leather jacket, inch by inch. I would never have let him do such a thing in reality, but…

"You have no idea how much seeing you at my mercy against this glass wall excites me," Kelen confesses in a husky voice.

"I'm not at your mercy, Wills."

"Yes, you are."

His impudent eyes travel down to the neckline of my light top. My nipples are so hard that their shape is even visible through my bra. With his index finger, he grazes the strip of bare skin visible between the top of my jeans and the bottom of my tank top, electrifying my hormones and frying my synapses. Despite myself, I arch against his tormenting finger, which makes him smile.

"Do you see this?" he says. *"Your body doesn't lie. It demands…"* He trails his index finger around my navel. *"All my attention."*

"Go to hell," I object weakly, my breath uneven.

"Tell me to stop, Myrina," Kelen murmurs, playing with the first button of my jeans.

My lips remain sealed.

He undoes the button. *"We're not doing anything wrong. You're not betraying your sister by dreaming of me."* Second button. *"I'm not even really here, I'm just a projection of your subconscious. It's just a harmless fantasy, without consequence."* Third. He spreads open the waistband of my pants. *"We all fantasize about the forbidden, you don't have to be ashamed. Ondine will never know. So… surrender to me for the duration of a dream,"* he suggests, brushing against the triangle of my black thong with his thumb, right at the level of my clitoris.

This fleeting contact electrifies my senses. I bite down on my tongue to prevent a damn moan from escaping. A rough chuckle rumbles from his throat.

"I couldn't look my sister in the eye when I'll wake up if I succumbed in dream to your perversion or… or mine," I challenge, cavalierly pushing aside his hand.

Before I can even comprehend what he's doing, Kelen seizes me roughly and spins me around to press me against the glass again. Not violently, but firmly. I exhale a small cry of astonishment and anger.

Yet another thing I would never have let him do in reality. I would have fought with all my might. I would have transformed into a hybrid demoness. I would have used my powers. And we would have battled on equal terms.

But I can no longer pretend otherwise: this is a damn erotic dream, and I have no damn desire for it to end. My Lustspawn side is winning the game.

With surprisingly delicate movements, Kelen pushes my hair behind my shoulder, and like the serpent in the Garden of Eden inviting Eve to bite into the *forbidden fruit, he whispers in my ear, "Look at all those demons down below… See the wonderful beauty of their union. Hear the heavenly joy of their moans. Feel their authentic emotions. The language of bodies coming together is a chaotic choreography that I'll never tire of. No rules. No inhibition. No restraint. They fully savor the present moment, brimming with confidence and freedom. They commune with the divine. It's a different form of love. I'll let you in on a secret, my little cat. That's not perversion. That, my dear, is true purity," he concludes, pressing his hot, muscular body against mine.*

Oh, god, he's so damn hard. I shiver in every limb, equally aroused by the caress of his deep voice as by the pressure of his arousal against my buttocks. I struggle to appeal to my Justspawn reason. I must resist on principle… Keep control… I can't do this to Ondine… I hate this guy… but… damn, it feels so good! It's horrible to admit, but no man has ever drive me crazy like this.

You're not being objective, Holmes, *grumbles my Justspawn conscience as Kelen takes my wrists and presses my hands flat against the glass.* You wouldn't react like this in reality.

Why fight against your womanly desires, Myri? *whispers my Lustspawn voice to the contrary as he hikes up the hem of my top to reveal the curve of my breasts.* It's just a little harmless fantasy. Let yourself go for once…

I press my forehead against the glass, closing my eyes to block out the disturbing orgy scene below. As Kelen traces enigmatic patterns with his palm, he begins to massage the exposed skin of my abdomen. Sparks of pleasure sizzle in the pit of my stomach. I arch my back, sighing deeply.

"Good girl. Listen to your body's natural needs. Let me caress you," he says in a sweet tone before running the tip of his tongue under my ear, eliciting a sort of plaintive meow from me. "Mm, you taste delicious, Myrina. I could devour you whole."

His right hand cups my breast over the lace cup of my bra. His left hand snakes toward my sex. He plants wet kisses along the exposed line of my throat, alternating between brief suckling and gentle nibbles. With a delayed realization, I notice I'm rubbing my buttocks against his stiff erection to encourage him to go further. He doesn't move his hips at all; stiff as a wooden stake, he lets me undulate slowly against him in total tranquility. I feel him smile against the moist flesh of my throat.

Just as he slips his hand into the opening of my jeans to access my inner thigh, I reopen my eyelids… and startle slightly.

She's alone and standing on the podium. My sister. Her eyes, red with tears of distress, are fixed on Kelen and me. The glass is not tinted! All the demons can see us from the outside. We've been putting on a show for several minutes.

I roar with rage, and in one swift motion, I push that bastard Hybresang backward with such force that he must cling to his desk to avoid falling. He bursts into laughter, proud of his dirty trick, as I hastily button up my jeans and readjust my tank top. I only have one desire now: to kill him. If only I had my sword!

"One day, I'll lay you flat on this desk and take you as violently as you hope, Myrina Holmes," Kelen says, eyeing me with a dark, predatory gaze. "I'll make you climax with such power that your scream will be heard all the way to Infernum. You'll even scream my name until you're voiceless. And it won't be in a dream. I promise you that. Now… wake up, my little cat," he declares, snapping his fingers.

I immediately open my eyes in my bed.

I'm. In. A. Terrible. Mood.

And to top it all off, my panties are soaked! Wonderful!

I glance at my phone to check the time. Five-twenty-five in the morning. Missed calls from Zagam: seven. Uh-oh. Shit, I forgot to take it off silent! He's not going to be happy.

I read the brief text he sent ten minutes ago.

> Holmes, call me back quickly. New corpse found tonight. A Charityfiend.

My heart skips a beat.

Kelen Wills was right.

CHAPTER 11

THE HOSPITAL THAT MOCKS CHARITY

"Charity in this life can always be increased until the last breath." ~French proverb

MYRINA

I take two Arcadus to get to the crime scene, making a brief detour through Infernum. Since the magical portals of Earth are not directly connected to each other, one must necessarily pass through the demon world if they want to travel from one distant point to another. Generally, I only use this means of transportation for work when there's no other option. I love riding my motorcycle, but in this case, the abandoned hospital where the Charityfiend's body was found is three hours away from the city where I live. A regular mode of transportation would have taken too much time.

It was two human kids who discovered the demon's body while exploring the old hospital, seeking a bit of thrill after a foolish dare with their classmates. Totally panicked, the kids called for help, but the operator on the other end thought it was a prank. He burst into laughter before hanging up. The CIT, which monitors all police channels worldwide, intercepted the call. One of our agents was immediately sent to the two children to erase their memories, as well as the photos they took with their phones. At least they won't be traumatized for life…

The Arcadus drops me off in the back room of a Slothling antique dealer who's dozing off in a rocking chair, snoring away. The guy opens one eye when he sees me, yawns so wide it looks like his jaw might detach, then closes it again, folding his hands over his belly. He's back asleep in seconds. Zagam is already at the hospital; he must have passed through here before me, briefing the Sinner and letting him know that more Trackers would be showing up at his shop. And when my boss personally shows up at a crime scene… it means serious shit's going down.

After a ten-minute walk down the street, I come into view of the building that's been abandoned for years. Creepy as hell, it could double as a set for a horror movie about the ghosts of deceased patients. Dirty walls riddled with cracks and graffiti, windows with broken panes or blocked by old boards teeming with mold, unruly vegetation resembling a wasteland, and sooty black stains on the facade indicating that the hospital was once ravaged by fire.

Sean approaches me outside the building. The grin he flashes contrasts sharply with the surroundings and the situation.

"Hey there, Myrina! How's it going? Did you sleep well?" he chirps cheerfully as if he's thrilled to see me.

"Do you ever get tongue cramps from all that ass-kissing, Sean?"

The young Virtuous bursts into a hearty laugh, which seems out of place. I was being serious, though.

"Oh, you're so funny, Myrina!"

What was I saying?

"Where's Zagam?" I grumble.

"I'll take you to him. He asked me to wait for you outside. You're going to be impressed by the crime scene, I bet. This serial killer doesn't mess around!"

"Yeah, a real psycho megalomaniac. Have they identified the victim this time?" I inquire as I follow Sean inside the hospital.

"Apparently so, Myrina. His wallet with his ID was lying on the floor, so we just had to pick it up. His name is John Blane, a minor Charityfiend living on Earth for about twenty years. Married to a Faithfiend, three kids. He worked as a nurse in a nursing home. In his free time, he volunteered at a homeless shelter and also with a charity that helps children with leukemia. He hasn't been home for two days, and now we know why."

While I don't like the Sinners who are deeply malevolent like Kelen Wills, I also struggle with the Virtuous who act like samaritans at every turn. These two extremes really get on my nerves.

We advance through the vast hospital hall, stepping over rubble and avoiding unhealthy puddles. The gloomy echo of our footsteps fills the room. A rusty gurney is overturned against a wall, and shards of glass are scattered on the floor. Sean illuminates our path with a powerful flashlight.

Indeed, the perfect setting for a crime scene.

"By the way, Myrina, I have an assignment due in three weeks to pass an exam," the intern prattles cheerfully, which contrasts with the heavy atmosphere. "I have to interview a personality from Infernum who I admire. Would you be willing to grant me—"

"Sean. If you want me to keep liking you, never ask me something like that again."

"Oh. Okay. Sorry."

"And stop apologizing, it annoys me."

"Sorry, I won't apologize anymore."

I glare at him. He purses his lips, looking contrite.

We turn left at an intersection. A few minutes later, I see lights at the end of a corridor and catch a whiff of burnt flesh. A standing spotlight has been set up in a room to illuminate the crime scene. Zagam, his sharp nose framed by glasses, stands next to a charred corpse lying on an operating table. In his human form, he's much less intimidating: a balding head and tanned complexion, thin as a rail. He collects tissue samples with a long metal clamp, placing them in transparent tubes to be analyzed later at the CIT. The deceased Virtuous, presented as such, could pass for a Sinner, as his silver scales have turned black from the flames' bite. Some have melted onto his flesh, indeed.

"You're late, Myri," my boss grumbles without looking up from his thorough examination.

"It's not like this guy's going to complain," I remark, eyeing the Charityfiend's body, whose wrists and ankles are tied to the table's four legs with silver handcuffs. "What do we have here?"

"Combustion."

"Thanks, I noticed. Wow, he's got a serious hole in his chest!"

The bones of his ribcage were shattered because… the nasty demon ripped out his heart. Nice. Then he was roasted like a suckling pig.

"Damn, but where's the heart?" I mutter.

"Missing, Myri. Before you got here, we searched the hospital and the surrounding area from top to bottom for clues. The murderer must have taken it when he left; it must be a trophy. And just like in the church, he left nothing behind, no fingerprints, no DNA traces. He also didn't use the Arcadus from the antique shop; I checked the badge access logs. Either he came by conventional means of transportation, or he took another Arcadus farther away, or he teleported with his victim, or he flew here. His profile is confirmed: he's cautious, organized, thoughtful, and meticulous."

"And insane," I add, leaning over the disgusting, gaping wound. "He didn't do this with a saw or a blade, Zagam. Look, the bones are sticking out as if the heart was ripped from his chest by telekinesis."

My boss nods, confirming my suspicion.

"John Blane, you must've suffered before your demise," I conclude, staring into the empty eyes of the forever-staring corpse.

"An open-heart surgery," Sean comments from behind us. "Fits well with the hospital. The killer played the mad surgeon. Operation game! I used to love playing that game when I was a kid. You know it, Myrina?"

"Shut up, Sean. Zagam, did you check his file? Did John ever have any health issues, just in case?"

"No, none, like most demons. But he was a nurse, which explains the choice of location."

"That means the killer ensures that we find his targets in places that correspond to their species. A Faithfiend, virtue of Faith, a church, a dove. A Charityfiend, virtue of Charity, a hospital, and… a missing heart. It's literally the hospital mocking charity!"

"Not quite. Turn around."

I turn around and raise my eyebrows.

A gigantic flaming heart covers half of the room's wall. Its contours are composed of dried golden blood.

It's terrible to say, but the killer has a knack for drawing. He managed to depict the four arteries, the three ventricles, the veins…

Yes, demon hearts are more elaborate than those of humans. Fourteen flames, corresponding to the fourteen legions, crown the top of the organ. It's indeed the emblem of the Charityfiends, the symbol of their virtue. So, we have an *image* of a heart… But not the *real* heart. Would he have also taken something more discreet from the unnamed Faithfiend's body? A canine, a scale, a feather, for example? To embark on a morbid collection, perhaps? I'll have to ask our forensic pathologist, Lexi, what she thinks about it.

"Let's reconstruct the timeline of events. The murderer brings his apparently unconscious prisoner here, handcuffs him to the operating table, injures him somewhere to make him bleed, draws the flaming heart on the wall with his blood, telekinetically extracts the heart, and burns it with pyrokinesis," I summarize as I put on my gloves.

"Indeed, that seems most plausible in terms of chronology," Zagam grumbles. "We'll have to question his circle now. You'll handle his wife, Myri. I'll take care of the owner of the nursing home where he worked. Sean, you'll visit, one by one, all his friends, colleagues, and patients, along with Malphas, to gather their statements. This case is becoming a priority. A serial killer targeting the Virtuous, damn it… We need to take him down before he strikes again, that bastard."

I approach the corpse and plunge my hand into the hole, lifting residues of burnt flesh to grope inside the body. I thought I saw something blue.

"This is awesome, feels like we're in the thriller *Seven!*" Sean exclaims cheerfully. "Virtuous demons edition! Maybe the killer is a Sinner who hates the Virtuous and wants them to pay for their moral sense, who knows?"

"No, Sean," I contradict through gritted teeth as I extract my finding from the Charityfiend's chest. "First, this is not *awesome*. Second, he's not just targeting Virtuous demons. His next target will be a Sinner."

I show Zagam the bloodstained golden peacock feather I just unearthed from John Blane's thorax, where the heart used to be.

The peacock feather happens to be the emblem of the Pridefiend Sinners, the demons of pride.

In other words, this damn serial killer plans to murder twelve more demons. And he's mocking us in the process.

CHAPTER 12
CODE 13.1

"At least affect the appearance of virtue."
~William Shakespeare, Hamlet

MYRINA

Bree Van de Kamp, in a brunette version, pulls tissues from her pink box, sobbing heartbreakingly on her couch while her three kids squabble in the kitchen, adjacent to the living room. I hear bestial grunts and shrill cries, sounds of blows and broken glass. They're fighting over the last piece of chocolate cake, creating an absolute mess in the room. These little monsters, in the literal sense, are testing my already shaken patience with their mother's tears and wails. Normally, I struggle with human children, but demon kids are living calamities. If it were up to me, I'd hang them by their scaly tails from the ceiling or lock them in a closet to calm them down! Strangely, Virtuous children are worse than Sinners, probably because their parents generally instill a more lenient upbringing.

My exasperated gaze returns to Saraya Blane, the grieving widow of our latest corpse. I was going to say *fresh*, except that in this case, it's not the most appropriate term, given his state of carbonization.

Her mother, silent, rubs her back to comfort her. Saraya's tears seem genuine, but they disgust me, nonetheless. Her makeup has run, and her swollen eyes are smeared with black. She blows her nose with the slimy discretion of a sniffling elephant. *Once...* every time. Then she tosses her tissue onto the coffee table before grabbing another one.

Damn, it pisses me off!

Clarification, I'm not entirely devoid of compassion and empathy, but I'm more sensitive to the pain of people who suffer with dignity. Those who stoically absorb the bad news at the moment, and then collapse when they're alone, I truly admire. Because that's exactly how I react to trials. I hate displaying my emotions, especially in front of strangers. It's too intimate, humiliating, degrading, even… pathetic. It shows a lack of self-control and self-respect, thus weakness.

As for me, my grief belongs only to me, and upon reflection, I don't even share it with my family. Besides, it's better to have nerves of steel in my line of work. Therefore, the wet and noisy displays of this drama queen Faithfiend don't affect me one bit. I just want to get out of this oppressive bourgeois mansion with its floral tapestries and old mahogany furniture adorned with baroque decorations. There are *three* crucifixes in the living room, hell and damnation! Wasn't one enough? Three tiny Jesuses glaring at me as if I'd nailed them to their wooden crosses myself! Not to mention the symbol of the Faith demons, the huge porcelain dove spreading its wings on the sideboard. The kitschy sculpture has such a strange beak shape that it looks like it's smiling. I'd love to shoot that feathered bitch with a silver bullet, that silly smiling bird!

Zen, Myri.

"Do you know if your husband had any enemies, Mrs. Blane?" I ask, seizing a momentary lull between sobs.

She shakes her head with a sigh and directs her watery, clear eyes toward a giant framed photo of her husband on the wall. With a dazzling smile, a radiant gaze overflowing with sympathy, and his shirt collar buttoned up to his Adam's apple, this Charityfiend looked like a pastor with a stick up his butt. Good lord, all that's missing is the golden halo to complete the portrait.

"Everyone loved my John. Everyone," she assures in a quavering whisper, confirmed by a nod from her mother.

Yeah right, Bree Van de Kamp. Not me, and yet he's as dead as a doornail.

"Have you noticed anything unusual with him lately? Any

strange behavior? New acquaintances? Out-of-place remarks?"

"No, nothing out of the ordinary."

There's something fishy going on. This Charityfiend was too… altruistic. Nurse, volunteer, member of an association—and an involuntary organ donor. The very embodiment of Charity… or so it seemed. Hm, I need to dig deeper. Perhaps he was hiding things from his wife. Or maybe not, actually. Her pain doesn't seem feigned, unless she's an excellent actress. In this investigation, it's best to tread carefully.

"Where did he go two days ago?" I ask. *Before he got roasted without seasoning*, I add mentally, sparing the widow.

"The homeless shelter. It was around three-thirty PM when he kissed me goodbye at the door and got into his car. That was… that was the last time I… saw him… oh, my god, I can't believe he's gone!" she exclaims before breaking down in her mother's arms, just as I jot down the information in my notebook to reconstruct the timeline of events.

My phone vibrates on the armrest of my chair. I glance at the screen and nearly choke on my saliva as I read the text from an unknown sender.

> I was right, my little cat.

Kelen. Wills. Has. My. Personal. Number.

I should block him immediately. The problem is, I can already picture his smug smile, like *told you so*… and it's getting under my skin.

"Mommy!" cries a whiny little demon in its birth form as it barges into the living room, hands covered in blood. "Durant bit my butt, tore off a piece of flesh, and ate it because I ate the last piece of cake!"

Seriously, who names their kid Durant? Not even a human would dare! This Faithfiend must hate her brood.

"That's not true, I didn't do anything!" another voice shouts from the kitchen. "It was Dupont who pulled my tail, it really hurts! He's taking advantage of Dad being dead to get sympathy!"

At these words, Saraya Blane collapses on the couch, burying her head in her mother's lap, her perfectly styled hair being stroked. Puffing out my cheeks, I quickly retreat to the laundry room and close the door. This place is a nightmare! Case in point: even the dish towels are ironed, folded, and lined up on the washing machine. A shiver runs down my spine.

I call the other idiot of my horns, who picks up on the fifth ring.

"Good morning, my wild little cat," purrs his smooth voice. "What an unexpected morning pleasure."

"You better have a solid alibi for tonight after our meeting at the 1001 Nights of Lust, Wills," I retort without preamble.

"But I do, Agent Holmes. I was fucking your sister."

Zen, Myri!

"How did you get my number? And how do you know about the investigation?"

Unsurprisingly, he doesn't answer either of my questions. He yawns blatantly into the receiver.

"I'm still in bed. Do you want to come search my room so we can continue this verbal exchange in a more comfortable setting? As a special exception, I'll waive the need for a warrant. I'm feeling generous today."

There it is—I'm picturing him with his smug *told you so* grin… and naked in his king-sized bed. Leaning against his soft pillow, one lazy hand caressing his chiseled chest, the sheet taut from a monumental erection. I bang my fist against my forehead three times to banish these impudent and parasitic thoughts just as my phone vibrates against my ear again, signaling the receipt of a text. My eardrum rings.

"Your silence speaks volumes, my little cat. Did you know I dreamed of you last night?" Kelen continues in a drawling tone.

Oh, fucking shit.

"Please tell me I was skinning you alive with a silver blade dipped in holy water."

"No, Myrina. We were both in my office at the club. And it was damn… intense."

Double fucking shit.

Could it be…

No, it's not possible!

He just threw that out randomly.

Or…

I've heard rumors that major incubuses, particularly powerful ones, have the ability to infiltrate the subconscious of their prey to generate fantasies while they sleep. I took it as an urban legend… until today.

Triple fucking shit.

Which would mean that I'm not immune to the powers of the Hybresang.

This news distresses me. If I find out this asshole can also read my thoughts, it'll be the final blow.

"You implanted a dream remotely into my brain," I murmur in an icy voice.

A hoarse laugh echoes through the phone. "Do you believe me capable of such villainy?"

"I believe you capable of all villainy, Wills."

"Then you're pragmatic. My Virtuous Sinner, tell me, one detail nags at me… Do you intend to reveal to your sister that you soaked your panties dreaming of me last night?"

I hang up, furious.

Why won't he leave me alone, for fuck's sake? What have I done to have the king of pervs on my ass? Doesn't he have better things to do, like planning his election campaign, commanding his legion, and honoring a million responsibilities? I don't understand why he's coming on to me like this. We barely know each other, and he could have any other demoness. He must have dipped his dick in half of Infernum's Sinners, babes way hotter than me at that.

That's probably the crux of the problem, actually. Some men are so full of themselves that they can't fathom being rejected, just like Malphas, who's been hounding me for months without letting up. Given the choice, I'd rather deal with my colleague's clumsy advances than Kelen's. Because I'm not tempted to hook up with the Pridefiend, whereas the Hybresang sends my hormones into overdrive like nothing else… I must have been cursed by a witch to attract guys like them! If Wills doesn't back off soon, I'll tell Ondine her new boyfriend is hitting on me behind her back. I hope that'll open her eyes and she'll dump him once and for all.

I also need to talk to Zagam about my suspicions regarding Kelen poking his nose into my confidential investigation. He already knows way too much about these two murders, which is more than fishy. I'll ask my sister if she was indeed with him last night to verify his alibi, but even if she was, I won't remove him from my list of suspects. He has a horde of sleazy Ragebeasts under his command and ready to carry out his Machiavellian whims.

I read the text received during the call. It's from Lexi, our talented forensic pathologist at the CIT, a Temperling—the virtue of Temperance. She's also an expert in weapons and technological gadgets. A gem, this girl. I owe her a lot. Honestly, I don't know what I'd do without her.

> I reexamined the Faithfiend's body as you asked, Myri. Bingo, he's missing two feathers at the base of the wings in exactly the same spot. Right and left, mirrored. Removed before his death.

Our serial killer is indeed a collector of morbid trophies. Faithfiend feathers, Charityfiend heart… Gross.

"I like collecting beautiful and unusual things," Kelen Wills told me last night at the 1001 Nights of Lust while we were looking at the painting hanging in his office.

I write my response to Lexi.

> And the peacock feather found in Blane's chest?

> Currently being analyzed. I'll start the autopsy of our roasted corpse in a few minutes. By the way, are you satisfied with your new AA?

> They're perfect. The adjustments you made are spot on. Thanks again.

A smile forms on my lips.

> You're welcome, Myrina Holmes. At your service. Just remember, these ones aren't waterproof.

> No problem, I'll be careful.

"Mrs. Blane," I say as I return to the living room, "did your husband personally know Magistrate Kelen Wills?"

The widow glances at me with a hint of confusion. "No. Everyone knows that Mr. Wills considers the Virtuous as unworthy sub-demons to associate with," she states with a touch of disdain.

Thanks to her aversion to the Hybresang, the Faithfiend scored some points. I wouldn't say I suddenly wanted to be her friend, but she annoyed me a little less all of a sudden.

It's imperative that I uncover the connection between the Faithfiend with broken wings in the church and the Charityfiend immolated in the hospital to get a serious lead. Perhaps the two victims knew each other or frequented the same circles…

I show Saraya a close-up photo of the anonymous Faithfiend's scaly face. She shakes her head darkly, stating she's never seen this demon before.

I'm stuck in a rut.

My phone vibrates again. By the fiery trident, they all seem to conspire to annoy me today! I read the new text with a frustrated grunt. But it wasn't from Kelen, Ondine, Lexi, or Zagam.

Oh, this spells action!

It was one of the Tracker's automatic emergency codes. A lottery number that rarely falls and that all CIT agents dread receiving due to the danger of the intervention.

Code 13.1.

In other words, a Soulless attack on Infernum.

I crack my neck to warm up.

"Mrs. Blane, do you have an Arcadus in your house?"

She points to her husband's portrait, just as I suspected.

Great. I'll have to enter John Blane.

CHAPTER 13
CARNAGE

"Anger is a fire kindled, he who restrains anger extinguishes the fire; he who gives vent to it is the first to be consumed by such fire." ~Hazrat Ali

MYRINA

The Arcadus I borrow after fetching my arsenal leads me to the lobby of a luxurious skyscraper, which happens to be the headquarters of Colton Hallow. The Magistrate of the Envyfiends, demons of the sin of envy.

He's also one of Kelen Wills's rivals, the one who disparaged him in the press. One of the candidates for the Federators election with whom he was speaking on the phone before our meeting at the 1001 Nights of Lust. Quite a coincidence, isn't it?

The commotion is at its peak in the lobby, dominated by a tall glass sculpture in the shape of a pyramid. The Envyfiend Sinners working in the building are being evacuated and placed safely outside by my slightly on-edge Tracker colleagues. Sean, the intern, has been assigned the dirty job of cleaning up. Equipped with latex gloves, the Virtuous one is collecting all the bloodied pieces of corpses scattered on the floor and assembling them in three large, wheeled bins. My buddy, Lexi, will have a blast piecing together all these 3-D puzzles at the CIT morgue. The Soulless one has wreaked havoc on its path.

Seeing me here, Sean brightens up with a radiant smile and waves. Well, not with *his* hand. He shakes in my direction a severed limb adorned with black scales and clawed phalanges.

I ignore him, struck by a significant detail. Amid the chaos, I spot several Ragebeast demons in armor, preparing for a commando operation, charging their weapons and, amid the turmoil, two figures that are not unfamiliar to me: Malphas, the Pridefiend Tracker, and Sammael, the Ragebeast officer. A cockfight. As if now were the time to squabble! I approach them to learn more about the situation.

"You have no business here, Daniels!" my colleague shouts haughtily. "Go back to your stinking hole with your hotheads; you'll only get in our way! We'll handle the Soulless."

"We are enforcing Article 7.3 of the Infernum National Security Code," Sam retorts dryly. "'*Ragebeast soldiers are duty-bound to neutralize any threat to the lives of one or more Magistrates.*' My legion's soldiers are trained to intervene in such attacks. Let the pros handle it, Pridefiend. You're already out of your depth," he emphasizes, gesturing angrily at the chaos surrounding them.

Malphas's face twists with skepticism. Given his memory is like that of a goldfish, he doesn't even remember the National Security Code.

"Daniels is right," I interject, joining them. "A Soulless attacking Infernum's leaders is considered a case of force majeure by the law. The CIT doesn't have jurisdictional priority in this case."

"I hope you're joking, Myri. Those guys are brutes; they're going to cause a lot of collateral damage, and we'll end up cleaning up the mess!"

"I won't allow it, Malphas. Is Wills sending you, Daniels?"

"Indeed, Miss Holmes," he confirms with a small smile. "Nice sword, you wear it with style."

"Thank you. Nice watch." His flashy gold Rolex stands out against his armor, almost like an anachronistic element. "So, what do we have?"

"A rampaging Soulless, part-Envyfiend, part-Braveryfiend, and hungry," Malphas responds. "Have you faced these creatures before, Daniels? Because they don't mess around!"

"I've taken down three Soulless in the past, and you?"

"I saw one on TV once."

"I see."

They're exhausting.

"Hey, you two idiots!" I bark, snapping my fingers to get them back on track. "Where is this Soulless?"

"Last we heard, he was causing havoc on the twenty-fifth floor. We evacuated and sealed off the floors below," Malphas boasts, puffing himself up.

"And where is Magistrate Hallow?" I grow impatient, annoyed at having to drag information out of them.

"On the thirty-third floor, barricaded in an office with his two secretaries and his assistant. I spoke to him on the phone; he's wetting himself," Sam informs me with a mocking smirk.

"Why didn't he teleport to escape, the idiot?"

"Because he caught demon flu."

Ah. Tough luck. Demon flu only lasts a few days, but it significantly weakens the powers of Sinners and Virtuous, including major ones. Once again, it's a strange coincidence that the headquarters of the Envyfiends are under attack by a formidable creature just when the Magistrate is most vulnerable…

"But damn, what are you waiting for? Shouldn't you go take down that Soulless?"

"The official authorization from the boss," they reply in unison before shooting each other looks.

All right, enough wasting time! I push my way between them toward the elevator. I discreetly slip Sam's luxury watch into the pocket of my jacket. It's been a while since I stole something, but I haven't lost my touch.

'Myri, don't charge in solo, you're going to mess things up! We still haven't received permission from Zagam—we need to organize a plan before taking action!' Malphas warns from behind me.

Yeah right. Why not play a game of cards in the lobby amid the corpses to kill time? The Magistrate will die if we delay in intervening. I press the button to call the elevator and say over my shoulder, "Don't worry, my horned sweetheart! I've got a solid plan!"

Well, almost. I'll think about it in the elevator.

***

KELEN

While I devour a delicious and gargantuan breakfast in bed, my lieutenant calls me. I lick my fingers and wipe them on my sheets before answering.

"Kel, we have a problem," he announces in a low voice. "We probably should send our guys to the front earlier than planned."

"I told you to wait until I finish my breakfast, Sam. We're not on a tight schedule, the Soulless is only on the twenty-fifth floor. Let the pressure build up on Hallow until the last moment; he deserves it."

"It's the twenty-seventh floor now, judging from the camera footage. And your Amazon is also heading up, Kel. Alone."

I set down my waffle that's dripping with rhubarb jam on my plate. "By all the sinful saints, Myrina is already there?" I say, dismayed by this unexpected development.

I didn't think she would be so quick to react, let alone play the daredevil with such a creature. That demoness is reckless.

"She rushed over here in a flash and didn't wait for the green light from the CIT director. She left all of us in the dust. And before that, she swiped the Rolex you gave me, I just noticed. Given the profile of the Soulless, the Tracker is going to get slaughtered, Kel. What do we do, do we move?"

"Yes, follow her and cover her," I order, teleporting in front of the wardrobe a few feet from my bed. "I'll gear up and be there in three minutes."

A stunned silence settles on the other end of the line.

"Sam, are you still there?" I growl, opening the doors.

"You're going to show up in the field, Kel? *You?*"

He's not wrong. It's been ages since I've taken part in a fight of this caliber; it's not like me to do the grunt work of my subordinates. It's not that I don't want to—I love fighting as much as I love fucking—but I can't: for the past few decades, I've been overwhelmed by my duties as Magistrate. However, this morning, I have nothing better to do.

And, incidentally, I have no desire for that stubborn, mixed-race woman to die in such a stupid way.

***

MYRINA

A soft jazz tune fills the elevator cabin as I notch six bolts into my crossbow, keeping an eye on the floor numbers scrolling on the digital panel.

Thirteenth floor.

It always gives me a strange feeling to fight a Soulless. Every time, I think I could have become like them. The rotten fruit of a crossbreeding against nature, an animal creature incapable of reason. A sort of demonic zombie, powerful, driven by its thirst for blood and death, immune to silver bullets, hence the need for a sharp sword to decapitate it or heavy-caliber weapons capable of shredding it to pieces. I've also wondered many times if they ever experience primitive emotions or possess a form of primitive intelligence. Everything leads me to think that's not the case, but I still harbor a microscopic doubt deep inside, probably because I'm a half-breed myself.

The monster I'm about to track is half-Envyfiend and half-Braveryfiend, which is not particularly reassuring. Envyfiends have corrosive blood and saliva, a bit like the xenomorphs from the movie *Alien*. You don't want to miss your shot, that's for sure. As for the Virtuous Braveryfiends, they have tentacles studded with spikes like the Greedling Sinners. All in all, it's an extremely dangerous genetic combination.

If it's a young Soulless, it should be easy: they're dumb as a bag of rocks. If it turns out to be a bit older and more experience, it might give me some trouble. However, Soulless with Envyfiend genetic heritage have a big weakness: their sin of Envy. Like magpies, they're attracted to anything shiny, especially gold. They can't resist it: it's stronger than them. That's why I snatched Sam's Rolex. It's the little shiny bait that might eventually lure him away from his other prey.

Ah! That reminds me, I absolutely must demand a risk bonus from Zagam. Every time I go on a mission, I remember it, then I forget to mention it to him. I jot down the idea in a corner of my brain. An extra 200 Forks per month, no less.

After cocking my crossbow, I take off my heavy boots. Gravity is my friend in this somewhat perilous situation. Darn it, I have a hole in my right sock!

"Twenty-fifth floor. Have a nice day," the robotic female voice announces through the elevator speaker as the doors open.

"Same to you, bitch," I reply as I cautiously advance into the upside-down room with flickering neon lights.

Crossbow in hand, I follow the trail of freshly mutilated corpses, sidestepping the dark Envyfiend blood puddles eating away at the wood floor… heading toward the stairwell. I'm also following his scent trail. The Soulless has moved to the upper floors.

He has a purpose. He wants Hallow's hide.

Well, isn't that unusual. *One* specific target? Normally, these creatures attack anything that moves just to fill their bellies.

Hmm, there's a Pridefiend fishy in the Gluttonfiend's soup.

On the twenty-sixth floor, there's nothing to report except a few corpses and a chaotic mess in the offices. But I hear disturbing noises above me. Screams of pain and fierce roars.

I notice a huge claw mark streaking the wall next to the door as I pass by. Judging by the size and depth of the four dark streaks, the beast has a good size. Very reassuring. Which implies it wasn't just born. A surge of adrenaline rushes through me. *Focus, Myri.*

I climb the stairs stealthily, all senses alert.

Now I'm on the twenty-seventh floor.

I position my crossbow against my shoulder, eye on the scope.

In the open office occupied by about twenty desks, I spot a massive figure on all fours, shaking the badly mangled corpse of an unfortunate demoness. Its powerful jaws are lined with fangs and closed around her leg. Its spiked tentacles undulate above its back as the monster tears into its prey, emitting guttural growls. Its gray, viscous scales gleam under the artificial light of the neon tubes, and its ivory horns on its forehead are equivalent to elephant tusks. A lethal weapon on all levels. Ah, indeed, this one isn't a lightweight. Nine feet long, including the tail, and weighing in at 400 pounds of muscle—pure joy! In short, the Soulless is at least three years old, an exceptional case. Of course, exceptional cases always fall to me!

Drawn to a bright point, my eyes land on its neck and widen like saucers.

Holy hell, what the hell is this now?

The Soulless is wearing an electronic collar displaying a red indicator. The object resembles the training collars that dogs sometimes wear around their necks, delivering painful electric shocks when they bark.

By the frigid succubus, this is the first time I've seen something like this.

Domesticating a Soulless. The insane thought makes me shudder with horror.

In other words, if I'm not mistaken… Someone is attempting to assassinate the Envyfiend Magistrate Colton Hallow through a Soulless.

Lifting my gaze, I meet the abominable creature's heterochromatic eyes, which have abandoned its all-you-can-eat buffet to turn toward me. One red eye and one silver eye, like me in my demonic form, our only common point. Its tentacles and tail whip angrily through the air, its sharp teeth dripping with black blood, and its immense claws sink into the ground.

I curl my finger around the trigger of my crossbow.

You and me, buddy, we're not gonna be pals.

CHAPTER 14
CLASH OF TITANS

MYRINA

I release my bolt. It slices through the air with a whistle. I aim for the Soulless's leg to pin it to the ground and immobilize it.

In a tangle of tentacles, the creature leaps to the side, dodging my projectile, which embeds itself in the wall behind it. Undeterred, I shoot another bolt. This one grazes the curve of its back, cutting through its scales. A few drops of acidic blood spatter to the ground, and it emits a raging roar. Good lord, it's incredibly agile and swift! It propels itself against a wall, crouching low, and lunges at me with claws outstretched and jaws wide open. My third bolt lodges in its throat, but it does nothing to slow its wild charge.

No panic. Let's drop the crossbow; it's not suited for this beast!

I grasp Feather's golden handle and draw it from its sheath. A spiked tentacle hurtles toward my skull. With a swift sword stroke, I sever its tip while sidestepping to avoid being sprayed by the corrosive blood flow, but immediately, another appendage slams into my abdomen, knocking the wind out of me. I tumble backward— fortunately, not releasing my weapon—and sprawl onto my back, shouting in pain. A tentacle tip has pierced me above the navel.

But I don't have time to dwell on how much I'm hurt. The Soulless lunges at me, its open jaws ready to crush my head like a grapefruit. I roll on the ground to evade its snapping jaws, which miss my skull by mere inches. What a damn nasty creature!

Gripping Feather with both hands, I drive my silver blade into its chest with all my might. It screams in agony. So do I, because its toxic blood is trickling down my legs. It steps back to extract my sword, but Feather is deeply embedded in its scaly flesh. Consequently, as it tries to escape, it drags me along. I slide on the floor, dragged by the furious beast for several feet. I writhe under it as best I can to avoid being trampled in its frenzy. Teeth gritted, I reluctantly release Feather. The Soulless retreats into a corner, wrapping a tentacle around my sword and yanking it out of its body with a roar. It hurls Feather to the other end of the room, out of my reach, then glares at me with its purple and mother-of-pearl eyes brimming with hatred.

Well done, you idiot! It's even more enraged, barely weakened by its injury… and you're unarmed and in bad shape.

I really prefer to avoid reverting to my natural form because if I do, I won't be able to mutate for several days, I'll be too drained and weakened for that. But I might not have a choice, given how things are going…

Oh shit, it's opening its jaws. It's going to spew a jet of acidic saliva at me!

Driven by my reflexes, I crouch down to propel myself as high as possible. Thanks to Infernum's gravity effects, I perform an impressive acrobatic leap over sixteen feet and land on a solid oak desk, legs and arms spread out to maintain my balance. Unfortunately, the Soulless entwines two tentacles around the feet of the furniture and lifts it abruptly. I topple from my perch, whimpering, collapse like an old rag on my belly like an old rag, and roll onto my back just in time to see the heavy secretary, barely missing the ceiling, hurtling toward me. Swearing, I shield my head with my arms, curling up. This is going to hurt like hell.

Not as much as expected, as it turns out.

Something falls onto me without crushing me. It's not the desk; *it* has a different texture and, uh… *it* has arms, I think. A rush of air sweeps over me just before the furniture crashes down on me. I don't understand, what just happened? What's this big steel thing pressed against me? Did *it* teleport me just before impact?

"The reinforcements are here, my little cat," purrs a mischievous voice in my ear.

Oh, no—anyone but him!

I quickly move my arms away from my face, gaping. Two golden-brown eyes lock with mine.

"By all the hells, what are you doing here?" I bellow, outraged by his intervention.

"I'm saving your life, ungrateful Tracker, isn't it obvious?"

"I didn't ask for your help, you prat! I'd rather be squashed by a desk than rescued by... *you!*"

"To be honest, I'd have preferred that, too, to spare me the current reproaches you're showering me with, but I did it primarily for Ondine. She'd have been saddened by your loss and, since I'm an exemplary boyfriend..."

"Exemplary? I'll have you know you have a hand on my ass right now, Wills!"

"Was that your rump? In my eagerness to come to your rescue, I hadn't paid attention to that detail," he assures with a devilish smile. With that, he squeezes one buttock indiscreetly, making me blush to the roots of my hair. "By the way, you should do more exercise, Agent Holmes. This big area lacks firmness."

What do you mean this big area lacks firmness?

That's it: I'm going to kill the Soulless, and then, I'll kill Kelen Wills.

First step: break free from the firm embrace and wandering hands of the king of perverts. I push him away with a shove.

Second step: find the Soulless. I look around perplexed. The two suns of Infernum loom over us in the amber sky. The Hybresang has brought me to the roof of the skyscraper.

"Quick, let's get back there! He'll take advantage of our absence to go up to Hallow's office floor!"

"No, my men are temporarily distracting him while I take over," Kelen assures, straightening up to his full height.

He wears his warrior armor of red metal, which reflects the orange glow of the clouds. The breastplate bears the golden lion holding a silver dagger in its mouth, the symbol of his legion. I've always found this emblem ridiculous... on other Ragebeasts. But I must admit that Wills possesses a certain class. Vaguely. From afar. Well, okay, up close, too.

"*You*'re taking over?" I repeat, blinking, torn between incredulity and absurdity.

"Indeed, my little cat. You'll stay here safely out of harm's way. I'll come back for you after the battle."

"Is this Hybresang humor?" I choke out.

Since I became a Tracker, I've never stayed *safely out of harm's* way during a battle. For me, passivity and inaction are two... inconceivable concepts.

"Not at all. You're seriously injured," he specifies, nodding toward my tank top and pants, which are stained with gold-flecked, black blood, characteristic of my mixed heritage. "So, you're off duty until you regenerate."

"Don't talk nonsense, it's just a scratch. I don't feel a thing!" That's a lie. I probably have a hole in my stomach, and it feels like I have an iron poker rummaging through my guts, but I don't care, I'll recover. "I'll be off duty the day I'm dead. I won't let you take all the credit for this operation, Wills. It's up to me to kill the Soulless, not you!"

"Swallow your competitive spirit and your misplaced pride, Myrina. You fought well, but it's over for today," he decrees in a strangely softened tone. "Rest, soak up some sun, do some yoga if you feel like it. I'll handle this minor issue in a few minutes."

"*Wills, god da*—"

The end of my shout echoes into the celestial void. He dematerialized to return to the field and left me stranded on the skyscraper rooftop like a poor fool.

I'm livid with anger.

I, unlike him, don't have the power to teleport, and this building has over a hundred floors. It would take me ages to descend the stairs; I would arrive long after the battle ended. I need to find an alternative way to join the bloody festivities. Injured or not, I fully intend to neutralize the Soulless. It's my mission, not Kelen Wills's.

I stride to the edge of the building with determined steps, despite the pain gnawing at my abdomen and part of my legs. I lower my shadowy eyes to the void, fists clenched on my thighs. The skyscraper is so high that a blanket of clouds conceals the other buildings in the city.

So, *I'm off duty*, huh?

That Hybresang bastard will see if I'm *off duty*.

Kelen

I arrive in the room just in time to save Sam's hide.

My disapproval darkens as I discover my lieutenant struggling with the Soulless, ensnared by a writhing tangle of tentacles scraping against his armor. His complexion is bluish, and he's choking like a tin can being flattened by a steamroller. In my opinion, he already has several fractured ribs. On the other hand, he made the monumental mistake of keeping his human form to engage the beast in close combat, so he can only blame himself. His negligence disappoints me. He seems to have left his brain at home. I'll give him a lecture later.

While I teleported Myrina to safety on the roof, the creature had time to massacre four of my soldiers. They lie on the ground, dismembered, slit throats, or decapitated. It doesn't faze me in the least; demonic losses are always inevitable. A dozen of them hide behind furniture and shower the beast with silver bullet salvos, in vain. The projectiles hardly affect it. The demon is more riled up than ever.

Bunch of incompetents. Bullets are useless against Soulless. They regenerate much faster than the Sinners and have a higher pain tolerance.

Violence begets violence.

In a matter of seconds, I assume my original form. The mutation takes longer for ordinary demons, but I'm not one of them. In my case, it's just a formality. My men stop firing and look up. The Soulless turns its eyes toward me, growling. Perfect, I have their full attention.

My enchanted armor swiftly adapts to the physical changes, expanding and elongating. Two slits form in the metal to allow my immense wings of black feathers with scarlet tips to expand on either side of my back. My bones crack as my limbs stretch considerably.

My horns, spikes, and claws grow in less time than it takes to say it. I grow several feet taller, my skin covered in scales that shimmer like black jewels… and my power reaches its zenith. Flames sizzle beneath my carapace. I roll the muscles of my shoulders as I stare down the Soulless with my flaming eyes. As I'd hoped, it loses interest in Sam and releases him from its grip; it lets him slide to the ground to face an opponent of its own size. My lieutenant takes a gulp of air and crawls a few feet.

An acidic spit shoots out of my future victim's mouth. Since I don't try to dodge it, the saliva projectile lands on my cheek… without corroding my scales. Wiping it off with a paw, I let out a sardonic laugh as the Soulless appears bewildered. Yes, kid, in my natural form, I'm immune to eighty percent of the powers of the Sinners demons.

I swiftly grab a nearby chair, then transform it into a flaming projectile before catapulting it toward the creature, which turns around in a leap and clings to the ceiling to avoid being hit in the head. Perfect, that's precisely what I wanted: by reacting like this, it has lowered its guard. I grab the Soulless by the dangling tentacles in front of me, spin around, and hurl it against the right wall. The impact is such that it partially demolishes the wall. Half-dazed, it shakes itself off while grumbling.

I give it no respite. Spreading my wings and bending my legs, I take off to swoop toward it and pounce on it. I deliver a phenomenal punch to its jaw to stun it, breaking four or five teeth. One of its tentacles starts to coil around my neck in an attempt to strangle me, but I quickly grab the appendage and bite it fiercely. My fangs pierce its gray scales and tear through its elastic flesh, inflicting excruciating pain. Its acidic blood tastes like death, it's truly disgusting. I spit out a piece of tentacle on the ground, a hand compressed around its throat. My Ragebeast power burns its scales. It struggles under my grip, squealing like a pathetic little creature and banging its numerous tentacles on my sturdy body. I take it without flinching.

I'll finish it off in less than thirty seconds. I haven't decided how yet, but…

Something I hadn't anticipated happens before I can make my decision.

A gigantic creature from outside shatters the bay window into a thousand pieces with a deafening crash, smashing all the windows in the room with the speed and brutality of the collision. Another demon.

Or rather, I should say a demoness.

Myrina is so extraordinary in her natural form that I can't take my eyes off her. I'm mesmerized by this hybrid female who looks like nothing I've ever seen in my existence.

She lands gracefully in front of us, folding her splendid bichrome wings with silky ivory and ebony feathers.

Good heavens, she's a bit taller than me. She must bend her head forward to avoid touching the ceiling, and I already stand at eight feet two inches. On the other hand, she's much slimmer than me. She's as feline and supple as a panther while I'm as sculpted as a golem.

In addition, I have never had the opportunity to admire such a hue of scales. I can't determine the exact color because they display a thousand nuances. They are iridescent as if they were set with tiny crystals that reflect the light. I would like to caress her scales and wings to savor their texture. A dark and icy vapor emanates from them; in their demonic form, the Justspawns have the power to freeze their opponents. Her horns form two elegant arcs on her skull amid a mass of long black and white dreadlocks. Her slender, swaying tail reminds me of a silver whip. Her eyes are so large that they occupy a third of her feminine and elegant Lustspawn features. A ruby of sin and an opal of virtue, separated by vertical pupils… which lock onto me.

I'm completely captivated by her enchanting yet fearsome appearance. To me, she resembles more of a goddess than a demoness. Myrina is a natural diamond.

This only reinforces my belief that I must possess this alpha female. I'm even more determined to have her. At least *once*. It cannot be otherwise.

The saucy minx doesn't seem immune to my demonic charm either, as she delicately wraps her slender tail around my waist. I give her an appreciative smile, trembling with surprise.

She returns my conspiratorial smile. I'm conquered.

Then, with a sharp tug backward, she separates me from my prey and sends me spinning across the room as if I weighed no more than a human.

The bitch!

Nevertheless, I manage to unfold my wings to slow my momentum and cushion my fall.

I prepare to teleport near the Soulless, but I see the Tracker brandishing a claw with Sam's gold Rolex attached to it. She shakes the sparkling watch to taunt our common enemy.

The damned Soulless loses control of its Envyfiend instincts and charges at it like a bull.

The demoness stops him dead in his tracks by grabbing him by the horns. She has a herculean physical strength; it's damn impressive. At the same time, she wraps her tail around her opponent's neck skillfully. Black ice gathers on the creature's scales, attacking its flesh. While flexing the sinewy muscles of her arms, the Amazon pulls on its horns with a bestial war roar.

Suddenly, she tears off its head.

With her bare hands.

My demonic jaw drops.

I'm astonished, and that doesn't happen often.

The body of the Soulless collapses on the ground at her feet, convulsing, while Myrina casually tosses the hideous head out the broken window.

Well. I stand corrected.

I won't have her at least once.

This woman is worthy of becoming my official mistress.

✳✳✳

MYRINA

Here comes the inevitable backlash of my mutation…

I stagger, trembling. My heart races. My vision blurs. Buzzing fills my ears. I'm completely drained of energy and exhausted as if I had been fighting nonstop for days. As I revert to my human form, I slump near the Soulless's carcass. But I don't hit the ground. A soft, fluffy surface slides under my back, like a mattress of dark feathers.

A second later, I feel warm arms enveloping me, as sturdy and thick as tree trunks. I look up at Kelen's demonic face through my blurred vision. His mouth forms fervent words that I don't hear, but I can guess. "Myrina! What's happening to you? Answer me!" The ringing in my ears intensifies painfully, drilling into my brain. I'm about to faint. I've pushed myself too far; it's my fault.

Under his Hybresang mutation, the Magistrate of the Ragebeasts is as frightening as people claim. He looks like some kind of… Balrog. But at this moment, he seems surprisingly taken aback by my vulnerability. His incandescent eyes display an almost human gleam. He tightens his scaly arms around my body. It's not so bad after all to be comfortably nestled against him within the folds of his giant wings. Overall, it feels rather cozy and secure.

"Wills," I call out in a voice so quiet that I can barely hear it myself.

With a solemn expression, the sinful demon lifts me slightly, leaning over my face to listen to me. Perhaps he thinks I'm about to die and therefore, uttering my last words… I triumphantly smile inwardly before murmuring, "I… beat… you… you bastard." And I lose consciousness.

CHAPTER 15
HOME VISIT

"Virtue is the mean between two vices."
~Aristotle, Nicomachean Ethics

KELEN

After returning to human form, I teleport into Myrina's room, the young woman unconscious in my arms. A disgusting, greasy stench lingers in the middle of her bed. Damn, I hate cats. This one would win hands down in the ugliest animal contest. The foul creature glares at me menacingly, claws out. I glare back at it.

"Scram, you rat. Shoo!" I growl authoritatively.

The whiskered horror begins to spit and hiss aggressively, fur bristling, daring me to evict it from its territory. I consider, for ten seconds, using my telekinesis to toss this repulsive thing out the window, but I'm forced to abandon that delightful idea. If I were to kill this vile, dim-witted furball, I would undoubtedly diminish my chances of scoring with its mistress. I lay the Tracker down on the bed, then grab a pillow to throw at the black feline, which leaps to the ground, shooting me a dirty look, and rushes out of the room. I close the door behind it with my psychic power.

Good riddance. Begone, Satcat!

Sitting on the edge of the bed, I systematically scan Myrina's wounds, which are already almost completely healed. The demonic mutation has accelerated the regeneration process; a thin pink line streaks her flat belly, and her thighs, burned by the corrosive blood of the Soulless, are only marked by a few rednesses. I place my fingers on her jugular to check her pulse. Strong and steady. The diagnosis is reassuring enough, although I struggle to understand why she's so exhausted. I've seen very young Sinners falter after their transformation, but this phenomenon remains rare. It may be related to her disability.

With my hand around her velvety throat, I inspect her naked body with a curiosity tinged with desire. I see no reason to deny myself this little pleasure.

I notice no apparent deformities. She's as enticing in her human form as she is in her hybrid form. She has an ideally proportioned slender silhouette. Slim and athletic, yet with beautiful full curves. Her breasts rise and fall with the slow rhythm of her breathing, delicious golden apples crowned with small caramel peaks that would immediately harden under my tongue. They're larger than Ondine's, but I had already noted that. She has a charming beauty mark near her right areola. *Very sexy, Agent Holmes.*

My electrified eyes linger on her pubic mound. Brazilian wax—I approve of this sensible choice. It's a shame her thighs aren't a little more open so I could contemplate the most interesting part of her feminine anatomy. But I'll make up for that when she'll offers herself to me.

Her long, tapered legs are also worth mentioning. Sublime. I can easily picture them adorned with black garter belts and dark red stiletto heels, or even thigh-high boots.

Cruella De Vil truly has a hell of a body, and I have to muster all my willpower not to get hard—and not to touch her peachy skin, which looks so velvety, something I'll only do with her consent.

One detail catches my attention. She has a small tattoo near her pubic area on the inside of her thigh. The infinity sign, a horizontal eight… I furrow my brow, puzzled by this conventional symbol on a woman who is not like that. Two initials are engraved within the arabesques. An *M* and an *O*. If the *O* is the first letter of the name Ondine, why is it located in such an intimate place? Nevertheless, the sight of this tattoo troubles me. It doesn't suit her personality.

I pull a blanket over Myrina's body to no longer see this pathetic drawing. I have wasted enough time here; I need to return to the

Envyfiends' skyscraper to discuss the Soulless attack with Hallow. Before leaving, I ordered my men to take and hide the electronic collar encircling the Soulless's neck before the CIT noticed. I'll have it examined by my own experts. I admit I hesitated to take Myrina back home with me, but I quickly dismissed such an unwise option. If I had taken that initiative, she would likely have been in a state upon waking up. So, I behaved like a true gentleman toward her.

Let her make the most of it: it was the first and last time.

I write a message on a piece of paper and leave it on the bedside table before teleporting back to Infernum.

MYRINA

"My little cat,

I'll bring back your sword, crossbow, and clothes on my next visit. Until then, I wish you a speedy recovery.

However, know that you did not "beat" me: I let you defeat the creature because I knew my charitable act would please you.

I recommend you have your coypu euthanized as soon as possible; its stench turned my stomach so much that I refrained from vomiting on you.

Nice beauty mark, but make sure to have it checked by a competent dermatologist, just in case… I heard of a Virtuous Justspawn who died of scale cancer.

Lastly, I hope you don't hold it against me for not giving in to your pleas like a repressed nymphomaniac; I had other priorities than staying to indulge you with a pity cunnilingus. You should be ashamed of your scandalous behavior. I'm a Magistrate, not a gigolo.

See you soon,

Your favorite Hybresang."

Ondine raises an eyebrow after finishing reading Wills's note. Nestled in my pillows, I stroke Putrid, who purrs on my lap. When discovering the note upon waking up, I was so furious that I almost tore it into a thousand pieces. However, in a moment of clarity, I thought better of it. I decided to show this evidence to my sister so that she finally kicks him out of our… her life.

"Did you hit on Kel?" my sister inquires, doubtful.

My fingers tighten in my cat's fur. Is *that* all she got from the letter?

I won't lose it. I got this.

"Of course not, sis! He's lying. I've been trying to explain this to you for ten minutes. He's hitting on me behind your back, that bastard. And on top of that, he saw me naked."

"You did, too, so you're even." Hell and damnation, succubus are hopeless! "If you didn't want him to see you naked, you shouldn't have mutated in front of him," she argues calmly with a bad faith that mortifies me.

"Ondine, listen—"

"Honestly, Myri, you're reading too much into it," she interrupts with a shrug. "You misinterpreted his words. Maybe Kel is just flirting lightly with you, so what? It's not serious, he's just playing around. I flirt with my friends without even realizing it. He's a natural-born seducer like all the Lustspawns. Just because he flirts with every woman he somewhat likes doesn't mean he sleeps with each one of them. Don't get offended, but you're not his type of demoness. You're too—"

"I'm too what?"

"Tall. And temperamental."

Temperamental, me? I've character, it's not the same!

"He sent me an erotic dream the other night, and I can guarantee you he wasn't flirting *lightly*."

"No, you *fantasized* about him, Myri. Admit it. It's not a big deal, I assure you. I'm not mad at you. In your place, I would fantasize about him, too. What sensible demoness could resist a handsome man like him?" Her complicit smile is making me hallucinate. She taps my hand with solicitude. "It'll pass, don't worry. You should have sex with a major demon to take your mind off things. I'm sure Sam wouldn't mind helping you out."

By the name of a three-headed hydra, he's lobotomized her brain! She's not usually this naive! I'm speechless. I thought she would have a furious meltdown after reading the letter, then dump the Magistrate in a masterful way…

The ringing in my ears has diminished, my vision has almost

cleared up, and my wounds have healed, but I'm not feeling great. I slept for nearly six hours straight, and despite that, I'm still exhausted. My limbs ache, a migraine is pounding in my skull, my mouth is dry. I'm in survival mode. Imagine the morning after a mega hangover to give you an idea. Since I was starving when I woke up, I devoured half the contents of the fridge while talking to Zagam, who briefed me as I ate. When I brought up the topic of the Soulless's electronic collar, my boss seemed surprised. The object has disappeared, apparently. Concealing evidence—just great! It's a safe bet that Wills is behind this mischief. Or maybe Hallow. I don't know why they're keeping secrets from the CIT, but I'll find out as soon as I'm back on my feet.

Speaking of Magistrates… My phone screen lights up. Well, I received a text from my grandfather.

> Honeybun, I heard about the incident at the Envyfiends' HQ. Can I come see you?

> Sure.

Three seconds later, before I even have the chance to announce his visit to my sister, he teleports into my room.

Grandpa Amon, my father's father, former Justspawn Magistrate retired for about one hundred years, is a force of nature both in his demonic and human form. I only see him once or twice a month since I became independent because he has a schedule like a minister, but we've remained very close. We often call each other to exchange news. I share with him—and my banished father—my strange, piercing purple eyes. His long silver hair cascades down to his waist, and his features, though angular, exude aristocratic beauty. He's even taller and broader than Kelen Wills. He stands as straight as an *I*, hands clasped behind his back. If I remember correctly, he was born during the time of Clovis, the first king of the Franks. Despite being fifteen centuries old, he doesn't have a single wrinkle. I call him Grandpa, but he barely looks forty. I never knew my grandmother, his wife: she passed away long before I was born.

Amon took me in and raised me after my parents were exiled to the Limbo. He was my legal guardian until I came of age. I lived in his residence in Infernum for eight years—the duration of my Tracker training—then I returned to Earth to live with my sister after I became a full-fledged Tracker. I see a lot of my father Arthur in him. As for Ondine, she's the spitting image of our mother, Lustspawn Lysippé. Like mother, like daughter…

"Honeybun, you look terrible," he says, examining my tired face.

This welcoming statement perfectly illustrates the personality of the Justspawn. Honesty, integrity, and righteousness dictate their conduct. He didn't say it out of concern; he did it in a formalistic, almost stiff manner. As a true representative of the rigid virtue of Justice, Amon doesn't bother with pretenses. His sense of humor is non-existent, and he hardly ever laughs because he's what Ondine and I call *team face value*. You either worship him or despise him. Personally, I worship him. He amuses me at his own expense, and even though he annoys me at times, he's endearing in his stuck-up, old-fashioned, paternalistic way. My sister, on the other hand, despises him… and the feeling is mutual. They can't stand each other, and I often find myself caught between them. In summary, I'm their only common ground.

"Yeah, I always look like crap after decapitating a Soulless barehanded," I grumble, scratching Putrid under the chin.

"Your impulsiveness and recklessness will be your downfall, Myrina. You need to take better care of yourself at work; don't forget that your demonic form is unstable. And moderate your language in front of me, please. I didn't raise you like this. Don't let yourself be influenced by certain individuals with vulgar tendencies." He narrows his eyes toward my sister. His antipathy is palpable. "I'd like to speak to my granddaughter alone, Ondine."

"You've got some nerve, Amon Holmes!" she retorts immediately. "I live here, after all."

"True, but this isn't your room. Don't you have some humans to drain?"

"I filled up my tank yesterday."

A disgusted look appears on my grandfather's face. Let's just say sex isn't his cup of tea.

My sister bursts into laughter, tossing her jet-black hair back. "Oh, Amon, you should get drained yourself from time to time to get rid of your long-standing bitterness and negative energy. I have a Lustspawn friend who's into old snobs; I can give you her number. We call her *The Sucker* among ourselves."

"I thought you nicknamed her *The Vacuum?*" I venture.

"No, Myri, that's someone else," she informs me with a smile. "All right, Amon, I'll lick you."

Grandpa pales, eyes wide.

"Oops, Freudian slip. I meant *I'll leave you.*"

I snicker discreetly as my sister exits the room.

My grandfather shakes his head disdainfully. "It's hardly surprising she's gotten chummy with Kelen Wills. She's just as insufferable as that scourge Sinner."

"Grandpa, don't say that, you're exaggerating. Ondine has qualities. He has none."

"He intervened during the attack of the Soulless."

I confirm with a slightly curt nod.

"For what reason, Myrina?"

"To show off to his future voters through the media and boost his popularity like crazy," I grumble as I fidget with my cat's ears. "Magistrate Kelen Wills, saving his Sinner rival Hallow, from an assassination attempt at the risk of his own life would have been great publicity for him. Too bad for him I'm the one who finished off the Soulless."

"Were there any other witnesses nearby?"

"Yes, his men."

"No security cameras in the offices? No Trackers?"

I furrow my brows sensing something fishy. "No, why?"

"His agent just made a statement on television, honeybun," my grandfather admits with a hint of pity. "According to him, not only did Kelen Wills kill the Soulless with his own hands, but he also rescued an injured Tracker whose name wasn't mentioned. He gained five points in the polls in a few hours: the Sinners consider him a homeland hero. In three days, he'll be awarded the honorary Horn of Plenty for services rendered to the authorities of Infernum."

"Son of a bitch, what a fucking asshole!" I shout so loudly that Putrid scurries under the bed to hide. I don't give a damn about glory; he can shove his Horn of Plenty up his ass for all I care. But to deliberately sideline me and take credit for *my* work, relegating me to damsel in distress status? I won't tolerate such lowliness; it goes

against all my Tracker moral values!

I don't know how, but I'll get revenge. He's crossed the line!

"You should avoid that man in the future, honeybun," advises the former Virtuous Magistrate. "He's profoundly harmful. He'll crush anyone in his path to serve his ambitions. Allies and enemies alike."

"Not everyone, Grandpa. I'll be in his path," I decree with bitterness.

Amon gives one of his rare smiles, half-hearted, as he enfolds my hands in his. I discern intense emotional conflict in his purple gaze. Nostalgia, pride, disapproval, and sadness intertwine.

I already know what he's going to say. I've heard this refrain throughout my adolescence. It sounded sometimes like a compliment, sometimes like a reproach, and sometimes… both combined.

"Myrina Holmes, you're your father's worthy daughter."

CHAPTER 16
A TWISTED LOGIC

"Moral is the weakness of the mind."
~Arthur Rimbaud, A Season in Hell

MYRINA

"Oooooooh yes, Keeeel, moreee!"

My eyes roll for the umpteenth time. I squirm in all directions on my bed. My fists clench the pillow, muffling my groans… of fury.

It's impossible to sleep. My sister is *very* expressive and shameless during sex, and her room is adjacent to mine.

I haven't said a word to Wills since he showed up unannounced at the apartment two hours ago. Knowing myself, if I had opened my mouth, the confrontation would have escalated, and I would have ended up smashing his face in. I only restrained myself for Ondine's sake. I snatched my weapons and clothes from his hands, glaring at him. He just smiled as if he expected my reaction. Then I went straight to my room with my cat to avoid his abhorrent presence. I could have gone out, of course, but on one hand, fleeing my own territory would have been a sign of weakness. On the other hand… I was still exhausted from my shift, and I couldn't be bothered.

Sitting cross-legged on my bed, I put on my earbuds and start watching the movie *Constantine*, adjusting the volume to the max. Keanu Reeves is much better company than Kelen and Ondine.

After an hour, I'm distracted by a text message that makes me roll my eyes. Great, Malphas is feeling frisky tonight. Just what I need to complete my disastrous evening! He sent me a selfie of himself shirtless on his bed, his muscles glistening and flexed, in a pose of a languid heartthrob, with half of his pinky finger in the corner of his mouth. As if his pseudo-seducer pose would make me wet! If I weren't in a bad mood, I would have burst out laughing at this ridiculous portrait.

> My beautiful Amazon, if you need anything to help you feel better, I'm your demon.

> No thanks. I just need everyone to leave me alone, Malphas.

> I'm sure a little phone sex session would cheer you up. Just writing this text got me rock hard. Want to see it?

Too bad for him, he asked for it! To cool down the enthusiasm of my horny colleague, I lift Putrid's tail, take a close-up photo of my cat's rotten anus, and send it to Malphas with the caption:

> Enjoy your jerking off.

He doesn't respond. Perfect.

When I take off my earbuds at the end of the movie, there is silence outside my room. Relieved, I believe Kelen must have gone back home, and I go to bed with a smile on my face.

Big mistake.

A few minutes later, Ondine starts moaning. Whimpering. Mewling. Grumbling. Screaming. Her cries then escalate into shrill screams. I can't hear the other bastard, Hybresang, at all.

I pound on the wall with my fists as hard as I can, shouting at the top of my lungs, *"Shut up, damn it, I want to sleep!"*

And *then*, I'm hearing Kelen's raucous laughter.

Two seconds later, the headboard begins to thud against the wall in a fast, steady rhythm, as if to provoke me even more. The impacts are so violent that my own bed shakes, and Putrid wakes up hissing, as outraged as I am by this nocturnal commotion. It's horrible. Infuriating. Revolting. These noises and vibrations are anything but exciting. I'm not jealous of my sister; I'm just seething with anger toward *him*.

I almost want to go to her room with a bucket of ice-cold water. What stops me? The thought of seeing Kelen bedding my older sister. I would never be able to erase that traumatizing image from my memory. If it had been another male demon in his place, I would have done it without hesitation. I would have even forced him out, dragging him out of our building by the skin of his ass.

Just as I'm resigned to leaving the apartment, furious that he has once again won the battle, Ondine loudly orgasms, hissing his name… and the racket subsides. Finally.

I pray he doesn't stay the night here, and they don't fuck again.

Unfortunately, I can't fall back asleep, haunted by my sister's cries of pleasure and her lover's sinister laughter. After about thirty minutes, my stomach rebels with a growl. Nighttime hunger, fantastic! I won't be able to sleep until I've had something to eat.

I cautiously get out of bed. I unlock my door as quietly as possible, glance vigilantly into the dimly lit living room to make sure the coast is clear, and tiptoe to the kitchen, as stealthy as a burglar. I crack open the fridge door, taking inventory of the items. Plain yogurt? Not substantial enough. Asparagus? Poison. I settle on a quarter of roast turkey, a slice of cheese, a jar of mustard, and a jar of pickles to make myself a sandwich. I take out the ingredients one by one, arranging them on the counter to my left. As I grab the last item, I close the fridge door with a little kick… and nearly have a heart attack when I spot a tall figure to my right, silently observing me from less than six feet away. In a stupid reflex, I brandish my jar of pickles in his direction as if it were a gun.

Honestly, I feel pretty stupid for being startled by such a predictable jump-scare. The psycho guy hiding behind the fridge door has been done a hundred thousand times in horror movies. But in my defense, when that kind of scene happens in real life… it's a whole different story.

"Agent Holmes, lower that jar of pickles, it'll be of no use to you against me," murmurs the amused voice of my worst nightmare in the shadows.

"It depends on where I stick it in you," I retort in a grumpy tone, placing the jar back on the countertop.

"I'm sorry to dampen your enthusiasm, but it's a bit premature to consider that kind of practice at the beginning stage of our relationship."

I turn away with a grunt to switch on the small light above the stove and grab the loaf of bread from a cabinet to continue what I started. It's probably childish, but I don't want to show him any attention. He deserves nothing but my indifference tonight. To be honest, I don't even feel like insulting him. I'll get my revenge when I've regained all my physical and intellectual abilities. Right now, all I want is to satisfy my hunger, go back to bed, and sleep to put an end to this shitty day.

But Kelen Wills has decided to annoy me.

From the corner of my eye, I see him bend forward next to me, resting his elbow on the countertop and propping his chin in his palm as he turns his head to scrutinize my hardened face while I spread mustard on my bread slices. I'm starting to lose my temper. Under these circumstances, it's difficult to ignore his proximity and not speak up.

"Don't you have anything better to do, Wills?"

A sly grin appears on his lips. "My little cat, know that I always have a ravenous appetite after sex."

"That's none of my business. Grab something to eat and go back to Ondine's room to choke on it," I say, unwrapping the aluminum foil containing the roast turkey.

"I might wake her up, that would be a shame. She's sleeping so deeply. I've exhausted her, poor little thing."

"She exhausted herself by faking it, you mean."

"Women never fake it with me."

"My sister is an excellent actress."

"I remind you that I'm a telepath. I guarantee she wasn't faking it."

"So you hypnotized her to orgasm, then? Pathetic. But I'm not surprised, coming from you."

"I have no need for such methods. I only hypnotize my enemies," he asserts, grabbing the slice of turkey that I just laid on my slice of bread and stuffing it whole into his mouth.

"Next time you steal my food, I'll stab you in the hand with my knife. I'm not joking, Wills," I coldly threaten, tightening my fingers around the handle.

He chews his bite while inspecting my nightshirt mockingly. "I love your T-shirt," he remarks, changing the subject. "It fits you like a glove.

Okay… This Sinner Hybresang turns out to be a perpetual adolescent behind his facade of a formidable man of power and merciless demonic warlord. If I hadn't seen it with my own eyes, I'd have a hard time believing he resembles a monstrous balrog in his original form. He has multiple facets, each more unpleasant than the last. *Probably as many facets as sins.*

The white T-shirt in question reaches to the top of my thighs. Ondine ordered it online last year and customized it as a gift for me. It features a large paw covered in iridescent sequins as scales and equipped with sharp claws… raising its middle finger. Below the drawing is written, *Fuck you demon.*

Seeing his eyes drift over the line of my bare legs, I quickly tug on the hem of my T-shirt. I know he saw more earlier in the day when he brought me home after the fight with the Soulless, but I can't help it. If I had known I'd run into Wills in the kitchen, I would have put on old, oversized, ugly sweatpants, plaid socks, a puffer jacket, and even a balaclava before leaving my room. And still, I'm not sure all those unflattering clothes would have been enough to deter him from flirting.

Closing my sandwich, I move away from him and head to my couch. I feel his dark eyes weighing on my backside, making me shiver. I tuck my legs under me as I sit down, trying to show as little skin as possible.

"My sandwich isn't going to make itself, my little cat," Wills teases playfully.

Biting fiercely into mine, I flip him the middle finger, which makes him chuckle. Abandoning the food on the counter, the Magistrate teleports to the other end of the couch, then stretches his long, muscular legs to cross them on the coffee table. He leans back comfortably against the backrest, head tilted back, fingers intertwined behind his neck.

Here comes the devil encroaching on my territory *again.* What a nuisance. Note to self: find the contact information of a seasoned priest to exorcise him.

I wish I had enough willpower to not ogle this wicked and sultry individual who refuses to leave me alone.

His tousled dark hair attests that he just came from my sister's bed. His sculpted body is bathed in the pale glow of the range hood, and his half-closed eyelids give the impression of drowsiness, although I know he isn't actually sleepy. As for his body odor, it could be named *Incubus Fever* and sold in an Infernum perfume shop to excite demonic schoolgirls. The epitome of sexy nonchalance, Kelen Wills sits nearly naked a foot away from me, relaxed in his boxer shorts. This Hybresang jerk has eight perfectly sculpted abs and pecs that would make Henry Cavill envious. A slight patch of brown hair covers his broad chest and continues down in a thin line on his stomach. Even at rest, his package is so imposing it forms an enticing bulge in his black boxer shorts. I swallow my bite of my sandwich with difficulty. I've never seen a guy this well built. Even his skin doesn't have a single flaw. Inwardly, I groan with frustration.

Do you believe in destiny? I believe this guy was born to annoy me—and tempt me, because those two verbs are inseparable in my situation.

"I really like it when you look at me that way, Agent Holmes," he comments sensually, without even turning his head toward me.

I lower my gaze to my sandwich, jaw clenched and face burning. And not just my face, unfortunately. There's no point in denying I was ogling him since he caught me. So, I come up with a verbal counterattack. "I was wondering how a guy who thinks he's the center of the universe could have such an ugly belly button."

Staring at the ceiling, Kelen sketches a faint smile that deepens the dimple in his chin, which I find incredibly charming.

"My navel is just as perfect as the rest of me, my little cat. You should lean over me to inspect it more closely. I'd gladly hold your hair while your pretty purple eyes travel slowly over my skin. This way, you'll see that every part of my masculine anatomy is worthy of your delightful attention," he assures in a bewitching, openly sexual voice.

Good god, he's insufferable. For a split second, I'm starting to be wet imagining myself sucking him off. And I'm not talking about sucking his navel, as you've probably guessed.

To stave off this damned fantasy, I conjure another: Kelen tripping over a red carpet and falling flat on his face in front of hundreds of laughing demons. I start giggling to myself. The Magistrate frowns, his piercing gaze returning to me.

"What's so funny about what I said, Myrina?"

"Nothing, I didn't listen to a word of your babbling. I was thinking of a good joke my boss told me the other day."

"That's convenient, because I have a good joke for you, too. Earlier, I took your sister doggy style and came inside her while thinking of you. Isn't that hilarious?" he asks, removing his hands from behind his neck to place them flat on his bare stomach.

My laughter dies in my throat. He's killed my mood… and my appetite. I toss the rest of my sandwich onto the coffee table.

"You… you're disgusting, Wills."

"I was secretly hoping you'd come watch me pounding Ondine to satisfy your Sinner's curiosity. I even left the door ajar for that purpose. My orgasm would've been even more intense if I had looked you in the eye while coming inside her," he adds softly, with a malicious smile that sends a chill down my spine.

What a first-class bastard. He was *only* going at it with her to taunt me because I was in the next room. And if he stayed to *sleep* here… it was probably to annoy me, too. Next time, I'll secretly record his vile words and let my sister listen to them. How can he be so odious when she's peacefully sleeping just a few feet away? She deserves so much better than this demonic jerk!

"One more word, and I'll get my sword to castrate you!"

"No need to go to such extremes, my little cat. If you're frustrated, I'll buy you a dildo that looks like my noble phallus."

"Great idea! I've always wanted a pocket-sized vibrator."

Instead of getting offended, he emits a sardonic laugh.

"But really, who still says *phallus* nowadays? Are you that old?"

"I'm not old. I'm experienced."

"You're old, and you can't accept your age."

"I accept my age. In fact, I've been twenty-eight for over thirteen hundred years."

"I hope you die in agony and guilt for all the harm you've caused people over thirteen centuries, you old jerk."

The change in Kelen's demeanor at my words is radical. His whole body tenses, a brutal violence replaces the nonchalance, and he fixes an intensely hungry gaze on my mouth. My breath catches somewhere in my lungs.

"I'd better warn you, Myrina, if you keep rubbing me the wrong way with such hostility, I can't guarantee anything. I've been holding back my hard-on for minutes now, dying to kiss those exquisite lips of yours and bite them until they turn blood red," he abruptly interjects. Taking a deep breath, he shakes his head, closing his eyes before reopening them, his gaze once again distant, pinned to the blank TV screen. "So, how was your day?"

And he's bipolar on top of it! I cross my arms over my chest to conceal the pointed peaks of my nipples under my T-shirt. Yeah, I'm ashamed, but his anger turned me on.

"Drop the act, Wills. You're the last person I'd want to tell about my day, and I know you couldn't care less."

"Anything related to you, directly or indirectly, interests me, Myrina," he counters with an odd seriousness.

"Is that why you're making my life miserable?"

"If making your life *miserable* is the only way to get through to you, then yes. Given the choice, I'd rather be the object of your hate than your indifference."

Damn it all! Where does that even come from?

"You've got a seriously twisted logic, Wills," I grumble, growing increasingly uncomfortable.

"My logic adapts to my interlocutors. You're not sensitive to virtue; I've already told you that in your dream. Your moral sense is purely artificial, constructed from scratch by your Justspawn grandfather and your tutors at the CIT to cage and restrain your wonderful hybrid potential. I had my suspicions confirmed when I saw your sumptuous demonic appearance and your fainting spell. This weakness, if I may call it that, is primarily mental. It's a placebo effect reflecting your guilt for embracing your most powerful form. Your physical symptoms are real, but they primarily stem from your inner turmoil and doubts. If you were more Virtuous than Sinful, we wouldn't feel such a strong attraction to each other, I'm convinced.

"Myrina, think for a minute, how many Virtuous people have you slept with? None, right? Because it's sin that stimulates you the most and conditions your well-being. I'm trying to demonstrate it to you unequivocally by pushing you out of your comfort zone and shaking you up a bit. The day you stop denying it, you'll thank me for opening your eyes. And I'll be there for you, my little cat." He glances toward Ondine's bedroom door. "For you exclusively."

His ambiguous words hit me viscerally. And I hate it.

I realize that I'm having a discussion with the Magistrate Kelen Wills in my living room in the middle of the night. While he was fucking with my sister half an hour ago in the room next to mine, and he's on my list of suspects in a demonicide case.

I'm seriously losing it.

I've already made the painful mistake of getting attached to the wrong person. It's out of the question for it to happen again.

I abruptly stand to end this conversation that's making me so nervous. Kelen grabs me by the wrist in a burning grip. A fiery shock spreads along my arm at his steely touch. His expression, shadowed by the darkness, mirrors mine: grave, hard, and tense.

"Myrina."

"Let go of me, Wills."

"First, tell me who the man was who hurt you." It's not a question, but an order.

"And who says it was a man?" I whisper.

He meets my gaze without flinching. "I can't read your thoughts, Myrina. Your mixed heritage largely shields you from my telepathic powers. But sometimes, I catch the murky echo of your emotions. And there's one closely linked to a male figure from your past. Is it your father?"

"No."

Gently, his thumb begins to trace small soothing circles on the middle of my forearm, as if to influence me, igniting that cursed desire nestled in the pit of my stomach.

"Who was it, Myrina?"

"What does it matter to you, damn it?"

"I wonder who managed to infiltrate your Amazonian armor and cause you such pain." A spark of cruelty ignites in his eyes, which take on a reddish hue. "To kill him."

With a sharp movement, I break free from his grip, staring at him with contempt. "You can't kill him."

"I'm the most powerful demon in Infernum. I can kill anyone."

"Not him, Wills," I breathe out with a cynical smile.

"Why not?"

"Because he's already dead," I coldly drop before returning to my room.

I welcome the ensuing silence with relief.

CHAPTER 17
KELEN'S PRESENT

"Repentance is the child of virtue."
~Antoine Claude Gabriel Jobert, The Treasure of Thoughts

MYRINA

Kelen sends me a weird text early this morning. I read it in the bathroom while doing my business. It only contains one name.

> Aydan Smat.

Thinking he must have made a mistake, I respond:

> I suppose your message wasn't meant for me.

Three minutes later, he replies:

> Yes, Agent Holmes. I'm offering you a beautiful golden gift package. It's up to you to unwrap it and discover its contents.

> A golden gift? What's the occasion for that?

To apologize for his behavior yesterday? suggests a perplexed voice in my mind.

Apologize, him? No, that didn't sound like him. This man is unaware of the very meaning of the phrase *self-reflection*.

Without much conviction, I type *Aydan Smat* into my search bar. Nothing useful comes up; the name is unknown. So, I check on the demonic net.

And there, I get a result that makes me freeze.

There's a short biography and two photos in the official directory of Infernum, WikiDemonica. One portrait in human form and another in demonic form.

I immediately recognize the demonic form… and almost drop my phone into the toilet.

Aydan Smat is none other than my Faithfiend stiff, the guy from the leap of faith found in the church.

The first victim of the serial killer I am chasing.

****

Finally, I had a lead!

Aydan Smat, one hundred and four years old. No family. Former priest in a Faithfiend temple on Infernum. After the accidental fire that ravaged his sanctuary a decade ago, the Virtuous man packed up and left. One of his disciples, who I managed to reach by phone, revealed Aydan had renounced his faith as a Faithfiend following the tragedy that cost the lives of three children and two adults. He became homeless… on Earth.

He renounced his faith. That element was puzzling me.

I spoke with the human manager of the homeless shelter where Aydan occasionally stayed.

The center where John Blane the Charityfiend used to volunteer, my burning corpse from the abandoned hospital.

Yes, the two victims knew each other! According to my source, it was John who introduced Aydan to the shelter. The two Virtuous had been friends for about fifteen years. The Charityfiend had even offered to host the Faithfiend at his home and help him reintegrate into active life, but apparently, Aydan wasn't interested. He was described as *a solitary, taciturn, and reserved man, often lost in thought, who seemed to carry the weight of the world on his shoulders*, according to the shelter manager.

How did John Blane and Aydan Smat meet? No one knew, not even John's widow, Saraya Blane—the weepy one who looked like Bree Van de Kamp. I had gone back to see her as part of my investigation. When I had shown her the photo of Smat's corpse after her husband's death, she hadn't recognized him because he was in his demonic form, not his human one. But presented with the human photo, she recognized him instantly. She explained her late husband had never mentioned Aydan before bringing him home for dinner about two years ago. She had no good feeling about the other Faithfiend because she was very devout… and he wasn't anymore.

During dinner, they had even argued about their faith. Furious, he had blasphemed against their religion, telling Saraya that if God existed, he wouldn't have let Virtuous children die in terrible pain, during a fire. Saraya described Aydan Smat as: Bitter, sour, and melancholic, the kind of man who lives in the past. A lost and wandering soul. After the departure of the heretical homeless man, she told her husband John that she didn't want his friend in their home anymore.

After gathering all this information, I felt both euphoric and unsettled. Euphoric because I had found a link between my victims. It could mean they both knew the murderer. At the same time, I was unsettled because it was Kelen who had led me to this promising new lead. I had to find out how he knew the name of my corpse… and what else he knew about this story. The same went for the attack on the Soulless at the Envyfiends' HQ and the electronic collar that had unfortunately disappeared.

And I wasn't ruling out the possibility of getting some revenge on him for his antics along the way. I send him a text around noon.

We need to talk face-to-face in a private place, Wills. It's urgent.

You're seriously annoying me, Myrina. I'm eating, and I'm only on my third main course. Food is sacred to me.

In an hour, then!

No, at two PM. I always take a digestive nap after my meal.

I burst out laughing. *A digestive nap?* Oh wow, how glamorous! His demoness groupies would be horrified to hear that Kelen Wills has grandpa habits.

Okay for two PM, dinosaur. How about at the 1001 Nights of Lust?

It's during the day, so there won't be anyone at the club except us. The setting is perfect for what I have in mind.

That works for me, Myrina. Be punctual. I have a meeting with my staff at three PM. And stop calling me *dinosaur* if you want to stay in one piece for the next few days.

Oops. Sensitive about his age.

***

KELEN

Two-ten PM. Myrina is late for our meeting.

This greatly irritates me. I've already been at the club for fifteen minutes, and I'm not used to being kept waiting. Usually, I'm the one who makes others wait. If she stands me up, someone is going to get massacred.

While waiting for my enchanting *sister-in-law* to deign to show up for our meeting, I take the opportunity to sign the papers handed to me by my secretary, leaning over the glass bar in the main room. Mostly pacts. I don't read them; I neither have the time nor the inclination. Sam has been handling that chore for a while. My secretary drafts them, my lieutenant reads and approves them, I scribble my signature, and my Ragebeast envoys have the humans who dared to summon them sign as well. When the involved mortals perish, I reclaim their souls.

For what use? Professional secret. I might reveal it if you make a pact with me, but be prepared to pay dearly for your curiosity.

As I sign yet another contract sealing the death of a human who wronged another, there's a vigorous knock at the door. Paymon, who I brought in just for the occasion— thank goodness, I'm not a doorman!—unlocks the door and lets my visitor in. I straighten up, smoothing the wrinkles in my shirt with a swipe of my hand. Ten seconds later, my bouncer and my Tracker appear in the room.

I can't take my eyes off her. It takes me a few moments to recognize her and get used to her new look.

She's wearing a tight miniskirt. High heels.

And even… makeup.

As she walks toward me with a panther-like stride, an alarm goes off in my mind, like a plane hitting turbulence. *Trouble ahead.*

Gorgeous trouble that I'd love to get into, by the way.

"Paymon," I call out, without breaking eye contact with Myrina, "you can leave."

When I don't get a response, I shift my attention to the idiot demon working for me. He didn't listen. Standing still behind my future mistress, this pervert is staring at her rear, rubbing his jaw with a stupid grin on his face.

"Paymon," I repeat louder to snap him out of it, "you have thirty seconds to get out of the club before I rip your eyeballs out and make you swallow them like appetizers."

"Y-yes, boss."

He leaves. I'm alone with Myrina. She climbs onto a stool next to me, places her handbag on the neighboring seat, and slowly crosses her lingerie-model legs. The hem of her black skirt hikes up with the movement, revealing a strip of dark lace that makes my mouth water. She's wearing stockings. My cock suddenly feels hot.

"Mm, did you go all out just for me, kitten?" I ask lazily, though I remain on my guard.

She gives me a haughty look as she unbuttons her tailored jacket. "Of course not. I have an infiltration mission later," she retorts sharply, sliding the fitted jacket off her shoulders.

She's wearing a backless purple top that matches her eyes. It ties behind her neck and is outrageously low-cut in the front. And she's not wearing a bra.

Startled, I snap the silver pen in my hand, staining my fingers with black ink. An angry curse escapes my throat. Proud of her effect on me, Myrina smirks as she watches me wash my hand in the sink behind the counter and dry it with a towel.

"Which circle are you supposed to infiltrate, exactly?" I growl, my eyes straying to the tantalizing curve of her breasts in the provocative neckline.

"If I tell you, Wills, I'll have to kill you," she says, leaning on the bar.

Her evasive answer irritates me slightly. "You're not going to let a demon infiltrate *you* to complete your mission, I hope."

"Who knows? Might as well make it useful and enjoyable."

"I'm the best suited to infiltrate you both usefully and enjoyably."

"You're exhausting, Wills. Get me a drink; I need it to face our upcoming discussion."

"Damn it, Myrina, do I look like a bartender?"

"No, you look like an ass. But you'll make an exception for me, won't you? Your bad reputation won't suffer, I promise. No one will catch you in the act of chivalry."

This hybrid bitch still challenges me. I dream of punishing her, tying her up, gagging her, spanking her, feasting on her Lustspawn energy, annihilating her Justspawn will, subjecting her to all my desires. No woman has ever shaken my self-control like she has. And needless to say, I haven't let anyone else address me like this. I'll put her in her place when the time comes, ensuring she repents for every slight against me. A blowjob per insult, fair game. Besides, she's painted her plump, insolent lips in crimson. She keeps pinching and moistening them as if it were a tic. I gather she's not used to wearing lipstick, and the texture bothers her. I might suggest removing the excess with my tongue, but there's a ninety-nine percent chance she'll tell me to fuck off.

I grab two whiskey glasses and a bottle of Dragon Bile. The Tracker doesn't take her eyes, accentuated with black eyeliner, off my face as I pour the strong alcohol into our glasses. Her lovely analytical gaze ignites me. She observes me in that undecided way every time she's torn between wanting to fuck me and needing to eviscerate me. Her spirit of contradiction is pleasurable for the Sinner that I am.

I push the glass toward her. She doesn't touch it. Surely, she doesn't expect us to toast like two miserable humans, does she?

"Got any sugar?" she asks with a soft voice.

"Sugar?" I repeat, not understanding.

"I always put sugar in my Dragon Bile, Wills. Like in my coffee."

It's a weird habit, but good to know.

I have no clue where my employees stash the sugar behind the bar, but I'll find it; I'm resourceful. I crouch down to open the lower cabinets and rummage through their mess. Eventually, I unearth the object of my search. With a victorious smile, I straighten up to place the package on the counter, along with a spoon. Myrina thanks me with a nod and incorporates three sugars into her glass before stirring her concoction with a hypnotic motion. I watch thoughtfully as she stirs while swallowing half my Dragon Bile.

"Wills, how did you find out the name of my deceased Faithfiend?"

I would have much preferred she had told me she was up for sleeping with me, in which case I would have dumped Ondine in a minute via text. But her question doesn't surprise me.

"If I tell you, my little cat, I'll have to kill you." I smile, parroting her line to tease and annoy her.

She smiles back at me. I've learned from experience that when Myrina Holmes returns my smile… it's not a good sign. I wouldn't go so far as to say I'm worried, but I'm not particularly calm either. I send a meditative glance toward her handbag. Could she have a weapon in there?

"I suspected you would reply with something like that," she confesses with a placid voice. "You know, Wills, the seven sins you so proudly boast of make you sadly predictable. The advantage of the virtue of Justice is that it's not so predictable."

She sticks her spoon into her beautiful red mouth to suck it greedily. By the four horsemen of the Apocalypse, she's openly teasing me! My heartbeat and breathing accelerates. I'm tempted to fuck her on the bar to stop her from infiltrating who-knows-where with who-knows-who.

"What do you have planned for me in the near future, Agent Holmes?"

She gives me an innocent smile as she taps the end of her spoon against my glass. A crystalline sound rises, like a gong signaling the start of a match in the ring.

"My darling, it's already done," she says.

I look down, somewhat surprised, at my glass of Dragon's Bile.

"You drugged me, didn't you?" I ask.

The demoness nods with a sadistic delight.

I burst out laughing. What nerve!

"Myrina, Myrina, come on… I'm a Hybresang. Human drugs have no effect on me," I say.

She joins her clear laughter with mine. "Wills, Wills, come on… Who says it's a human drug?" she replies.

I immediately stop laughing.

She didn't.

My legs wobble. My vision blurs. Damn, what is this crap? I try to teleport elsewhere. It doesn't work. I can't even morph. The substance she dispersed in my glass while I was looking for sugar has neutralized all my demonic powers. She's got some follow-through, this damn Tracker. I grumble in protest, even though I'm secretly impressed… because she was brilliant with this move. I had sensed something fishy, but I hadn't seen it coming in this way.

As I cling to the bar to keep from collapsing, I glare at Myrina. Except my vision doubles. *Two mixed-race vixens for the price of one.* I vaguely make out the diabolical twins reaching out with four hands toward my collar. I feel them gently pulling on my tie to bring my face toward them above the bar. Devoid of my strength, I'm unable to offer any resistance.

"We're going to play, Wills," Myrina whispers in my ear, her silky cheek brushing against mine. "But by my rules."

In a titanic effort, I try to steal a kiss from her lips to at least have the last word before fainting, but she quickly jerks her head back, flicking my temple… and I collapse onto my own bar, sinking into darkness.

CHAPTER 18
A VENGEANCE GONE AWRY

MYRINA

To detain a Sinners Magistrate for an interrogation of this kind… I've never before committed such a serious offense against the laws of Infernum. For this crime, I could be sent to prison or banished to the Limbo, or even executed by my colleagues at the CIT.

Between us, I couldn't care less. I take the risk. I believe the end justifies the means in certain contexts. Kelen Wills thinks he's above everything. They've all been crawling at his feet for centuries, and it's time for him to come down from his pedestal. He treats my sister like a whore and devalues her shamelessly. He appropriated the death of the Soulless I decapitated to increase his political popularity. He drives me crazy, tests my patience, and pushes me to my limits with the sole purpose of getting laid. And most importantly of all, he could be a serial killer.

If this hypothesis turned out to be true, I would slit his throat without batting an eyelid.

As I planned my trap before heading to the 1001 Nights of Lust, I told myself this: Desperate times call for desperate measures. Wills is a great evil. Therefore, I do nothing wrong if I inflict harm upon him. QED.

I thought I would feel guilt, uncertainty, and stress when the time came. However, it turns out I don't. On the contrary. Truth be told, I'm so excited to have Kelen at my mercy that I almost freak myself out. I shouldn't be rejoicing at the unhealthy idea of torturing him to extract information—or better yet, confessions. Yet, that's the case. It seems this scumbag full of vices brings out the primitive malevolence lurking within me. I'm impatient for him to emerge from unconsciousness to start implementing my little program. I want answers to my questions, and I will get them.

I had dragged him by the ankles to the stage of the club room. This muscular bastard weighs a ton! Fortunately, I've regained all my physical strength. Holding him against me, I lifted him onto a chair leaning against the pole dance bar and bound his wrists behind the bar with my silver handcuffs. The drug provided by Lexi is a sedative that Trackers administer to demon criminals to knock them out and prevent them from using their powers. As for Kelen, who is much more powerful than other Sinners, I downright put a triple dose in his drink. Even after he wakes up, the effects of the drug should persist in his body for several hours. Well... in theory.

After filling two champagne buckets with crushed ice—in case the first one isn't enough to pull him out of his coma—I get to work on the staging. I press various buttons to adjust the spotlights on the stage. Red light? No, he might see a sexual connotation in it. I want to scare him: I need an oppressive atmosphere to put pressure on him. I activate a green light. That's not it either, it makes me nauseous. Blue spotlight... Perfect. Cold, impersonal, unsettling. I turn off all the other switches; thus, only the cerulean light envelops the stage.

I climb back onto the stage to approach my prisoner slumped in the chair, hands tied to the dance pole. I grab him by the hair to forcefully lift his head and gaze upon his peaceful face. Even when he's unconscious, he's as beautiful as a dark angel. He looks asleep and... harmless. I sigh despite myself. *Come on, Myri. Don't falter.* I steel my mind. This is not the time to be superficial, let alone sentimental. It's just a beautiful exterior wrapping around a rotten core, I must not forget that.

Releasing his head, which sways on his shoulder, I unbutton his shirt while focusing my attention above his disheveled mane. If I give in to the temptation of detailing his enticing chest, it'll distract and derail me from my mission.

On to the next step.

Without mercy, I hurl the ultra-fresh contents of the bucket at my captive's face… who jerks awake. Grumbling, he shakes his head vigorously to clear his foggy mind. A few fragments of crushed ice remain stuck in his hair and shoulders. I bite my lower lip in dismay. Darn it, I hadn't thought that Kelen would be even sexier half-drenched. He raises his sparkling eyes to me, clicking his silver handcuffs against the metal bar. To my surprise, he's not angry at all. Nor frightened. It's a bit… bewildering.

"A dominatrix," he comments with Olympian calmness, his onyx orbs running over my body. "I should have guessed. In fact, it's not displeasing to me, Cruella De Vil."

"You misunderstand, Wills."

"Absolutely not, my little cat. The olfactory language of your pheromones tells me that you're particularly excited to have drugged and handcuffed me to gain the upper hand. It's a new situation for me, you know. I've never let a woman take control over me before, not even during foreplay. But when it comes to you…" An approving smile lines his full lips. "I confess I'm very curious to see what you're going to make me endure and especially how far you're willing to go in this spicy new game. Go ahead, unleash yourself, Myrina, I give you my blessing."

His provocation fuels my anger when I'm supposed to keep my cool. That's exactly what he's looking for.

It all comes down to this invisible tug-of-war between us. A dark power struggle. Who will exert control over the other through action and speech.

But this isn't a game. He'll realize that soon enough.

"Tell me everything you know about Aydan Smat," I demand in an uncompromising tone.

"That name means nothing to me," he replies, unfazed.

I swing my arm back and slap him with a powerful backhand, splitting his lower lip. The smack on his cheek echoes ominously in the room. Kelen plunges his predatory gaze into mine as he cleans his bloodied lip with a sensual flick of his tongue. This simple gesture makes my clit pulse as if he just ran his tongue between my legs.

Lord, this is off to a bad start.

"You can do much better," he murmurs with a hoarse voice.

For once, I agree with him.

I give him a violent punch in the lower part of his face, making his jaw crack. His head slumps to his shoulder. Yet, he takes the pain without uttering a sound. He moves his jaw from side to side. If I had hit a human like that, I would have dislocated it.

I won't lie: taking out my anger on him after what he did to Ondine and me feels incredibly satisfying and feeds my thirst for justice. The rage burning in my veins and the hatred freezing my heart ease somewhat, even though this guy deserves way worse than a bucket of crushed ice, a good slap, and a punch in the face. Behind my back, I massage my numb fist. It feels like I've punched a wall.

"Not bad, my little wildcat. I saw stars—you're getting better," Kelen compliments me.

The bluish spotlight highlights the coldness of his expression, contrasting with the heavy, suffocating atmosphere surrounding us.

"Where's the Soulless's necklace, Wills?"

"Up your ass, Agent Holmes."

The bastard stole my line.

I draw the silver knife I've tucked into the silk waistband of my skirt.

The sight of my weapon doesn't faze him much. In fact, a spark of interest lights up in his perverse eyes.

Hell and damnation! If he's a masochist, this is going to be even more complicated than I thought.

"Ask me that question nicely, Myrina. With the respect I deserve, on your knees between my legs. Open my zipper and blow me with at least as much skill as your sister. If you manage to satisfy me like she does, I might answer you," he suggests, his eyes caressing my mouth, then my chest.

My nostrils flare. I see red. He gives me a crooked smile that only intensifies my fury.

He disgusts me.

Breathing heavily, I lean forward to grab him by the throat. My human nails extend into demonic claws. I press the tip of the knife into the hollow of his cheek. I suddenly have the urge to carve his smile Joker-style and disfigure his handsome, caustic face. I can be cruel, too. "Do you have a connection to these sordid murders, Wills?" I hiss, squeezing his throat in my grip.

He doesn't lose his smile.

"It would suit you if I were your murderer, Agent Holmes… That way, you'd have the perfect excuse to unleash your resentment on me and absolve yourself. While you secretly long to enslave and destroy me since our memorable encounter… Don't be afraid to enjoy it, my little cat. Let your Sinner instincts run free. You can express all your hybrid power with me, and I'll never hold it against you. Unleash your anger, your pain, your need for domination. Take your revenge on me, pretend to be the hand of Justice if it pleases you. My shoulders and back are strong enough to endure all the torments your delightful mind could devise. Brutalizing me makes you feel better, doesn't it?"

"No," I refute in a low voice. "You're wrong. I'm not like you."

"Indeed, Myrina, you're not like me. Not yet. But you could be worse than me if you wanted to be. In your impressive true form, nothing would resist you," he says, his voice as smooth as honey.

"Last chance before I step it up, Wills!" I growl, positioning the tip of my knife under his chin. "Did you kill those two Virtuous ones?"

"Do it, Myrina," he murmurs, challenging me with his gaze. "If you have the guts, do it."

Slowly, I draw a long scratch across his throat with my silver knife, extending it down his chest between his contracting pectorals. He flinches, his jaw clenched, and his features twisted. The drug in his system probably makes him more sensitive to pain than usual. His blood runs over his muscular flesh in a black rivulet, sharpening my own darkness, my insatiable thirst. My heart pounds. My cut traces down his abdomen, between his abs. This path is fascinating.

When I lift my knife from his skin, just above his navel, we both exhale, but not for the same reasons.

He then taunts me, "You're tickling me, my little cat. It's official, you're a terrible torturer. You didn't press the blade deep enough or angle it properly. I could teach you a lot about how to flay a demon."

A chilling certainty hits me. Violence won't work on the Magistrate. He won't crack. Even if I amputated his fingers, even if I broke his bones. He has tortured. He might even have been tortured before. I'm an altar girl compared to him and everything he's been through.

"No," he continues after a heavy silence. "I'm not your murderer. When I kill someone, I claim it loudly, for the sake of my reputation. I despise psychopaths without balls and horns like that lunatic you're chasing."

"I don't believe you. Your insinuations about my investigation—"

"Myrina, I just wanted to get your attention. It worked beyond my expectations," he says sarcastically, tapping his handcuffs against the bar to illustrate his point.

"What-what do you mean by that?"

"I'm a hunter, like you, my dear. I know what makes you tick. It's not the execution, it's the hunt. The chase. If I hadn't made you think I was a suspect in your investigation, you'd never have come after me."

Damn it. He manipulated me to *chase* him!

"If I hadn't baited you like this, you'd have dismissed me from the start, relying on your prejudices against me," Kelen continues in a horribly detached tone. "If you weren't so independent and stubborn, we could catch this murderer together by working complementarily. My offer still stands, by the way. You've seen that I have a knack for finding clues that elude you. Without my help, you won't catch this killer. He's far more intelligent than any criminal you've neutralized in the past. In return…" He leaves the sentence hanging.

And then he shifts into aggressive seduction mode, unleashing his incubus pheromones, which apparently haven't been affected by the drug… and they wreak havoc on my thoughts.

I'm supposed to be immune to these chemical tricks of a Lustspawn male because of my hybridization. The problem is that Wills isn't just any demon. He's a Hybresang with powers sharpened by centuries of practice. A ticking time bomb. And I'm already a burning fuse of desire for this particular bomb. In short, his lust demon scent is the match threatening to make me lose my mind. His golden-brown, magnetic eyes bore into mine, fueling the flame of desire that pulses more and more intensely in my lower abdomen. *I'm immune to his pheromones. I'm immune to his pheromones.*

But then again, when you look at it from another angle… since violence has failed, perhaps a different approach might be more effective. Why choose between playing the good cop or the bad cop? I can do both at the same time.

So, I straddle my prisoner, seating myself astride his knees. In my movement, my skirt rides up my hips, fully revealing my thighs adorned with stockings and the lower part of my thong. Kelen's breathing suddenly becomes heavier, but this reaction has nothing to do with the knife I'm now pointing at his heart. Now, that's more what I want.

"A counteroffer, how typical of you… What is it exactly?"

"I want you, Myrina."

"For a half-day temp contract between two missions?" I mock, poking his chest with the tip of my blade.

"No, my beautiful hybrid. For a permanent, exclusive contract."

My smile fades. He's not joking.

"My Virtuous half doesn't bother you anymore, all of a sudden?"

He shakes his head.

"Wills, you're insane. I have no desire to partner with you. Professionally or personally."

"Really no desire?" he inquires, his amused eyes glancing down at our thighs.

Without even realizing it, I had moved closer to him during our conversation. The epicenter of my spread legs was now just an inch or two away from—

"You're hard," I whisper, incredulous.

"Such keen insight, Myrina."

"I drugged you, cuffed you, beat you, cut you. And you're hard!"

"It's not the torture that gets me like this, devil woman. Come closer, let's negotiate the terms of our trial period."

"I'm not negotiating anything with you," I breathe, pressing my wet sex against his indecent erection. "I'm imposing my conditions. If you answer my questions, Wills, I'll let you fuck me."

Once. Maybe. If the occasion arises.

At my words, his pupils turned blood-red in an instant. He's all in. And me… I'm getting more and more wet. My brain is short-circuiting. His pheromones are driving me crazy; I'm two steps away from going full nympho.

"Fuck you here, Myrina?" he repeated in a deep voice that made me shiver, lifting his hips to grind his impossibly hard bulge between my legs.

It feels so good to finally have him against me, so rigid, so powerful, so massive. A wonderful torment. A guilty pleasure. I press my hips against his in return, riding his erection and rubbing it between my thighs. Oh yes, I want him to fuck me right there. Deeply.

His lascivious lips brush my throat while his nose inhales the scent of my skin. The tip of his tongue is tracing my jugular. My free hand, trembling, tangles in his thick hair, inviting his face to nestle in my neck. He kisses me delicately. Bites me fiercely. Sucks me passionately.

My heart is racing at two hundred beats per minute. The only sounds breaking the silence of the room are our ragged breaths and his eager kisses.

Growing feverish, I throw my knife to the ground to better join our heated bodies. My swollen breasts under my tank top press against his powerful chest, wet with cold water and warm blood. My hands clutch at his shoulders, and my claws dig into his trapezius muscles through his shirt. As he throws his head back, letting out a deep, masculine groan of satisfaction, I dive onto his throat to lap up his slightly sweet blood that's as intoxicating as wine. I devour every square inch of his coppery skin, scratching it with my fangs. I can't stop; my Lustspawn instinct has taken over. I rub my aching clitoris against his prominent cock with reckless, animalistic frenzy. I'm so wet that my desire soaks both my thong and his pants.

Oh god, it's terrible. I desperately need to come. But I don't care about him. He's nothing. He's merely the instrument of my unbridled pleasure. I don't even want to remember his name. Or his identity. He's just a body I'm using to release the anguish that consumes me, the void inside me.

"Did you know there's an entire galaxy in your violet eyes, Myri? Your pupils are black suns. Your irises are studded with stars. Every time your eyes draw me into their mysteries, my heart implodes in my chest," interjects a masculine voice, whose softness and tenderness pierce through my confused memory.

No. No. No. Shut up. Not now. Please. Go away.

"Save your barroom poetry for your wedding vows," I had replied, laughing.

With my throat tightening from overwhelming sorrow, I slow the movement of my hips. *What am I doing?*

The glowing red orbs of Kelen's eyes lock onto mine. Reality crashes down around me, pulling me into its depths. Panicking, I pull away from him.

A sound of breaking metal immediately echoes in my ears. His palms smack down on my buttocks, slapping against my flesh to pull my hips back toward his.

He broke his handcuffs in one swift move.

Shocked, I realize he could have done it much earlier. He let me hit him and torture him!

The moment the Hybresang takes control, pressing me against him with possessive fervor, my breath hitches. His demon eyes bore into mine as he guides my hips against his to resume our erotic dance and finish what we started. A desperate moan escapes my lips as my unyielding desire surges back, overwhelming me. A ball of intolerable heat swells deep in my belly. I wrap my arms around his neck, squeezing my swollen clit against the hard bulge of his cock. I need to come to release my searing pain. And Kelen feels it through my emotions.

"Let go for me, my little cat," he whispers in my ear, kneading my bare ass under my skirt with tender voluptuousness.

With a final thrust harder than the rest, I shatter into a thousand delectable pieces, arching against Kelen. A piercing cry bursts from my throat at the first spasms. My soul fractures like crystal. An exhilarating energy courses through my taut muscles. My eyes are still closed, but I know he's watching me intently as I surrender to this cathartic orgasm. I collapse against him, panting, clinging to his biceps. He strokes my hair with one hand, planting a gentle kiss on my jawline.

What a nightmare. I can't stay another second.

I get up from his lap, tearing myself away from the warmth of his body. This time, he doesn't stop me.

We didn't kiss, we didn't have sex, he didn't even climax. Still, I'm overwhelmed with shame. I messed up royally. I behaved like a slut. He's probably right, I'm worse than him. And Ondine... God, I'm a terrible sister.

"You don't have to feel guilty, Myrina. I was a willing participant, if not delighted."

"Shut up, Wills. Shut up!" I glare at him. "All of this is… it's your fault! You pushed me to the limit!"

He raises an eyebrow, pulling the silver cuff off his wrist as easily as a simple ribbon. "My fault? Let me remind you that you're the one who physically mistreated me before using me like a giant sex toy." He smiles while dabbing the blood on his chest with a piece of his shirt. "I loved our little SM bondage session, my little cat. Next time, I'll be the one tying you up."

"There won't be a next time. You're a monster."

"Yes, by the standards of the Virtuous. But I own it, unlike you. By the way, how did your fiancé die, Myrina? Did you kill him by accident?"

I lunge at him, ready to beat him to death.

But the second bucket of crushed ice—now melted—rises into the air, carried by Wills's willpower, and dumps its entire contents over my head to stop me in my tracks.

"Remember, those aren't waterproof," Lexi had warned me.

I gag. I panic. The water has seeped in, it's too late. There's nothing to be done.

They don't work anymore.

"No!" I scream hysterically, clutching my head as tears well up in my eyes. "No, no! Not that! What have you done? They're ruined! They're ruined!"

The face of the Sinner Magistrate freezes in surprise and incomprehension at my horrified expression. He mumbles something unintelligible and takes a step toward me.

"Don't come near me! Never come near me again!" I shout, turning away.

I run as far as I can from this demon who brings out my darkness like no one ever has before.

CHAPTER 19

KELEN LEADS HIS INVESTIGATION

"Pride is presumptuous, eager to glorify itself." ~Alfred Auguste Pilavoine, Thoughts, Miscellanies, and Poems

MYRINA

Once back home, I send a text to my friend from the CIT.

My AAs got wet, Lexi. They're toast, I'm so upset!

Ouch! What happened?

A walking disaster named Kelen Wills, that's what happened!

I'll tell you later.

While omitting a few compromising details, like the fact that I held him captive in his own swingers club and that his incubus pheromones turned me into a crazed nymphomaniac.

Can you repair them?

No, Myri, I'm sorry, water is unforgiving. I'll have to make new ones for you. I'll prioritize it, but it'll take me several days. I need to order the parts and assemble them in my lab. I'll graft them for you as soon as they're ready. Didn't you keep your old AAs as a backup just in case?

I shoot a nasty look at Putrid, who is licking his paw, his rolls of fat spilling over the edge of my couch. One day, cats will rule the Earth. While they massacre and enslave humans, this particular specimen will be napping on his back with his snout buried in a can of tuna.

Don't even get me started, Lexi. I made the mistake of leaving the old ones on a shelf. My cat thought they were kibble.

What a naughty kitty, he never misses a chance. As soon as your new AAs are ready, I'll let you know.

Thanks. Can you explain the situation to Zagam for me? I won't be able to go back to work until this is sorted out.

No problem, Myri. I'll inform the boss. He'll understand.

Zagam, understanding? My Lexi is quite the optimist.

***

KELEN

I didn't sleep during my meeting at the Ragebeasts' headquarters, but I barely listened to any of their babble. I kept clicking my pen button at irregular intervals, which tends to get on the nerves of all my demon officers. I love annoying them with that little noise. It's as grating as a sharp claw screeching on a chalkboard. The most satisfying part is that none of them dare to say anything about it. But today, I was indulging in this habit more out of routine than a real desire to piss everyone off. I was preoccupied with my altercation with Myrina at the 1001 Nights of Lust, her expression of distress, and her hasty departure.

Don't get me wrong, I didn't feel the slightest bit of remorse. I was just intrigued by the extent of her reaction after I drenched her with ice water. The Tracker had really lost it. It vaguely reminded me of a cheesy and bizarre '80s movie with little creatures that should never get wet, which I stumbled upon one night while flipping channels as I was banging a circus performer with incredible flexibility. *Grabelins* or *Gressins*, something like that. I even had a good laugh over the scene where a curly-haired mother throws one of the diabolical little creatures into the microwave to cook it until it explodes. I sent the contortionist home once I was done with her so I could watch the movie alone, munching on green apple-flavored candy ribbons. Sometimes, humans create beautiful works, I must admit. I really enjoyed that movie, but that's not the point. The Amazon Myrina Holmes, with her badass exterior, had a problem with water. *"They're ruined!"* she had wailed, clutching her head in her hands. What on Earth was she talking about? Her hairstyle?

Or, more likely, it was related to her disability.

She had forbidden me from approaching her again, but this mystery was gnawing at me.

Since my contrarian nature can't stand being told what to do, I teleport to her place after my meeting. Damn, I've been visiting this dump way too often lately; I need to start spacing out my visits.

At least the black nutria is absent; I don't smell its musty stench in the apartment. Good, I won't have to resist the temptation to kick its rear. As for Ondine, she's at her dance class right now, if I remember correctly.

I don't have to go far to find my beautiful Tracker. She's asleep on the couch, curled up with her head on the armrest. Preparing for the confrontation ahead, I loudly clear my throat to wake her, expecting her to startle instantly—and maybe point a gun at me, why not. But she doesn't react at all.

"Myrina."

Still nothing. I frown. I don't rule out the possibility that she's pretending to sleep to try to catch me off guard and lunge at my throat. Watching her closely, I approach the couch. My gaze is drawn to the bare, graceful curve of her shoulder peeking out from the neckline of her oversized, pale blue, cashmere sweater. Struggling against the urge to press my lips there, I lift my eyes to her angelic face, which is softened by the haze of sleep. A dried trickle of blood on the upper part of her neck, just below her jawline, catches my attention. She has bled from her ear.

Struck by a doubt, I turn toward the coffee table.

Three objects resting on a handkerchief confirm my suspicions: a kind of plastic tweezers with curved ends, and two tiny, black, glossy eggs with long, dirty needles inserted into them. These are highly sophisticated little devices, products of demonic technology— unique, extremely discreet, and custom-made, since no other demon has this kind of auditory deficiency... except her.

This complicates matters. I'm torn between conflicting feelings. First, I think about my reputation as I look to the future. If it were to be discovered that I'm involved with a woman who bears such a handicap, it could greatly discredit me. The public opinion of the Sinners of Infernum is not known for its tolerance toward individuals with severe disabilities. For instance, demons who become blind after losing their eyeballs in combat—some species don't have regenerative abilities—are ostracized from society. The same goes for amputees missing a wing, a leg, a horn, or a tail. Strength and power are the norm for us. A demon who doesn't possess all their physical capabilities is considered weak and unreliable by their peers. So, if I were to take Myrina as a mistress and her infirmity was exposed, it would inevitably reflect poorly on me and tarnish my reputation. The Sinners' leader in a relationship with a deaf woman? Let's be realistic; I'd be the laughingstock of the legions.

Second, I realize this new revelation makes Myrina an even more exceptional and remarkable demoness. Despite her disability, she has managed to become the best Tracker at the CIT, a seasoned warrior, a young woman of strong character, and a leader with an iron grip. In a way, the fact she has a failing sense makes her journey twice as admirable and her profile even more interesting. And when I look at things from this perspective, I find her more attractive than ever. Such fragility in her underscores all her other strengths and awakens within me an ancient protective instinct I haven't felt for centuries, since… well, I'd rather not think about it.

In thirteen centuries, I've never backed down from a challenge. Should I cross her name off my list of conquests and give up on seducing her just because she's deaf?

Kelen Wills, failing? Admit defeat? I frown at the thought.

These two verbs don't align with my name.

And damn it, I desire her so intensely! I loved feeling her lose control and ride my cock wildly. Feeling her passionately bite into my neck as if she was holding back from sinking her teeth in. Feeling her sharp claws rake my scalp and shoulders. I relished every second of her magnificent, guilt-tinged climax and adored all her screams and moans. The taste of her skin is so much more delectable and aphrodisiac-like than in my dreams… I couldn't even control my erection, which hasn't happened in a long time. My cock was so hard it was painful. I imagined ten times over thrusting into her with a single brutal stroke and basking in her incredible succubus sexual energy. If she had kept riding me with such fervor, there's no doubt I would have ejaculated in my boxer shorts.

I need to think things through, gain some perspective… and most importantly, learn more about her.

I'm not the only one having a good time.

Ondine's dance class ended fifteen minutes ago, so I went to the locker rooms, following her scent. Unsurprisingly, I find her being fucked from behind by her dance instructor against the lockers, her pink Lycra leggings pulled down to her knees. The Lustspawn often has a carnal appetite after sports. Since I'm a considerate boyfriend and they're almost done, I lean against the wall with my arms crossed to let them finish their business. I note with prideful satisfaction that despite his good thrusts, the human doesn't make her moan like I do.

As they reach orgasm, I decide to make my presence known in the worst possible way to really drive the point home. I slam the ajar door shut with all my telekinetic might. The human jolts, yelling and jumping back.

"Ondine? What… what are you doing?" I feign shock, my voice dripping with indignation.

The two lovers turn toward me. The guy, beet-red, hurriedly stuffs his now flaccid member back into his pants in record time. Behind him, Ondine bites her lips to stifle her laughter as she pulls up her thong and leggings.

"Oh, my god, how long have you been cheating on me with this jerk?" I exclaim, placing a hand flat on my chest.

"Don't get upset, Kel. Think of your blood pressure."

"My blood pressure was just fine until now."

"Wow, I'm so sorry, man! I didn't know she had a boyfriend!" the instructor apologizes, raising his hands contritely, overwhelmed with shame.

I glare at him murderously. Faced with my size, he's not putting on airs. "I'm not her boyfriend, I'm her husband," I say.

"Damn it, what a slut!" the guy spits over his shoulder.

"Shut up, asshole!" Ondine cries out, scandalized by his insult.

"You call my fucking wife a slut, motherfucker?" I roar, clenching my fists until my knuckles crack.

"No, no, shit! I didn't say that!" He panics, turning pale.

"Then you're calling me a liar?" I add.

The Zumba instructor is on the verge of pissing on himself, and I'm already tired of this game. I have no intention of beating him up—what's the point in stomping on a mollusk?

"Get out of my way, dickhead!"

He runs off. He won't be screwing another one of his students anytime soon.

Ondine skips over to me like a pretty little goat and brushes my lips with a languorous kiss to greet me. "You're a very naughty boy, Kel," she coos, caressing my chest.

On the contrary, I've been adorable, kind, and patient. Not only did I not tear apart the other idiot in the locker room, but I also let my girlfriend finish before stepping in.

Grabbing her by the shoulders, I push her away from me,

wrinkling my nose. "Damn it, Ondine, you reek of human cum."

"If you had arrived a bit later, I would've had time to shower."

That would have been preferable. Like all demons, Lustspawns are immune to STDs and can't reproduce with humans, so they never use condoms. The succubus's vagina must be a real breeding ground. Until she thoroughly cleans it, there's no way I'm dipping my dick back in. But let's leave these little hygienic considerations out of why I'm here.

"Are you taking me to the Italian restaurant tonight?" Ondine asks with a coquettish smile.

"No, I have other plans. You should go home and see your sister."

"What has she done this time?"

Aside from drugging me, handcuffing me, torturing me, and riding my dick like a rodeo? Nothing. "She had an issue with her hearing devices."

The succubus's smile vanishes. She pales, looking at me with wide eyes. "What? She told you?"

I'm sure Myrina will come up with a credible story to justify this *problem* without mentioning our steamy games.

"Yes, Ondine, but she didn't go into detail. She was embarrassed. I was caught off guard; I had no idea she was deaf. Why didn't you tell me?"

"Because it's her business, Kel. She hates talking about it; it's her Achilles's heel. And she's not deaf, she's hard of hearing."

"So she can hear without her hearing aids, then?"

Ondine is reluctant to provide details. She hesitates, thinks it over, looks at me, and then agrees to answer. "Under certain conditions. You have to be in front of her, within about six feet, and speak clearly. Not too fast and not too low. She can read lips well. If you say something from far away, if she has her back to you, or if there's too much background noise, she probably won't hear you. She also has tinnitus, ringing that greatly disrupts her hearing. It's a genetic and degenerative anomaly that gets worse every year; there's nothing that can be done. It's the same every time she reverts to her demonic form: her hearing deteriorates a bit afterward." She sighs. "In about ten years, she'll be completely deaf. She's very dependent on her devices; she couldn't be a Tracker without them."

"How long has she been wearing them?"

"Since she joined the CIT, after her mother and her father were exiled. It changed her life. She told me that when she lived on Earth in her youth, she suffered a lot because of her condition. She was reclusive, sullen, withdrawn, uncomfortable in her own skin. She lived in a dark bubble. Since the kids in her neighborhood didn't know about her disability, they called her retarded whenever she left the house. She couldn't go to school like the others, so she had a tutor at home. He taught her sign language and lip reading so she could communicate better with her family. Regular hearing aids weren't suitable for her condition; they didn't work."

That doesn't surprise me. The inner ear of demons doesn't have exactly the same anatomical configuration as that of humans.

"At the CIT, they made and implanted very sophisticated in-ear prosthetics for her, which she has to wear all the time. They cost a fortune."

"But these gadgets, as sophisticated as they are, aren't waterproof."

"No, not these ones. She can't take them off whenever she wants because they were grafted onto her auditory nerve via an electric needle and meticulously adjusted during a minor operation. Myri has to wear special ear protection before showering or put on a hat when it rains to keep water from seeping into her eardrums."

That explains everything. Judging that they were no longer useful, that little idiot didn't wait for the surgical intervention and removed them herself with tweezers, hence the bleeding. Damn, that must have hurt like hell. That's probably why she was sleeping so deeply on her couch. The pain must have exhausted her.

If I had known it would mess up her implants, it goes without saying I never would have spilled water on her head.

At least now I know what's going on. And I'm going to find out how to say *fuck* in sign language.

CHAPTER 20
PROVOCATION AND REACTION

MYRINA

Silence isn't a source of peace for people like me. It's a source of anxiety from my earliest memories.

One day, when my condition progresses too far, hearing aids will no longer be effective. Silence is inevitable. And it scares the hell out of me.

Far more than death, to be honest.

Imagine no longer hearing all those little everyday sounds that ordinary people don't even notice anymore.

No longer hearing the rustling of leaves under the caress of the wind.

No longer hearing the melodious chirping of birds.

No longer hearing the pattering of rain on a window.

No longer hearing your favorite songs.

No longer hearing the laughter of those you love… nor your own voice.

I'll only hear those damn high-pitched whistling sounds, like a pressure cooker, sometimes so powerful that I want to bang my head against the wall and scream at the top of my lungs. My tinnitus never leaves me; they're only muffled thanks to the devices that counterbalance my deficiency. These phantom buzzings taunt me with their mere existence. They correspond to the sound frequencies I've lost over the years due to the progressive destruction of my auditory cells. Sounds I'll never perceive naturally again.

It's said that humans born completely deaf cope with their disability better than those who gradually lose their hearing. Without my hearing aids, I'd be a very different woman. For one, I couldn't have trained as a Tracker: to do this job, you need all your senses to be fully operational. I might have become a depressive and agoraphobic hermit. When I was little, I was afraid of people and the outside world. I was only comfortable at home and could only rely on my parents. I couldn't handle anything; I was passive, isolated, morose. I envied the other kids I watched from my bedroom window playing in my street. I wished I had enough courage to overcome my fears and join them, but I thought it was useless because we wouldn't have been able to communicate properly.

A few years ago, Ondine said during a conversation that it's better to lose your hearing than your sight and that I should put things into perspective. I almost slapped her. I reasoned she didn't mean any harm by such a comment. She didn't realize the impact of her words because she wasn't directly affected, that's all. Of course, blindness is a terrible disability, but so is deafness. To me, sight, hearing, and touch are the three most important senses of the five. We could do without smell and even taste; it would be annoying, sure, but not dramatic. Anosmia and ageusia wouldn't stop us from thriving personally. But living without sight? Living without hearing? Living without feeling the sensations of physical contact? I can't imagine my life without one of these three senses.

I suppose I lack objectivity, but that's my opinion. And being the victim of a progressive degeneration over which you have no control is horribly frustrating. I have no control over my hearing loss. My devices have become my lifeline, my only portal to normalcy. Deprived of these two technological aids, my confidence evaporates. I'm lost and vulnerable. I'd go so far as to say I'm just a shadow of my former self.

If Owen were still alive, he'd take me in his arms and comfort me with his unshakable natural optimism that exasperated me more than once when we were together. He'd tell me in sign language that it's only temporary and that I'll have new devices soon. He'd add, with a mischievous smile that this interlude would allow me to take a break from work, and he'd take the opportunity to spend time with me. Between two passionate embraces, he'd distract me by buying me the latest popular books or playing our favorite films in their original language with subtitles. A Quentin Tarantino marathon, for sure. But Owen's been gone for three years, I'm feeling down, and I don't have the slightest damn desire to read a book or watch a movie. I miss my human every day, and even more so in these moments when crushing loneliness overwhelms me.

As I uncork a bottle of Dragon's Bile in the kitchen, a hand gently lands on my arm. The tactile precaution is unnecessary: although I didn't hear her footsteps, I sensed my sister's scent before she approached. I grab a second glass from the cupboard and pour the liquor into the glasses under Ondine's concerned gaze.

For fuck's sake, if there's one thing that pisses me off, it's being pitied. Especially by *her*!

Considering I just got off rubbing against her boyfriend's dick like a desperate slut… I don't deserve her compassion.

"Myri," she calls in a loud, clear voice that seems to reach me from afar as if my ears were stuffed with cotton, "what happened with your devices?"

"I screwed up. Again," I reply bitterly, downing half my glass.

"No, sis. Accidents happen to everyone."

I let out a cynical laugh. If I hadn't been playing the hot torturer with her man, this *accident* wouldn't have happened. I should have kept my distance from Kelen instead of grilling him hard. That's exactly what he wanted, and I fell into his trap like an idiot. I should have realized he was baiting me about my investigation just to get me to chase him. As a result, I've spat on my principles for *nothing*, and I'm stuck in my apartment for several days like a leper, waiting for new hearing aids. Meanwhile, a demon serial killer is still on the loose and planning a third murder—unless he's already committed it.

"Is there anything I can do?" Ondine offers, gently stroking my tension-ridden back.

Leave Wills. He's screwing us both over.

"No," I reply curtly, trying to shut down the conversation with a tone that, despite everything, isn't directed at her.

"Myri, it's not a big deal, Lexi will make you new ones. Be patient. You're so caught up in your job and obsessed with this investigation that it'll do you good to take a break and rest. The other Trackers can cover for you."

She's speaking softer now without realizing it, but as I'm watching her lips, I catch every word and don't need her to repeat.

"Damn it, Ondine, you sound just like Owen," I mutter before grabbing the bottle and heading back to my room quickly, so she won't notice the wetness in my eyes.

***

KELEN

The Horn of Plenty award ceremony is set for tonight at the Magistrates' Palace in Infernum. I teleport into the vast amphitheater with Sam, who's in charge of security, for a preliminary inspection of the venue.

Dozens of winged demons zigzag through the air, hanging our legion's flamboyant banners on the walls. Engineers adjust the lighting, and journalists set up their equipment in front of the stage. I even notice a pretty art restorer using a brush to touch up the silver scales of a demon in the giant fresco on the ceiling. I loathe this symbolic piece; it drips with hypocrisy.

Seven Virtuous and seven Sinners feast around a banquet table as if they were blood brothers. It's inspired by Leonardo da Vinci's *Last Supper*.

Backstage, Hallow is berating his young Envyfiend agent, spraying spit in his face and pounding his chest with a rigid briefcase. Apparently, they have a difference of opinion over the speech Hallow will give just before mine.

"*Eternal gratitude?* Do I look like I want to polish that Hybresang trash's shoes with my forked tongue? Your stupid speech is political suicide! Rewrite it from scratch!"

I exchange a wry smile with Sammael. The Magistrate of Envy

is a caricature of himself. He's as short, skinny, and ugly in his human form as he is in his demonic one. He reminds me of a leprechaun on amphetamines.

"*Eternal gratitude* is a bit much, Hallow," I say cynically while adjusting my suit jacket. "*Immeasurable appreciation* would be more fitting. As for polishing my shoes with your bifurcated tongue, I'll pass. They were made by a Florentine cobbler, and I wouldn't want your corrosive saliva ruining the leather."

"Wills!" my Sinner rival screeches, his red eyes glaring at me. "Enjoy your moment of glory; it will be fleeting."

"That's not what the polls suggest. The number of my supporters is growing day by day."

"Just like your ego! Polls aren't representative of public opinion, and you know it as well as I do. The mentality of Infernum's voters is fickle. They still have plenty of time to come to their senses and change their minds about you."

"I agree with Hallow's point," a gravelly, sensual feminine voice rasps against my scales. "Hello, Kelen. I thought I detected the distinctive scent of perversion that always accompanies your arrival somewhere."

I silently curse. There's no avoiding my ex this time.

"Beliale. At least the smell of my perversion masks your stench of whore queen."

"Oh, Kelen, I've missed you, too." She sighs, brushing her dark, red-painted lips against my cheek, likely leaving an ugly smudge on my clean-shaven skin.

Damn it, I didn't even have time to dodge her damn cheek kiss! I'd rather have kissed a praying mantis. I pull a handkerchief from my pocket to wipe my cheek under her amused gaze. She relishes our verbal sparring. I don't. If she weren't a Magistrate, I'd have killed this Lustspawn bitch centuries ago.

"What do you think of my new dress?"

"The cut is unflattering. It makes you look twenty pounds heavier, and not in the right places," I say, tossing the lipstick-stained handkerchief to the ground.

"But you didn't even look at me, Kelen," she chides, feigning amusement.

"Because every single one of your outfits makes you look stuffed, Beliale. Your stylist must have it out for you."

She laughs heartily. I know she loves when I'm cruel to her. Unfortunately, I can't help it—it's an old reflex. This twisted woman believes that flogging and humiliating her is my way of showing affection. Not many demons in Infernum can truly anger me, but Beliale is one of them. She's a pure dominant, like me. She's arrogant, ruthless, ambitious, treacherous, egocentric, vicious, and sadistic. These traits, which I admire in other Sinners, are intolerable in her because she pushes them to their extreme. This black widow uses and abuses her art of seduction to manipulate everyone, both men and women.

The Blood Countess, sometimes called *Countess Dracula*, have you heard of this legend? Elisabeth Báthory, a Hungarian criminal who lived in the 16th century, known for torturing and murdering young virgin girls before bathing in their fresh blood. Elisabeth is Beliale's middle name. But she didn't bathe in blood to preserve her youth, as the myth suggests. No, she did it just for the pleasure.

The only two people she has ever cared about in her life are herself… and me. She considers me her male alter ego. She still hasn't realized that she doesn't even come close to me and that I never want to sleep with her again, even if we were the last two survivors after the Apocalypse.

Needless to say, if any man other than me had insulted her appearance, she would have slit his throat in a second with a swipe of her claw.

"I was disappointed not to see you the other night at the 1001 Nights of Lust, Kelen," she begins in a caressing tone. "In truth, I had hoped you would participate actively in my orgy like you did in the past. Are you turning into a Virtuous one? It certainly seems so, since you're playing the hero, saving the lives of your rivals and… the Trackers."

Hallow grumbles something under his breath.

"Be careful, my dear," she continues, "those beautiful black scales you're so proud of might take on silver hues if you don't cultivate your seven deadly sins more diligently."

My gaze, inflamed with restrained rage, finally lands on her. A smile curves her venomous lips. That was precisely what she wanted: for me to look at her. By calling me Virtuous, the worst insult anyone could hurl at me, she got what she wanted.

There was a time when just looking at her would make me hard. Everyone who has crossed her path swears she's the most beautiful demoness in Infernum. If the Greek goddess of love, Aphrodite, had existed, she would have undoubtedly taken on Beliale's human appearance. Six feet of sensuality and grace. Hair cascading to her hips like a golden waterfall, eyes sparkling with translucent green, peachy skin with an indescribable softness, and a body with perfect curves wrapped in an obscene red silk dress. I once compared our conquest tallies out of sheer boredom. Believe it or not, her list is even longer than mine.

Now, I don't desire her at all, simply because I've realized this girl is nothing more than a toxic, pestilent turd wrapped in golden satin.

"I hope you enjoyed your night at my club with your cronies because it was the first and last time you'll ever set foot in there."

"You'd turn away the future Leader of the Sinners at the door of your establishment?" Her eyes twinkle with slyness. "That's not very sportsmanlike of you, Kelen."

"Even if you became the Federator—which won't happen—I'd rather bulldoze my club to the ground than let you in again."

"I can't wait to see your face when they announce the results of the second round, my dear."

"Beliale…"

"Mm, Kelen?"

I lean in to whisper in her ear, "Call me *my dear* one more time, and I'll fill a fountain with your blood and bathe in it."

With that, I teleport elsewhere in the Magistrates' Palace with Sam before making good on my threat.

MYRINA

First text message:

> Myrina, I stopped by your place earlier while you were asleep on the couch.

I don't reply. He can go to hell! I'm busy drinking, wrapped up in my blanket.

Five minutes later, a second text:

> You shouldn't have removed your devices by yourself.

Ah, he's aware. Do middle finger emojis exist?
Third text. I shouldn't even read it, but…

> I know you're mad at me. To prove that I'm worthy of your trust, I'll answer one of your questions.

I raise an eyebrow as I set my half-empty bottle back on my nightstand.

Fourth text message.

> I got the name Aydan Smat by contacting Magistral Faithfiend Azath. Since he owed me a favor, he went out of his way to identify him. I sent him a photo of your corpse, which he forwarded to several Faithfiend dignitaries in his legion. One of them recognized a former priest who once served at a temple in his district. Aydan Smat.

Heart racing, I immediately type on my phone.

> And how did you get his photo, Wills?

> Agent Holmes, I said I'd answer *one* question.

> Bastard Hybresang!

> Don't you have more original insults in your repertoire?

> I'm not going to list them all; it would take me hours.

> Please do. I could spend hours reading your sweet words, my little cat.

> Wills, leave me alone once and for all. You're wasting your time and mine! I don't see why you keep insisting; we'll never get along.

> We already do, Myrina. We're on the same wavelength. You just haven't admitted it yet.

> I'M HARD OF HEARING.

> Is that supposed to scare me or make me run away?

Unknowingly, a smile spreads across my lips. I give myself a mental slap to erase it. When I'm drunk, I smile for no reason. And when I'm drunk… I write nonsense.

> Wills, seriously, what do you see in me?

> I won't list everything; it would take me hours.

I let out an incredulous giggle, shaking my head. Smooth talker, that one! A few seconds later, he continues:

Everything about you is sexy. Your face, your eyes, your hair, your mouth, your body, your scent, your way of moving, your demonic form, your independence, your courage, your tenacity, even your nasty temper. And the most arousing thing of all? You can decapitate a Soulless with your bare hands.

A strange lump forms in my throat. Damn, I must be really wasted to be moved by a sleazy compliment from Kelen Wills. *Myri, you've hit rock bottom!*

Anyway, you and I are a perfect match, since everything about me is sexy, too.

Reading this text, I laugh out loud.

You always turn everything back to yourself, Wills, it's pathetic.

Not pathetic. Sexy.

All you've got going for you is your looks.

So, you think my looks are sexy.

Stop saying the word *sexy*, it's not sexy at all, it's actually outdated.

By the way, I'm looking forward to finding other ways to communicate with you. I won't need to talk to make myself understood, my little kitten.

Yeah, right, as if you know sign language!

True, I don't know it. But I can draw letters on your body with my tongue.

A wave of heat surges between my thighs as I visualize the scene. I bite a corner of my blanket to stifle a groan.

An *S* on the beauty mark adorning your breast. An E on the valley of your stomach. An *X* on the tattoo inside your thigh.

Breathing heavily, I clench the blanket in my fist, waiting for more… which doesn't come.

And the *Y*, jerk? Where would you trace the *Y*?

Are you still there, Agent Holmes?

If he thinks I'm going to ask him where he'd write the last letter, he's got another think coming! I snicker while quickly typing my response.

You know, Wills, it would take a lot more to turn me on. I'd rather go clean up my cat's vomit and diarrhea from its stomach bug than read your crappy sexts that give me acid reflux.

Oh, no! Shit! What an idiot—I sent it!

What have I done? I provoked him, challenged him. Minefield, Holmes! Out of ammo, retreat immediately! I pull the blanket over my head, groaning in despair. I should always turn off my phone when I'm tipsy.

Suddenly, something tugs my blanket away from me with a sharp pull. Eyes wide open, I find myself face to face with Kelen, who has materialized a foot away from me. My god, he's shirtless, built like a walking fantasy, and he's… he's in jeans. I've never seen him in jeans, and damn, it's a sight to behold! My throat goes dry, and my thighs grow wet. The three open buttons reveal the waistband of his white boxer briefs and the top of the bulge of his erection. He must have been in the middle of dressing or undressing while texting me. He dropped everything after reading my last message.

His fiery eyes, like blazing garnets, trigger a red alert in my brain.

He places a knee on the edge of the mattress, then leans forward, his fists planted on either side of my legs. Veins ripple through the taut muscles of his arms. His fierce gaze locks onto mine, matching his predatory expression.

Instinctively, I scoot back on my elbows until the top of my back hits the wooden headboard. He moves closer to me on the mattress, crawling like a lion preparing to pounce. He looms over me with his full physique, one knee between my thighs, hands on the bed on either side of my hips. I open my mouth to call for Ondine, who must be in the living room or bathroom, but he immediately clamps his large, burning hand over my lips. I'm paralyzed with fear and trembling with desire.

His ravenous eyes drop to my heaving chest. That's when I realize I'm only wearing my *Fuck you demon* T-shirt and boy shorts as armor to protect me from an especially hot-blooded incubus, to whom I foolishly wrote, *It would take a lot more to turn me on.*

Okay, buddy, you've won this battle! I'm already horribly turned on, no need to go overboard, bye!

My desperate, almost pleading look must be eloquent enough, because Kelen gives me a surprisingly gentle smile that makes my chest tighten.

Then, the demon leans forward at the level of my right breast and extends his tongue to draw an *S* over the fabric of my T-shirt. Very, very slowly. My breath catches in my lungs. Without breaking eye contact and without removing his hand from my mouth, he deliberately traces around the erect peak of my breast, whose shape is clearly visible. His tongue snakes around the edge of my areola, right where my beauty mark is. The fact that he remembers its exact location ignites all my erogenous zones.

With his free hand, he lifts my T-shirt up along my waist to my ribs, revealing my stomach. He continues his demonstration by writing a large *E* that starts below my navel, rises up my midline, and ends at my diaphragm. The sensation of his hot, silky tongue caressing my bare skin makes me moan against his palm, which presses harder against my mouth in response. Despite myself, I arch on the mattress.

Overwhelmed by the devastating power of my desires, I both dread and crave what comes next.

Kelen moves down my stomach, his lips brushing my trembling flesh. Carefully, he places his hand on my knee to part my legs. I don't resist; I feel strangely weak. His breath on my intimacy electrifies me. Delicately, the tip of his tongue sketches two intersecting lines on the inside of my thigh, over my tattoo, to form a small *X* right near the seam of my boy shorts. Damn, he must have an unobstructed view of the damp spot that betrays my state, not to mention the scent of my sexual pheromones.

Our gazes collide once more. His contains an unspoken question to which I refuse to respond. Since I don't make any move to push him away, he decides for me.

When his tongue fails on the edge of my panties, which cling to my moist flesh, I bite his palm violently to stifle a scream. He doesn't remove his hand from my mouth, however, and unperturbed, he continues the upward line of his impudent Y along my slit. He pauses insistently at the center of his letter, pressing his torturous tongue on my swollen and hypersensitive clitoris, causing my hips to jerk abruptly off the mattress. Then he finishes with the upper strokes one by one, returning to lap at my innervated bud in between. He even takes the liberty to trace three tiny circles to bring me to the edge of orgasm. I swear inwardly, my fists clenched on the sheets.

I'm breathless when he deigns to withdraw his head and rise to his knees between my legs. He removes his hand from my mouth as he contemplates my frustrated face. For the first time since we met, I sense hesitation and doubt in him, as if he doesn't know whether he should stop there or go further. His irises are a dark red, filled with gravity, fever, and... confusion?

It's really strange. He doesn't gloat, doesn't smile with a swaggering and triumphant air. He just scrutinizes me, lost in his enigmatic thoughts. I feel the tips of his fingers snake along my neck, then trace the outline of my ear. His features become impassive again in a fraction of a second, and without warning… he vanishes from my bed and my room, leaving me prey to the most terrible unsatisfied desire of my entire existence.

Despite my confusion, I don't lose my composure. It's better this way; he did well to leave. Because of the alcohol, I lowered my guard again with that bastard. Anyway, if he had started to undress me, I wouldn't have let him.

Well, I'm almost sure of it.

Now, I need to gather my wits enough to remember where I put my damn vibrator.

CHAPTER 21
BYE BYE BIRDIE

"Humanity takes itself too seriously; It is the world's original sin." ~Oscar Wilde, The Picture of Dorian Gray

KELEN

Sometimes, my Pridefiend side revels in the social recognition from my peers.

Sometimes, my Slothling side couldn't care less.

At the moment, as I adjust the microphone on the lectern in front of hundreds of Sinners and Virtuous demons from the jet-set of Infernum, I'm having some difficulty concentrating because of the lingering taste on my tongue. I had three drinks and sucked on a mint before the ceremony, but it feels like the flavor is embedded in my taste buds. The worst part is, I only licked Myrina's pussy through her lingerie. Hearing her softly moan against my hand, watching her gorgeous body arch under my lips, feeling her sharp teeth bite into my palm, all of it got me hard as a rutting bull.

Let's face it, it's the first time a woman has ignited my sins of lust, envy, and gluttony all at once, like a stick of dynamite with multiple fuses. Earlier, I was inches away from tearing off her panties and taking her forcefully on her bed, keeping my hand over her mouth to stifle her cries of pleasure. She wouldn't have resisted for a second, I'm sure of it. Her eyes blazed with desire, her breasts pointed through her T-shirt, her thighs trembled with anticipation, her panties were soaked. She wanted me as much as I wanted her.

What stopped me? I don't have a clear answer to that question. Maybe it was the proximity of Ondine, which would have amplified Myrina's guilt. Maybe it was her vulnerability due to her disability. Or maybe it was both at the same time. I prefer not to dwell on it too much; overanalyzing might give me a headache.

After leaving the Tracker's room, I teleported to Lilas's place, my little barmaid from the 1001 Nights, always up for a quick and dirty session with her revered boss. She greeted me with an enchanted smile, arms, and thighs wide open. I fucked her on her coffee table like a brute. It was good, as usual. I left once I was done, as usual.

It was… as usual. Nice, relaxing, but nothing more. On my way home, I remembered with a delayed realization that Lilas looked at me strangely when I came inside her, groaning her name. She was scowling, which was out of character for her. Could it be that I accidentally said Myrina's name instead of hers at the moment of orgasm? It's quite possible. I was distracted. Whatever.

Hallow's pathetic thank-you speech was enjoyable. He didn't mean a word of his declaration. The Envyfiend Magistrate spoke in a nasal, monotonous voice. He read his notes without looking at the assembly and sniffled regularly because of his demonic flu. I loved his insincerity; it gave me butterflies in my stomach.

Next, The Braveryfiend Magistrate Archibald Remington approached me, the solid gold Horn of Plenty in his hands. By Satan and Lucifer, the trophy celebrating my heroic courage is hideous! The engravings depicting the fourteen emblems of our demonic legions are rudimentary at best. The goldsmith deserves death by decapitation. I wouldn't even want to display this thing in my restroom.

Remington's hypocritical and pompous smile irked me considerably. The demon of Courage is the most popular of the Magistrates on the other side. According to polls, he's expected to become the Federator of the Virtuous. His main rival is Azath the Faithfiend. I abhor him almost as much as Beliale, this Remington.

When he handed me the Horn of Plenty, he turned his head toward the cameras with his old silicone smile, posing for the journalists' photos. As for me, I neither turned my head nor smiled as the camera flashes bombarded us and the spectators applauded so vigorously that every seat in the amphitheater shook. Without saying a word to him, I forcefully took the solid gold Horn of Plenty from his hands and loudly placed it on my lectern. Remington stood there like an idiot for a few seconds, arms still outstretched, before smiling at the crowd to save face and returning to his seat behind me.

Silence soon returned to the room. Everyone is now eagerly awaiting my speech; it's the highlight of the evening. The cameras are focused on me. I feel like teasing all these fools. I clear my throat slightly, my eyes raised to the ceiling as if contemplating, smoothing out the nonexistent wrinkles of my black jacket. There are discreet coughs behind me; Remington subtly hints that I should speak. Do I piss him off? Good.

I place my hands flat on the lectern on either side of the Horn of Plenty, which glimmers like a gold ingot, scanning the crowd with my gaze. I wink at a beautiful baroness Sinner in the front row, who bites her black lips while smiling, then I bring my mouth to the microphone to finally speak.

I decide to play it modest, for once. Just to gain more points in the polls. I place a solemn hand on my chest as my powerful voice resonates throughout the room. "My demon brothers and sisters, I am infinitely honored to receive this prestigious Horn of Plenty, which will be the centerpiece above my fireplace so that I can proudly gaze upon it every morning when I wake up. I thank each and every one of you from the bottom of my heart for this magnificent symbol. It may not show on my face because I've acquired perfect control over my emotions over the centuries, but I'm crying tears of joy deep inside. It's nothing less than a childhood dream come true."

Several female spectators sigh, touched. In the back, near the doors, Sammael chuckles in the shadows, hand over mouth.

"But as the commander of the Ragebeast Legion, I have only fulfilled my duty to protect Infernum and saved the life of a friend in dire straits." I shoot an ironic glance at Hallow, stiff as a board in his seat. "I'm convinced he would have done the same for me if our roles had been reversed." I turn back to my audience, puffing myself up. "You all wonder who orchestrated this attack of despicable cowardice. I will reveal it to you today. The Soulless who infiltrated the headquarters of the Envyfiends was *trained* as a weapon of war."

I pause to build suspense, relishing their surprise, worry, and confusion. Thanks to my heightened hearing, I hear Hallow grinding his teeth behind me. Backstage, the other Magistrates and I had agreed not to disclose certain details to the public and media. Frankly, I couldn't care less. I have no interest in not using this information to my advantage in my election campaign.

I pull the Soulless's necklace from my pocket, rolled up into a ball, and unfurl it, brandishing it high. I display it to the assembly. "I pledge before you to eradicate the clandestine scourge threatening Infernum if I become the Federator of Sinners!" I exclaim with determined aggression. "I will spare no effort to find and kill the leader of the Rebels and all the followers who seek to sow chaos on—"

On stage, footsteps sound to my right. Furious, I pivot toward the Ragebeast soldier who has deserted his post and, more importantly, dared to interrupt me. His vacant, bovine stare raises my suspicions. I make a telepathic incursion into his mind just as he abruptly parts the folds of his cloak to reveal his chest bristling with explosives. Panic-stricken screams shake the crowd.

The moment he presses the detonator button, I think with dismay, *Damn, my credibility is going to take a serious hit.*

MYRINA

As I take my second slice of goat cheese and honey pizza, the annoyingly loud Skype ringtone blares from my smartphone on the coffee table. I mute the TV and pick up my phone to see the caller ID. Malphas. I hesitate to answer, but you never know, it could be work-related.

Holding the screen up to my face, I answer. My colleague is busy fixing his hair with a comb, using his phone's camera as a mirror to tame a rebellious tuft on top of his head. More high-maintenance than a woman, that guy. I'm almost certain he spends more time than me in the bathroom in the morning getting ready. Once, I even saw a trace of orange foundation on his jawline, and of course, I teased him about it relentlessly. Offended, he retorted that it was tinted moisturizer to give him a healthy glow. Whatever.

"I hope someone's dead," I snap aggressively.

He mutters something under his breath while still fixing his hair. I increase the volume of the video call. He's not aware of my partial deafness, and I have no intention of letting him find out.

"What?" I demand. "Repeat that, Malphas, I didn't hear you."

"I said yes, precisely," my colleague lazily replies. "We have a third murder. So, you're not feeling well? PMS, is it? If you want, I can come massage your uterus. I have a degree in physiotherapy and gynecology."

What a sexist jerk! As soon as a woman isn't feeling her best or is in a bad mood, most guys attribute it to her period.

"Or you can massage your rectum with a silver stake," I mutter under my breath.

"I already tried it a century ago during a night of drunken debauchery. I didn't particularly enjoy the experience; the next day was really tough."

Damn, he's serious. This guy is sick.

"Okay, Malphas, about this third murder!"

"Hey, Myrina!" Sean's voice shouts as a smiling head pops up over my colleague's shoulder. "Wishing you a speedy recovery! If you need anything, even an ultra-sweet coffee at four in the morning, don't hesitate to call me!"

I furrow my brow and straighten my shoulders upon seeing black splatters on the wall behind the two goofballs.

"But… you're at the crime scene?"

"Of course," confirms Malphas. "That's why Zagam told me to call you. We're going to let you enjoy the slaughter live; it's even gorier than a season finale of *Reality TV Demons* here."

He moves his phone closer to the corpse as I finish eating my slice of pizza.

A demon has been nailed to the wall by the framework of its spread wings and arms. It looks like a gigantic butterfly pinned to a board.

No, not a butterfly, a big transgenic chicken prepared before cooking.

Because all its scales have been torn off; it has been meticulously skinned. Demons don't have a layer of skin under their natural carapace, so its black, raw flesh gleams under the spotlight. You can see all the muscles, tendons, and veins. Its wings have also been meticulously plucked. Its horns and claws are gone, too. This particularly sadistic treatment must have taken the murderer a long time.

"Take a look at this, Myri," Malphas says, zooming in on the floor that's completely covered in bloody feathers and scales. "He scattered them all over the room to make a carpet. And right in front of the stiff…"

He angles his smartphone toward a large mirror. Holy shit. I gulp down my bite.

"He skinned him alive and forced him to witness the entire torture session," my colleague finishes, raising an eyebrow at the screen, with a rather incongruous little smile.

"Two wounds were cauterized by fire, Myrina!" Sean chirps enthusiastically, who I don't see on the screen. "In the location of the frontal horns, a highly innervated area that would have caused significant bleeding. Lexi will confirm it, but judging from his injuries, I believe this guy agonized for hours, facing his reflection. The murderer undoubtedly wanted him to see himself dying slowly."

What cruelty. What inventiveness. Jack the Ripper can eat his heart out.

"Where are you, by the way?" I ask.

"In the offices of an abandoned factory on Infernum in the suburbs of Neethoraa. We received an anonymous email with the address of the building. We had our computer experts on it but couldn't locate the sender's PC; their IP address is encrypted. He's taken all precautions, the bastard. He knows what he's doing. We sent a patrol of Trackers to the factory, and they found the body," answers Malphas.

Hmm. This time, he killed on Infernum, not on Earth. In the bustling capital of the Ragebeasts. He can easily move from one world to another, apparently. And he's now keeping us informed of his macabre activities…

Your murderer is a nasty poker player who wants to include you in his card game, my dear, Kelen had warned me at the 1001 Nights of Lust.

"What did the factory produce?"

My colleague mutters something, lowering his head, so I can't read his lips.

"Damn it, Malphas, speak up, there's interference!" I lie to justify not hearing him.

"Suck," he says without raising his voice.

"Huh? What do you mean, I suck you? I won't allow it, Malphas!"

"No, dummy, buses!"

"A bus factory?"

"*Arcadus*, Myri! Are you dense today or what? Ears need cleaning, just like your ass."

"Have you ever tried cleaning your ass with a cotton swab, asshole? Speak up, I told you there's interference!" I yell into my cell's mic.

"Yeah, chill! You're not easy when you're on your period. The mirror was made here; it was already on-site. But this Arcadus is no longer operational. It was deactivated and abandoned in the offices when the factory closed its doors. The company went bankrupt years ago, due to competitors offering more competitive prices."

"Have you identified the new stiff?"

"Not yet, we're on it. As you can see, our victim is disfigured and unrecognizable. He's a Sinner, judging by his black blood. From the smell, I'd say he's from my legion, but I'm not one hundred percent sure. I don't have as much of a nose as you do."

Of course, it's a Pridefiend! The peacock feather found in the previous body is the emblem of the pride demons, and the whole setup confirms it. Pridefiends are extremely full of themselves—just look at Malphas. In their demonic form, they're as beautiful as the Lustpawns. They tend to show off their magnificent shimmering scales, their pretty raven feathers with midnight blue highlights, and their silver horns that are larger than those of other Sinners. The murderer has thus attacked the vanity and self-esteem of this Pridefiend to punish his sin of pride... by confronting him with his own unsightly image in the mirror. But if, as Sean thinks, the victim agonized for a long time before succumbing, why didn't he regenerate? His scales and feathers should have reformed, even if his horns and claws were lost. Besides—

"Guys, where are the horns and claws?"

"The claws are on the ground. The horns, vanished into thin air."

"They probably went into his morbid collection, in my opinion. Don't skimp on crime scene photos and send them to me. The body, the nails, the floor, the walls, the mirror. Ask Lexi to take a blood sample when she receives the body at the CIT—he may have been poisoned to prevent regeneration. Once we've discovered his identity, I want to know if he knew the other two victims, Aydan Smat and John Blane. Have you found any clues revealing his next target?"

"No, we searched, but we didn't see anything out of the ordinary. Well, relatively speaking," Sean interjects, appearing in front of the screen with his perennial stupid grin.

"Go over the perimeter with a fine-tooth comb, Laurel and Hardy! He must have slipped past you! And the peacock feather? Any drawings or images anywhere?"

"Nothing, Myri," Malphas says, shoulder-checking the intern roughly. "Get out of here, Virtuous, you're encroaching on my personal space!"

"Good god, but search again, godam—"

I don't finish my curse, my eyes fixed on my TV. On the banner scrolling across the bottom of the screen…

Special Breaking News Flash.

Terrorist attack by the Rebels at the Palace of the Magistrates during the Horn of Plenty ceremony. Kamikaze explosion. Thirty-seven dead, including two Magistrates—Colton Hallow, and another whose identity has not yet been revealed.

I end my call with Malphas and dial Kelen, my mouth dry.

First ring.

Second.

Third.

Fourth.

On the fifth, the voicemail kicks in. A woman's voice rings out.

"His Dark Eminence is not available at the moment, due to torture, meeting, or interview. Alternatively, he may simply not want to talk to you. Please make an appointment with the Ragebeast headquarters secretary at 0666-666-69-69 or leave a voicemail after the beep, bearing in mind that His Dark Eminence will probably not call you back."

I curse and hang up. I call his personal number.

"Answer, you asshole. Answer, damn it!"

I land on voicemail again. I hang up.

On the TV screen, I see him giving his speech behind a lectern, holding the Soulless's necklace. A Ragebeast soldier breaks away from the others and reveals an explosive belt by parting his cape. When the guy explodes into a thousand pieces, I startle on my couch, and the camera cuts off. I didn't see which Magistrates managed to teleport.

For the third time in a row, I call him. I don't understand why I'm freaking out so much for him. Kelen Wills, dying in an explosion? He's way too arrogant to perish in such a mundane and conventional way! But why isn't he picking up, for god's sake?

Ah, I got it! He's doing it on purpose to make me freak out. It amuses him. He must be chuckling right now, his phone in hand, relishing seeing my name on his screen and… Oh!

"Yes, Agent Holmes?" His calm voice comes through the phone.

"Wills, go to hell!" I yell into the phone, the torrent of my fury immediately overwhelming the wave of relief that washes over me. "Do you get off on making me wait, you asshole! I hope you die in excruciating agony!" And I hang up on him.

I sigh. He's still alive.

Then I realize.

Damn, he's still alive.

CHAPTER 22
CONTRARIETIES

"The soul endures the hardships it is prepared for." ~Seneca, On Anger

KELEN

Damn Rebels!

I had a damn piece of Horn of Plenty lodged in my right thigh, and now I've got second and third-degree burns all over my body. In less than an hour, I'll be good as new, thanks to my regeneration ability, but for now, I'm in agony, and I can't calm down. I've returned to my demon form at the Ragebeast HQ. I extracted the gold fragment from my thigh myself and wreaked havoc in the meeting room.

When I indulge in this kind of spectacular outburst, no one dares to try to calm me down or even talk to me. With her hands crossed behind her back, Serena patiently waits for my rage to subside while Sam is on the phone with his friend and occasional lover, the lieutenant of Magistrate Valafar—another potential Sinner candidate—his finger buried in his free ear to avoid hearing my fierce screams during his conversation. I smashed the meeting table with my fists, set fire to the curtains by touching them, sent all the chairs flying against the walls, clawed at the tapestries like a wild beast, demolished the lamps with a sweep of my tail.

"No, I can't pass you to Kel right away. He's busy rearranging the furniture and decor here, it helps calm his nerves," Sam explains over the phone, sending a glance in my direction as I relentlessly smash my throne against the floor.

Yes, I still have an ear between two material destructions.

"The terrorist? Unfortunately, yes, I can confirm it was indeed one of our guys. Nobody suspected; we only searched the spectators. They're becoming damn bold, these sons of bitches. If they start infiltrating our own ranks, we're in trouble. The guard was hypnotized by the rebels to act as a walking bomb and cause as much damage as possible. They really pulled it off this time. I can't explain the chaos, it was everywhere. No, buddy, you're kind to ask, but I wasn't injured at all, I was too far from the blast. Kel, on the other hand, got a piece of Horn of Plenty in his thigh before teleporting away."

He lets out a bitter laugh. "Ah, you're not wrong about Envyfiends! If we look at the bright side, it's one less candidate for the elections. Only our bosses and Belial are left in the race. On the other hand, let's be realistic: Hallow didn't stand a chance of becoming a Federator. It's clear, demonic flu can kill! If he had been able to use his powers, Hallow would have made it out."

"Not necessarily," Serena interjects, running a hand through her short hair. "Magistrate Faithfiend Azath didn't have the flu, and he wasn't fast enough to get away, remember."

"He was too busy ogling Belial's cleavage, that's why," Sam replies. "Every time I looked at him during the ceremony, he was leering at her. That old Virtuous pervert probably didn't even see the Rebel flashing his explosives; he was eyeing the succubus's assets. At least he died with a nice image burned onto his retinas!"

I revert to my human form as there's nothing left to wreck and limp over to my lieutenant.

"Oh man, you should see Kel's face, it's like Chernobyl! He looks like an extra auditioning to play a charred zombie in *The Walking Dead*. A photo? Hold on, I'll ask him if he's okay with it. It's not looking good though, he seems really pissed."

I abruptly seize Sam's phone and crush it, tightening my fist around it.

"Damn it, Kel, that's not cool! I paid over 2,000 Forks for that device!" my lieutenant laments, casting a pitiful glance down at the scattered pieces at our feet.

"You should consider yourself lucky he didn't do the same to your balls," Serena astutely remarks with a mocking smile.

"Ragebeasts, I want you to find me the Rebel who approached our guard and hypnotized him! Conduct your investigation internally, question his fellow guards and his loved ones, retrace his last hours—in short, do your *damn job*!" I thunder, slamming my fist against the wall behind Sam with all my might, smashing the stones upon impact.

I don't wait for their response. I teleport home, I need to be alone.

Otherwise, I might end up killing someone from my own camp.

MYRINA

I'm working on the case of the three murders at the table in my living room. After further investigation, Sean discovered a peacock feather under the scales and black feathers that dotted the floor of the last crime scene. He has been identified, indeed he's a Pridefiend... and known, moreover! He's an actor who has appeared in several human X-rated films, including the famous *Pride, Sex, and Prejudices*. His stage name? G. Latrique, which in human French sounds like *I have a hard on*—Yes, I promise, not a fib!

His real name? Gabriel Bariballarik, which is a tad less marketable. When I saw his photo, I realized he was a pure hottie. This Pridefiend looked like the actor from the *Game of Thrones* series, Kit Harington. *You know nothing, Jon Snow!* I also studied a few sequences of *Pride, Sex, and Prejudices*. As part of my investigation, naturally! Nice costumes, beautiful sets, big... production. Yes, Gabriel was very handsome, narcissistic... and it's precisely for these reasons that the murderer targeted him. As soon as I get my new hearing aids back, hopefully the day after tomorrow, I'll go gather testimonies from his circle.

Furthermore, I was right about another point: he was drugged so his tissues wouldn't regenerate. By analyzing his blood, Lexi found a high dose of sedative capable of neutralizing powers, with a composition very similar to the one used at the CIT to calm down the most cunning criminals. It's not the kind of product you can buy at the corner pharmacy on Infernum. I wonder how that damn murderer got hold of it. On the black market, perhaps… So, Gabriel agonized for hours in front of the mirror before dying from his horrible wounds. Ultimately, his torturer must have let him die alone; I doubt he stayed in the same room all that time.

However, we haven't found the clue that indicates the next victim. Even the autopsy revealed nothing on this matter. I keep examining the crime scene photos and the corpse in case an important detail jumps out at me. In vain.

For a nanosecond, I consider showing the file to Wills to get his opinion.

A *nanosecond*.

Because it wouldn't be professional at all. It would be unreasonable, even.

At that moment, my sister emerges from our Arcadus, looking gloomy and weary. She was just with him. She wanted to check on him after the attack at the Magistrates' Palace.

"Back already, sis?"

"Yes," she says shortly.

"Ondine, what's wrong?"

As she speaks, she starts signing with her hands so that I understand all her words.

"Kel was unbearable, Myri. He seemed completely fed up that I was there. I wanted to do the right thing, you know! I thought he would be happy to see me, but he was cold as ice," she confesses, choking me up.

"He's a jerk, that's nothing new."

"No, I assure you, he's not usually like that. He's really upset with the Rebels. Sam told me the other day that he doesn't like losing control. When things don't go as he plans, he tends to lose it and let his sin of wrath take over the other six."

"That's no excuse for taking it out on you; you're not to blame!" I growl, already imagining giving Wills a piece of my mind for his attitude toward her.

But what are they still doing together, damn it? It just doesn't click between them. Besides sex, they have nothing in common.

"Ondine… do you have feelings for him?"

She purses her lips, playing with the curved tip of her hair. "I don't know, Myri. He annoys me sometimes. But most of the time, I love being with him, he's so… I don't know, I can't explain it. It's complicated. It's not just physical, anyway. I want to give him a chance."

"He won't change. Not for you, not for anyone."

"We'll see," she evades, shrugging. "Well, I have to go shower and wax before going to work at the club. By the way, he said he was planning to call you tonight. He has information for you about the Rebels."

With these perplexing words, she heads into the bathroom.

I'm not going to wait around who knows how long for Mr. The Magistrate to deign to give me a call. I go out onto the balcony to call the ill-tempered one, leaning on the railing, and take the opportunity to light a cigarette. I've cut down a lot on smoking lately, but I can allow myself this one, it's only my fourth smoke of the day. He picks up on the third ring.

"Agent Holmes," he says curtly over the phone as I inhale my first drag. "Sorry to disappoint you again, but I haven't had the chance to perish in excruciating agony in the past two hours."

He took my words badly, obviously. I should be glad, but I can't manage it. He's so often in control of himself and detached… that it troubles me to have impacted him with a few insults. I've said much worse to him before, though.

"You're hurt, Wills?"

"Don't overestimate yourself. The demon who could hurt me with a mere threat hasn't been born yet," he snaps in a sour tone.

His response catches me off guard. "No, I… I meant… physically. Because of the explosion."

Sepulchral silence on the other end of the line.

"I was, but my regeneration is complete."

"You weren't nice to my sister."

"Tsss. It was her choice to visit me; I didn't force her. It wasn't the right time. Are you really lecturing me about being unkind to her? Shall I remind you of a couple of recent events that—"

"I'm going to hang up, Wills!"

"Then do it, Holmes."

Another silence. I nibble on the end of my filter. This strange conversation makes me uncomfortable. It's easier to handle when he's flirting with me and I'm brushing him off, or when we're trading biting remarks back and forth. Now, I feel like I'm stepping out of my comfort zone. Ondine was right—he's not usually like this. It's unsettling. I take another drag while observing the twilight sky.

"You had the Soulless's electronic collar in your possession, Wills."

"Indeed. I wanted to deal with the Rebels myself, but they turned out to be better organized and more dangerous than I thought. They even tried to hack into my personal computer some time ago. I compiled a dossier on them. I made a copy for you to pass on to your superior at the CIT."

Now that's surprising.

"Why's that?"

"Because I'm capable of setting aside my pride to fulfill my duty under the best conditions, unlike you. I don't appreciate the CIT's methods, but I trust you—even if it's not mutual. I will only deliver this file to you. If you tell me you're not interested, I will destroy it. You'll be my sole intermediary; I don't want to deal with your colleagues or your boss. The Ragebeasts and the Trackers should help each other catch the Rebels. They've killed two Magistrates; it's become a state affair today. The elections are fast approaching, and I don't want them to continue messing up my affairs. I can't run my political campaign with a sword of Damocles hanging over my head. You have information on them, I have information on them, so let's cross-reference them to get more conclusive results. And if you need my occasional insights for your investigation, I'm always on board."

"I'll think about it."

"Don't think too long. My offer has a short expiration date," Kelen says briskly. "Come to my residence on Infernum tonight to pick up the dossier or don't come at all, but make up your mind. Let me know your acceptance or refusal via text. I need to call Magistrate Remington."

And he hangs up on me.

Fair game. Well, I think.

I don't know what to make of this conversation. I don't know if I should go to his place or not.

I don't know much anymore, to be honest.

CHAPTER 23
MOONLIGHT SONATA

"In music, poetry, and the fine arts, there is something supernatural that can only come from the heavens." ~Pierre-Claude-Victor Boiste, The Universal Dictionary

MYRINA

Even the world's best hunter would be nervous before entering the den of the lion king. In fact, they would be even more alarmed than ordinary people for a simple reason: unlike them, they would be fully aware of the degree of danger they are exposed to, danger linked to the unpredictable nature of the beast. So, do I have a huge knot in my stomach at the thought of going *alone* to Kelen Wills's place? You already know the answer.

Nevertheless, there's no way I'm going to show any trace of anxiety in front of him. He would revel in it.

I thought he would greet me outside his Arcadus, but that's not the case. Emerging from the portal, I enter a living room larger than my apartment… where there's no one.

Breathtaking.

He wasn't bluffing when he claimed at the 1001 Nights of Lust that he owned a vast collection of artwork. It feels like being in a museum. Every wall is adorned with masterpieces and priceless ancient relics—elegant Japanese swords, formidable medieval weapons, Asian daggers with gem-encrusted handles, large Scandinavian perforated axes, armor pieces dating from different eras. Life-size marble sculptures stand among the dark and imposing furniture. One of them, in particular, catches my eye. It depicts an Pridefiend demon embracing a curved Hopeling demoness against him, one leg raised on his hip, in an attitude of carnal abandon. They gaze into each other's eyes, nose to nose, lips parted. Their tails and wings are intertwined as if they were one. They are about to kiss. A Sinner and a Virtuous in a position suggesting lovemaking? It's a sacrilegious symbol on Infernum, to say the least... Wills has no legal right to own this kind of artwork, but I suppose he couldn't care less. If I were to file a report with the CIT just to annoy him, this statue would be seized by my colleagues and destroyed at headquarters, and the Hybresang would incur a hefty fine. However, I won't do it.

Oh, it's not to be nice to him or grant him some kind of favor... It's just that I find this sculpture sublime, and it would be a shame to demolish it. I must undoubtedly project subjectively onto my parents. After all, if my Virtuous father hadn't loved my Sinner mother, I wouldn't have come into the world.

Floor-to-ceiling windows run along one wall. Above the horizon line, you catch a glimpse of the majestic silhouette of the volcano, Vésave standing amid a rocky chain in a barren plain. The golden and silver glimmers of the two moons illuminate the jagged peaks of the mountains. This means that Kelen's abode is perched on the heights at least thirty miles away from the nearest city. He values his solitude and tranquility, apparently.

My gaze falls upon the pure and elegant shape of a black piano near a long purple leather couch, which accentuates my sense of surprise. Well, well, Kelen Wills is an art *and* music enthusiast? Demons who play instruments are extremely rare on Infernum, and the music lovers I've heard of are exclusively Virtuous. I would never have guessed that Wills was part of this virtuoso elite. Unless the piano is just a decorative element... Or it belongs to someone else.

Increasingly curious, I pivot toward the Arcadus from which I emerged. Ominous dark colors, a raft, contorted bodies of shipwreck survivors, injured and corpses, stormy skies, a raging sea... Wills definitely has a taste for gloomy and tragic scenes. The poor humans wave clothes as flags to call for help as threatening waves prepare to engulf their fragile vessel.

"Theodore Gericault, *The Raft of the Medusa*. A masterpiece of a major artistic movement of the 19th century called Romanticism. My favorite painting."

His deep, powerful voice startles me as it resonates just behind me. If I had my hearing aids, I would have heard him approaching. I turn toward him, shooting him a glare.

Of course, shirtless as usual! Disheveled ink-black hair, hands in the pockets of his black satin lounge pants. Super handsome, naturally. And super annoying, naturally. The two adjectives go hand in hand when it comes to Kelen.

"Try not to sneak up on a deaf person from behind if you don't want to get a good punch in the face, Wills!"

"I'm starting to get used to getting punched by you, Agent Holmes." He pauses, staring at me. "I was wondering if you were going to come tonight. I was reading Dante's *Inferno* before surrendering to the comforting arms of Morpheus. Accompany me upstairs so I can show you my room. I'll take the opportunity to read aloud Canto III of *The Divine Comedy* on my bed. One of the verses of this poem reminds me of you. '*Lasciate ogne speranza, voi ch'intrate.*' Translation: 'Abandon all hope, ye who enter here.'"

I sigh exasperatedly, shaking my head.

"Perhaps another time."

I feared he would be as cold and rude as he was on the phone earlier, but his behavior is more in line with what I'm accustomed to. Apparently, he had time to calm his anger and take a step back. In any case, he doesn't look like someone who almost died today in a terrorist attack—he looks superb.

"I told you by text that I had no intention of lingering. I'm not here to have tea with you, marveling at your strange collection, or organizing a book club in your bedroom! Where's the file on the Rebels?"

Kelen gestures with his chin toward a nearby sideboard. A gray briefcase is placed there. I walk toward the object of my visit, open it, and flip through it under the stoic gaze of my host. The information he promised me is there. Perfect, I'll go through it at home before bringing it to Zagam.

I dedicate a small nod of thanks to him and return to *The Raft of the Medusa*. He doesn't even try to stop me. It's suspicious and… a bit insulting, I must say. I slow down, casting a wary glance over my shoulder. He hasn't moved an inch. He just stares at me, hands in his pockets. A question unrelated to my investigation or the Rebels pricks my tongue.

"You play the piano?"

He affects a small, crooked smile and slowly nods his head.

"You're kidding me, Wills. Demons are terrible musicians. There are only a few Virtuous ones on Infernum who manage to—"

"I have the gift of perfect pitch, thanks to my Hybresang DNA. It greatly facilitated my musical training. I also play the violin and guitar when the mood strikes, but I always return to my noble instrument of choice, the piano."

I grimace. I was born with impaired hearing, and he with perfect sound and pitch perception. Diabolical irony.

"I must admit, it's hard to imagine you playing epic war music in front of your legion of Ragebeasts to boost their fighting spirit."

"My little cat, I only indulge in this activity in private, alone. It's very rare that I invite anyone to listen to my music. I don't share my secret gardens with everyone, only with those I trust absolutely. I consider it even more intimate than sex."

"You're teasing me."

"Not at all. Music is too personal. Too emotional. Too revealing."

"And do you compose as well?"

"I composed a piece once. But I never let anyone hear it." He casts a darkened glance at the piano. "Anyway, I burned the sheet music."

"Why did you do that?"

"Too many questions, Agent Holmes."

"Occupational hazard. I'm a Tracker, you can't blame me. Especially when you drop vague hints left and right without elaborating."

"I believe you find my case interesting and want to delve deeper into it."

"That's not what I said."

Paradoxically, I enjoy these freewheeling conversations with him, even if he doesn't want to confess all his little secrets. He speaks calmly and clearly, not too loud, not too soft, not too fast, not too slow, so that I can understand all his sentences. For once, my conversation partner is adapting to me, not the other way around. It's a relief not to have to think too hard to decipher or interpret someone's words, or to make them repeat things because certain words, whispered or poorly articulated, would have escaped me. And I really like Wills's baritone voice, which doesn't hurt. It resonates in me like the strings of a musical instrument. I pick it up better than others, and I almost never need to read his lips. Which is convenient, since looking at his mouth tends to excite me. When I'm not wearing my hearing aids, I have more trouble hearing women's voices and high-pitched sounds.

As these thoughts cross my mind, a heavy silence falls between us. Tearing myself away from his unsettling gaze, I turn to head back through the Arcadus, but Wills declares in a ceremonious voice, "Beethoven began losing his hearing at twenty-seven, Myrina. That didn't stop him from composing many masterpieces that have marked the history of classical music, even before he became completely deaf. At thirty-one, he produced the most admirable and poignant piece of his entire career: Sonata No. 14, more commonly known as the *Moonlight Sonata*. It was originally a funeral march, but he dedicated it to a young countess he was in love with. Do you have seven minutes to spare to listen to me play the first movement?"

I stop short in front of *The Raft of the Medusa*. My heart skips a beat. *It's very rare that I invite anyone to listen to my music*, he told me thirty seconds ago.

"If you consider it more intimate than sex, this isn't a good idea."

"I'm not suggesting it to get you into my bed, Myrina. I want to show you through this beautiful sonata that your disability doesn't define you as a woman, and your hearing impairment doesn't condemn you to a life that's isolated, dull, and unhappy. You're much stronger and more determined than you think. True weakness is resigning yourself to your own weaknesses; I'm convinced of that. Never give up on what matters most to you—it would be a betrayal of yourself."

"Those are generic words, Wills," I say, with feigned indifference.

"Then let's set aside words and let the music speak, my little cat," he replies, taking my hand firmly.

He teleports us immediately in front of his magnificent, gleaming piano, just a few steps from the bay window.

"Okay, let me hear your sonata, but I might not perceive some of the notes," I murmur, placing the folder on the couch.

He runs his palm over the lid protecting the keyboard, as if caressing a living being, before lifting it. A pianist's quirk, I presume.

"Of course, you will. You won't miss a single note. You'll stay close to the piano, and my living room is an excellent soundbox."

Kelen sits at the instrument and taps the spot next to him. I sit at the end and on the edge of the bench, legs facing out, leaving some space between us. I notice he doesn't have any sheet music in front of him; he must know the piece by heart. Out of the corner of my eye, I see him position his feet above the pedals and spread his fingers over the black and white keys of the keyboard.

I've never heard anyone play the piano in real time, and no one has ever played an instrument for me. The fact that Wills is the one doing this makes it even more unique, surreal even. It doesn't look like the Hybresang I know. It's so… human. And also so… romantic?

Except you don't seduce a woman by playing her a funeral march.

Moreover, he's no longer looking at me. His face is focused, his features have closed off, and his gaze is meticulously examining the keyboard. He's already in his own bubble.

When he starts the first notes, as soft and sad as an autumn night, I hold my breath.

I stop breathing. I'm mesmerized by the music that takes me to another universe from the very first seconds. I tense up on the bench, my hands clenched on my knees, struck by an invisible lightning bolt.

I am overwhelmed by the powerful flow of these harmonious notes, both dark and intense, smooth and mysterious, exquisite and desperate, coursing through me like the waves of a freezing torrent. They slide across my skin, raising the hairs on my forearms. They caress my back, sending a shiver down my spine. They quicken my heartbeat to an unimaginable rhythm. They tighten my throat, twist my insides, burn my lungs, and make my synapses crackle. They make every fiber of my being tremble, tear me apart, permeate me, exalt me, transcend me. Because they seem to speak directly to me.

To my experiences. To my doubts. To my memories. To my pain.

My captivated gaze falls on Kelen's hands, undulating over the keys with unparalleled grace. All his movements are precise and hypnotic. His long, powerful fingers press delicately on the keys to make them sing. He transitions between different chords with dexterity and agility born of long practice. His tendons and veins stand out on the backs of his virile hands while his muscles ripple beneath the tanned skin of his arms. My eyes travel up to his profile. His head moves slowly back and forth, his mouth set in a thin line, and his eyelids almost closed. A rebellious lock of hair sways on his furrowed brow, teasing his frowning eyebrows. The golden and silver lights of the two moons dance on his chest, blending together, creating moving shadows and patches of light. It's a spectacle both auditory and visual. He's completely possessed by the music he plays, like a professional pianist. He feels it, too. He lives it. He understands every nuance and conveys them to me perfectly. I no longer exist for him, yet he brings me into his bubble through the *Moonlight Sonata* of a human artist who died centuries ago.

No present.

No reality.

Just the piano and us.

A balance as fragile as it is strong, as fleeting as it is eternal. There's no physical contact between us, but our souls have never been so close, connected by the fluid notes of this music. It is undoubtedly the most beautiful, the deepest, and the saddest sound I have ever heard.

Seven minutes.

Seven hours…

Seven years?

I don't know anymore. I've lost track of time.

I surrender to my buried emotions, crystallized by the music. I almost never cry in front of others; my pride won't allow it. But in this moment, I can't suppress the warm tear that slides down the curve of my cheek as I look back at the starry sky beyond the bay window. I think of Owen, my lost love. I think of my parents who I will never see again. I think of my sister. I think of my life. I think of my death. I think of Kelen.

He has suffered, too. The way he immerses himself in this piece expresses it more clearly than any words. It is obvious.

Too personal. Too emotional. Too revealing, he had said

I agree.

Driven by an irresistible urge and drawn to the musician's aura, I move closer to him on the bench. Gently, I rest my hand on his thigh. Without stopping playing, he slightly turns his head toward me. He studies the tear rolling down my cheek, then locks his unfathomable gaze with mine. At the moment our eyes meet, he hits a wrong note. Just one, in seven minutes. I close my eyelids to protect myself from what he might read in me.

The final ethereal notes float through the room like a flurry of invisible feathers. Beethoven's *Moonlight Sonata* concludes.

The ensuing silence brings with it a sense of emptiness, mourning, and a refreshing coolness. I shiver all over, my fingers clenched on the demon's thigh.

More intimate than sex.

I confirm this, too.

I feel Kelen's warm palm cradle my cheek. I tilt my head to better nestle my face in his broad hand. He wipes away my tear with the tip of his thumb without saying a word.

My trembling hands rise to his face, which I cradle. I smooth his clenched jaws, feel his cheekbones. I explore the contours of his features, the texture of his skin. Then my index finger wanders over the fullness of his lips, soft and moist, which part at my touch. The tip of his tongue slides over my finger to taste it.

I melt with pleasure.

I don't even dare to reopen my eyes. I'm blind and deaf at this moment. I'm left with my three other senses. My touch. My smell. My taste.

Abandon all hope, ye who enter here.

Kelen closes the last distance between us. I feel his erratic breath on my mouth, the tip of his lock of hair tickling my forehead, his nose pressing against mine. And finally, his lips, which I can no longer resist, brush against mine, capturing my sigh of relief.

This kiss, full of gentle sensuality, contains neither haste nor brutality. With equal appetite, we savor it like a forbidden sweet we've coveted for ages. He explores every corner of my mouth with lazy languor, his tongue playing lasciviously with mine, his sharp teeth occasionally capturing my lower lip to suck and nibble it like his favorite candy.

I've exchanged passionate kisses with dozens of men, both humans and demons, but no one has ever kissed me like this. He makes me feel like the most delicious and desirable creature in the world. I melt under his eager tongue and dissolve against his mouth, which devours mine. A cascade of burning honey flows through my body, down my throat, spreads in my chest, fills my belly, and gathers between my thighs, radiating through my flesh as it passes.

Kelen's hand leaves my cheek, slips behind my head, and firmly grips my hair to keep me from escaping. My fingers travel along his thick neck, the tense line of his strong shoulders. His arm wraps around my waist and pulls me against him, pressing my breasts against his chest.

His kiss suddenly becomes more hungry and possessive. He no longer savors me, he devours me. His hand snakes down my neck, runs down the curve of my back, slides under the hem of my tank top. He unhooks my bra in two seconds and slips his hand under to grasp my breast. He squeezes it so hard that I bite his tongue while moaning. He growls into my mouth before cruelly pinching my hard nipple, making me shiver with pleasure and pain. I want his tongue everywhere on me, his fingers everywhere inside me.

A drop of sweat beads between my taut breasts. I dig my nails into his back, scratching his skin with growing ferocity. Our fangs elongate and clash. We engage in an erotic battle without catching our breath, attacking each other with tongues, teeth, and claws. Through our frantic kiss, I feel his infernal strength, his incubus power, and his electric Hybresang heat pour into my throat and belly, the precursors of the extraordinary sensations that magnify the sexual act between two demons bound by the sin of lust. But just as his hand presses between my parted thighs and begins to caress my sex over the fabric of my jeans, my elbow accidentally hits the keyboard, producing a series of discordant notes that act as a shock to my brain. Reality crashes into me like a slap.

I'm kissing my sister's man. I'm letting him touch me.

I jump to my feet, breaking free from his embrace and his kiss. Breathing heavily, Kelen and I stare at each other like mortal enemies. His blood-red eyes, filled with devastating lust and tinged with anger, burn me in place. He slams the lid down on the keyboard, steps over the bench, and stands up to face me. His hands reach for my hips. I pull back sharply as his fingers graze my sides.

"Myrina, come back. We both want this so badly," he argues, his voice much rougher than usual.

"I can't, Kelen. I can't, damn it!"

He grits his teeth, hearing his first name from my mouth. I've always called him by his last name until now.

"What we have between us is much stronger than attraction, Myrina. It's a deep connection. You felt it in our kiss, too. You'll never be able to kiss another man without thinking of me, I guarantee it. Every time you have sex with someone else, you'll only climax if you imagine me in his place. You think I'm saying this because of my sin of pride, don't you?"

He laughs bitterly. "Deny it if it makes you feel better! The more you resist and fight your desire, the more it will eat away at you. Why do you think I've been so distant with your sister since the explosion at the Magistrates' Palace, Myrina? Because I would have preferred *you* to visit me. But you didn't come, of course. You didn't even get back in touch after you yelled at me and threatened me while I was so damn happy to hear your voice after that fucking explosion. You only called and came here because I offered you this folder. Tell me to leave Ondine, and I'll do it in whatever way suits you best. Tell me, Myrina!"

"But most of the time, I love being with him, he's so… I don't know, I can't explain it. It's complicated. It's not just physical, anyway. I want to give him a chance," she said earlier.

As for me, I don't want to give him a chance. I don't want to be with him. It would betray my sister. It would betray Owen's memory. It would betray myself.

If he wants to leave her, let him leave her, but don't involve me in it. I don't want to be with him. Or any other man.

Feeling overwhelmed, I grab the folder and flee through the Arcadus without looking back.

CHAPTER 24

69 DEGREES IN THE MORNING

"Lechery, lechery; still, wars and lechery: nothing else holds fashion." ~William Shakespeare, Troilus and Cressida

MYRINA

I finally got my new hearing aids. I feel alive again.

As a bonus, these ones are waterproof. I won't have to protect my ears in the shower or rain.

Lexi performed a minor surgical procedure at the CIT to implant them before adjusting them using her PC software, just like an audiologist. My hearing assessment indicates everything is fine. I can hardly hear my tinnitus anymore thanks to the hearing aids—thank Satan, those whistling sounds were driving me crazy and keeping me from sleeping.

So, I've regained optimal hearing. I can hear all the little everyday noises again and, more importantly, every word from my conversation partners. I hugged my friend tightly, thanking her warmly for being so responsive.

Myrina Holmes is back in action. It's time to dive back into work.

I forwarded Wills's file on the Rebels to Zagam. My boss grilled me about the Magistrate, but I remained quite evasive. When the

Virtuous Justspawn mentioned he would give Kelen a call, I told him it was unnecessary trouble because the Hybresang wouldn't answer him. I made it clear that I had arranged things with him and that he would only deal with me to avoid multiple intermediaries. Zagam grunted that he didn't like the unofficial turn this matter was taking and that I had better bring results quickly on all fronts.

The information was confirmed: Gabriel didn't know Aydan and John, they've nothing in common. Apparently, there's no uniting connection between the Pridefiend, the Faithfiend, and the Charityfiend. I've scheduled a meeting with the director of the film *Pride, Sex, and Prejudice*, and I'm going to meet this human on a porn film set. I have to remain professional, but I confess that my personal curiosity is piqued to the highest degree. By the way, it reminds me that I really need to have sex to release my stress and tension. An ideal way to decompress. Masturbation is okay for a couple of minutes!

It's decided: tonight, I'm going to a bar in Infernum, and I'm going to hook up with a Sinner demon. It will help me forget about that dark asshole Kelen, and especially to prove him wrong about the last words he dared to say to me at his place. I'm sure that if I sleep with several men, I'll manage to put into perspective the desire I feel for Wills. If I'm so drawn to this guy, it's mainly because I'm super frustrated. My Lustspawn sexual energy is somehow making me pay for my abstinence. I've been so obsessed with my work that I haven't slept with a man in a good month. I'm going to fix that as soon as possible.

Here I am on the set of *69 Degrees in the Morning* in a luxurious mansion. I showed my fake police badge to be able to enter, and I'm waiting for the director in the garden, standing like a fool amid the bustling crew by the infinity pool. Cameraman, sound engineer, assistants…

Under a parasol, a hairdresser and a makeup artist are attending to a thirty-something actress, a bleached blonde with big boobs and wearing a fuchsia bikini, who is on the phone. I think she probably had a pretty face originally, but her eyes are so stretched by her facelift and her lips so swollen with silicone that she resembles the offspring of a reptile and a carp. Near her, sitting on a sun lounger, a young brunette actor—a bland pretty boy—is reading his script while nervously tapping his foot on the ground. I'm too far away to hear what he's whispering, but I can read his lips.

"Ah. Mm. Oh. Yes. It's so good! More! Yes!"

I shake my head, amused by his studious and focused look, like a diligent student.

"He always rereads his lines fifty times before a scene because he has the memory of a goldfish," comments a deep voice on my right.

I turn my head and look up at the smiling face of another actor who has approached. Oh, there's a real hottie, *69 Degrees in the Morning* lives up to its title!

Here stands a huge black man absolutely stunning in a mechanic's jumpsuit, his zipper lowered to his abs, holding a tube of lubricant in his hand. Muscles sculpted like those of a dark Apollo, face with strong yet refined features, full lips framed by a well-kept goatee, dark chocolate skin adorned with bad boy tattoos, and a gaze as dark as ink, not lacking in intelligence and depth. The dream of any normally constituted succubus. He has much more of an effect on me than the other actor. He's very sexy: if I had passed him on the street, I would have turned back to look at him.

"This is no longer just a goldfish memory at this point, it's more like a larva memory," I quip, eyeing him up and down with undisguised interest.

He chuckles and returns the favor, eyeing me up and down with the same interest. Perfect, we're already on the same page. I guess I won't need to go to a bar tonight to find myself a handsome demon after all. This human has assets as seductive as an incubus. And I suppose he must have a significant one under his jumpsuit.

"New in the industry, miss?" he asks.

"No, I'm not an actress. I'm with the police," I reply.

"Ah, you're here to see the boss about Gabriel. Too bad, I would have loved to work with you."

Well, the actor from *69 Degrees in the Morning* doesn't beat around the bush! Like me, he knows what he wants and he's confident, I love it. He's exactly my type for a one-night stand. His burning gaze wandering over my body ignites my desires and makes my mouth water. Apparently, the fact that I'm a *cop* doesn't deter him. It's exactly what I need to banish Wills from my thoughts.

"Work with me or in me?" I retort teasingly.

"Both, to be honest with you," he replies with a predatory smile.

"Did you know Gabriel?" I ask.

"Not very well. We worked together on a film scene a few months ago. A gangbang. I was saddened to hear about his death; he was a good guy." Yeah right, he doesn't mean a word of it. "What exactly happened?"

He was skinned alive, plucked, horned, and nailed to a wall by a sadistic demon.

"You can well imagine I can't tell you that, sir…"

"Nickolas Dick. But you can call me Nick. It's my real name. And you?"

"Myrina Holmes, spiritual daughter of Sherlock." We shake hands for a long moment. He has a firm grip, a large warm hand; it's engaging. "*Nick Dick the mechanic* sounds good."

He laughs again. He has a very… sexual laugh. Yum! This human exudes an appetizing vitality and a masculine fragrance that bodes well for some excellent sex.

"I don't see the connection with the film's setting though," I add, gesturing to his beige jumpsuit. "How do you fit into the script?"

"The lady needs to go shopping and can't get her car to start," he explains, glancing briefly at the actress on the phone. "She calls a breakdown service, I fix her car in her garage, but she doesn't have any money on her; her husband confiscated her credit card because she's spent too much lately. She offers to pay me in kind, and I accept, of course."

"And your colleague with the larva memory, what's his role?"

"The gardener and her son's best friend. Same deal, she pays him in kind, and we end up with a threesome."

I burst into such a loud, spontaneous laugh that all the humans on the film crew pivot toward us.

"The screenwriter is a genius. I admire his imagination," I comment, nodding in approval.

"I hope you'll appreciate my acting skills, Inspector."

"I'm sure I will, Nick," I murmur, holding his flirtatious gaze with a playful smile.

"How about grabbing a drink tonight after work?"

"At your place, yes."

He raises an eyebrow, pleasantly surprised. He probably isn't used to women outside his professional circle being so direct and confident. I mean, sleeping with a porn actor would likely make many women hesitate, right? It's exciting in a fantasy, but in real life, it's a different story. For me, it's not a problem at all. On the contrary, I see it as a challenge.

I pull a business card with my name and personal number from my jacket pocket and slip it into his jumpsuit pocket just as the director calls me from the house. I whisper to Nick to call me at six PM and join the man I'm scheduled to meet, an old, bearded guy in a gray suit who reeks of cocaine. We go into the living room to talk one-on-one and sit across from each other.

"How would you describe Gabriel?" I ask, pulling out a notepad to take notes.

"A spoiled brat diva," the director grumbles, sinking into his leather armchair. "He thought he was the best."

"What do you mean?"

"When he showed up on the set of *Pride, Sex, and Prejudices*, everyone had to bow to his demands, or he'd throw massive fits. He wanted to do everything his way, the little bastard! He'd change lines and positions at the last minute. He'd make us redo takes if he didn't feel he was highlighted enough in the scene. He constantly belittled his colleagues. The actresses and crew hated him; he created a toxic atmosphere on set. Not professional at all. If he hadn't been the spitting image of the guy from *Game of Thrones*, I would've fired him. His pretty face was my main draw, so I put up with it."

"This movie made you three million dollars, according to my sources.

"Thank God. It was a freaking nightmare to shoot. By the end, I swore I'd never work with G. Latrique again."

Given his blunt words, if the director had been a demon, I would have put him on my list of suspects. But he's not. My killer isn't human, that's clear.

While I'm writing in my notepad, the man eyes me lecherously. What is it with everyone today? My Lustspawn pheromones are on standby. I was flattered a few minutes ago when Nickolas approached me, but the creepy old guy's gaze isn't doing it for me.

"Tell me, Inspector, do you wear contact lenses?"

I shake my head sharply.

"You're very cute in your own way, you know. You have a unique look that catches attention. I'm sure you'd be a hit in one of my movies. The role of the bad girl who pretends to be a feminist but loves getting ravaged every which way."

I look up at him, put my notepad on my lap, and reach into my jacket.

"Cops don't make much money, I hear. Maybe you should consider a career change or… *Oh shit, are you crazy?*"

I've just pulled my revolver from its holster and pointed it at his forehead. He raises his hands, his face pale, eyes wide, legs trembling. *Well, buddy, looks like you've got a problem with bad girls after all.*

"Insulting an officer in the line of duty, sexual harassment, *and* drug use, asshole! You still have white powder under your right nostril. You've ten seconds to apologize before I haul you to the station and throw you in a cell."

Of course, he hastens to apologize, becoming all sweet and contrite.

That's better, we can now continue the interrogation under better conditions.

Or maybe not…

My gaze drifts toward the sliding glass doors. The scene shoot has started. Ms. Duckface is getting sandwiched by two actors, standing at the edge of the pool. With his mechanic suit around his ankles, Nick is in front of her, holding her up—what arm strength you have, my big guy, you're really my type—while the other guy goes at it from behind, grunting. She's screaming so exaggeratedly that I can hear her from inside. The cameraman circles them, his camera on his shoulder. A little shiver runs through me when I meet the feverish eyes of the hot black guy who intensifies his thrusts, every muscle in his body taut. Yes, I appreciate his acting skills, and even more, his hip movement.

I can't wait for tonight. I'm eager to fuck Nick.

✳✳✳

Nickolas lives in a modern loft tastefully decorated, but I didn't take the time to inspect the place because as soon as he opened the door,

I jumped on him and devoured his mouth. I kept my eyes open to scrutinize his face and make sure I didn't confuse him with a certain demon I know.

One might think a porn actor is just a rough brute who bangs like in X-rated movies, but that's not the case with Nick. I expected him to tear off my clothes and take me against the wall like an animal, but he carries me to his bedroom, hands under my thighs. Along the way, he kisses me gently, his tongue lightly brushing against mine; in truth, I'm the more passionate and impatient one between us. When he lays me down on his bed, I pull him down with me, legs around his waist, and tug his T-shirt over his head.

"I saw you threaten my boss with your gun earlier," he growls, tossing his T-shirt aside while I run my hands over his muscular chest. "It made me even harder during the scene."

Laughing, I grab him by the neck to pull him down and press my lips to his. I close my eyes, surrendering completely to the kiss as Nick unbuttons my black blouse between us.

You'll never be able to kiss another man without thinking of me.

Annoyed, I half-open my eyes. Shut up, Wills, get lost! I'm not thinking of you.

"My pants, Nick," I murmur, pulling my head back to break the kiss.

The human's mouth trails down the curve of my throat, nestles between my trembling breasts. His fingers unbutton my jeans, then he pulls them down my legs. His hungry lips follow the motion, traveling over my stomach, to the inside of my thigh. The same spots Kelen licked before the attack at the Magistrates' Palace. This association of thoughts makes me even wetter, much to my dismay.

My lingerie quickly disappears, along with Nick's jeans and boxers. Oh wow, he's huge! The tip of his dark member almost reaches his navel. I spit into my palm and grab him with both hands, stroking him so vigorously that he winces in pain. Oops, sorry, I didn't gauge my demonic strength. Sinners are much less sensitive. I soften my grip, making him groan with satisfaction. Sexy. Not as much as Wills, but—

Damn it, Myri, stop that!

We're going to skip the foreplay; I can't afford time to think.

Without even letting him touch me, I grab the condom from his bedside table, tear the wrapper with my teeth, and roll the latex down Nick's dick. He tries to slow me down.

"Myrina, wait, I haven't even—"

"I don't care, I'm ready, fuck me fast and hard," I cut him off coldly, glaring at him.

"But why—"

"It's this or nothing, Nick!"

With a frustrated sigh, he positions himself between my thighs and enters me slowly, one hand on my breast. An expression of intense pleasure crosses his face.

"Oh fuck, you're so incredibly hot, this is Nirvana!"

You've never slept with a succubus before.

I might even have to hypnotize him after our session to erase myself from his memory. Some humans get addicted to sex with Lust demons, like a hard drug, and I have no desire to have another Malphas chasing after me.

I thought his sexual energy would electrify me once he was inside, but it didn't. Oh, his thrusts are fine, I can't deny that. He has the technique and the rhythm. His tip hits the mouth of my cervix, his shaft massages my inner walls. But I'm nowhere near orgasm. In fact, I'm there without being there. The minutes tick by. We switch positions three times. He speeds up, panting. He's enduring, that's cool… But it's not enough. He seems disappointed by my lack of reaction. I'm not one of his usual partners; I never fake it. He slips a hand between us and captures my clit between his index and middle fingers. Ah, interesting initiative, impeccable technique but. he's more tickling me than anything else.

What. The. Hell!

God, it started so well!

I slap his hand away to take over myself, ordering him to pound me with all his might. He obeys, groaning, trying to hold back until I climax. He's all sweaty now. He's not that sexy after all. His gaze is dull. His smile, bland. His chin dimple isn't like—

Every time you fuck someone else, you'll only come if you imagine me in his place.

I close my eyes to block out his face, imagining Kelen pounding between my thighs. Suddenly, I'm on fire. I open my mouth to moan shamelessly, arching on the mattress, writhing beneath him. My free hand clutches his shoulder. I hear a sort of wheezing groan above me. His body grows heavier on mine, his movements less forceful. Ah, I'm going to come, I'm almost there!

"Myri… na…"

That's not Kelen's voice.

I reopen my eyes. Nick is on the verge of passing out.

Damn, I can't control my Lustspawn power; I'm draining all his energy!

Chilled by the sight, I shove my lover away roughly to avoid killing him. Then I make him forget our encounter by whispering a few hypnotic words, get dressed, and leave without a second thought, leaving him exhausted on his bed—but alive.

Damn it, if I had hooked up with a Sinner demon like I'd originally intended, I wouldn't have had this issue… and I would have come.

Without thinking of Kelen.

I return home in a bad mood, frustrated by this ruined evening. I pick up the mail on my way. Among the bills and flyers, there's an envelope for me. Label with words in printed letters. No sender's name.

In the elevator, I cautiously open the letter, my eyebrows knitted.

What the—

A photo.

Of *me*.

The hair on the back of my neck stands up.

I'm sleeping in my bed, my cat curled up next to me on the cover.

And at the bottom of the envelope, like a morbid, mocking offering…

A silver feather stained with golden blood.

CHAPTER 25
ORAL PACT

"Regret is an amplifier of desire."

~Marcel Proust, Albertine disparue - Posthume

MYRINA

With my arms crossed over my chest, I wait for Lexi's verdict as she leans over the microscope. It's equipped with a UV light that reveals fingerprints. She examines the envelope, the photo, and the feather from every angle.

"Nothing usable," my friend laments. "No trace, not even partial. And there are no indications or inscriptions on the paper; we can't determine its origin."

She scrapes a bit of the dried golden blood off the silver feather with a plastic stick, places it between two glass slides, and inspects the sample under the microscope, comparing it with another. A few minutes later, she confirms my suspicions, "It's the same DNA. The feather belongs to Aydan Smat the Faithfiend, the first victim. The killer took two from the base of the wings, and this is one of them." She looks up from the microscope, her worried clear eyes meeting mine. "You're in danger, Myri."

I let out a bitter laugh.

"If I had a Fork for every time I was in danger, I'd be the richest demon in Infernum."

"Myri, please, don't take this lightly. This psychopath knows where you live. He photographed you while you were sleeping," my Virtuous friend stresses, her gentle voice contrasting with her grim expression.

"Yes, from outside. The angle of the shot proves he was outside, on the other side of the window, between the curtains. Given the photo's quality, he didn't zoom in; he wasn't in the building across the street. He didn't break into my place, but he was flying a few feet from my bedroom, Lexi."

"You might be his next target."

I can't be one hundred percent sure, of course, but I don't think I'm part of his bloody plan. It's not his usual modus operandi. I feel like I don't match the profile of his victims. I mostly think this bastard is doing this to mess with my head: to scare me and put pressure on me to drop the case. Yeah, I'll quit my duty when pigs fly and lay ostrich eggs! I'm not afraid for my life; I can defend myself. But I do fear for Ondine, who lives with me.

He thinks he's so superior and untouchable that he provokes and threatens me personally. It only strengthens my resolve to hunt him down… and give him a nasty reckoning. I'm a real pressure cooker. He's poking the scales of the wrong demoness.

Given all the precautions we've taken from the beginning to keep this case under wraps and away from the media, it implies he's monitoring the progress somehow. He's spying on us, that's obvious. Or worse… The fact that he's so well informed about me could mean he's a member of the CIT himself.

This idea sends a chill down my spine.

That's why I decided not to mention this letter to my boss or the other Trackers. Only Lexi will be in on the secret.

Unfortunately, Ondine and I will have to crash somewhere else for a while. It's too dangerous to stay at home.

I leave my friend's lab. Holding my hand, she urges me to be careful. I smile and nod. Back at the apartment, I check every room with my revolver in hand to ensure no one's there. Then, I call my sister, who's still at the 1001 Nights of Lust. I explain the situation in a voice message while hastily packing our things.

"And don't come back, sis. I'm packing our bags, taking a quick shower, and then I'll join you at the club. We'll stay at a hotel tonight, and tomorrow, we'll crash at Grandpa's. I've briefed him, and he's cool with us staying. I'll ask our neighbor to take care of Putrid since he can't go to Infernum. See you soon, sweetie."

Fifteen minutes later, as I'm drying off after my shower, my sister calls back after her shift. Wrapping a towel around myself, I leave the steam-filled bathroom to answer her call in the living room. I recap the situation. Our tense discussion escalates into an argument. I pace around the apartment, circling the furniture. She outright refuses to stay with Amon, whom she can't stand.

Then she drops a bombshell as I walk into the kitchen. I freeze in front of the kitchen island as she declares, "Kel is right next to me in his office. I told him about it."

For fuck's sake, could she not keep her mouth shut?

"He wants us both to stay with him, Myri. He insists we'll be safer at his country house than at Grandpa's in the city. He'll even have Ragebeast soldiers guard the area."

Hell and damnation, living with *him*? And Ondine? The three of us together?

Abyssal horror, a nightmarish prospect!

"Damn it, no, absolutely not!" I choke out, clutching my phone tightly.

I hear her muttering something to Wills. I catch the word *stubborn* and… No, damn it, she just handed him her phone to try and persuade me, too!

"Agent Hol—"

I immediately hang up and slam my phone down on the kitchen counter with such force that it cracks the screen. Fucking hell!

Exactly five seconds later… *he* teleports right behind me.

And when I say *right behind me*, I mean it quite literally. Before I even have a chance to turn around, the intruder bumps into me and pins me against the counter, his bulky arms wrapped tightly around mine, preventing me from moving. A straitjacket of flesh and muscles.

Yet, I don't panic or struggle at first, because I immediately recognize the warm touch and intoxicating scent of Kelen, and I know for sure that he won't harm me. I feel no fear. In truth, I'm as limp as a rag doll in his arms. I should be furious that he presumes to hold me in such an intimate manner against him, but in reality, his iron grip provides me with a peculiar comfort, as if I've just donned armor that renders me invincible. I'll never admit this odd thought to him, of course. Anyway, I don't need that armor; I already have my own.

"Let go of me and step back, Wills. I'm really not in the mood to fight with you," I warn, my tone icy cold.

"If your sister hadn't informed me, would you have told me?" he growls in my ear, his voice as hard as his body.

"That's none of your concern. I don't owe you any explanations."

Tightening his grip on me with one arm, he lifts his free hand to grab my wet hair and sharply pulls my head back. I bite my lip to moan. If any other man had dared to do that, I would have killed him. Wills has a dangerous knack for both infuriating and arousing me when he unleashes his dominant macho attitude, which confuses my senses.

"I'm very, very angry with you, Myrina," Kelen murmurs threateningly, his mouth moving behind my ear.

Angry *and* aroused. I'm naked under my towel, half-drenched, and he's hard as a rock against me. It reminds me of the erotic dream he sent me the other night, when he pressed me against the glass of his office at the 1001 Nights of Lust. Except this time, it's real… Every sensation is even stronger, more intense. His fingers tangled in my hair feel like lightning bolts electrifying my nerves. His breath on my neck is as devastating on my skin as a tornado. His chest rising against my back ignites my flesh like a wildfire. His erection against my ass liquefies my lower abdomen to the point where I have to clench my thighs. How I wish I had a switch to turn off this suffocating desire over which I have no control!

"You'll get over it," I retort hoarsely as he sniffs the line of my neck with a low growl.

"And to top it off, you've slept with a human tonight. I can smell his disgusting scent on you!"

That's the big problem with the heightened sense of smell of major demons. Despite washing everywhere with soap, Kelen still detects the faint olfactory trace of Nickolas.

"I prefer his scent to yours," I lie.

"But you didn't climax," he purrs with a hint of satisfaction, rubbing his face against my throat, which quickens my pulse and my breath. "I sense your frustration."

"Leave."

"Not without you, my little cat."

"I'm not coming to your place, Wills! Host Ondine if you want. I'm planning to stay at my grandfather's, and I won't change my mind."

He lifts his head from my neck with a silent sigh that swells his chest. But his breathing slows noticeably behind me. His hand releases my hair and rests flat on the countertop in front of me. Even though he's still pinning me against my kitchen island, he's regaining control. *More or less.* His arousal is harder than ever against my towel as our vibrating bodies adjust like two puzzle pieces.

"If I listened to myself, Holmes, I'd kidnap you right away for your protection."

"You *would try*," I interject through clenched teeth. "You know where you can put your protection? Three hints: it starts with an *A*, ends with a *S*, and there's a *S* in the middle."

"You trust the wrong people, once again. Wake up, there are plenty of corrupt individuals in the CIT. I may not know all of them, but I'm well aware of how rotten your order is since I, myself, bribed some of your colleagues without any difficulty. Files disappear, evidence is falsified, data is altered or deleted. I'm almost certain now: either your killer has an insider… or, more worrying, he *is* the killer."

"What? But… damn it! Who did you bribe?" I articulate, horrified, turning my head toward him.

Lord, this explains how he got all the information about my investigation and the photo of Aydan Smat that Kelen then transmitted to the Faithfiend Magistrate to identify him! He's bribing one or more of my colleagues!

"I'll reveal it to you if you agree to stay with me until *we* eliminate this serial killer, Myrina."

More blackmail, ultimatums, lies, and manipulation. He doesn't know how to act otherwise. It's pathological in him. Inseparable from his deep-seated nature as a would-be Sinner.

"Zagam? Malphas? Sean? Lexi? Or perhaps—"

"Be reasonable, come with me."

"Be reasonable, go to hell."

"Let's have a truce for the greater good. I'll behave myself. I won't touch Ondine in front of you, I won't flirt with you," he enumerates with an irritated tone.

I burst into a sarcastic laugh. As if I'm going to believe him while he's pressing his hard-on against my ass right now! He can't help but tease me.

"Very well!" Kelen suddenly exclaims dryly, turning me toward him. "I'll let you go on one condition."

I raise an ironic eyebrow. *A petulant child pretending to be a grand lord!* "What's that?"

"A kiss, just one. I want to kiss you before I go back to finally erase the disgusting smell of that human from you, but I won't do it without your consent. I've received enough punches and rejections from you for eternity."

Strange. It's unlike him to give in so easily, let alone *ask for permission*.

"Are you reduced to this, Wills? Begging for a kiss to soothe your oversized ego?"

"I never beg. Normally, I take. But since you're more miserly than a Greedling and more stubborn than a Ragebeast, I have to adapt to your exceptional case. If you don't grant me this tiny favor, Myrina, I won't leave your side."

I swallow. My temperature starts to rise. "A… a kiss and… you'll leave?"

He nods slightly. The scorching memory of our kiss in front of his piano three days ago makes me dizzy all of a sudden. Let's not deceive ourselves, it wouldn't be a chore; this guy kisses incredibly well. If I keep control of the situation, it should be manageable.

"It will be the last time, Wills."

"So, you agree?" he deduces with a certain formality.

A little red alarm flashes in my mind. His detached behavior doesn't bode well. He's plotting something. I need to redefine the boundaries.

"I agree to *a* kiss. But nothing more. And then, you leave."

He gives a triumphant smile. I can tell I just messed up.

In a flash, Kelen grabs me by the waist, lifts me off the floor, and sets me on the kitchen island. Our faces are now level. We stare into each other's eyes. I shiver with anticipation, but he doesn't move. He just holds me by the waist, his thumbs resting on my ribs. I place my hands on his shoulders, licking my lips and glancing at his. Half-closing my eyes, I lean in to kiss him… and meet nothing but air.

Damn! He swiftly turned his head to the side and left me hanging!

"What are you playing at, Wills?" I snap, annoyed.

"My little cat, you agreed to a kiss." His sly smile widens. "But I never specified where I would kiss you," he murmurs, sliding his hands up my sides to grasp the edge of the towel at my chest.

My cheeks flush bright red and my mouth forms an *O* of shock. I catch his wrists just as he starts to untie the knot. "Are you crazy? I agreed to a kiss, not a clit polish!"

"In that case, you should have specified that you wanted me to kiss you on the mouth. You know Infernum's Civil Code Article 2.2, Myrina. You can't go back on your word, or you'll owe me a much heavier debt. An oral pact between two demons is equivalent to a written contract between a human and a demon. We set the terms of this arrangement together, and our mutual agreements serve as signatures."

"Wait, you're quoting legal texts to go down on me?"

"Exactly," he replies nonchalantly.

I stare at him, floored by his trap.

And, against all odds, I realize I'm wildly turned on by his Civil Code spiel—appealing to my Justspawn side—and his sexual machinations—appealing to my Lustspawn side. Seriously, what other man would pull off something so insanely bizarre?

On second thought, I'm an enforcer of the law, right? I can't back down. Professional conscience, I have to set an example. And at this point, a kiss or cunnilingus isn't that different. Or rather, it is. In the first case, I'd feel guilty and wouldn't orgasm. In the second, I'd feel guilty and would climax. If I had climaxed with Nick, I'd feel less guilty about brushing off Kelen.

Am I making lame excuses to justify my slutty tendencies toward him? Probably. But right now, I don't have the strength to refuse such a gift, no matter how twisted and immoral it is. If I'm going to hate myself and this Hybresang, it might as well be for something worth it. At least if he manages to make me see stars.

I release his hands with a sigh.

With calculated slowness, Kelen unties the knot and spreads open my towel. His red eyes light up with delight. Here I am, naked and offered under his piercing gaze, lying on my kitchen island like an all-you-can-eat buffet he's about to devour without restraint. The sin of gluttony in all its excess. By Lucifer, the way he hungrily eyes my body grips me in the guts and… everywhere, actually. My nipples are already hard, and I'm wet, but under his scrutiny, my vital organs quiver, my skin tingles with sensual goose bumps, and all my muscles tense. My heart races. My legs tremble as he starts to brush my thigh with his fingertips, tickling my now hyper-sensitive skin.

Say something, Myri. This heavy erotic silence is unbearable. To compensate for my vulnerability, my aggression surfaces, "Let's be clear, asshole," I growl, spreading my legs in front of him, "I still hate you, we're not having sex, and we will never talk about this again."

"I've never seen such bad faith in a demoness. You're wonderful."

"Shut up and get to work, Wills!" I snap, grabbing his hair and forcing his face exactly where I want it.

I hear a muffled laugh vibrate against my most intimate part, then his hot, devilish mouth gets to work, much to my delight.

Oh, that damn mouth! I'd much rather feel it here than hear it spout nonsense and—

What? Already done? This is a joke, right? I look down at him, frowning. He's lifted his head and is staring at me with a little smile, his chin above my pubic bone.

"Why are you smiling like an idiot?"

"My little wildcat, I've been wanting to eat your pussy since the day we met. Let me savor this moment."

With one hand under the curve of my ass, Kelen slides the other between my legs and penetrates me with two joined fingers, languidly, never breaking eye contact with his glowing red gaze. A low moan escapes my throat as I arch back on the island to better accommodate this unexpected intrusion. Fingers weren't part of our deal, but I have to admit they're useful. Panting, I lift one leg to rest it on his shoulder, making my position more comfortable.

He starts licking my dripping lips methodically, then circles his firm tongue around my throbbing nub. I melt like sizzling butter under this exquisite treatment. Absolutely fantastic. You can't say the Magistrate doesn't know what he's doing. His two fingers slide languidly inside me, igniting my inner walls while his delightful tongue caresses my swollen clitoris. His other hand digs into my backside, kneading it with a possessive roughness. I'm nothing more than a giant bundle of nerve endings all firing simultaneously. I desperately grind my hips against his mouth and clench my small muscles around his fingers, chasing the grand orgasm boiling in my belly. My vocal repertoire becomes limited. I growl, moan, babble unintelligible words, incoherent syllables, and in the midst of it all, I let slip his nickname in a pained, pleading tone. "Kel."

His fingers stop moving inside me, his moist lips peel away from my skin, and without a word, we lock eyes intensely. The long sigh he exhales lands on my clitoris, and I realize he held his breath when I said his nickname. I'm aware I've crossed an even more intimate barrier than what he's currently doing to me. I bite my lips in embarrassment, and he gives me a new kind of smile, both tender and roguish.

Then his hand leaves my rear and roams over my trembling breasts. His fingers play with my nipples, and his thumb lingers on my beauty mark.

"I won't lie to you, this might be painful at first, my little cat," he says gently, his fangs grazing my pubic mound. "But it won't last. Surrender, don't resist, and your orgasm will be even better. You have to go through it."

I don't react immediately, anesthetized by my sensations. What is he talking about? He better not be thinking of unzipping to fuck me, or I'll knee him in the face!

Kelen pulls his fingers out of my pussy and grips my leg firmly. His other hand spreads out and presses on my chest, pinning me to the island. What is he doing?

Then, without warning, he bites down hard on my groin, on the inside of my thigh, mirroring my tattoo. His sharp canines savagely pierce my flesh, actually drawing blood onto my towel. It feels like being bitten by a ravenous lion who could tear my thigh off at any moment.

I throw my head back and scream with all my might, drunk on the pain.

I claw at the demon's shoulders, gasping for breath, struggling beneath him, but he doesn't let go. He presses his full weight on me, pinning me to the countertop with his hand. He's fiercely sucking my blood, emitting small, animalistic growls. The wound burns horribly, as if someone is injecting sulfuric acid into my veins. Tears sting my eyes.

A few seconds later, the pain vanishes, transforming into ecstasy. I arch my back on the island, convulsing repeatedly. A ball of fire explodes in my lower abdomen, and I climax like I never have in my life.

Kelen gently laps at my wound, which is already starting to heal, before straightening up between my legs, his forehead glistening with sweat and his pupils dilated. He wipes his bloody mouth on his sleeve and takes a step back. I don't understand what just happened—why did he bite me so cruelly? Afflicted, exhausted, and drained, I look at the top of my thigh. A red, raised rune has appeared where the wound was. An arabesque with two dots. The most oppressive sight of my life.

NO!

A major demonic seal.

That son of a bitch took advantage of my weakness to mark me like an object that belongs to him.

He betrayed me. He chained me to him. He linked our souls. He connected our emotions and minds.

Without my fucking consent!

"You can now summon me at any time if you're in danger," he says softly, avoiding my tear-filled and horrified gaze. "You just need to say my name twice out loud while thinking of me."

"Take it off, Kelen!" I whimper, on the verge of a panic attack.

His expression hardens at my words. His red eyes turn back to amber. Impassive, unyielding.

"That's impossible. My Hybresang mark is irreversible." He heads for Ondine's travel bag to grab it. "You didn't leave me a choice, Myrina. Your stubbornness and spirit of independence could be your downfall. You don't seem to realize what kind of demon you're dealing with, but I do. I have a principle of always protecting those I care about, whether they want it or not."

"Wills, you bastard! How could you do this to me?" I scream, a mix of rage and sorrow in my voice.

He gives me one last, bitter look before dematerializing to go find my sister.

CHAPTER 26
CLARIFICATIONS

"When virtue seizes power, the executioner rubs his hands." ~Grégoire Lacroix, On ne meurt pas d'une overdose de rêve

KELEN

I teleport back to the 1001 Nights of Lust, Ondine's bag in hand.

While I had my head between Myrina's golden thighs, Sammael entered my office. I find the succubus nestled in his arms, her head resting on his broad chest. She's still in her stage outfit: a tiny, frilled thong. He's stroking her bare back, whispering words of comfort to reassure her, and she nods weakly. They're so close they didn't hear me arrive.

I've never seen Sam coddle anyone like this. It's clear now he has feelings for her. It's time to put an end to this.

"Ondine."

She jumps at the sound of my voice and quickly steps back as if caught red-handed. Sam shoots me a dark look that I ignore.

"Kel! But… where's Myri? She was supposed to come back with you!" exclaims the Lustspawn, crestfallen.

"She refused to follow me; she's determined to go to her grandfather's. Change of plans, you're not coming to my place anymore," I state flatly, tossing her travel bag in front of her.

"What?" Ondine and Sam exclaim in unison.

"I can't host you. No, let me correct that: I don't *want* to host you. I offered out of concern, but on reflection, it was a bad idea."

This is a lie, of course. Charity is a virtue I particularly abhor. Initially, I made the offer because I wanted both of them to come to my place. Since Myrina declined my generous invitation—which still stings—I see no reason for Ondine to stay at my place. She might get too comfortable, and I have no desire to cohabit with her, even temporarily.

"You'll stay with Sam; you'll be just as safe there as in my residence."

Their faces paint a picture of stunned disbelief.

"It's over between us, darling. I should've done this sooner. We had a good time, and you're a fantastic lay, but it's not working between us, and it never will. I could say I'm sorry, but I'm not, so… I won't."

"I slept with Sammael, you selfish bastard!" she snaps coldly, hoping to hurt me. "Several times. He's a much better lover than you, a thousand times more attentive!"

"Ondine!" my lieutenant reprimands her in a hushed voice.

"That's because I never gave my all with you, even when I was all in you," I reply indulgently. "I visited between your thighs out of courtesy, not as the master of the house."

I don't mention that I already knew she'd been hooking up with Sam for several days. In fact, I'm the one who asked him to do it. He was dying to be with her, and she wasn't immune to his charms, so I gave my explicit blessing to my second-in-command. I thought she'd leave me for him so I wouldn't have to dump her—so Myrina wouldn't hold it against me—but Ondine took her sweet time. I guess she was worried about losing her job. Anyway, I keep this little tidbit to myself so the succubus doesn't end up resenting Sam, too. Mostly, I do it out of respect for him.

"This has something to do with my sister, Kelen?" Ondine interprets, glaring at me.

Yet another sensitive topic to handle with care. I want to avoid dragging Myrina into this breakup to prevent discord between them. I'm willing to take on the bad guy role entirely in this story; it doesn't bother me. So, I mix lies with the truth, "Yes and no. Yes, because

I made advances toward her. No, because she rejected them every time. That's not the reason. In the end, I just can't pretend with you anymore, Ondine. You're wonderful… but not for me. Don't worry, this won't affect your job; I have no intention of firing you."

Her eyes blaze with legitimate anger. Retaliation is imminent.

I exchange a glance with Sam as Ondine grabs a metal letter opener from my desk. He looks at me, silently asking if he should intervene; I shake my head slightly, bracing myself for my ex-girlfriend's vengeance. I can allow her one hit. That's often how we resolve relationship conflicts among Sinner demons. Some family dinners are bloody affairs. The Lustspawn strides toward me, half-naked, with a martial step.

I thought she'd go for my throat, face, or chest, but instead… she plunges the letter opener right into my stomach, near my navel. I bend over, growling. *Very* unpleasant, though I can take it. When she pulls her makeshift weapon from my flesh, drops of black blood hit the floor. Tsss, my nice shirt is ruined, what a shame.

"I quit," she hisses. "I don't want you as my boss anymore, you're vile!"

"That's your choice, Ondine," I mutter, pressing my hand against my bleeding wound. "I won't stop you."

She turns to Sam and says in a softer voice, "I'm going downstairs to get dressed in my dressing room and say goodbye to the girls. Can you grab my bag and join me in a few minutes?"

He nods, smiling at her affectionately. She returns his smile before heading for the door. But at the last moment, she makes a detour, brandishing her bloodied letter opener and…

"*Ondine, no!*" I shriek, eyes wide with horror.

With three swift and fierce strokes, she slashes my second favorite painting, Fuseli's *The Nightmare*. My face falls apart as I see the gashes marring the canvas, disfiguring its surface. Damn, that little bitch! I could tolerate her stabbing me in the stomach, but ruining an authentic masterpiece is a real sacrilege. What an unspeakable waste!

"I always hated this painting," she remarks, letting the letter opener fall to the ground.

I curse like a sailor as the door to my office slams shut behind her.

Sam chuckles with sadistic amusement. "You definitely deserved that, Kel."

"The hole in my abdomen, sure. But the painting? That's going to be impossible to restore."

"At least you're avoiding the punch I was planning to land on your face before she grabbed the letter opener. I would have happily knocked all your teeth out."

Grimacing in pain, I collapse into my chair.

He sits on the edge of my desk. "Despite your questionable methods, you made the right decision for everyone, *finally*. So, tell me, what happened with the Amazon?"

"I did something impulsive that I maybe…" I clear my throat, my eyes on the slashed painting. "Shouldn't have done."

His blond eyebrows shoot up on his forehead. It's the first time he's ever heard that kind of admission from me. "Kelen, what did you do to her?"

"I marked her."

"You marked her," he repeats incredulously. "Wait, you *marked* her?"

"Damn it, in what language do you want me to say it, Mandarin?"

He hesitates, rubbing his neck. "But you haven't marked anyone since—"

"Shut up, Sam, I don't want to talk about it!" I snap, my tone angry.

"Was Myrina okay with receiving your seal?"

"What do you think, idiot? Do you think I'd doubt my choice for a second if she had been?"

"By all the demons of Infernum! Seriously, you've been off the rails lately. This is where obsessions lead! How do you expect to still seduce her if she hates you?"

I would have preferred if she just hated me, if I had the choice. It was worse than hatred: I disappointed her. My bite didn't just cause her physical pain, but also moral anguish. I felt it keenly through our new bond. Despite what she says, she was starting to trust me *a little* before I marked her. Not anymore.

From now on, I'll experience her most intense emotions. The closer we become, the stronger this sharing and connection will be. And what really pisses me off is that I've opened myself to her own torments by resorting to this act, driven by the irritating and growing concern she instills in me.

I made my decision suddenly when she told me she wouldn't come with me. In my mind, marking her was the necessary condition to agree to let her go, a sort of supernatural life insurance. That's why I negotiated the *kiss*. I wanted to imprint my seal in an intimate place that other demons wouldn't see, and the top of her thigh seemed like an ideal spot… at the time.

"Seducing her is no longer on the agenda, Sam. The dynamics have changed. I didn't do it to assert possession over her; I marked her solely to keep her alive."

"It's one and the same, Kel. You would never have marked another demoness; we both know that. It's a more serious commitment than marriage among humans. Whether you admit it or not, you've claimed her as yours on every level."

I grit my teeth, sinking deeper into my chair.

"She won't be able to sleep with other men at all while she bears your Hybresang mark."

That's good.

Just like the kiss by the piano, the mark wasn't planned. I acted on instinct in both instances. I kissed her the other night after *Moonlight Sonata* to absorb her pain because her tear got to me. Tonight, I bit her on the leg because I didn't want to lose her and couldn't tolerate her stubbornness anymore. So yes, to some extent, I've become attached to this damn half-breed with a fiery temperament, I can't deny it. I want to fuck her hard and make her my companion for a few months, maybe even years. But claim her as my other half, my soulmate? Let's not exaggerate! I'm not that crazy. It's a seal of summoning and protection, not possession in the truest sense of the word. Sam is wrong; he's jumping to conclusions because of my unusual behavior.

Maybe he even thinks I love her. Again, he's mistaken. Love? By Satan, I'd crucify myself before succumbing to such absurd weakness again! Loving someone other than yourself is for the Virtuous and humans.

"I told her it was irreversible so she wouldn't try to convince me to remove it. But I'll release her from it when that damn killer is stiff as a board."

"Really, Kel?"

"Really, Sam."

This two-tailed moralist doesn't believe me. I couldn't care less; he can go to hell. Anyway, my relationship with Myrina is none of his business. It concerns only her and me.

"You've really gotten yourself into a mess with her," the Ragebeast summarizes thoughtfully. "Then again, you've only got yourself to blame."

Struggling against the urge to rip out his tongue for his insolence, I gesture for him to get out of my office. He shrugs and obeys. A few minutes later, as I doze in my chair, recalling my nickname on the lips of my Tracker while my belly wound heals, I receive a text from my agent. The message informs me that they'll be talking about me on the news. Yawning, I use my telekinesis to turn on the wall-mounted flat screen.

"… the funeral pyres of Magistral Envyfiend Hallow and Magistral Faithfiend Azath. Thousands of Sinners and Virtuous were present today outside the gates of the Magistrates' Palace for the occasion. Following the attack, the people of Infernum have sharply become aware of the terrorist threat posed by the Rebels."

Images of me during the ceremony with the Soulless's electronic collar in hand flash on the television. There's no debate about it; I look fantastic on screen: I have an insane amount of class and charisma.

"Magistrate of the Ragebeasts Kelen Wills, who narrowly escaped death during his heartfelt and sincere speech, has become a symbol of the glorious order that survives adversity against all odds for many demons. Public opinion has faith in him to defuse the growing chaos caused by the rebels. He has particularly gained the loyalty of many Envyfiends who supported the late candidate Hallow. Polls place him comfortably ahead to win the first round of the Sinners' Federator election."

I smile with satisfaction at the percentages displayed alongside the anchor's words. Ah, what excellent news! It turns out the explosive tragedy has served my interests by boosting my sympathy capital with voters instead of discrediting me as I feared. A climate of fear and doubt hangs over Infernum: it's clear no one is safe from the extremists' acts from the Rebels, not even the Magistrates. So, public opinion seeks a demon strong, authoritative, determined, and powerful enough to eradicate these troublesome renegades.

A warlord.
Am I up to the task?
Undoubtedly.

CHAPTER 27

NIGHT TERROR

"Sometimes, only one person is missing, and the whole world seems depopulated." ~Alphonse de Lamartine, "Isolation," First Poetic Meditations

MYRINA

"Honeybun."

I turn toward Grandpa Amon, my knife bloody in my right hand, a piece of skin in my left. Clad in gray-striped pajamas that clash with his dignified posture, my grandfather scrutinizes me disapprovingly. His eyes lower to my scraped thigh.

"Come now, honeybun, what have you done to your leg?"

"Kelen Wills marked me," I explain, my tone vibrant with anger, as I toss the piece of skin bearing the demonic seal into the fireplace I just lit.

The smell of burning flesh makes me wrinkle my nose.

A brief expression of disgust crosses the Justspawn's features. His reaction has nothing to do with the stench emanating from the hearth; it's stirred by my revelation. But he quickly regains his usual impassivity.

"The Hybresang will pay for this outrage, Myrina. Unfortunately, your self-mutilation serves no purpose. When your tissues have finished healing, the mark will reappear."

Damn it. I suspected as much, but I figured it was worth a shot.

"If I rip off Wills's head, our bond will be broken, right?"

"Come on, honeybun, please."

"No one will know. I'll make his body disappear down to the last scale."

"There's no need to go to such extremes. I'll force him to remove that mark from you."

"That idiot told me it was indelible."

"He lied to you. He can erase it."

Why am I not surprised by this latest pettiness? Yet, a glimmer of relief washes over me. At least I'm not condemned to carry around this wretched demonic seal until death, that's something.

"Could someone else remove it for me?"

I'm not an expert in this field, I only know the basics. What I do know is that minor demons can't mark others; this power belongs only to major and intermediate demons aged over several centuries. Typically, it's more common among the Virtuous, between parents and children or spouses, and the bond is rarely one-sided. The demon marked marks the marker in return, if you get my drift. Reciprocity further strengthens the connection.

"No. Only the demon who inflicted such a mark can release the individual they bound. I seem to recall advising you to keep your distance from this Sinner," Amon lectures me.

"That's what I did, Grandpa, I assure you. But he…" *Gave me the best licking of my life on the central island of my kitchen.* "Tricked me."

"Hmm, did you have sexual relations with him, young lady?"

"What do you mean by sexual relations? With or without penetration?"

"Myrina Holmes, you're heading down a bad path."

"Grandpa, I already feel guilty enough, don't pile it on."

A heavy silence hangs between us. His gaze reminds me too much of my father's, so I avoid it. Mine drifts to the framed photo above the fireplace. It shows a little girl with messy brown hair streaked with silver, sitting on a swing, pushed by a handsome young man with short pearly hair, smiling broadly. He had violet eyes, like Grandpa and me. His name was Arthur Holmes.

There are pictures of him and me all over Amon's house. Sometimes, I feel like this place is a giant mausoleum.

In fact, I tend to talk about my parents in the past tense even though they're alive. They're in a parallel plane I know almost nothing about, the Limbo. My only consolation when I think about them is knowing they're together.

Damn, I miss them both so much!

When the CIT took me away from them, I was ten years old. I didn't understand why their love for each other and for me could be considered a crime. It took me years to accept our fate— our separation—and stop blaming the government and CIT. My colleagues were just following orders, after all. It's the archaic and stupid laws of Infernum that are to blame, not the enforcers.

At the beginning of my training as a Tracker, I was a loose cannon. I ran away several times, cursed my masters thoroughly, and got into fights with my classmates repeatedly. I even punched one of them and handcuffed him naked in the toilets because he made a cruel reference to my parents, blurting out in front of everyone that they were traitors and deserved to die. Some teachers claimed I was a lost cause.

But Zagam didn't want to give up on me. He was always there for me, scolding me when I messed up, encouraging me to get back up when I faltered, and congratulating me as soon as I succeeded. Over the years, I learned discipline and obedience. Well, to some extent… As I grew up and matured, I told myself that I had to overcome my reservations and restrain my emotions to follow in the footsteps of my father, who was an excellent Justspawn Tracker. Fully investing myself in my work is my way of honoring him and following the virtuous principles he instilled in me as a child. He was passionate about his job; at home, he would constantly talk to us about it, my mother and me. In sign language, he would recount chases, fights, arrests, anecdotes, toning down the violence in his stories so as not to shock me. His stories fascinated me. He was my hero, my role model.

My mother, Lysippé Holmes, was the gentlest and most affectionate of Sinners. Of course, like all succubus, she loved to seduce; but she did it with grace and elegance, never vulgarity. Lysi was a stunning fiery brunette with blue eyes, just like Ondine. A smile from her was enough to melt my father and me. We did puzzles and rode bikes together; it was our girl thing. My grandfather never told me to avoid hurting me, but I'm aware he didn't appreciate her. In his mind, it's because of her that my father, his virtuous only son, fell from grace. I presume she personifies for him the figure of carnal temptation and the evil that corrupts good. If he truly thinks that, he's completely off base.

My father and mother were my only anchors during the first ten years of my life. They pampered and overprotected me because of my deafness. They taught me not to let my disability consume me. In short, I had the best parents in the world, and I lost them abruptly fourteen years ago when the Trackers discovered they were a couple and had a hybrid child they were raising on Earth.

A closed-door trial with a select committee was held to decide their fate. There were only the two accused, Magistrate Justspawn Dickens—my father's chief—Magistral Lustspawn Beliale—my mother's chief—and fourteen impartial jurors randomly selected from the demon population, one representative per legion. Even Amon wasn't allowed to attend in person. Through the speakerphone on his phone, he pleaded my parents' case to spare them from death, like a passionate defense attorney. And Grandpa managed to save them from execution with his arguments and rhetoric. I will never thank him enough for that.

Have I tried to find a way to contact them in the Limbo, or even bring them back to Earth?

Of course.

In secret, I've sifted through hundreds of books and searched the demonic internet, all in vain. There is no Arcadus in the Limbo; it's a mysterious world reserved for banished demons, a gigantic prison stuck between Infernum and Earth. They are trapped in this zone until their death. Only the fourteen sitting Magistrates have the power to teleport there. I don't know which of them abandoned them there because it's a highly classified state matter. Logically, it would be Dickens or Beliale, who both presided over the trial. I've also considered Wills, of course, but I dare not ask him. Even if he agreed to answer me, which I doubt, I would be too afraid that he would admit to playing an active role in their exile.

When I lived here, I grilled Amon dozens of times about the Limbo. He would clam up like an oyster every time I brought up the subject. He would invariably reply that my father would have wanted me to move forward, definitely not to brood over their fate.

It's one of the most painful taboos of my adolescence. Neither he, nor Ondine, nor I have the right to communicate with them. I often think about my parents, though I keep these thoughts to myself. I don't know why, but I imagine them wandering in a misty plain, hand in hand, like lost souls.

"I'm going back to bed, it's late," my grandfather declares in a rigid tone. "We can discuss this tomorrow if you wish. If your thigh hurts too much while you wait for it to heal, there are painkillers in the bathroom. Good night, honeybun."

He teleports to his room, leaving me alone and defenseless in the living room, facing the photo of my father and me. Even the best medicine doesn't work on the deepest wounds.

I can't sleep. I scribble the three names on the bathroom mirror with my sister's lipstick to try and make sense of it.

Aydan Smat. John Blane. Gabriel Bariballarik.

Aydan, the former priest turned homeless after renouncing his faith following the fire at his temple. Virtuous Faithfiend. Defenestration. Church. Symbol: dove. Clue: flaming heart. Virtue: faith.

John, the nurse and volunteer, apparently loved and respected by everyone. Virtuous Charityfiend. Immolation. Hospital. Symbol: flaming heart. Clue: peacock feather. Virtue: charity.

Gabriel, the narcissistic and haughty porn actor. Sinful Pridefiend. Flaying. Factory. Symbol: peacock feather. Clue: unknown. Sin: pride.

"Mirror, mirror, on the wall, tell me who the murderer is," I murmur, gazing at the reflection of my darkened face behind the three red names.

Gabriel's name suddenly catches my eye.

Sin of pride…

Mirror…

Holy. Shit!

What an idiot I am for not getting it sooner! I was thinking of something organic, not an *object!*

That's the clue for the next murder: the mirror at the crime scene!

Because the mirror is precisely the emblem of the Virtuous Prudlings, the demons of prudence!

But how can I prevent the next murder if I don't know how he chooses his victims? Because he doesn't select them randomly. There's a link that connects them all. There's a coherence I'm missing. The places where the bodies were found don't make sense on their own; they correspond to the sins and virtues unique to each victim.

A Virtuous. A Virtuous. A Sinner. And soon, another Virtuous.

But why punish *them*?

Because their virtues or sins were more pronounced? No, that doesn't make sense. There are plenty of other Faithfiends who lost their faith like Aydan, hundreds of Charityfiends more charitable than John, thousands of Pridefiends more prideful than Gabriel.

Gabriel didn't know Aydan and John, who were friends. How did those two meet? I dug into their pasts and found nothing!

Unless the information was erased?

And the spy at the CIT, by the way? Zagam and Lexi have access to all our order's confidential data. I also know that Malphas has the password to my boss's computer, like all the senior Trackers. I've caught Sean alone in my boss's office, claiming he had to drop off a file or dust the place. Given his profile as a smart geek, I bet he could hack a PC easily.

Killer? Accomplice? Wills's informant?

This is so frustrating!

I wipe off my red writings with a washcloth soaked in water and soap, then head back to my teenage bedroom that Grandpa left exactly as it was when I moved out. I'm in for a sleepless night, tossing and turning in bed.

My phone vibrates. Anonymous call.

It must be Kelen calling from a blocked number.

I hesitate to pick up. A huge ball of rage and anxiety is growing in my gut because of this mark. I need to let it all out. So, I give in to my impulse.

"I'm going to skin you alive and eviscerate you, Wills," I announce in an icy voice.

No response.

I only hear slow, heavy breathing on the other end of the phone.

A cold sweat runs down my spine.

"Wills? Is that you?" I murmur, shivering.

No, Myrina. It's not him, my Tracker instinct whispers.

I glance up at the window. Grabbing my gun, I flick off the safety and rush toward it, the phone wedged between my shoulder and ear. On high alert, I peek outside between the curtains. My eyes dart back and forth across the deserted street. No shadows, no movement.

"Listen to me, you gutless piece of shit," I hiss into the phone's microphone. "If you think you can scare me, you've got your horn up your ass! Your time is running out. I'm going to find you and kill you, asshole. I'm going to—"

"Do you miss him, Myrina?" a robotic, distorted voice asks on the other end.

I freeze, my throat dry. My heart skips a beat.

My god, who is he talking about?

My father?

Wills?

Or… or…

No. You're losing it, Myri, it's impossible.

"Sometimes, only one person is missing, and the whole world seems depopulated," the altered voice whispers.

Click. He hung up.

Sometimes, only one person is missing, and the whole world seems depopulated. A quote from the human poet Lamartine that I once read on a wall, written in blood, by the worst demon from my past.

I pull the phone away from my buzzing ear. My eyes, wet and unsteady, are glued to the screen. I set the device on the windowsill, staring at it as if it were a homemade bomb. My fingers tremble on the grip of my revolver. My legs give way. I clutch the door frame. Acid rises, burning my throat. I'm suffocating.

This is a nightmare. I need to wake up. I *must* wake up.

Then, it hits me.

He's alive.

I was convinced I had dealt with him three years ago.

Now, I know who the serial killer is, and there's no longer any doubt that he has a personal vendetta against me.

I lied to him: I'm terrified.

CHAPTER 28

SHADOWS OF THE PAST

"Sometimes tears have the eloquence of speech." ~Ovid

MYRINA

Victor Cole.

That's the name tied to the face that has haunted my nights for the past three years. A specter I loathe with every crack in my fractured soul.

A Ragebeast Sinner.

In my nightmares, he murders Owen in his demonic form. In my dreams, I see myself killing Cole in *my* demonic form, driven by an unmatched thirst for blood and vengeance.

He couldn't have survived. At the end of our fight, which lasted only a few minutes because I quickly gained the upper hand mid-flight, I literally tore him apart in the sky with my teeth and claws, restraining him with my tail. I tore out his throat with my jaws. I even went so far as to dismember him. I still remember the acrid taste of his black blood on my tongue as it rained down to the ground thirty feet below us. I have never been as fierce and enraged during a criminal execution. I wished I had the cold blood to prolong his agony for hours and inflict the worst suffering of his long existence. But I had only one obsession then: justice for Owen.

However, Cole's death did not lessen the pain of losing my beloved.

I was engaged to a wonderful human. Handsome. Gentle. Kind. Tender. Funny. Considerate. Intelligent. A dreamer. An optimist. A scientist. My opposite in terms of character. The kind of man who would put spiders outside instead of squashing them. He had a lot of OCD; he washed his hands thirty times a day until they were chapped, and he couldn't stand dirt and mess. He wanted everything to be tidy, clean, sorted, and ordered. Coming from a middle-class family, he was pursuing his PhD in astronomy. After making love, he would talk to me about stars, planets, black holes, and stellar systems that I didn't understand at all.

I fell in love with him at seventeen; he was two years older than me. A shy smile, a sideways glance in a small neighborhood bookstore, and I was head over heels. It overwhelmed and even frightened me at first, but then I realized that love doesn't conform to any code or rule. I purposely bumped into him in an aisle. Our books fell and mixed on the floor. Astrophysics books for him, detective novels and thrillers for me. So cliché, right? He was my best friend and my lover. I didn't need to talk for him to understand me. He even lost his virginity with me; I was his first girlfriend. He insisted on learning sign language so we could communicate from a distance.

We were going to move in together at his place after our wedding. On a whim, we got tattoos of the infinity sign with our initials on our thighs the day he proposed to me. He wasn't aware of my secret; I was always extremely careful. Owen never suspected that I was a demon. I told him I was a bartender in a nightclub to explain my nocturnal absences. Every time he suggested visiting me at work, I hypnotized him to make him forget the idea.

Three days before the ceremony, Victor Cole took him from me in the most violent way imaginable. Owen had no notion of self-defense. A lamb facing a dragon. Against a major demon, he stood no chance.

I found my beloved's body when I returned from a mission one night. I often have horrifying flashbacks about it.

Our sheets soaked in liters of sticky, red liquid. My wedding dress, slashed by claws, draped over him like a morbid, mocking costume. His mutilations. His burns. His countless wounds. His hazel eyes wide open, staring at the ceiling. And that inscription in letters of blood on the wall: *Sometimes, only one person is missing, and the whole world seems depopulated.*

A message directed at me.

Why did Cole target my innocent human? For revenge. An eye for an eye, a fang for a fang. I had tracked and executed his lover, a formidable criminal like him. Together, they had terrorized Infernum for months. I killed the first demon, but his lover Victor managed to escape… and in his rage and grief, he took it out on my Owen a few weeks later. I had stolen the love of his life, so he did the same to me.

I hunted Cole for days without sleeping or eating. And I finally got him. I transformed and slaughtered my fiancé's murderer with a cruelty I didn't know I possessed.

After that, I said fuck off to everyone and took off on a solo road trip on my motorcycle. I didn't want to see anyone. Not Ondine. Not Amon. Not Zagam.

I cried until I had no tears left. I even cursed myself for loving Owen and regretted the mistake of getting so close to a fragile human when I had such a dangerous job, one that could put his safety at risk. I felt guilty to the point of vomiting for not being able to protect him and for hiding the truth about myself from him. I envied the Sinners who enjoyed life without ever getting attached to anyone. I wanted to rip my heart out because the pain was unbearable. I had suicidal thoughts. I slept with strangers picked up in bars, several a night, to drain their sexual energy like a junkie. It felt good at the time. I also considered quitting my job more than once.

I didn't, because my job was all I had left.

After a few weeks, I came back home and slowly climbed out of the abyss with the support of my sister and grandfather. More or less. I threw myself into my work as a Tracker. I buried the pain deep inside. I told everyone around me that I never wanted to talk about it again.

But Owen will be engraved in me forever. My love. My grief. My burden. My virtue. My sin.

Victor Cole can't be alive.

Unless he made a pact with an even more powerful demon before his death to transfer his soul into another body.

A sordid pact, forbidden by law, considered an act of high treason against Infernum.

Here I am now. Crushed. Lost. Scared. I feel utterly helpless. Collapsed on my bed, assaulted by memories, drowning in my macabre thoughts. Tears stream down my cheeks.

And, of course, it's at this most vulnerable moment that Kelen Wills barges into my old teenage bedroom. His sudden presence hits me like a scorching tornado through our new bond. An overwhelming energy radiates from him. He probably sensed my fear and sorrow.

Fucking demonic seal.

Clenching my hand around the grip of my revolver, I roll on the mattress to aim the barrel between his legs. He doesn't flinch, not even a little, remaining completely unfazed. He's lying on his side, facing me, propped up on his fist. On my bed. His hair is tousled. In his boxers. I should almost be grateful he took the time to put some on; he could have been naked. He studies my tear-streaked face with a puzzled expression.

"If you don't get out of my bed right now, I'll blow your balls off. Regeneration will be very unpleasant, Wills," I threaten, my voice trembling, far from my usual firm and cold tone.

Not convincing at all, Myri.

"Hmm, what happened, my little cat?"

I shake my head sharply. No way am I opening up to him.

He lets out a long sigh before grabbing my wrist and slowly moving the revolver away from his crotch. His touch sends delightful sparks across my skin. Carefully, he pries my fingers off the grip one by one, then takes the gun from my hand and places it on the mattress behind him. I fight back a sob, red with shame for not being able to hide my tearful weakness from him.

"My sword is under my bed and my knife under my pillow," I mutter weakly, trying to keep him in check.

"How many weapons do you have within reach, exactly?"

"You don't want to know."

"My little cat, come here and give me a hug, you need it."

I look at him in disbelief.

I must have misheard that. Are my hearing aids malfunctioning?

But no, Wills is dead serious. I shiver with revulsion. This guy freaks me out. Almost as much as Cole.

"A… hug?" I repeat, blinking.

It's a crude and absurd word coming from a Sinner like him. If he had said, "Come here so I can fuck you, you need it," I would have been far less shocked.

Kelen grimaces apologetically, waving his hand dismissively. "Don't get me wrong, I hate this unnatural idea as much as you do. But our bond has advantages. A platonic embrace will comfort you, and we can both regain our composure quickly. Your tears make me extremely uncomfortable."

He's not wrong. It pisses me off, too, crying in front of him.

But a hug? With *him*?

Courage, Myri. It's for a good cause. You can do it, I think, exhaling.

Kelen wraps his fingers around my arm to place it around his waist himself. I curl up against his bare chest, stiff as a board. I'm halfway to puking.

"I warn you, Wills, you better not get hard."

"I'll contain myself, Myrina," he whispers close to my ear. "Relax, I have no sexual intentions right now. Oh, and by the way, if you tell anyone about this, I'll kill you."

I nod slightly. Naturally, he can't handle hugs either.

It's not so bad, after all. My nausea has passed, and I'm feeling a bit less unsettled. The Hybresang is warm against me and smells incredibly good. His right hand is drawing small circles on my back, and his left is massaging my scalp. His deep, steady breathing calms me. I nuzzle my wet face into his firm chest. His heart beats slowly and powerfully in his rib cage. I think I might even fall asleep like this.

"For your information, I broke up with Ondine," he confides softly after a few moments of silence.

I swallow hard, torn by conflicting emotions. "Is she… is she at your place?" I murmur against his hot skin.

"No, she's with Sam."

I bite my lips in worry. "How did she take it?"

A low growl rumbles in his chest. "She stabbed me in the stomach with a letter opener before slashing *The Nightmare* by Fuseli."

A tender smile stretches my lips. I'm so proud of her. I'll buy her a gold jewelry set to celebrate this sweet revenge.

"She's having an affair with my lieutenant," Wills continues evenly.

Really? That's news to me!

My joy and surprise are short-lived. I swallow again as a thought strikes me. "And… did you tell her about—"

"No. I didn't want to drag you into this."

"Wills, even if you're not with her anymore, it doesn't change anything for me. I have no intention of becoming your girlfriend. And I still hold a grudge against you for the mark," I add, lifting my head to fix my dark gaze into his.

"I know, my little cat," he assures pensively, sliding his hand over my cheek to wipe away my remaining tears.

"You need to remove it. My grandfather said it's not irreversible."

He frowns. His fingers briefly tap along my jawline as if to buy time. "Once the killer is dead. Not before."

"Promise me!" I order, pinching his chin hard between my thumb and index finger. Damn that too-sexy dimple that I want to lick.

At my simple gesture, his pupils dilate. My breathing deepens. Our bodies heat up. Our invisible bond sizzles in my belly. Searing attraction, energy magnets, **RIP** dry panties. He hooks a hand behind my neck. The other hand moves dangerously toward the mark marbling the top of my thigh.

It's official, the *soft hug without sexual intentions* moment has jumped on a high-speed train and left me stranded on the platform of *feverish embrace saturated with depraved thoughts inappropriate for the context.*

"I never promise anything to anyone, my little cat," he murmurs in a suave tone, bringing his tempting lips close to mine.

"Not my problem. You're going to promise *me.*"

"I promise I'll think about making that promise."

My god, he's so annoying! Unfortunately, I start panting and arch under his fingers that graze the demonic mark, setting my freshly healed skin on fire. My Lustspawn hormones are going haywire. Oh my, these exquisite sensations…

"Wills, stop," I moan as his handsome face draws near.

"You can call me by my first name. It doesn't bother me at all, Myrina."

"It does bother me…"

He crushes my body against his without mercy, his hand pressing into the flesh of my thigh. Ah, Chibresang is back.

"See what your damn mark is doing to us!"

"It's not the mark, you little fool. It was already there before."

"Oh, shut up and kiss me on the *mouth*, bastard," I suddenly shout, closing my eyes.

He lets out a rough laugh… and stops just short of my lips. What the hell is he doing now?

"Wills?" I grumble, opening my eyes again.

Kelen has frozen, holding his breath. The barrel of a high-caliber black rifle with silver bullets is pressed into the hollow of his cheek. Oh, oh.

"Get your filthy claws off my granddaughter, Wills," my grandfather growls from beside the bed, his silver eyes clearly showing he's furious about the scene we're presenting to him.

Okay, I think my room has officially turned into a Magistrate teleportation meeting room.

CHAPTER 29
SOUL PACT

"Blood is inherited, and virtue is acquired, and virtue in and of itself has a value that blood does not." ~Miguel de Cervantes, Don Quixote

KELEN

"Good evening, Amon. It's been a while," I remark nonchalantly, pulling my hands away from Myrina's body.

The presence of her grandfather and his rifle does nothing to calm my hard-on. This whole platonic cuddle thing has messed with my head. Besides, every time she calls me a bastard, threatens me with a weapon, curses, or gives me orders, it turns me on like crazy. I bet the naughty demoness knows it and does it on purpose to provoke me. I've just made a crucial decision: the day I manage to fuck Myrina Holmes will be more explosive than an atomic bomb dropped into a volcano during a summer heatwave.

"And I would've preferred never to see you again, Wills!" the former Magistrate Justspawn fumes. "Especially not under these circumstances. Your Sinner stench woke me from my restorative sleep. How dare you intrude into my home and take advantage of my little honeybun?"

My eyes lock immediately with the Amazon's. I arch a mocking eyebrow, suppressing a snicker. "Honeybun?" I murmur, supremely amused by this incongruous nickname.

The young woman glares at me with her amethyst eyes, perfectly complementing the rosy hue of her cheeks.

"I wasn't taking advantage of your Hone—" *No, there's no way I can say that again, it's too ridiculous.* "Granddaughter, Amon."

"Then why is her face tear-streaked?"

"Why don't you ask her?"

"Honeybun, has this miserable individual harmed you?" the Virtuous one questions with smug assurance.

"If I say yes, Grandpa, will you pull the trigger?" Myrina inquires softly, never taking her eyes off me.

"Probably."

The little pest seems to ponder her answer. I darken. Damn, she's bold. I arm myself with patience and composure in the face of these two equally crazy Holmes.

"Amon, don't play the paternalistic tough guy. I'm not fooled. Your testosterone level is lower than that of a newborn Slothling. You know very well that I haven't harmed Myrina."

"You've defiled her with your mark, vile character," he notes in a sanctimonious tone, pressing the barrel of his rifle into my jaw.

Defiled? I've honored her, yes.

"To protect her from a bloodthirsty, sociopathic demon."

"She can protect herself. You saw her in her natural form at the Envyfiends' HQ before you took all the credit for her feats. I don't know why you pursue her with your despicable attentions, but it's time it stopped!"

"It's up to her to decide if my attentions are despicable or not, not you," I argue, flicking an invisible speck of dust off my shoulder.

"Oh, drop your gentleman act, both of you!" the Tracker interjects, rolling her eyes. "Why don't you just punch each other instead of yapping like a couple of old ladies in a retirement home?"

"Mind your language, young lady!" Amon scolds, gripping his firearm tighter.

I never liked this Justspawn's rigid mentality back at the Magistrates' Palace, and his infantilizing of Myrina only cements my disdain for him. If his virtue of Justice were tangible, it would be stuck in his colon. Despite her closeness to him, I bet Myrina won't last a week here with her independent spirit and strong temperament. I'll reiterate my offer to let her stay with me in a few days; she might be desperate and on edge enough to accept.

If Amon weren't her grandfather, I'd have bent his rifle with my hand and wrecked his face. Then, obviously, I'd have wrecked Myrina with *my* own rifle and given her the ride of her life.

"Grandpa, please lower your weapon." The young woman sighs, sitting up on the bed. "If anyone's going to kill Wills, it'll be me."

There she goes, teasing me again. My erection isn't going anywhere. Even the uptight Virtuous can't miss it, given how obvious it is in my boxer shorts. That's probably why he's glaring at me *and* looking pale as a ghost. I laugh inwardly as he reluctantly lowers his rifle, despite his extreme agitation. This guy must have stayed a virgin for centuries before dipping his biscuit in Grandma Holmes's tea.

With a broad smile, I lean back against the Tracker's plush pillow, arms crossed behind my head, exposing the glorious form of my Sinful phallus under my boxers without a shred of shame. I wonder if I can push him to the point of transformation, the Justspawn.

Myrina furrows her brow and growls as she catches onto my game. She throws a corner of the cover over my wild beast to hide it from Amon while muttering yet another insult at me.

"Will you tell me why he's here, honeybun?" the former Magistrate demands, casting a stern—and slightly stressed—look at her.

"Excellent question. Why am I here, *honeybun*?" I chime in, my tone dripping with sweetness as I turn my head toward her.

"Cole," she reveals in a whisper.

Cole? Who the hell is that? A colleague? A lover? The name rings a faint bell. I dig through my overloaded memory.

"Why are you talking about him?" the Virtuous one asks in an unsteady voice.

"I think he's alive, Grandpa. He… he called me earlier."

Amon slumps onto the mattress, shoulders sagging. Fantastic. I'm in Myrina's bed with her, her grandfather, and an erection. I couldn't have dreamed of a better night.

"That's not possible, honeybun," the Justspawn contests, staring into space.

"Grandpa, he quoted Lamartine before hanging up. His voice was distorted by an electronic modulator, but it could only be him."

Ah, I remember. Victor Cole. He was part of my legion. I didn't know him personally, but I heard about his murderous exploits a few years ago. He was pursued and eliminated by the CIT.

"Myrina, did you kill Victor Cole?" I deduce.

She nods weakly, wringing her hands. Impressive. Cole, the renegade, was known to be a formidable major demon. Cruel, ruthless, and sadistic, he committed dozens of savage murders on Virtuous, Sinners, and humans with his lover's complicity before being gunned down. Even other Ragebeasts who associated with him feared him because he was unpredictable—he killed on pure impulse, without distinguishing between his victims. He had some serious issues. He made headlines in Infernum's press many times over.

"Wills, leave us alone? You're not needed here!" demands Amon with a hint of delicious aggressiveness.

"Just when things were getting interesting?"

"He can stay, Grandpa," Myrina concedes, to my surprise.

"How can you trust him?" the former Magistrate grumbles skeptically.

She sizes me up with her solemn violet eyes. With her long brown and silver hair cascading in silky waves over her shoulders, she looks magnificent. Even the faint red streaks marking her cheeks, remnants of her tears, do not diminish the angelic beauty of her features.

"No, I don't trust him. But I know he's on our side. More or less. As long as it suits him."

"Glad you're finally realizing that," I reply with a hint of a smile. "So, Victor Cole?"

"Victor Cole assassinated of my fiancé, Owen."

My smile fades at her sad and troubled expression. Damn, everything makes sense now. "I'm sorry, Myrina."

I don't know what else to say, because that's all that comes to mind. I had sensed she was involved in her ex's death, but I thought she had accidentally killed him by losing control of her powers, hence her guilt toward him. I'd offer her another hug to console her and score some points with her, but with her grandfather around, it's better to refrain.

"Owen was human, Wills."

Damn. Wanting to marry a human, what madness! This tragedy was almost inevitable given Myrina's profession and the number of her enemies. But she's already aware of this, I can feel it through our bond. Voicing it aloud would only rub salt in the wound. Despite my sins, I'm not completely devoid of tact and manners.

Without going into details, she then recounts the chain of violent events that took place three years ago: the lover's murder by her hand, her fiancé's murder by the Ragebeast criminal's hand, Victor Cole's murder by her own hand. And that bloody inscription on the wall in her own room: *Sometimes, only one person is missing, and the whole world seems depopulated.*

Damn, it bothers me that she went through such a trial. And honestly, it bothers me even more to be bothered by someone else's misfortune. That's one of the main drawbacks of my mark: empathy. It's the most annoying emotion there is. This realization is almost depressing. I need to snap out of it quickly before feeling any semblance of compassion. By all the Sinners' saints, that would be abominable.

"And you think Cole called you earlier and quoted that line to you?"

She nods slightly.

"So, you're not sure you killed him, then?"

"Yes. I shredded that bastard," she asserts, her tone hardened as she clenches her fists on the sheets of her bed. "But if he made a soul pact before dying, he could have reincarnated into a new body."

"But soul pacts are strictly forbidden, honeybun," the former Magistrate refutes, shaking his head.

"And also extremely dangerous," I add, intertwining my fingers over my superbly defined abs. "They require stringent discipline and great power. They happen in two stages: the pact itself between the two parties and the transfer ritual between the old and new body. If there's the slightest hiccup in the mystical ritual, the soul of the demon who just died can disintegrate the soul of the master with whom he made the pact."

"Have you ever used this kind of pact, Wills?" the Tracker asks, staring at me.

"No. You'd have to be insane, reckless, or desperate to take such a risk. I once knew a major Sinner who tried it with his dying son. It ended very badly. One mispronounced word by the father, and both their souls self-destructed simultaneously. These pacts are very unstable and not made on a whim, Myrina. The master conducting the necromancy ritual must be extremely prepared before attempting it, especially since they're bound to the other demon until the final death of either one. In theory, the master can even transfer part of his power to the other… and influence them mentally, even control them."

"Damn, there are two of them," she murmurs to herself. "The master and the assassin, the puppeteer and the puppet. Victor Cole is probably the executioner, and there's another demon behind the pact, pulling the strings from the shadows."

"You think your serial killer is Victor Cole reincarnated in a new body?"

"Ninety-nine percent sure."

"And the other demon would be?"

"I have no idea, unfortunately. Same goes for their motive. I don't know what their criteria are for selecting victims or if there's any connection to me. But if I get my hands on that scum, Cole, the second one will follow."

I don't like this news at all. If there really are two of them, it complicates things considerably. In the end, I don't regret branding my little cat. Even if I'm not with her, I'll sleep more soundly thanks to our bond.

"That phone call you got—is there any way to trace the caller's location?" Amon asks, looking worried.

"I don't know yet, Grandpa. I'll take my phone to the CIT tomorrow, but…"

"But?"

"There might be a traitor there," she continues, casting me a sideways glance. "Is your informant trustworthy, Wills?"

"By definition, an informant isn't very trustworthy, Myrina. But he knows that if he were to cross me, he'd pay the price. He fears me and needs my money. So, I think in this situation, you can rely on him."

"Who is it?"

I smile at her. "An intern Prudling."

She returns my smile. "Thanks for the info, Wills." Her smile vanishes, and her gaze turns icy. "Now, asshole, get out of my room. As Grandpa said, you're not needed here."

Ah, the clever little bitch.

I feel used. She revealed her secrets about Victor Cole, her fiancé Owen, and her investigation just to get what she wanted: the identity of my informant. And I didn't see it coming. I should be angry, offended, or at least find this approach unpleasant… But actually, no. She's as devious as I am, and I love it.

"Good night, my little cat. I'll call you soon."

"Don't feel obliged!" Myrina and Amon exclaim in unison.

Laughing, I teleport home. Then I send a text to Sean, imagining the look on his face when he reads it tomorrow morning:

> She knows about you, my boy. I suggest you do everything she asks, or it'll be bad news for your scales.

CHAPTER 30
NEW STRATEGIES

"That laziness is one of the seven deadly sins that makes us doubt the other six."
~Robert Sabatier, The Book of Smiling Unreason

MYRINA

"Are you sure, ma'am?" I press, eyeing Sean's mother, a voluptuous Prudling in her demonic form, currently nursing her child in an old rocking chair.

The baby, Sean's little brother, looks like a plump shrimp with faded scales, retractable antennae, and tiny horns. My verdict? He's hideous.

"Yes, yes, Inspector, go ahead, upstairs! First door on the right. He'll be glad to see you. He was so bored not being able to go to work at the CIT because of his injury and… Ouch!" She winces and looks down at her little monster to scold him. "Sweetie, I've told you a thousand times not to bite Mommy's breast!"

Utterly disgusting. I congratulate myself for skipping breakfast before coming here. The demonic little creature beams up at his mom with a huge, toothy smile, his sharp teeth dripping with golden blood and bluish milk. The lady with the wounded breasts smiles back, tenderly stroking the wriggling antennae of the carnivorous little thing in her arms.

As I head toward the stairs, suppressing my nausea, I hear a monumental burp echo through the living room, followed by a high-pitched, maniacal laugh. Ugh. How can such a small creature produce such a loud noise?

Sean called in sick today. He emailed his medical leave to Zagam. Apparently, he *accidentally* cut off two fingers this morning by sticking his hand in the garbage disposal. Given the slower regeneration rate for demons of his species, the student is out of commission for now. Convenient excuse… My guess is the boy deliberately stuck his hand in the disposal to avoid running into *me* at the CIT. I'm sure Wills tipped him off that he'd spilled the beans to me about him.

I knock on the door indicated by his mother. No response from inside. Slowly, I open the door to his teenage bedroom. The intern doesn't hear me coming: he's facing away from me, sitting at his computer with headphones on. The floor is littered with stained Haitian boxers, holey white socks, and used tissues.

I glance over his head, intrigued, as I close the door behind me. Perfect timing, Myri!

With his good hand, the Virtuous is energetically masturbating, moaning in front of a hardcore Infernum porn video full of unrestrained succubus and playful tentacles. His other hand, wrapped in bandages, rests on the edge of his desk. Indeed, he's missing his index and middle fingers, but he doesn't seem to be in much pain. It's the first time in my life I've felt torn between the urge to laugh hysterically and the need to puke my guts out.

Approaching his chair, I notice he's alternating his gaze between his computer screen and his phone near the keyboard. He keeps glancing at a photo of… *me?*

In the picture, I'm crouched next to a piece of a broken wing, disheveled, with a pale face and tense features, wearing rubber gloves… not my best look. I frown, recognizing the image I thought I had deleted from *my* camera. It was from the day we met in the church where Aydan Smat the Faithfiend was found. I had ordered Sean to take pictures of the crime scene and the corpse; he had blinded me with the flash, and I had scolded him. He must have sent this photo to his own number while I was busy with something else.

Oh, the jerk. He's jerking off thinking about me. That's seriously creepy.

I abruptly yank his headphones off. He jumps three feet in the air, screaming at the top of his lungs, nearly having a heart attack.

"Oh, my god! Oh, my god!" Sean squeals, his face turning green as he clumsily stuffs his now flaccid penis back into his filthy boxers.

"Call me by my name instead," I growl, grabbing his phone and letting it fall to the floor. I stomp my boot heel on the device, shattering it. There, that's done.

"Please, don't kill me, Myrina!" the perverted intern whimpers, falling to his knees in front of me. "I'm too young to die! My mom needs me to help around the house since my dad ran off with the babysitter! And Mr. Wills made me do it!"

"Wait, he forced you to jerk off to my photo?"

"No, the… the spying and all that! He said he'd have me fired from CIT on the spot if I didn't secretly give him info, tips, and copies of documents about your investigation, and… and that I'd end up scrubbing the HQ bathrooms for the rest of my life!"

I smile inwardly. Threats and intimidation, classic Wills.

"Sean, Sean, Sean…"

He hides his head in his hands, trembling with fear and shame like a scared little herbivore. I almost feel sorry for him. If he wants to become a Tracker, he'll need to toughen up, and I'm not talking about the little thing he was handling just a minute ago.

"Sean, you pathetic little Prudling wimp, look at me."

He complies hesitantly, his tearful eyes pleading, as if saying, *I'll do anything to make it right.* Perfect. The Hybresang told me last night that Sean is scared of him, but I'm willing to bet all my savings that Sean is even more terrified of me. And rightfully so.

I grab him by the collar of his T-shirt with both hands and haul him to his feet. "Repeat after me, you idiot. You won't reveal anything to Wills behind my back."

"You… won't reveal anything to…"

I growl.

He gets it. "*I* won't reveal anything to Wills behind your back."

"Good," I approve, giving him a friendly pat on the shoulder. "I've got a job for you, geek. How would you like to be my shadow partner?"

∗∗∗

KELEN

"No, sir, I don't have any more information on Victor Cole, and we've never made a soul pact within our legion," Serena confirms as she consults our archives on her tablet.

"Can you check if it's the same in the other legions, Captain?"

She looks up at me, horrified. Sitting at my desk at HQ, I'm amusing myself by balancing a pen horizontally on the point of a pencil that's levitating vertically thanks to my telekinetic power.

"It's illegal," she whispers.

"And so?"

Serena, looking stern, steps closer to my desk and places her finger in the path of my makeshift spinning propeller. The whirling pen stops dead.

"If the other legion leaders realize we've accessed their confidential data, kiss your ambitions to become Federator of the Sinners goodbye. You could even be removed from your position as Magistrate and dragged to court by CIT," she murmurs gravely.

She's worried about me. How sweet.

"My little Ragebeast, do you really think I've reached my eminent status without ever taking risks? The goddess of luck smiles on bold Sinners, rarely on Virtuous ones who always follow the rules."

"Your Dark Eminence, why are you so keen on getting this information, exactly? I don't see how it relates to the elections," she points out suspiciously.

"Because it doesn't. I'm doing a favor for someone."

"*You?* You're doing someone a favor?"

I give a brief nod, setting my spinning pen in motion again with a mental nudge.

"In exchange for what?"

I'd love to answer with, "Probably the best lay of my life," but I won't; it'd give away it's my Tracker. By the way, why do all my close ones think I always act out of self-interest, no matter what I do?

"Who is this *someone*?" my captain inquires.

"No one," I respond lazily.

"Sir, this someone is not no one."

"Everyone is someone and no one is everyone, Serena."

"You're trying to confuse me to change the subject."

"Not at all, my dear enraged Ragebeast," I refute, adopting my incubus seducer voice. "I forgot to tell you, that beige suit really highlights your curves; you almost make me hard."

I say *almost* because I've never wanted to sleep with Serena, even though she's charming in her way. It would be like sleeping with my sister, and I'm not that twisted.

"And now you're trying to flatter me!" she accuses, squinting in my direction.

"Your scales are quite lovely in your demon form. I've noticed they seem shinier and blacker than before. Hmm, have you molted recently?"

"Sam and I have noticed you've been behaving unusually since you started hanging around a certain mixed-race warrior."

"I'm not hanging around her; I can barely tolerate her."

A slight, irritating smile spreads across Serena's lips. I darken with displeasure as she slowly nods, giving me a knowing look.

"Is it me making you smile?" I growl, on the defensive.

"Oh no, it's no one. Very well, Your Idle Malice, I'll get to work hacking into the other legions' data to see if any rogue demon has made a soul pact in recent years… to do someone a favor," she adds mischievously before turning on her heel.

Damn. All these sinful women are devils.

MYRINA

"So, what's the news?" I ask.

"According to my research, the phone number belongs to a disposable prepaid phone, integrated with a ready-to-use, non-subscription mobile that was stolen three days ago from a large supermarket in Infernum. The device was deactivated last night shortly after the call you received and was probably destroyed right after. I can't trace it or determine who it belongs to; the demon took all necessary precautions."

"Okay, Sean. Do they have surveillance cameras in that store?"

"Yes, but they don't record; they run live continuously. The security agents use them to spot thieves and troublemakers in real-time."

Damn, this lead is useless. I'm fed up, I have nothing solid to work with to make progress!

"What are we going to do now?" my Virtuous partner asks over the phone.

When I'm at a dead end, I think about my Tracker father and wonder what he would do in my situation. Arthur Holmes would refocus on the common thread between the victims to trace back to Victor Cole and his accomplice. Because there is a damn connection, I'm sure of it.

"I'll call you back," I promise before hanging up and dialing Kelen. "Wills, is this a good time?"

"No, I'm in the middle of—"

"Good. I just had an idea, but it's bold and risky."

"I already love it."

"The media, Wills."

"The media?"

"Expose the three murders to the press in an anonymous email. Bring the journalists and the public opinion into play."

"Bad publicity for the CIT, Myrina. A monstrous mess in the making. Your boss would be furious, and your murderer would be more than thrilled to be thrust into the spotlight."

"I don't give a damn about Zagam's mood. He won't know it was me who contacted the press anyway; it wouldn't be the first or the last time a case leaked. I remind you that there are still eleven victims out there waiting to be killed. If they knew Aydan, John, and Gabriel, they'd be scared realizing there's a serial killer after them and they'd come forward to the CIT."

"First, there's nothing to say. All the victims know each other. Second, what if Cole has already captured them?"

"Nothing. It's a gamble. You suggested during our meeting at 1001 Nights of Lust that he wanted to play with me, and your theory is proving true, day by day. So, I'm going to play, too."

"You're overlooking the problem of the traitor at the CIT. Imagine one of Cole's future targets calls your order to shed light on the situation: the informant will know before anyone else.

"In that case, we'll have to be faster than him. Sean can put all the CIT's phone lines under surveillance without my boss noticing, but I'll need several reliable people to listen to all incoming and outgoing calls 24/7 and filter the testimonies."

"And that's why you're calling me, right? An espionage operation where I would put a few trustworthy Ragebeasts from my legion on the job."

"Exactly."

"I can do that, but on one condition."

"Wills, I won't sleep with you," I anticipate with weariness.

"Myrina, behave yourself. I'm in a meeting with my staff and put your call on speaker."

I gape, stunned.

He bursts out laughing. "I was joking, my little cat. I'm alone in my office." His voice becomes deeper and more sensual, penetrating my skin. "What are you wearing?"

And you, asshole?

"An old plaid jumpsuit, size sixty, I lie to throw him off."

"Mm, and you're naked underneath."

"Wills, you're exhausting."

"Is your hair down?"

"No, I shaved it with clippers, completely bald."

"Completely shaved. Interesting."

I roll my eyes.

"Be nice. Just tell me what you're wearing, it's not that hard."

"A white tank top and black shorts," I reply mechanically.

"Underwear?"

"Not matching today. Black lace bra and white cotton thong."

Silence on the other end of the line. I smile; he sighs. *Serves him right.*

"You want to kill me, Myrina," he breathes, his voice hoarse with desire.

"That would suit me just fine, yes. To free me from your stupid mark."

"You're the first woman I've met who exacerbates all my sins at once."

His confession catches me off guard and piques my curiosity. I shift positions in my grandfather's chair, who is away, nestling into a corner and crossing my legs over the armrest. *Don't ask him why, dumbass*, my somewhat rude reason advises.

"Hmm, why do you say that?"

I get a strange feeling, as if I can *sense* him smiling. Must be because of the demonic link.

"When you come into my view," he admits in a low, lascivious voice, "seven parts of your body stir my vices. For example, your pretty violet eyes tickle my greed."

"I don't see the connection at all," I grumble, skeptical.

"Their color is a unique treasure that stirs my covetousness. So, I want them to look only at me, filled with a golden desire reserved for me. Never again on another man."

Pffft. Lame. I'm disappointed; I thought he'd be more inventive than that. A unique treasure—

"My sin of envy," he continues with languorous indolence, "awakens at the sight of your neck when you have your hair up. I'd love to bury my nose in that enticing little hollow and inhale your scent deeply. I'd let my lips brush against the velvet of your skin. I couldn't resist. My little cat, just thinking about it gives me a raging hard-on; I'm really very cramped in my pants."

Ah. My troubled gaze darts to the fireplace, where no fire burns. Suddenly, it's so hot in here! I consider using my Justspawn power to cool my body down a bit.

Automatically, I rub my neck under my thick mane. Indeed, I have a small dimple in the middle. He's observant, I'll give him that.

"Your thigh marked with my seal inflames my sin of pride," Kelen murmurs over the phone. "Right now, I imagine extending my claws, then violently tearing off your shorts and thong. I'd proudly gaze at my mark, so close to your wet little pussy, quivering with impatience and craving my attention. I'm sure your thigh and its twin would grip my hips tightly as I prepare to thrust very, very slowly into you…"

A painful jolt of electricity tears through my lower abdomen. I squeeze my thighs tightly, focusing on my breathing, which threatens to spiral out of control, and on my heart, which is racing in sync with the throbbing of my clitoris. I'm both exhilarated by his words and irritated that he can get me into this state just by sharing his ridiculous fantasies. Because, much to my dismay, my brain is working overtime. Not only can I vividly picture what he's describing, but I can also imagine him as he speaks. Slouched in his chair, legs spread wide, one hand on his obscene erection. His shirt sleeves rolled up to his elbows, the top buttons of his collar undone, his tie carelessly loosened, and his eyes red with lust. Licking his lips like a hungry big cat. Despite his physical absence, he exudes so much sex appeal that if I wrung out my thong, my damned arousal could fill a basin.

"Should I stop here, Myrina?" he asks after ten seconds of silence, with a hint of cynicism. "The next part is even more enlightening, but you might not be ready to hear it…

Damn tease.

"Keep making a fool of yourself, Wills."

My voice is probably lower than usual, giving me away, because he lets out a laugh.

"My sin of sloth is accentuated by your sultry chest, my little cat."

What the hell is he babbling about?

"I burn with the desire to pull up your tank top with my teeth, remove your bra, and rub my face against the swell of your breasts until my beard leaves a mark. Then I'd suck and nibble your delightful nipples one by one to make you purr and meow with pleasure. Next, I'd place my cock between your globes. I'd fuck your breasts and make sure to spray them with my cum. After licking your soiled skin clean, I'd use your feminine assets as a pair of comfortable pillows to take a little recuperative nap."

My breathing hitches. My eyes widen in indignation, my cheeks flush scarlet, my fingers tighten around my phone, and I press a hand against my chest with its hardened tips. He'd lick his own cum off me? I knew he was a pervert, but this is too much!

"Let's move on to my sin of wrath now," Kelen decrees with authority. "I associate it with your ass."

Oh, my god. Hang up, Myri. Hang up!

I can't end the call, though. My body wants to hear the rest…

Could he be hypnotizing me over the phone?

"Two tempting apples that deserve a punishment to learn what it costs to defy me all the time," he growls on the other end while I squirm in my chair, struggling with waves of intense heat that obstruct my airways. "Know that I'm an expert in spanking. I even train my Lustspawn employees at the 1001 Nights of Lust to master it perfectly for demanding clients. I dispense pain and pleasure with rare virtuosity. I have a lot of strength in my wrist and arm. I'd only need my palm smacking your sexy ass to make you cum a thousand times more powerfully than all your former lovers combined."

"Wills, I… enough, shut up, I get it!"

"I still have two sins to cover, Myrina. Gluttony and lust."

I let out an uncontrollable groan of despair. He saved the worst for last. I hate him.

"Your sweet, luscious mouth symbolizes my gluttony," he continues in a honeyed voice. "Or rather, I should say my voraciousness… It stirs a ravenous hunger in me. Because I wouldn't just taste and nibble on your sugary lips… No, I'd ravage it with my tongue as if I were fucking it with my cock."

I brush my lips with the pad of my middle finger, recalling our wonderful kiss at his place, in front of his piano. I stifle a small sigh of regret. The pressure and taste of his lips were so—

"Are you excited enough to hear the details of my final sin, Myrina?"

"N-no."

"Make an effort. I'm sure you can easily guess which part of your body corresponds to my lust."

I won't say it.

"My pussy."

Damn, I said it.

"Your pussy," he confirms in an infinitely satisfied tone, laden with a sensuality that crucifies me. "The warm, wet source where your hand is right now…"

Bullshit, what a poor excuse for a guy!

By reflex, I look down and shiver. Oh, crap. He's right. I didn't even realize it, but my naughty fingers had slid between my thighs.

Might as well leave them there since they're trapped by my legs.

Heart pounding and breath ragged, I wait for him to hit me with his ultimate fantasy, lightly rolling my hips to rub my aching clit against the edge of my hand. Is he touching himself at this moment, too? Has he unzipped his pants and wrapped his fingers around his thick cock under his desk?

"My little cat," he whispers as if confessing to me, "your pussy…"

"Mm?"

"I'll let you imagine *everything* I would do to it."

And he hangs up on me with a chuckle.

I let out a scream of rage that echoes through the entire house, as furious with him as I am with myself.

CHAPTER 31
CHANGE IN MODUS OPERANDI

"When devils will the blackest sins put on, They do suggest at first with heavenly shows." ~William Shakespeare, Othello

MYRINA

Holy shit!

Cole has clearly changed his modus operandi. If the clue at the previous crime scene was indeed the mirror, he was supposed to target a Prudling.

Except now I'm dealing with two new murders. Both Justspawns. And one of them is a celebrity.

Carl Dickens, Magistrate.

Okay, so he's also targeting Magistrates… And to successfully take one down, you have to be seriously skilled. I don't know which damn demon Cole's soul has reincarnated into, but it must be a major powerhouse who might resist hypnosis and telepathy.

I'm even starting to wonder if his host body has hybrid DNA. That would explain how he could burn Aydan Smat's heart inside his chest and wield several formidable abilities.

The other victim is being identified, but apparently, she wasn't part of Dickens's circle. She's a young female. Just an ordinary Justspawn like so many others.

I glance over my shoulder at the sound of raised voices. Zagam, scales bristling, bellows into the phone with Dickens's lieutenant, demanding explanations. Around us, about fifteen trackers flutter, securing the area and scouring the surroundings for clues—footprints in the dirt, claw marks on tree trunks, overturned rocks or broken twigs. Yeah, with a Magistrate involved, the boss has mobilized all available colleagues on the case. The investigation has become top priority for the CIT and the pressure is at its peak.

Zagam laid into me when I arrived at the scene, criticizing my inefficiency and threatening to pull me off the case if I didn't produce concrete results quickly. I took it on the chin before assuring him that I'd double down on my efforts. I didn't want to reveal to him that I suspected Victor Cole of being behind the murders because I trust no one at CIT except Sean (and to a lesser extent because he was Wills's informant!)

I'm getting paranoid with all this. I've often thought Zagam, despite being Justspawn, has the damn temper of a Ragebeast... And Cole was precisely a Ragebeast in his past life.

"Two Virtuous for the price of one," comments Malphas beside me, arms crossed. "But why this setup?"

Hm, Malphas... Braggart, idiot, harasser... What if he's playing the role of a hindrance to perfect his cover? A collector of beer bottle caps *and* morbid trophies gathered from crime scenes? Victor Cole inhabiting the body of an Pridefiend Tracker, that would be ironic! Or perhaps Malphas is the murderer's spy, hiding evidence to aid his accomplice? Could it be to get back at me because I rejected him after our utterly dismal night of sex? I can't rule anything out, not even the most eccentric theories.

"The balance is the symbol of the justice virtue among the Justspawn, idiot," I retort wearily, nodding toward the two corpses in front of us.

"Ah, smart," my colleague admits with an approving nod.

When it comes to stupidity, though, he's quite the expert!

Yes, this time we're dealing with a double hanging.

The two victims were killed on the spot, in a forest on Earth about a hundred kilometers from the city where I live. Once again, just like with Gabriel, the CIT received an anonymous call to report the murder scene.

In the middle of a small clearing bordered by ferns stands an ancient oak tree. The two Justspawns sway gently on either side of the tree, rocked by the wind, in a tableau of macabre poetry. They are suspended at the same height from two different branches, by ropes around their necks. The trunk separates them, resembling the central beam of a balance with the corpses as the scales. Below them, two overturned stools lie on the ground.

"Myrina!" Sean calls out as he approaches Dickens's strangled body to photograph it. "Come see this!"

I join my young Virtuous teammate, who seems particularly proud and excited to show me his discovery. He's a bit crazy, this kid. Following his gaze, I stiffen.

Cole must be the most diabolical son of a bitch in Infernum.

A thin transparent cord connects Dickens's right wrist to the leg of the girl's stool. And vice versa: another thread is stretched between the girl's left wrist and the leg of the Magistrate's stool. In other words—

"He wanted to force them to kill each other," I murmur, shivering.

"What do you mean by that, Myrina?" Malphas inquired over my shoulder.

"He must have promised them that he would spare the first one who pulled on the cord."

To kill or be killed, what a vile dilemma… Especially for a Virtuous Justspawn who believes in justice.

"It's not really a dilemma. I would kill without hesitation to survive." God, if only he could shut up! "But why did they both die then?"

"Well, if they had both pulled the cord at the same time, the two stools placed facing each other would have tipped forward, since the attachment is knotted at the top of the leg… But the stools were overturned backward as if the murderer had kicked them. I think both victims refused to participate in his twisted game, so he executed them one after the other."

I mentally reconstruct the scene. Under the threat of a gun or similar weapon, they climbed onto the stools and looped the slipknots around their own necks. The killer must have tightened each one before slipping the cords around their wrists and giving them the instructions for his survival game. But neither of them gave in to his atrocious blackmail. The murderer lost patience and finished them off. With the height not sufficient for a brutal fall, the victims' cervical vertebrae didn't break. Given the position of the rope around the neck, the facial edema, and cyanotic complexion, death was caused by progressive asphyxiation from the compression of the carotid arteries. I hope the two Virtuous quickly lost consciousness, but one thing is certain: the actual strangulation lasted several minutes. They must have struggled, convulsed, and passed out before dying.

I order some hefty Trackers to take down the Justspawn corpses so I can examine them more closely. My colleagues cut the ropes and lay the bodies side by side on the ground. Bodily injuries, multiple cuts, fractured ribs… They were both beaten before they died. Unfortunately, I don't find any tiny scale fragments under the victims' claws, and their fists aren't bruised, which would have indicated that they struck their attacker.

If this is how it happened, Cole wasn't alone. He must have been working with an accomplice. The two victims, conscious before their execution, would have tried to resist and fight if he hadn't been supported by someone else. One threatened with a ranged weapon, the other handled the operation in a concrete manner.

And this time (with a small reservation to be confirmed after the autopsy), no trophy was taken, and no clue points to the next victim.

In short, all this supports the idea that they've changed their modus operandi. Why kill two Justspawns and not a Prudling as the previous crime suggested?

What happened between this double murder and Gabriel's?

Damn, wait a minute.

Cole called me in between!

Could he and his accomplice be at odds?

What if his demon master wasn't aware of his phone call? After learning that Cole contacted me, he could have decided to speed things up and disrupt his original plan. Impulsively, Cole might have taken the initiative to call me and taunt me without consulting him, and as a result, the other adjusted his plan to better throw me off the scent.

Another unverifiable hypothesis at this time. However, my instinct tells me I'm getting warmer. I feel like I'm getting closer and closer to the truth.

By trying to act differently than before, they're starting to make small mistakes…

I don't need much more to corner them.

Deep down, I know it. Not where, not when, not how… But I'll get them.

As I'm thinking this, several demons in human form burst into the clearing. Excited journalists, cameras and microphones in hand. The cavalry.

They got my anonymous message. The investigation is going public.

Zagam starts barking orders, gesturing wildly, furious. Trackers intercept the journalists to prevent them from entering the crime scene and filming. But it's too late; they weren't quick enough. The hanging bodies of Magistrate Dickens and the female Justspawn are already on tape.

Some will see it as a political murder since Dickens was a candidate in the Virtuous Federators election. There will likely be various interpretations in the media, given that my boss won't comment.

I exchange a knowing look with Sean, who is aware of my schemes, and return his smile.

I can only hope my gamble pays off.

KELEN

"Myrina."

"Wills, you again?" She sighs over the phone.

I'd rather make her sigh with pleasure than with annoyance, but a reaction is a reaction.

"Hide your excitement. I'm probably going to need close protection, my little kitten."

"Do you have news for me? Has Cole attacked you?" she asks with a hint of hope that dismays me.

"No, but your killer is targeting the Magistrates, and I'm defenseless. I'm offering you 10,000 Forks per week to be my personal bodyguard day and night. Room and board on me, bonuses in kind, weapons provided. I'll reserve a room in my home for you and buy you a fitted leather uniform with my emblem embroidered on the chest. You're a size ten, right?"

"You have thousands of Ragebeasts ready to defend you tooth and nail," she retorts, not appreciating the generosity of my offer.

"Dickens also had thousands of Justspawns ready to defend him. I received a death threat letter in the mail today, believe it or not."

"From whom?"

"No idea. I get dozens every week; I make paper planes out of them."

"Be serious! You're the last demon in Infernum who needs protection. I'm not worried about you. So, the surveillance of CIT calls?"

"The lines are swamped with questionable testimonies that give little away. However, I have another piece of information that might interest you regarding a soul pact, but I won't talk about it over the phone. May I come over?" I ask politely.

"No, I'm training at my grandfather's, and he doesn't want to see you anymore."

Exit the irascible grandfather. I imagine my little hybrid skipping rope, all shiny with sweat, her chest bouncing with each movement, her firm buttocks molded into micro shorts. Am I having inappropriate thoughts? Well, it's only natural, considering I'm a Sinner.

"Wills, you're fantasizing," she finally growls as the silence stretches on.

A smile tugs at my lips. She's starting to know me well.

"I'm shooting my crossbow, you perv. Want to know what target I picked? A photo of you."

Adorable. She's crazy about me.

"The one from *Playdemon* last month, where I'm lounging naked by a lava pool?"

"What? Y-you posed for an adult magazine?" she stammers.

Never in my life. I have my dignity.

"Page sixty-nine. No photo edits, all natural. I give you permission to hang this masterpiece in your room so you can look at it every time you masturbate."

"You're impossible. Sometimes I wish I were completely deaf so I wouldn't have to hear your nonsense."

She doesn't deny it. I'm sure she's already thinking about me while touching herself. Anyway, she doesn't have many options to relieve herself sexually, with my mark. If she tries to sleep with another man, demon or human, she'll experience such intense brain pain that she'll pass out. But she hasn't tried this physical discomfort yet. I would know if she had.

Let's get back to our demons. Will she take the bait regarding my information?

"Where and when are we meeting, Myrina?"

"In a public place not frequented by demons. On Earth. In two hours. It's chaos in Infernum, and journalists are sticking to me like glue because of the investigation. Some are even camped outside Grandpa's house. I don't want us to be followed."

And she probably doesn't want us to be alone together, if I'm reading between the lines correctly. She must be afraid of jumping on me if we were in a more intimate setting. At the same time, given my physique, I can't blame her. If I were her, I wouldn't resist myself either. Especially since I really turned her on the last time on the phone; she must have been hot as a firecracker.

"A bar, maybe?"

"Okay, but not where I live. I have a place in mind in the next town over, I'll send you the address by text. There aren't many demons around there, so we'll be able to talk peacefully."

Tsss, talk, always talk… Myrina Holmes, a little less talking and a bit more blow jobs!

"You do realize that I wouldn't make the concession of mingling with humans for anyone else but you, my little kitten," I emphasize, hoping she'll thank or compliment me.

No such luck. She hangs up on me. As usual.

All right, now an existential question…

What am I going to wear for our date?

CHAPTER 32
A NOT ROMANTIC DATE

"Greed is the punishment of the rich."
~Oriental proverb

MYRINA

"Grandpa, I'm heading out!" I call over my shoulder, slipping on my jacket in the living room.

Huddled in his antique Louis XV-style armchair by the fireplace with a glass of Dragon's Bile in hand, my grandfather doesn't respond. It's unlike him not to ask questions.

"Grandpa?" I approach him. His vacant, fixed gaze is lost in the contemplation of the flames. In my humble opinion, the murder of Dickens, who was his second in command when he was Magistrate and succeeded him about a century ago, has dealt a heavy blow to his spirits. They hadn't seen each other at all in recent years for reasons unknown to me, but Amon and he were once friends.

"Hey," I call softly, gently placing my hand on his shoulder."Are you okay?"

He tears himself away from his vision to look at me with a distant gaze. For heaven's sake, I hope he doesn't fall into depression… Sometimes, he worries me. He dwells far too much on the past, brooding over everything that happened with my parents.

"I'm sorry about Carl, Grandpa."

He gives a slight shrug. "Don't be sorry for him, honeybun. It was bound to happen sooner or later; he offended to many people. He was a real piece of trash. That's why I cut ties with him. He gradually let himself be corrupted by power. Even though he didn't deserve such a violent death, I'm not particularly surprised he ended up in such a tragic manner."

Ah, that partly explains why the murderer targeted that Justspawn. He was a corrupt Virtuous politician.

"He wasn't corrupt in the end," I point out. "He could have killed the girl to save his own skin, but he didn't. Yet, he had grievances against her."

We identified the Justspawn female. She was actually Dickens's ex-lover. They had an adulterous affair, but she spilled everything to the press, causing the Magistrate's divorce scandal. Let's just say the last two of Cole's victims weren't on good terms with each other.

"One act of kindness doesn't erase hundreds of harmful acts," mutters Amon. "In some ways, Dickens wasn't much better than a Sinner. Where are you going?"

"For a drink."

"With whom?"

"A guy you don't know."

"Myrina Holmes, don't lie to me. I heard you talking to Kelen Wills on the phone in the training room," he retorts sharply.

"Don't jump to conclusions; it's a professional meeting."

"Your attraction to that demon baffles me. Wills is the complete opposite of Owen."

"You're getting on my nerves, Grandpa. Why do you care about what I do with my life?" I retort, stung.

"Your father isn't here anymore to watch over you, Myrina. It's up to me to take care of you when you stray down the wrong path."

"First of all, you're being dramatic. And secondly, I didn't ask for your opinion."

"Don't get attached to him and don't let his mark blind your judgment, Myrina. He will cause you pain. That's all he's good for: spreading evil around him."

I know, thanks for the useless moral lesson.

"I have to go. See you later, Grandpa."

As I walk away, I feel his critical gaze on my neck, and I realize

I'm almost relieved to be leaving this house… even though the idea of enduring the lewd insinuations of the Hybresang is as pleasant as a hemorrhoid flare-up.

***

Back on Earth, I pass through the underground garage of my building and hop on my motorcycle to head to the neighboring town. There's no Arcadus near the bar where we're meeting, but that's fine because I felt like riding my bike. The rush of speed and freedom is so exhilarating!

Around eleven-thirty PM, after a half-hour ride, I turn off at a slow intersection and pull into the parking lot of the human bar I indicated to Wills. I had a drink there with Ondine a year ago during a shopping spree. The facade isn't much, but the interior is nice. Taking off my motorcycle helmet, I look up at the green neon lights that make up the establishment's name.

O'Brien's. An Irish pub.

I walk in. It's not very crowded tonight, maybe three or four customers at most. Good. I recognize the warm, rustic decor that hasn't changed since my last visit. Wooden paneling, stained glass lamps, paintings depicting wild and lush Irish landscapes, a solid oak bar that stretches sixteen feet long, and an old traditional billiard table. Ambient music fills the speakers on the walls: "Rocky Road to Dublin" by The Dubliners.

I spot Kelen at the back of the room. He's playing billiards, waiting for me. I'm a few minutes early, yet it's surprising he's already here. He hasn't seen me yet. I watch him lean forward over the table, focused with his cue stick in his hands. His dark hair is tousled as usual. He's dressed in black jeans and a vibrant royal blue shirt that accentuates his tan complexion and muscular build. I sigh. He's really attractive, that jerk. He embodies raw temptation. Humans probably don't hesitate to make pacts with him upon meeting this man of unreal beauty. He reminds me of a dark star drawing his targets in like a magnet, luring them into the abyss of his perversion. A splendid mirage destined to corrupt and defile. I'm probably the only woman who has ever managed to resist him in thirteen centuries of existence.

His black ball strikes two yellow balls powerfully, each landing in a pocket before bouncing off the edge and falling in, too. A bit of telekinetic help, perhaps… Judging by his self-satisfied look, it's his first time playing billiards. *This idiot Sinner didn't understand the rules at all.*

I approach. While polishing the tip of his cue with a small piece of blue chalk, the demon turns toward me, undressing me with his eyes, a sly smirk on his face. And here we go again… He hasn't even spoken yet, and he's already getting on my nerves.

"If you sink the black ball, you lose, Wills."

"In that case, teach me how to put the right balls in the right holes, my little cat."

Lord. I should have smoked a joint to relax before facing this evening.

"I'm not here to play billiards."

"Shame, I would have gladly lent you my cue. Look how beautiful and stiff it is, just waiting for your delicate touch. I'm sure you'd handle it better than me," he says smoothly.

"Forget it, I'm too clumsy; I might snap it in half."

"You're in a bad mood. More than usual, I mean."

"I guess you've noticed that my mood always matches your despicable company."

"Agent Holmes, you're turning me on again. Not the place or the time."

"Go fuck yourself."

"I've also noticed you have a language OCD. You tend to tell me to go fuck myself when you're out of clever comebacks."

I open my mouth, indignant. But seriously, go fuck himself!

With a fierce glare, I sit down on a nearby bench. Kelen puts away his cue and takes a seat opposite me. Without breaking eye contact, he slowly unbuttons his shirt collar, then his cufflinks, rolling up his sleeves one by one. And he dares to claim that I'm the one turning him on?

"This place is even worse than I feared," comments Wills, sweeping a disdainful glance across the common room that sets my teeth on edge. "The owner has no taste for matching colors and materials. It feels like we're in the tavern of some village of congenital bumpkins lost in the depths of Connemara."

"I prefer it a thousand times over the 1001 Nights of Lust."

"Don't compare my club to this human dump, it's insulting."

"Aren't you tired of being a complete asshole, Wills?"

He flashes me a radiant smile. I don't know why, but every time I call him an asshole, he seems to relish it as if I've paid him the greatest compliment. I bet if I said something nice to him, he'd get offended. I'll have to test that out one of these days.

"Welcome, guys!" chirps a cheerful female voice. "What can I get you?"

Kelen and I turn our heads toward the overly cheerful waitress wearing a black top printed with a four-leaf clover and the pub's name. Well, she certainly doesn't have a typical look. Neck, arms, and legs adorned with colorful tattoos, long red hair with red-tipped ends, large green eyes framed with black eyeshadow, and a milky complexion. A striking beauty in her own right. A *girl next door* version of a curvy pin-up.

I notice Wills scanning the human waitress up and down with a lascivious eye, lingering on her ample chest and olive-colored skirt that reveals her tattooed legs. By Cerberus' name, what a bastard. I don't know if he behaves like this because he can't help himself or just to annoy me, but… I suddenly feel like breaking the billiard cue over his womanizing ass.

"It depends, darling, are you on the menu?" Kelen replies smoothly, deploying his full arsenal of charm.

To my surprise, the girl isn't affected by his pheromones. There's only one possible explanation for a human resisting Lustspawn's pheromones: she's hopelessly in love with someone else. Her friendly smile melts away, and her delicate eyebrows furrow. She casts a stormy gaze down at the Magistrate.

I actually quite like her.

"I beg your pardon, sir?" she says, narrowing her eyes at him.

"Are you deaf, too?" he retorts casually. "I asked if—"

"No, I'm not on the menu," she cuts him off curtly. "And if you don't want me to kick your misogynistic ass out of O'Brien's, I suggest you keep those inappropriate remarks to yourself in the future, for fuck's sake."

Oh, she's got wit and character, this little redhead! Smarting in his pride, Kelen shoots the girl an angry glare, then turns to me as I burst out laughing without restraint.

"So, is your fucking order for tomorrow?" the waitress continues, her tone colder than a freezer.

"A Guinness for me, please," I say with amusement.

"Noted, miss. And for you, Discount Casanova?"

"Absinthe," he states coldly.

"We don't serve absinthe here," she snaps, tapping the menu in front of him with her index finger. "Everything we offer is spelled out clearly. Besides not understanding the rules of billiards, are you illiterate, too?"

A flash of murderous anger gleams in my reluctant partner's eyes; his irises are on the verge of turning blood red. I clear my throat sharply to remind him to keep his cool with the bartender.

"Irish coffee," grumbles Kelen, visibly making a considerable effort not to explode.

"There you go, see? It wasn't that hard!" She turns to me. "Good luck."

"Thanks, I'll need it," I reply with a slight conspiratorial smile.

The redhead returns my smile, then scrutinizes Kelen up and down with a caustic expression. "By the way, sir, your fly has been open for a good ten minutes."

With that, she retreats behind her bar while I fight to stifle my laughter.

Grumpily, Wills squirms and grumbles on the bench, trying to zip up his pants under the table. "She can dream on if she expects a tip, that vulgar bitch," he grumbles in the language of demon.

"Well, I'll leave her a generous one just for standing up to you," I tease him in the same dialect.

And if she spits in his drink, she'll get a double tip.

"That stupid human wouldn't have done it if she knew who I was. She would've wet herself."

"Yeah right, *Discount Casanova*. So, I'm getting impatient, what about this soul pact?"

He gazes at me in silence, figuring out how to broach the subject. Oh boy, I don't like where this is going.

"My captain, Serena, combed through the pact archives of other legions over the past decade," he begins, clasping his hands on the table before him. "She didn't find any soul pacts."

"What? You're telling me you made me come here for nothing?"

"Let me finish, Myrina. It's possible that the pact between Cole and his master was sealed orally to leave no written trace. You know what that means, my little cat? Such pacts can only be made by Magistrates. Your latest victim, Dickens, was a candidate in the Virtuous Federators elections. He only had two rivals: Remington the Braveryfiend, who's still alive, and the other Faithfiend Magistrate Azath, killed in the Rebels' attack. As a result, Archibald Remington will be appointed Federator by default: there won't be any elections among the Virtuous Magistrates."

His words leave me skeptical.

"Are you suggesting that Remington is behind all these murders *and* leading the Rebels' uprising? That doesn't make sense! Why kill his two rivals in different ways? Especially since he's been leading the polls for weeks. It doesn't add up, Wills. The Rebels wanted to eliminate as many Magistrates as possible; they didn't have a specific target. And Remington wouldn't have any reason to kill Hallow either."

"My little cat, just imagine the scenario where thirteen Magistrates are assassinated one after the other in various circumstances that initially seem unrelated... Soon, Remington would be the only one left in power in Infernum, with no one left to challenge his all-powerful legitimacy."

"A political conspiracy would be too massive, Wills. I don't believe it. And how do you explain the choice of the other victims? Aydan, John, Gabriel, and Amanda, Dickens's former mistress?"

"Those victims are just there to muddy the waters and confuse the CIT. Purely random, in the end. Archibald Remington orchestrates these little murders to cover himself; Victor Cole carries them out."

"No. There's a real connection between them. I'm certain of it. Aydan and John knew each other, just like Dickens and his ex-Justspawn. I read the woman's testimony in a gossip magazine when she revealed their affair to the public. She said she met the Justspawn Magistrate at the Magistrates' Palace during a judicial case where she was a jury member, and he was a judge."

"What case was that?"

"It wasn't specified in the article. Sean searched through the CIT data, but it's a confidential state matter accessible only to Magistrates. Could you maybe take a look for me?"

"You're scattering yourself and wasting your time. Knowing that information won't bring you anything more."

"When I was little, my father used to say that good Trackers explore all leads, even those that seem insignificant. The more meticulous you are, the more likely you are to find a crucial clue."

"I'm taking great risks for you, Myrina, and I'm not entitled to any compensation."

Spontaneously, I place my hands on his. Kelen watches me attentively, his head slightly tilted to the side.

"I feel like I could learn to appreciate you a bit more if I didn't have this mark. You have countless flaws, but I think over time, I'll manage to put them into perspective. You still have two or three qualities—"

"Which ones? Tell me."

Damn, he's got me! I rack my brains. If I tell him he's built like an Adonis or that he gives top-notch oral, he'll get cocky. If I say he plays the piano really well, that's off-topic.

"You managed to take in and not kill that waitress. I'm impressed, I swear."

Chuckling, the Magistrate gently tightens his fingers around mine. "My little cat, when you try to manipulate the king of manipulators, be believable," he murmurs, bringing my hands to his mouth to kiss them slowly, causing a double sensation of tingling in my stomach and a burning wave between my thighs.

Just as the redheaded waitress returns with our order on a tray, I quickly withdraw my fingers from Kelen's. She gives me my beer with a friendly smile and clumsily places the Irish coffee near Wills's arm, splashing his nice shirt with drops of whiskey, making him curse under his breath. Without flinching, the girl pulls the bill from her skirt pocket and places it in front of him. He furrows his brow as he reads the amount written.

"What? Thirty euros for two drinks? That's robbery!"

"I'm applying the special asshole rate," she argues before walking away.

"These damn humans, they should be on the verge of extinction," he hisses in our language. He digs a hand into his pocket, fumbles for a moment, then gives me a falsely complacent smile. "Myrina, I'm sorry. I forgot my wallet; you'll have to pay the bill. Let's say it'll cover the umpteenth favor I'm going to do for you."

Damn Hybresang. I thought I'd never collect on his avarice sin, but I was royally wrong.

CHAPTER 33
THE VIRTUE OF JUSTICE

"Justice is the mistress and queen of all virtues; it shines with admirable brilliance; it is from it that men of virtue derive their true name." ~Ambroise Rendu, The Treatise on Morality

UNKNOWN DEMON

I spy on them from a distance in the parking lot of the Irish pub. None of them have noticed my presence, of course. Thanks to my powers that allow me to approach my victims discreetly, no one ever notices me.

Outside the door, Myrina brings a cigarette to her mouth. Kelen Wills says something to her and touches the end of the cigarette with his fingertip, causing a tiny flame to burst from his skin. She takes a drag, nodding in thanks before exhaling a swirling cloud of smoke into the air.

He walks her to her motorcycle. She zips up her jacket while talking to him, the cigarette dangling from her lips. I watch them, concealed in my cloak of darkness. Physically, the Tracker has hardly changed. Her hair is a bit shorter, her body slightly thinner, but she's still as beautiful as ever. The possessive way he looks at her annoys me. She belongs to me, not to him. When I think that he marked her with his seal, it makes me want to shred him even more with my claws.

I'll soon have the opportunity. I'm just waiting for *his* approval now.

After two minutes, Myrina flicks her cigarette to the ground. She grumbles as Wills takes the helmet from her hands and playfully shoves it onto her head. With a delicate gesture, he fastens the strap under her chin, his fingers brushing against her throat. She shivers, fluttering her eyelashes. Her violet eyes shine far too brightly for my liking.

Oh, yes, I will savor every nuance of the Hybresang's pain.

She abruptly lowers the visor of her helmet as if to create a barrier between her and him. Then she swings her leg over the saddle of her motorcycle, starts the engine with its headlights on, kicks up the stand with her boot, and drives off after giving the Sinner a final glance over her shoulder. Hands in his pockets, Wills remains standing in place for several seconds after she disappears, staring thoughtfully at the spot where she vanished.

I could transform and attack him now, catching him by surprise. It's tempting. I would love to see his black blood pooling on the ground. But I must stick to the plan we've prepared, no matter what. I can't afford the slightest mistake anymore.

Wills turns in my direction, his body tensed. His perplexed gaze scans the parking lot as if he sensed something. But he can't see me. His vigilant eyes don't stop on me. He shakes his head slightly and teleports home, I suppose.

I walk to the spot where they were both standing and crouch down to pick up the Tracker's cigarette butt. A trace of coral gloss stains the white paper. I inhale the stick, closing my eyes. My heart palpitations increase.

Myrina Holmes. My greatest sin. My most tenacious obsession. My sharpest pain.

For three years, I've been preparing for this moment in the shadows. Three years of waiting, training, enduring these violent memories that torment me. Several times, I've almost succumbed to madness, overwhelmed by all this power tearing me apart from within. But tonight, I'm more lucid and determined than ever to see our plans through to the end.

Only one person is missing, and the whole world seems depopulated.

Soon.

I grab my phone and dial the familiar number.

"They've just gone their separate ways," I inform in a low voice.

"What did he say to her?"

"He suspects Remington is the pact master. She doesn't. She's close to the truth and asked him to research the trial. When he reads the file, he'll understand everything."

A grim silence at the other end of the line.

"Then, we must act tonight; it's time. You know what you have to do."

I smile as I hang up.

Finally.

I can't wait to kill Kelen Wills and present my new trophy to Myrina. I think I'll bring her his head wrapped in gift paper to celebrate our reunion.

And undoubtedly, I'll keep his balls as a souvenir to add to my impressive collection.

KELEN

In front of my computer screen, alone at home, I read through the trial report Myrina mentioned at the pub, munching on barbecue chicken wings.

Boring. Boring. Boring.

As I start the second paragraph filled with numerous names, I nearly choke on my bite. I cough, pounding my chest with my fist, spit a small chicken bone onto my desk, and reread the lines causing my distress.

Damn. Damn. Damn!

This can't be true!

Just a half-hour ago at the Irish pub, Myrina claimed, *"When I was little, my father used to say that good Trackers explore all leads, even those that seem insignificant. The more meticulous you are, the more likely you are to find a crucial clue."*

Unable to continue reading, I jerk myself out of my chair,

fists clenched in my hair. After pacing in circles for a few seconds to regain my lost composure, I return to read the rest of the file, somewhat jittery.

"There's a real connection between them. I'm certain of it."

The connection she mentioned is right in front of me.

There aren't just fourteen names in the paragraph.

There are sixteen.

And among those sixteen names, six of them jump out at me.

Aydan Smat, jury member of Faithfiend.

John Blane, jury member of Charityfiend.

Gabriel Bariballarik, jury member of Pridefiend.

Amanda Woods, jury member of Justspawn.

Carl Dickens, Judge of Justspawn.

Beliale, Judge of Lustspawn.

Next paragraph.

Crime. High treason against Infernum.

Accused. Two names.

Lysippé and Arthur Holmes.

Sentence…

Double execution.

Just as I'm about to teleport to Amon, I sense a threatening presence behind me.

I don't need to see him to guess who it is.

Victor Cole.

✱✱✱

MYRINA, FIVE MINUTES EARLIER

"I'm glad you're back, honeybun," Grandpa says from his armchair where he hasn't moved since I left. "I was afraid you'd spend the night with him."

"You shouldn't have waited for me," I grumble.

He stands and turns toward me, his silver eyes showing deep sadness. He holds tightly to the frame containing the photo of my father pushing me on the swing. God, he breaks my heart. I'm exhausted and dreaming of going to bed, but I can't leave him like this.

"Honeybun, we need to talk," he says in a somber tone. "I've put off this moment for years to protect you, but it can't wait any longer. You need to hear the truth, however painful it may be. Sit down, my child."

My heart races. He's really freaking me out now.

"The… the truth?" I repeat hesitantly.

"About your parents and what happened fourteen years ago," he says, placing the frame back on the seat of his chair.

I remain standing, silent, tense, waiting, arms crossed over my chest. I have no desire to sit down.

My gut tells me something, but I can't believe it.

Or rather, I don't want to believe it.

My grandfather stands before me, his gaze full of bitterness locked with mine. "It was I who kept your father's double life on Earth hidden, Myrina. I knew about his secret love affair. I disapproved, of course. I tried more than once to convince my son to end the madness. He wouldn't listen; he was bewitched by your succubus of a mother."

My jaw clenches so hard I feel like I could break my teeth.

Amon gives me a faint smile. "When Arthur told me Lysippé had just given birth to a mixed-race child who wasn't a Soulless, I resigned myself to the situation and helped them as best I could. You were a little miracle of nature, after all… He worked at CIT during the day and sneaked back to see both of you on Earth in the evening. I couldn't even visit you. I so wanted to see you grow up and get to know you before you turned ten, but I didn't want to risk you all being discovered.

"Unfortunately, my worst fears came true. The Justspawn Magistrate Carl Dickens was my friend at the time, or so I thought. One evening, when he came to dinner at our house, he stumbled upon that photo your father had given me. I had forgotten to put it away before his visit. I blamed myself so much! Because my forgetfulness had very serious consequences, Myrina. A girl with hair like yours doesn't go unnoticed; it raised his suspicions.

"Dickens hired a demon detective to investigate. And that man found you on Earth, unfortunately. My Virtuous son in a relationship with a Sinner, father of a uniquely hybrid child: Dickens couldn't believe it. Out of *friendship* and *respect* for me, as he put it, my former lieutenant didn't want to expose me or involve me in the affair. So, he concealed my involvement from the judicial authorities. That was his only concession."

I uncross my arms, blinking rapidly as I grasp the weight of his final words. "What do you mean, his only concession?" I ask.

Amon lets out a long sigh that swells in his chest. Meanwhile, my breathing becomes irregular.

"The verdict was decided in advance between the two uncompromising Magistrates who served as judges, my dear. Dickens and Beliale never intended to decree your parents' exile. They interpreted Infernum's ancient laws to suit their own agenda. They bribed all the jurors for that purpose so the sentence would be unanimously voted upon. Even the Virtuous, who preached integrity and righteousness, shamefully allowed themselves to be influenced.

"It turns out my phone call during the trial was completely futile. The demons involved didn't want this affair to leak out, knowing they would face public outrage. So, they twisted the truth, claiming your parents had been sent to the Limbo like other criminals before them. Only those sixteen knew the truth. I only found out months later from one of the Virtuous jury members who, stricken with remorse, confessed everything to me behind their backs. Through my telepathy, I read all the other juror's names involved in this elaborate bloody hoax. They tricked us. They lied to cover their crimes. Myrina, your parents have been dead for fourteen years."

I take a step back, stunned as if I've just been punched in the face.

I stammer in an unrecognizable voice, "N-no… no… you're wrong…"

"You can't imagine how sorry I am," he laments, taking me by the shoulders. "I wanted to tell you the whole truth, but you were so young, so sensitive… I only thought of protecting you. I waited for you to grow older and stronger emotionally to handle the shock of this news. But just as I was about to tell you, you faced another ordeal: Owen, your beloved, murdered by Cole. So, I postponed it again, waiting for you to rebuild yourself."

A moment before he pulls me close, I glimpse the fierce gleam that ignites in the depths of his eyes, but I'm so overwhelmed that I don't grasp its meaning. Tears stream down my cheeks, and I let out a mournful whimper, limp like a ragdoll against his chest. The moral pain paralyzes me.

Then my own words echo ominously in my liquefied mind, *"Aydan and John knew each other, just like Dickens and his ex-Justspawn. I read the woman's testimony in a scandal magazine when she exposed their affair to the public. She said she met the Justspawn Magistrate at the Magistrates' Palace during a trial where she was a jury member, and he was a judge."*

My parents' trial.

And *finally*, it hits me.

"G-grandpa, what… what have you done?"

His thick arms tighten around me in a steely grip. I tremble. I gasp for air. I suffocate.

An indescribable terror engulfs me.

"When the virtue of Justice itself is tainted by vice, there's only one solution left," he decrees with a hardened voice that sends chills down my spine. "Revenge."

Before I can even struggle, I feel a needle pierce my neck and inject a substance. My vision blurs, my legs wobble, my stomach churns. Reflexively, despite the repulsion and horror flooding over me, I cling to Amon's sweater.

No! No! screams a panicked voice in my head as my body stops responding.

"Don't worry, honeybun," he whispers in my ear, gently stroking my hair. "Everything will be fine. It's just a sedative I obtained from the CIT by using a fake copy of your Tracker badge. Now you, too, are ready to commit to this noble cause and punish the real criminals. You'll be able to settle scores with those who took your parents from us. We'll mete out justice in our own way, as a family. This revenge is as much mine as it is yours, my sweet girl."

Devastated, I begin to lose consciousness in the arms of the demon who'd orchestrated all these murders and forged a soul pact with the instrument of his vengeance.

My own grandfather.

CHAPTER 34

A FORMIDABLE ADVERSARY

"The corruption of what is best is the worst." ~Latin maxim

KELEN

I throw myself flat on the ground to dodge the intruder's blow, roll onto my back at full speed, and deliver a powerful kick… into thin air.

Where the hell is that bastard?

Something lifts me powerfully off the ground and hurls me against the ceiling. My back absorbs the impact harshly, cracking like a wooden plank. I crash back down on my hardwood floor amid a shower of debris. On all fours, I shake myself off with a growl. This method would be more effective than a chiropractor!

"I'm still the leader of your legion, and I don't appreciate this kind of insubordination directed at me, Cole!" I thunder in an aggressive tone.

A chuckle reaches me from a corner of my living room. My narrowed eyes dart toward the sound. Just as I suspected. This low-grade psychopath is capable of turning invisible like the Virtuous Prudlings *and* masking his body odor. So, he's reincarnated as a demon of Prudence. A major one, since I can't read his thoughts with my telepathy. He was spying on us in the Irish pub's parking lot. I had sensed a strange presence at the time. My warrior instinct was right. Regardless, Prudlings can't remain invisible indefinitely; this primary power drains too much energy from them. He won't be long before reappearing, and I'll enjoy massacring him.

But first, the crux of the matter: mutation.

"You'll appreciate even less what I'm going to do to you next, Wills," retorts a sardonic, cavernous voice about six feet away from me as I transform.

He wants to play soldier in demonic form, apparently. Otherwise, he would have attacked me again by now. If this presumptuous Ragebeast locked in the body of a lowly Prudling truly thinks he can defeat a Hybresang Sinner, he's sorely mistaken. He poorly carries the name of the prudence virtue characterizing his new form.

"Approach," I murmur, on high alert.

A projectile the size of a fist suddenly surges from my right. I spread my wing in front of my face to shield myself, but my feathers begin to freeze in a dark vapor. A sharp pain shoots through my nerves.

By Satan, Prudlings can't do *this*! I immediately raise my temperature to melt the black ice. My scales and feathers glow red, emanating heat. I shake my damp wing, scattering steaming droplets on the ground.

He possesses a Justspawn power, like Myrina.

I cringe. Something's not right.

"What are you, exactly?" I bark, glaring furiously around me. "Show yourself, you coward! Unless you're afraid to face me?"

A demonic silhouette as hefty as mine takes shape before me. Its silver scales shimmer under the lamp light. Its massive gray wings beat at its sides. Spikes protrude from its muscular arms and swaying tail. Its horns brush against the ceiling.

I'm rarely surprised. In over thirteen hundred years of life, I've seen many incredible and dreadful things.

But I've never seen a creature like this…

…except in the reflection of my mirror. My scarlet eyes widen at a much lighter version of myself. Its silver eyes fill with an ironic gleam. I'm about to fight a Virtuous Hybresang.

***

MYRINA

I slowly emerge from unconsciousness, senses dulled by the sedative, mouth dry, stomach queasy, heart pounding against my rib cage.

Amon. How could I have screwed up so badly and gotten it so wrong?

A muffled scream chills my blood. It's not coming from me.

I jerk my head up so fast I feel dizzy. A slender figure squirms in the back of the room near the wall. There are three other people, inert and unconscious. Four prisoners, bound and gagged, hang suspended from the ceiling by silver chains binding their wrists. Their feet don't touch the ground, their arms are raised above their heads. They're too far away for me to identify their demon race by smell. Anyway, it wouldn't change anything.

Four jury members from my parents' trial, likely drugged beforehand. The only one who's already awake, a young brunette woman, wriggles about wildly, emitting small squeals of terror behind the gag tied over her mouth.

They were all kidnapped at the same time by my grandfather and his accomplice. That means there are seven demons left to *punish*. Including Beliale the Lustspawn Magistrate, who isn't here.

I shift a leg to try to get up. Metallic scraping on the concrete floor. I'm a captive, too. A long chain, about six feet long—give or take—connects the wall to my ankle.

I survey the surroundings and recognize the place. We're still on Infernum, in Arcadus's abandoned factory where Gabriel the Pridefiend's corpse was found. An isolated location. The Trackers have no reason to return to the crime scene, which has been thoroughly searched and cleaned for days.

No sign of Amon anywhere.

One foot against the wall, I lean backward, pulling desperately on the chain, straining to rip it from its ring. With no success, I only exhaust myself. I don't have enough strength yet to break it or to transform. Amon injected me with quite a dose designed to neutralize my powers. Maybe in a few minutes, if I'm lucky? I've never experienced the sedative they administer to CIT criminals myself, of course. I don't know if its effects will be as intense on me as on other demons. I remember Wills regained his abilities very quickly at the 1001 Nights of Lust during my interrogation, but I'm not a Hybresang, so… I have no certainty about myself. In any case, I need to think and buy some time. And the other woman, who seems to be having a panic attack and is sobbing more and more, isn't helping me focus.

"Hey, back there, calm down. What you're doing is pointless except for wasting your energy," I advise calmly, though inwardly, I'm as stressed as she is.

She suddenly stirs less and looks at me with distress, breathing heavily behind her gag. Yes, I know, sweetheart. This situation is *slightly* trying. This damn creepy scene reminds me of the horror movie *Saw*.

Leaning on the dark wall, I rise on shaky legs.

I don't even want to dwell on my parents' death. Otherwise, I might let myself be overwhelmed by grief and end up lying prostrate on the floor, shedding all the tears of my body like a little girl. If I start pitying their fate and completely surrender to the pain gnawing at my heart, I'm done for.

I must stay in Tracker mode at all costs.

At that moment, my grandfather teleports into the middle of the room, crossbow in one hand… and four bolts in the other.

Not one more. Not one less.

One per prisoner, I deduce with a great shiver of apprehension.

"Finally awake, honeybun," he says in a neutral tone.

I hide the disgust and anger he inspires in me. He can go to hell if he thinks I'm going to do his dirty work! But if I can convince him to hand over the crossbow, I could target *him* instead. I absolutely must buy time and make him talk while I regain my demonic strength. Without losing my self-control, preferably… and making him believe I'm going to join his cause.

"Yeah, thanks for the nap, Grandpa, I really needed it. What have you done with the other demons?" I ask, eyeing the prisoners.

"The Sinners will follow suit," Amon assures, glancing at the panicked girl with a bored eye. "We had to speed up and modify our program to adapt to the recent turn of events. Since we didn't have enough time to kidnap them all, I established priorities. These are the last four Virtuous jurors of the secret tribunal: the Prudling, the Temperling, the Braveryfiend, and the Hopeling. We still have to eliminate two Lustspawns, one Ragebeast, one Slothling, one

Greedling, one Envyfiend, and one Gluttonfiend." His periwinkle gaze darkens. "That bitch Beliale is giving me a hard time; I can't locate her. When the investigation went public in the media, the Lustspawn Magistrate realized she was in trouble and went into hiding somewhere on Earth. But it's only a temporary reprieve; I'll find her. I'll torture every member of her staff until one of them breaks. Ah, I have a sublime death reserved for Beliale, my honeybun. Cut from crotch to chest with a silver saw and hung upside down. She'll bleed out in terrible pain, and it will be exhilarating."

Honeybun. And to think this lunatic still dares to call me by my affectionate nickname!

"Where's your assassin buddy?" I whisper, struggling to contain the black fury rising within me.

"He's dealing with your buddy."

"R.I.P Cole! Wills is going to flatten him."

Amon gives a sly smile that sends a chill down my spine.

"My honeybun, first of all, your Sinner is no match for my warrior. I've taken steps to enhance all the natural abilities of the body that received his essence and even added a few extras along the way. Secondly…" His smile widens. "How could you believe I would make a soul pact with Victor Cole to bring that abomination of the Ragebeast back to life?"

My face falls apart.

He couldn't have…

He didn't—

"You didn't do that," I whine in a low voice, casting a distressed look into his eyes.

"Oh, but I did, Myrina," he replies softly. "I did it. I've accomplished what no other demon has done before me. I reincarnated a human soul into the body of a Virtuous, a major Justspawn."

I collapse to my knees, half-slumped against the wall. My legs can't hold me anymore. I clutch my head in my hands, moaning. No. No!

"Then, thanks to the wonderful alliance of modern science and ancient black magic, I transformed him into a Hybresang dedicated to the seven cardinal virtues," Amon continues calmly as if explaining his new recipe. "I made sure he was guided by four dominant virtues:

justice, fortitude, faith, and hope. Naturally, the other three virtues are present in very negligible quantities because I couldn't afford for him to exhibit charity, prudence, and temperance; it would have thwarted my plans. However, as I had hoped, he developed a power for each Virtuous legion. You see, for this pact, I needed a pure, noble, malleable soul, and that of a demon wouldn't do. Three years of hard work so that he could master all his remarkable abilities and be ready to start our beautiful work! The armed hand of justice, implacable, devoted, determined, daring, designed to abolish the evil and vice that rot our world. And the icing on the cake—you get to reunite with the one love of your life you thought you'd lost! Aren't you proud of me, honeybun?"

Devastated, I swallow my nausea to keep from vomiting bile onto the floor. This is a fucking nightmare from start to finish!

"We're going to accomplish great things, the three of us, on Infernum," my grandfather concludes with a hint of enthusiasm that disgusts me even more. "By combining our respective powers, we will purge it of its most unacceptable sins, even among the Virtuous. You, me… and Owen."

CHAPTER 35

DEMON DUEL

"If your opponent is of choleric temper, seek to irritate him." ~Sun Tzu, The Art of War

KELEN

A Virtuous Hybresang. I sure didn't see that coming!

Cole gives a half-smile at my surprise. I'm going to wipe that smile off his—

An invisible weight suddenly crashes down on my back. My legs buckle without resistance, and I find myself pinned to the ground, face down, as if my body weighs a ton. No matter how much I resist, I can't get up. I strain all my muscles, trying to move my arms, but it's no use. Damn, he has a Temperling power: he can even manipulate gravity! Out of the corner of my eye, I see Cole taking a medieval weapon off my wall.

A flail made of a handle, a chain, and a spiked steel ball.

He walks toward me, whistling, while keeping me immobilized from a distance. It looks like I'm at his fucking mercy... or so it seems.

Yeah, come on over here.

"It might sting a bit," my enemy warns, twirling his weapon.

Speak for yourself.

Behind Cole, all the weapons from my collection have quietly detached from their mounts as he approaches me. They levitate in the air, waiting for the right moment… and aim at his back. I smile inwardly the moment he raises the flail, and I give the mental command for my babies to fiercely defend their demon daddy.

Thirteen sharp blades fly toward the silver-scaled Hybresang. He spins around at the sound of their whistling and lets out a huge curse.

At the last second, he generates an invisible shield around himself, a Faithfiend force field that blocks all my weapons and makes them veer off course.

By all the hells, he's got some moves!

However, my telekinetic counterattack has broken his concentration. This disrupts his Temperling trick that's been keeping me pinned to the floor, since he can only use one power at a time. Freed from his hold, I spring at him as soon as his force field dissipates.

I wrap my arm around his thick neck to strangle him while pummeling his ribs with wild punches, pouring all my violence and physical strength into each blow. He drops the flail, struggling. He manages to grab one of my wings and flips me over him in an acrobatic move. I smash a 3,000 Forks light fixture with my tail as I land on the glass coffee table, which shatters under my weight. If not for my protective scale covering, I'd have shards of glass embedded all over my body.

As I'm still lying on my back, I see him raise his two fists wrapped in black ice above my head. I teleport just before his frozen limbs smash into my face. I reappear behind him while he's crouched, his fists embedded in the floor. Without thinking, I hurl a fireball at point-blank range between his shoulder blades to scorch his wings. However, my attack doesn't have the desired effect. The impact propels him forward, but it doesn't burn a single feather or scale. Damn, he's immune to fire because of his Justspawn and Braveryfiend genes! I should have guessed. It's logical, since he incinerated Aydan Smat's heart inside his chest. This ability has been amplified by his Hybresang DNA. He can manipulate both ice *and* fire.

But I have two significant advantages over him, powers he doesn't possess: teleportation and telekinesis. Given his profile, I need to wear him down, exhaust him, and destabilize him, while waiting for an opening to deliver a masterstroke and finish him off.

Just as I decide to adopt this combat strategy, he becomes invisible again.

He's really starting to piss me off.

The other Hybresang lifts my beloved piano.

"*No not the piano, you son of a bitch!*" I roar as he hurls it toward me.

Unfurling my wings and stretching out my arms, I dash toward my precious instrument to minimize the damage. Catching my heavy piano, I stagger back several meters, grumbling, muscles straining under the effort.

I feel something coil around my ankle. An invisible tail.

Cole suddenly yanks me to the side. I collapse onto my flank, and my piano crashes onto its feet, emitting a discordant musical clatter. Damn, it's scratched!

My enemy drags me across the parquet floor, which I claw at wildly, before hurling me across the room like an athlete throwing a shot put. I slam into a stone wall face-first, inadvertently smashing one of my favorite paintings, *Starry Night* by Vincent van Gogh, an impressionist masterpiece. This serial killer has no respect for anything or anyone!

It's high time to show him what I'm made of.

As I get back up, I summon my telekinesis again, mobilizing all my collection of weapons. They zip through the air around me as if they're alive, their blades reflecting the lamplight as they slice through the void.

Golden blood splatters to my right, and I hear a growl of pain. Victory, I've hit him.

He reappears, raising his force field to better protect himself. I've wounded him: a deep gash now mars his scaly thigh. His mobility is reduced.

"Surrender, Cole!" I command, simultaneously slamming all my weapons against his invisible shield to weaken it. "I'll be merciful, I promise. I'll grant you a relatively quick death; you'll hardly suffer."

"I'm not Victor Cole," he growls, flashing a predatory grin, his palm pressed against his bleeding thigh.

"Yeah, right. And I'm the demonic reincarnation of Jesus of Nazareth, minus the beard and with more sex appeal."

"Since you marked the Tracker on her thigh, you must have seen the tattoo she has on the other leg, Wills. The infinity sign with the two initials," he murmurs.

I furrow my brow, bewildered. He's trying to confuse me. That traitor Amon must have told him.

"Your mark means nothing. Myrina belongs to me, body, heart, and soul. I'll rid her of you to break your sham of a bond, and she'll return to my arms as if nothing ever happened. Some bonds are so powerful they even withstand death, Sinner."

God. Damn. It.

Sometimes, only one person is missing, and the whole world seems depopulated.

He didn't say that on the phone referring to Cole.

He was talking about his own feelings for Myrina.

That bastard Amon Holmes reincarnated her human fiancé's soul into a demon's body!

"Owen!" I gasp, stunned.

Unfolding his wings, the deceitful iconoclast takes advantage of my shock to attack again. He takes off from the ground and charges at me like a madman. My reaction time is too slow to teleport away, and he slams into me head-on, carrying me with him through my bay window as we grapple with each other.

Our deadly fight continues in the sky. We pound each other with punches and kicks, scratching and biting like two wild beasts, spilling each other's blood repeatedly. I teleport behind him, but he whips me with his scaly tail, causing me to lose altitude. He flies at full speed toward Vésave, and I chase after him for a few seconds. Then, as we near the volcano, I materialize in front of him, head down, flapping my wings to stay airborne. He brakes when he sees me appear in his path, but it's too late.

He impales himself on one of my horns, which pierces through his stomach. His body convulses violently, and a strangled gasp escapes him. He tries to pull away, scratching my shoulders and cursing me out. Grabbing him by the waist, I drive my horn deeper into his abdomen, reveling in his agony.

Then it's my turn to suffer both physically *and* emotionally when he delivers a massive punch to the base of my horn, breaking it off clean.

Mutilated. He's mutilated me! Horns never grow back, not even for demons with regenerative abilities. Now I'm a unicorn, *permanently handicapped!* I feel my stump with supreme horror as Owen gasps for breath, pulling my severed horn out of his abdomen. A stream of golden blood gushes from the gaping wound.

I'm now boiling with rage, as intense as the glowing orange depths of the Vésave crater beneath us. I am nothing but hate and fury.

And… sorrow?

But it's not my own sorrow.

Myrina.

I was so consumed by adrenaline and the heat of battle that I hadn't paid attention to my Tracker's emotions, who is undoubtedly also in a dire situation. She's in danger. I must swiftly eliminate Owen, locate her using my demonic mark, and go to her aid. She might not have the strength to kill her grandfather. So, I'll do it for her.

Unfortunately, concern for others is a weakness…

I fully realize this when Owen comes at me like a madman. Instead of teleporting behind him as I would normally do to continue wearing him down from a distance—especially since he's seriously injured—I engage in close combat, bombarding him with brutal blows to finish him off quickly. A rookie soldier's mistake.

The Virtuous Hybresang seizes the opportunity to twist the bones of my wing at an impossible angle… before stabbing the joint with my own horn.

I scream in agony. It's torture.

My wing is out of commission: I can't fly until I've regenerated. I cling to my adversary, who gives me a sadistic, triumphant smile. Since I'm touching him, if I dematerialize, I'll take him with me. I see only one way out. Let myself fall into freefall and teleport before landing in the crater. I've never tried it, obviously, but in my opinion, the lava won't make an exception for me. When a depressed demon wants to commit suicide on Infernum, he generally dives into the Vésave. The lava will melt my scales, my wings, my organs, and my bones. It will be very hot for me, and not in a good way.

"Ragebeast Magistrate, here's your one-way ticket to hell. I suggest you say your last prayers! Let's see if there's any virtue behind all your sins. Do you think you have any chance of surviving the lava? I don't. Your turn to test the leap of faith, Wills!" Owen exults.

He punches me in the head, stunning me, tearing me away from him, and hurling me into the void, using his Temperling gravity power to prevent me from teleporting mid-fall.

During my descent, I realize faith is a virtue I despise almost as much as charity.

✳✳✳

OWEN

I lower my gaze. Thanks to my gravity power, Kelen Wills's demonic silhouette is instantly absorbed by the boiling lava. Despite my wounds in the abdomen and thigh, I rejoice at witnessing this unprecedented spectacle. I've loved watching each of my victims die, but this sight has an even sweeter taste. I've defeated the most powerful Sinner in the world. It's only natural; justice always prevails in the end.

Finally, there's no longer any obstacle between Myri and me.

A job well done.

I just regret not being able to take another trophy besides his horn before settling his account. Oh well, I'll have to make do.

Now that the Sinner Hybresang is dead, it's time to find my future wife.

CHAPTER 36
MYRINA'S CHOICE

"No virtue can dwell in hate." ~*Victor Hugo, Prose Philosophy*

MYRINA

When everything you've believed in for years collapses around you in just a few minutes, how do you not sink into an ocean of unleashed darkness? What lifeboat remains when you suddenly realize that the people you trusted most have lied to you and are even worse than the monsters you usually track?

Like in Wills's favorite painting, *The Raft of the Medusa*, by Géricault, I am nothing but a helpless castaway in a storm, prey to destructive forces closing in on me. Hopeless, I weakly signal to a ship sailing far beyond my reach, while a massive deadly wave prepares to engulf me.

Fatality. It's the first time in twenty-four years that this word has entered my mind.

Owen is alive. Under the control of my grandfather, my ex-fiancé has become a bloodthirsty demon with the aim of avenging my parents' death. And they want me to join them so we can continue what they've started together. I could never have imagined such a catastrophic scenario.

Owen, once the embodiment of kindness and goodness, corrupted by the dark enchantment of a forbidden soul pact, transformed into a sadistic killer fueled by his master Amon's twisted thirst for justice.

I'm so tense that my muscles ache everywhere. A sharp pain has just surfaced at the top right of my skull, where my demonic horn used to be. I wonder if it's actually a side effect related to Wills's mark, which he must be fighting Owen. I also feel an intense fury that isn't my own.

Hybresang Sinner versus Hybresang Virtuous... Lord!

"How were you able to create a Hybresang from a Justspawn?" I ask in a hollow voice, still trying to grasp what eludes me.

"By balancing various infusions, I injected him with blood from the other six Virtuous species before performing the magical ritual that merged their powers within him. I've been studying this complex subject for years, honeybun. As soon as I learned about your parents' execution, I began my research and planned all of this."

Planned. I take note of the term and store it away in my mind.

"When did you make this soul pact with Owen?" I murmur, staring into emptiness.

"It doesn't matter, Myrina."

He doesn't want to answer. Clearly, he has something to hide...

Keep him talking, Myri.

New pain, even sharper. At the level of my left shoulder blade. Where my wing is located in my demon form. My stress shoots up.

Damn it, Wills, hold on, don't let me down!

"An artificial Hybresang with a human soul darkened by evil," I summarize. "You manage to keep him in check? He must be somewhat disturbed, no?"

My questions make Amon uneasy. He clears his throat, a shadow clouding his eyes.

So, I'm right. The murderer isn't the obedient robotic servant who blindly follows every directive. The phone call he made to me the other night confirms this. It wasn't part of their plan, but Owen couldn't help himself.

I even believe he still has feelings for me.

"*Artificial* is redundant. Hybresangs are artificial by definition," grumbles Grandpa.

"What?" I gasp.

"Did you really think your Magistrate was born a Hybresang,

Myrina? No demon can *naturally* combine the seven sins or virtues—you don't need to be a genetics expert to figure that out. Like Owen, Wills underwent a mutation. Originally, he wasn't a Hybresang."

"But… what was he originally?" I croak, astonished.

"I don't know, and I don't care, honeybun. He's going to die any second now, anyway. Come to terms with it."

The moment he says that, I let out a huge scream of pain, curling up on myself. My skin burns horribly for a few seconds…

Then nothing.

As quickly as it appeared, the overwhelming wave of agony disappears.

I don't feel anything anymore.

I don't feel Wills anymore.

I blink, incredulous.

No, my asshole can't be dead.

I lean against the wall, closing my eyelids. A warm tear rolls down my cheek. I wish the ceiling would collapse, the walls would tremble, the floor would swallow me.

I wish I could be anywhere but here.

"Are you crying for *him*?" Amon questions with obvious disgust. "Damn it, honeybun, I thought you were smarter than that! He enchanted you with his pheromones and his mark. You're free now."

Shut. Your. Fucking. Mouth.

My strength is gradually returning, which proves that the sedative is becoming less effective. Just a few more minutes to hold out before I can maybe go on the offensive…

Don't falter now, Myri.

Keep stalling.

Illuminate the shadows.

Find the weaknesses.

"I still have questions, Grandpa. Who is the juror who confessed to you about my parents' death?" I ask calmly, almost detached, contrasting with my inner turmoil.

"Aydan Smat, honeybun."

I would have bet on that, damn it. The first victim! Following his confession, Amon could have decided to spare him, to forgive him… But no. Because of those sixteen demons, his son Arthur was executed. So, in his mind, all the guilty ones had to pay the price without exception. My grandfather didn't care about Aydan's remorse.

"Do you have any connection to the fire that ravaged his temple years ago?"

He hesitates for three or four seconds before responding. I imagine he wants to gain my trust, but at the same time, he doesn't entirely trust me—the drugs and the chain on my ankle are evidence of that. Grandpa is the personification of contradiction.

"Yes. I set fire to his temple on impulse to punish him. But he escaped."

And children died instead of Aydan, who later renounced his Faithfiend faith.

"But why Gabriel the Pridefiend? You only targeted Virtuous jury members, except him."

"I initially planned to start with all the Virtuous jurors, then the Sinful jurors, and finish with Judges Dickens and Beliale. But I encountered that little bastard Gabriel by chance at the Magistrate's Palace after Aydan's murder. Just seeing him strutting through the halls with a demon on his arm enraged me. He was boasting to her, puffing his chest out. I wanted to shut him up for good. So, I slightly modified my plan to make him the third victim."

"The same goes for the two Justspawn, Dickens and Amanda. The judge wasn't supposed to be killed so soon, but the media's involvement changed the equation, and you adapted your plan accordingly." I glance at the prisoners at the back of the room, illustrating my point. "Why leave clues at the crime scenes to signal the legion of subsequent victims? And the trophies, are they part of your collection or Owen's?"

His square jaw tightens. He remains silent.

I read between the lines. The clues and trophies are solely Owen's doing. Individual slip-ups. Like the phone call.

Owen wanted to play with me by leaving breadcrumbs as if he wanted me to catch him. He was probably eager to see me again. Eager to the point of being reckless and undisciplined.

I'm on to something.

"Was it your idea or Owen's to take the photo in front of my apartment while I was sleeping, Grandpa?"

"Mine," Amon responds curtly, exasperated by my questioning.

The photo, yes. It was to scare me into coming to live with him so he could keep an eye on me. However, the bloodied feather from Aydan was Owen's personal touch in the envelope.

Earlier, Grandpa mentioned a fake badge. He duplicated my card to access CIT data and steal sedatives from Lexi's lab, which he used on several victims.

Oddly enough, the more the pieces of this damn puzzle come together, the more composed I become. I'm filling in the blanks of the investigation by analyzing my grandfather's reactions.

"Honeybun, it's time," he reminds gravely, handing me my crossbow and four silver-tipped bolts. "It's up to you to dispense justice this time."

Without a word, I take hold of the crossbow and the projectiles, hands trembling. The Virtuous woman who is now awake whimpers behind her gag. As I load one into the weapon…

My grandfather draws a revolver from under his jacket, removes the safety, and presses it against my temple. I flinch.

I shouldn't be particularly surprised. He doesn't fully trust me.

"Sorry for this little precaution." Amon sighs. "But it's necessary. It might be a bit tough for you, knowing yourself. But once you've taken them all down, you'll feel relieved, I promise. And you'll thank me for pushing you to do it. Think of your parents, honeybun."

My parents would never have wanted this.

"Do you think your son, my father, a Justspawn Tracker, would have condoned all this, Grandpa?" I emphasize, staring at him unwaveringly.

"We'll never know, Myrina," he replies evenly. "It is what it is. Start with her."

He swims in total denial. The emotional argument I just used won't dissuade him from carrying out his macabre plans. Amon won't feel guilt, and I don't see how I could reason with him. He's already gone too far. The pain of his loss has half scrambled his brain.

I raise my crossbow, breath ragged and throat tight.

The cold barrel of the gun against my temple. My clammy finger on the trigger. The crossbow feels so heavy in my hands…

I aim at the girl's head, who cries, pleading with her eyes and whimpering like a wounded animal.

I've scraped by with all the time I could, but I don't know if it will be enough. I'm not yet at the top of my game. If I rebel now, I'm not sure I can overpower my jailer.

On the other hand, I think this bitch showed no mercy toward my parents. She condemned them to death like the other jury members.

"You're thinking too much, Myrina!" Amon urges, taking on his most authoritative tone. "Pull the trigger! Shoot!"

Shoot now, or he'll do it for you! my panicked Lustspawn voice urges.

Never forget your principles as a Tracker. Fight with all your might and die if you must, orders my stern Justspawn voice.

Kill or die.

Give up or fight.

I've made my choice in both cases.

"No. No, I can't," I whisper, lowering the crossbow.

"Myrina, don't persist in your folly. Last chance! Don't make me liquidate you," growls the former Magistrate, growing increasingly agitated.

"But you'll have to do it anyway, Grandpa! Because I'll never be a part of your damn stupid vengeance." I lock my defiant polar eyes with his. "But will you have the balls to kill your own granddaughter, the last remaining member of your family? What will you have left when all these demons and I have perished, Grandpa? Your bitterness? Your hatred? Your loneliness? Your despair? Your grief? Will you commit suicide to atone for your own crimes, perhaps? Don't you find your behavior contradictory? Washing away others' sins while revealing yourself to be a repressed Sinner supposedly working for Virtue? Look at yourself in the mirror, for god's sake! You're out of your mind!"

He shakes his head vehemently, brows furrowed.

"Dad would never have wanted people tortured and murdered for him, Grandpa. It goes against all his moral values. He would never have lowered himself to this. He would have been ashamed of you!"

"Shut up immediately, Myrina Holmes, you're talking nonsense!" he spits out, furious.

"*Amon!*" a third voice exclaims, male.

We turn our heads. I hold my breath.

My god. He's here, in human form.

He emerges from a wall mirror, an active Arcadus.

A young man in his twenties, with a handsome, sweat-glistened tan face. Shirtless, only wearing half-torn jeans. His abdomen and thigh hastily bandaged. I don't know him, but I recognize him.

My eyes, clouded with sorrow, meet his. His eyes, both strange and familiar to me, are a bluish-gray, topped by a curly chestnut mane streaked with silver threads, as if he'd aged prematurely.

If Owen is alone here…

It confirms that Wills is dead.

Do you know the sound of a heart shattered into a thousand pieces?

Despite my deafness, I do.

CHAPTER 37
BLOODY REUNIONS

"Love tolerates absence and death better than doubt or betrayal." ~André Maurois, Climats

OWEN

"What are you doing?" I bark at Amon, who is pointing a revolver at Myri's temple.

"She's a bit hesitant. I'm motivating her," he retorts.

"We didn't agree to this!"

"After all your deviations, you dare say that to me, Owen?" he counters, glaring at me.

I don't respond to his jab. This isn't the time to argue. I look back at Myrina, who is examining the object in my hand. Wills's horn. A smile forms on my lips.

"You were supposed to bring back his head," Amon reproaches, suddenly dampening my joy of defeating the Sinner Hybresang.

Always lecturing me, directing me, infantilizing me. Even in front of her. He doesn't care about the wounds on my belly and thigh that I hastily bandaged after returning to human form. He is obsessed with his plan.

"I saw him fall into Vésave," I explain, watching Myrina's strangely stoic and silent reaction.

She must be in shock from our reunion, no doubt. I wish the old Justspawn would leave us alone to be together, but it's not possible right now. I'll make up for it later. I'll take my future wife in my arms and kiss her passionately.

"Are you sure he's dead, Owen?" Amon presses, tense.

He's starting to annoy me more and more. "Yes! I saw him go under. No demon can survive lava. Remove the gun from her temple, Amon."

"Once she eliminates our four targets."

"For god's sake, give her a break! She'll kill the next ones if you insist. Put yourself in her shoes for thirty seconds: she just found out her parents were dead and I was alive. She's not in a state to shoot."

"Owen," Myrina calls softly, addressing me for the first time.

My gaze immediately returns to her. It feels strange to hear my name from her lips again. I've dreamt of this moment for three years. It's not quite how I imagined it, but I'm with her, and that's all that matters. I've missed her so much. Her incomparable beauty, her lovely starry eyes… Right now, I'm simply happy. All these sacrifices were worth it.

"Why did you do that, Owen?" she asks sadly.

"For you, Myri. I did it for you, of course," I answer.

An expression of incomprehensible pain paints her face. I frown. Well, so my answer wasn't what she expected? Amon repeatedly told me during training that she would be proud of me once she understood the truth. She must be even more confused than I thought.

"My Myri, did you miss me?"

She nods faintly. I smile, reassured. But she doesn't return my smile. She stubbornly avoids my gaze. Frustration gnaws at me.

"Owen, did you… did you know what I was before you died?"

"Yes, Myri. Your grandfather told me."

"You spilled that to him?" she wonders, looking at Amon.

"I explained we were demons one day when you were at work," Amon answers.

"He reverted to his natural Justspawn form to show me," I interject with a light laugh. "I was terrified the first time I saw it! Then my initial fear gave way to almost scientific fascination, I'd say. I wanted to know everything about your world, your legions, your traditions. Amon spent hours telling me everything. Including the appalling death of your parents."

"And when was that, Owen?" she asks slowly.

"A few days before my death."

"A few days before your death," she repeats, coldly eyeing Amon, who purses his lips.

"I don't blame you for hiding your double life from me, Myri," I continue, shrugging. "I understand why you did it. It's true that, at first, I didn't feel adequate as just a human. I wished I could have helped you, protected you, and shared every aspect of your life, not just what you showed me. I was waiting until after the wedding to have this discussion with you, but that bastard Victor Cole" — I grimace at the painful memory — "ruined everything by showing up at the house to bleed me dry. I hope you made him suffer when you caught up with him."

"Oh yes, darling, Cole suffered a lot," she assures me without taking her eyes off her grandfather. "And your soul pact? When was it made?"

She called me *darling*. Just like old times. Wonderful. Things will sort themselves out now, I'm certain of it. Everything will go back to how it was between us. It might even be better, now that I've become a demon capable of understanding and watching over her.

"Don't tell her," Amon intervenes abruptly, gritting his teeth. "She's trying to pit us against each other, Owen."

"No, you're being paranoid!" I refute defensively.

"Owen, please answer me," Myrina says softly, locking her purple gaze with mine.

"Right before I died, angel. Cole left me for dead after torturing me, wanted me to bleed out on our bed. Your grandpa found me, dying in the room…"

The young woman's eyes darken and fill with tears.

"And offered me this pact so I could reincarnate into a demon's body. To come back to you after avenging your parents. He saved me, Myri."

"Okay. So, Amon teleported to our place while you were dying, Owen. Lucky coincidence. Perfect timing!" she snaps sharply.

What's she implying?

Several troubled voices swirl in my head.

Amon said she was trying to sow discord between us.

But Myri would never do that. Myri wouldn't lie to me.

She said she missed me, so Myri still loves me.

Amon saved me and made me powerful. Amon is my master and friend. I owe respect and obedience to Amon Holmes.

My fiancée's moist purple eyes suddenly change color. Her left eye turns red. Her right eye, silver. Enthralling.

"You bastard," she hisses at her grandfather. "You *planned* everything, huh? You didn't just jump at the first chance to seal your vile soul pact, you *provoked* it! You needed a *human* for your ritual, you told me!"

"No, you're insane! It was Owen's choice, I just offered him an exit. I hadn't originally chosen him; it was a twist of fate! I had picked another human, but misfortune struck your fiancé before I could finalize the pact with—"

"You're lying!" she screams in his face despite the menacing presence of the revolver. "The details don't add up, there are too many inconsistencies! You hypnotized your scapegoat Victor Cole to attack Owen without finishing him off so you could have time to finalize your damn oral pact before his death! You wanted your Virtuous Hybresang to dirty his hands in your place, because you never had the guts to kill all those demons alone! Owen, it's because of him that you're dead, he's responsible for your murder. For three years, he's been manipulating you to carry out all his wishes, damn my horns!"

Lies. Scapegoat. Cole. Soul pact. Create Hybresang. Mastermind behind your murder. Manipulate, my confused mental voices buzz.

An abominable migraine starts pulsing in my head, as it does every time I'm on the verge of losing control of my emotions and impulses. I massage my temple with my index finger.

Out of the corner of my eye, I notice Amon wrenching the crossbow from Myrina's hands.

"Owen," he addresses me in a frigid tone. "I regret it deeply, but she will never join our cause. And if she's not with us, my boy… she's against us."

He's going to kill her, all my voices chant in unison.

***

MYRINA

"Amon," Owen interjects.

My grandfather stares at me with a mix of sorrow and determination. Breathless, I meet his unbalanced gaze.

"Amon," Owen repeats firmly. "She's your granddaughter. Lower. That. Weapon."

"She's no longer my granddaughter!" Grandpa shouts, seemingly losing his mind like never before. "My granddaughter would have understood the beauty and greatness of our deeds! My granddaughter would have—"

He never finishes his sentence.

With his right hand, Owen swiftly grabs his wrist to lift the gun. The silver bullet flies from the barrel, grazing the top of my head and embedding itself in the wall behind me.

With his left hand, Owen forcefully drives Kelen's horn into his skull.

Amon's golden blood splatters across my face. I open my mouth, but no sound emerges from my throat. A silent scream echoes in my mind. My eyes are as wide as my grandfather's, who falls to his knees before me, letting out a wheezing groan. I am deeply shocked by what has just occurred.

With Olympian calm, Owen extracts the sticky horn from his head. The former Justspawn Magistrate sprawls on his side, limbs limp. He resumes his demonic form as he passes away.

Without hesitation, the Virtuous Hybresang eliminated his master and accomplice to save my life.

"Karma, Amon," murmurs my ex-fiancé, eyeing the inert scaly body at our feet. "You kill me, I kill you. Except you won't reincarnate." He looks up at me, wiping the bloody horn on his jeans, and smiles tenderly, a flicker of unpredictability in his eyes. "Don't worry, sweetheart. If you don't want to do it, I'll kill those four for you. They're witnesses, we can't let them live. It'll be my wedding gift, okay? And as for the other jury members and Beliale, we don't have to hunt them down. If you want to drop this vendetta, no problem, we'll do as you wish. We'll flee together to Earth, and the CIT will never find us."

He extends his free hand toward me to embrace me. I take a step back and hit the wall.

His smile fades.

"Myri, you don't have to be afraid of me. It's me, come on."

No, it's not him. It's not my Owen. The man I loved would never have committed all these heinous crimes. My Owen died three years ago. This psychotic, sick demon… is not him.

I have to kill him.

To release *my* Owen's soul.

So he can finally be at peace.

"Take… take me in your arms," I plead with a choked voice, my heart infinitely heavy.

His smile returns instantly when he hears my request. He drops his deadly horn, grabs me around the waist, and pulls me close to him. I suppress a shiver of disgust as I feel the hands of a sadistic killer on me.

I take advantage to release the three bolts I've gathered in my fist… toward his throat.

But I wasn't fast enough because of the drug slowing down my reflexes.

Owen grabs my arm and the three silver points stop just an inch from his Adam's apple. He looks as shocked as I am.

"Myri, what's gotten into you?" he exclaims, bewildered by my action. "Have you lost your mind?"

I elbow him in the forearm, hoping to make him let go… but without success. His fist crushes my wrist, and my bones crack. I groan through clenched teeth.

"You'll come to your senses," Owen declares, his eyes blazing, twisting my wrist until my fingers open and the bolts slide to the ground. "There's no other way, Myri. You've been mine since the day you bumped into me at the bookstore seven years ago."

"You've become a damn torturous monster!" I protest, punching him in the chest, which doesn't even make him flinch. "I'll never be with you, *never!*"

My acidic and radical words plunge him into a furious frenzy.

Owen grabs me by the throat, lifts me off the ground as if I weighed nothing, and slams me harshly against the wall. I kick wildly at his shins, but it's utterly futile. He doesn't budge. His fingers tighten, strangling me. I gasp for air; my complexion must be turning blue. I scratch his arms, fiercely struggling… but he's still far too strong for me.

"Whether you like it or not, Myri, nothing and no one will ever separate us again!" roars the Virtuous Hybresang.

"Wrong, idiot," interjects a gravelly voice behind him. "I will."

And someone forcefully pulls Owen backward, tossing him to the other end of the room like a sack of potatoes.

I gulp a huge breath of air, grabbing onto a long, feathered wing spread out in front of me. Through my blurry vision that sharpens with each passing second, I make out a towering figure with black scales, standing four heads taller than me and looking like… a smoking and battered Balrog.

Damn, Wills is alive!

Thank god. I've never been so happy to see that complete bastard!

And I admit that the demonic seal that helped him find me has its relative usefulness in the current context.

"Are you hurt, Agent Holmes?" he asks, examining me with his red gaze.

"I… I'm okay, and you?" I stammer, squinting at the multiple burns covering his body.

He smiles in response. He's terrifying when he smiles in his demonic form. Especially with one horn missing… But I must be crazy because this sight comforts me.

However, my joy and relief are short-lived: like on the phone after the Rebels' attack, I realize I'm *so furious* at him.

"But what the hell were you doing, Kelen Wills?" I burst out, shaking his half-broken wing, eliciting a small groan of pain from him.

"I was relaxing in a lava bath, my little cat," he replies, breaking my chain with a telekinetic impulse. "You should try it, it's quite invigorating."

"No kidding! Why are you only showing up now?" I ask.

"I make it a principle to always arrive late, but always at the right time. If you'll excuse me, I have another ass to kick besides yours." He turns to Owen, who has straightened up and begun to metamorphose. "By the way," he adds over his shoulder, "I've discovered a new high-level power that helped me survive in Vésave. Would you like a sneak preview?"

"Go ahead, asshole," I mutter.

"I'm glad to see you, too, Myrina," Kelen affirms, brushing my cheek briefly with the tip of his intact wing.

He gently touches my skin with his feathers, soft in texture, in an affectionate gesture that warms my cheeks despite the circumstances.

A moment later, Wills literally evaporates, transforming into a column of red and black smoke.

I'm astonished.

So *that's* why I couldn't sense his presence through our link anymore: he managed to abandon his solid form and adopt a gaseous consistency!

Incredible. He's developed a major Slothling power, an extremely rare ability in Infernum.

It can only mean one thing: faced with mortal danger, his Hybresang genes *evolved* and underwent a lightning-fast mutation to adapt to his hostile environment.

The demonic smoke cloud hurtles toward Owen, who has completed his transformation. He erects a Faithfiend force field around himself at the last second. In his mist form, Wills swirls around him like a whirlwind, violently ripping him from the ground and hurling him repeatedly against the factory ceiling—likely weakening his invisible shield. Boom. Boom. Boom.

With raised eyebrows, I lower and raise my head to follow the movement. Owen roars with each impact, chilling me to the bone. Cracks form in the ceiling, and chunks of stone break loose.

The Sinner finally ceases his onslaught. The Virtuous falls flat on his stomach, badly beaten. But his force field still holds, and Wills returns to his solid form, his new Slothling power likely consuming a great deal of energy.

There's only one way to break through a Faithfiend shield like that: ice.

Owen's Justspawn body may be immune to ice, but not his force field.

I crouch down and pick up my still-loaded crossbow. I close my fist around the bolt just as Owen recovers, takes flight, and dives toward Wills like a giant eagle. My projectile coats with a thin layer of frost that cracks. Damn, this isn't going to work! My human form is cruelly hindering me.

If I manage to mutate, it will accelerate the restoration of my powers and amplify them.

If I manage to mutate.

I struggle to regain my focus as they battle like two fierce beasts. Light scales begin to appear on my arms… before melding back into my skin.

Damn it, fucking drugs!

I try again and again.

Yes, between giving up and fighting, I've made my choice.

To hell with fate.

KELEN

Here I am again in a precarious position. Twice in the same day—it's extremely frustrating. My sin of pride, already battered by my mutilation, will have a hard time recovering. Sure, I gained a new power, but if I had been given the choice, I would have preferred to keep my horn.

At least, my little Tracker is safe and sound. And Amon is dead, so half the job is already theoretically done.

In practice, Owen proves to be a terribly tough adversary.

His fists hit me. Sometimes I counter, occasionally I dodge, often I take the hits, sporadically I strike back. But he has the advantage of intact wings and a force field that dampens all my counterattacks. And he's very upset by my survival and arrival. I must say, I enjoyed witnessing the shock on his face when I sent him flying backward, interrupting his little love tête-à-tête. Almost as much as I enjoyed seeing Myrina's delighted expression when she saw me.

As vicious as a Sinner, the Virtuous Hybresang relentlessly strikes my injured wing with all his might. I teleport around him because I no longer have enough energy to transform into black and red smoke, but he's increasingly able to anticipate my movements and preempt my assaults.

He finally traps me in a corner of the room and bites into my throat like a rabid beast, his claws buried in my chest. My blood flows copiously over my beautiful scales. I bombard him with vigorous punches and elbows to make him let go, but his force field protects him, so he holds on. The pain is unbearable, I see stars. He sinks his fangs deeper into my flesh, growling. He's bleeding me and crushing me with his powerful jaws. What a hell, the bastard is going to tear my throat out!

Then suddenly, his grip loosens, and he trembles all over. He gurgles against my neck.

Over his muscular shoulder, I discern a black and white wing that doesn't belong to him. My gaze meets two mismatched eyes: one scarlet, one silver. Then I hear a soft, sorrowful voice behind my attacker.

"Forgive me, Owen."

He spits blood as he half-collapses against me. I push him aside. He crumples like a sack.

His force field has been shattered. There's a gaping hole in his back. His ribs are completely fractured.

Myrina stands before me in her demonic form. In her fist, made of black ice stained with golden blood, she holds Owen's enormous, still-pulsating heart.

The Virtuous Hybresang breathes his last breath, looking at her with a burdened expression.

She immediately drops the organ, which stops beating, and steps back, closing her eyes. Tears flow freely down her iridescent cheeks.

It breaks my heart that she had to do this. *That wretched empathy tied to the mark again.*

With a hand on my shredded throat, I spread my wings around hers to form a cocoon of feathers.

Without reopening her eyelids, the young woman draws closer and spontaneously nestles against me with a sigh. Her arms wrap around my waist. We're both covered in black and golden blood, our four wings intertwined around us.

After a long, unbearable silence, hoping for a compensatory passionate kiss—also to distract her, even if I might come off a bit unbearable—I casually remark in a whisper, "I lost a horn for you, my little cat."

"Hm."

"I almost died in Vésave," I add, aiming to make her feel slightly guilty.

"You survived," she mutters harshly, her scaly cheek against mine.

"I'm a true hero," I insist softly into her pointed ear.

"No, you're a real jerk. I'm the one who saved your life."

"I saved your life before."

"Just shut up, Wills," she concludes wearily.

I wrap an arm around her and hold her tight against me, stroking her smooth, cool dorsal scales. A hug will do for now; I can grant her that favor.

CHAPTER 38
DAMNED KARMA!

"Virtues are sisters; vices are comrades."
~Diane de Beausacq, Maxims of Life

MYRINA

After freeing the four Virtuous, Kelen teleported them one by one to CIT. The conscious demoness was overwhelmed with gratitude toward us. She kept thanking us between emotional sniffles. I remained silent while Wills watched me, unconcerned about the chick.

While the Magistrate took the survivors to headquarters, I called Zagam to give him a quick rundown. My boss was stunned; there were a lot of pauses on the phone. I cut short the awkward conversation by promising to call him back tomorrow, once I was rested. He said I could take as many days off as I needed to recover from this ordeal and that he would be there if I needed anything.

Right now, I only need one person.

My sister.

On the other hand, I dread the moment when I will have to tell her that our mother has passed away.

"Myrina, I'll handle it," Kelen murmurs as several Trackers wrap Owen and Amon's corpses in body bags under my disheartened gaze.

I look up at him, not understanding at first. Then I realize he's offering to speak to Ondine on my behalf. He must have sensed my reluctance through our demonic link. Normally, his intrusion into my emotional privacy would irritate me. But right now, I feel somewhat disconnected from reality.

"No, I'll do it," I emphasize in a monotone. "Can you take me to Sammael's?"

"Of course. Just let me swing by my place to change."

Both of us are draped in blankets brought by my colleagues, as clothes never survive the mutations. We've also received first aid from a Tracker medic. Kelen's wounds have all been bandaged; he looks like a mummy. Owen really did a number on him, and I can sense his physical pain even though he doesn't show it. For me, the pain is mostly moral.

He teleports us directly into his bedroom, where elegant, antique, cherrywood furniture lines the walls, which are adorned with black tapestries delicately patterned with silver arabesques. My theory is confirmed as his bed, draped in light Egyptian cotton sheets, is as massive as I imagined. Opposite the bed stands a magnificent six-foot-tall mirror with a finely carved golden frame. The owner's disproportionate pride is evident even in this object. If he brings his conquests to bed in this room, it's clear to me that the strategically placed psyche mirror allows him to see himself when—

Anyway, let's not dwell on that.

As he drops his cover to the floor and heads toward his wardrobe, I reflexively turn away. I hear rustling fabric, a zipper being pulled up, and soon he joins me, offering a handsome white silk shirt. Our intense gazes lock, fingers brushing as I take hold of the garment, feeling a tad embarrassed. I head into the adjacent bathroom and hear him sigh behind me.

Seriously, what did he expect? As if I'm going to strip naked and change in front of him! Fortunately for him, he doesn't make a comment.

When I return to the bedroom, Kelen is texting his lieutenant to let him know we're coming. His amber eyes lift from the screen, lighting up as he examines me with a mixture of approval, pride, and possessiveness. I roll my eyes. Typical macho reaction from a Neanderthal demon: he clearly likes seeing me in his shirt, which, by the way, is way too big for me. He starts to compliment me, but I cut him off with a raised, imperious hand.

"Don't say it, Wills."

"You don't know what I was going to say, my little cat."

"Yes, I do."

"Well, what was I going to say then?"

"That you find me sexy in your shirt."

"Wrong, I was going to say that I find you sexy, period."

A slight twitch at the corner of my lips. He feigns shock, pointing a finger at my face like a mischievous kid setting up a lame joke.

"But… but… by Satan's forked tail! Agent Holmes, are you *smiling*?"

"It's an optical illusion, jerk."

His warm laughter seeps into me, soothing some of my sorrow.

I can't lie to myself anymore: whether I like it or not, I care about this man. But I don't want to think about it too much, he might sense it through our connection.

"Let's go, Wills."

He teleports us to Sam's place.

✳✳✳

That's it, I've told Ondine everything.

Her hand nestled in her lover's, she didn't look at me once during my recounting. She seemed distant even before I started explaining. Her reception was cold and withdrawn. When Kelen and I arrived at Sam's apartment, she lingered for a few seconds on the shirt I was wearing.

"At the end of my story, a tear escapes from her eye. I move closer to embrace and comfort her, but she pulls back sharply, fixing me with a look overflowing with resentment that freezes me in place.

"Ondine, I—"

"Sam, Kelen, leave us," she commands firmly.

The Ragebeast and the Sinner Hybresang exchange furtive glances.

"That's not a good idea," Wills retorts, a worried crease forming on his forehead.

"It wasn't a question, Kelen," my sister cuts in with tangible aggression toward him. "Myrina and I need to talk alone."

"That's right," I confirm, despite the knots in my stomach and throat. "Leave us."

Reluctantly, Kelen obeys, grabbing his lieutenant by the shoulder. They dematerialize.

"I'm not coming back to the apartment," Ondine declares, her voice highly strung. "I'm moving in with Sam."

Just as I feared. She's angry with me.

"I'm so sorry about Mom, sis. If I could—"

"It's not about Mom, Myrina. And before we get to the other point, know that I'm also sorry for you. For Mom, your father, Amon, Owen, all that shit. You didn't deserve any of that, and I hope you find a way to get through it on your own."

On my own…?

"But that doesn't change how I feel about you. I can't keep all this inside any longer just to spare your feelings. Compassion is one thing, betrayal is another."

"Betrayal?"

"You think I'm an idiot, Myrina? Sam slipped up, hinting in front of me about Kelen's mark."

Karma, Owen said just after stabbing Grandpa.

Okay, fucking karma, I can get that. But not now, damn it!

"Unbeknownst to me, yes."

"*Unbeknownst to you*, huh? 'Inside her thigh, right next to her pussy?'"

Ah. She must have grilled Sam for details. I swallow hard. What do I say to that?

"Dare to claim he didn't leave me for you and that you haven't been screwing him behind my back for weeks!"

"I swear I'm not with him."

"But you don't deny the rest."

Hellhound's name, we're supposed to support each other, not fight over a guy!

"I messed up, I admit it. Several times, Ondine. It doesn't excuse anything, but I've beaten myself up over it. However, I can assure you we haven't slept together."

"You know what?" she says with bitter disappointment that

tears me up inside. "It doesn't matter whether you slept together or not. What matters is everything surrounding it. Frankly, I don't care about Kelen Wills anymore. I've moved on from him. As you said from the start of our relationship, he's a first-class jerk," she declares with a bitter laugh.

"But it seems you've changed your mind about him! I was fooling myself about that guy. I was naive, it's true. I had this teenage crush on him. It was ridiculous, especially when I see Sam, who was right in front of my eyes and who treats me like a queen. I'm not surprised Kelen acted like a jerk to me; he's always been like that. In fact, he could have slept with every Sinner demoness in Infernum, and it wouldn't have really affected me. But when I think that *you*, my beloved sister, did dirty things with him while urging me to dump him? It's so pathetic! You were jealous of me, admit it."

"No, not jealous. I was weak, mostly. And I am deeply sorry."

"Oh, you should be. You're selfish. If you're not happy, no one else can be, especially not me! Poor Myrina, eternal victim of fate who lost her parents and her human fiancé, with her shortened life expectancy, her deafness, and her problems! You always turn everything back to yourself. You have a pathological need for attention, and you don't even admit it, unlike pureblood Sinners. You hide behind your moral Justspawn facade, which is the height of hypocrisy! Never questioning yourself, just like your psychopath grandfather! You're neither a Sinner nor a Virtuous one; you just imitate sins and virtues to try and hide the emptiness inside you. But I lost my mother, too, Myrina, you're not the only one suffering here!"

I'm stunned. I'm completely taken aback. This belligerent speech didn't come out of nowhere. Ondine had been harboring these resentments for years. The breakup with Wills was the last straw, and the news of Lysippé's death heightened her emotional sensitivity. I had no idea she had such a negative view of me. My heart aches even more.

"Go ahead and sleep with him to forget your pain and recharge your Lustspawn batteries, Myrina, I don't care. Mark or not, he'll toss you aside like an old, used tissue once he's done with you."

She's wrong. At least I'm sure of one thing now: Kelen wouldn't do that.

"But don't count on me to wipe your tears afterward; I've had enough of you two. I've always tried to be there for you, to fulfill my role as the older sister, but you're no longer worthy of my trust. If you weren't family, I would cut ties with you. Maybe someday I'll be able to forgive you, Myrina… but right now, I don't want to see you anymore, and I'm sick of your crap. Get out."

"Do you really mean that, Ondine? Are you sure that's what you want?"

She nods coldly, despite her trembling hands on her thighs.

I leave Sam's apartment cursing karma, tears in my eyes.

***

It's been a week since Ondine started giving me the cold shoulder and ignoring my texts.

It's been a week since I've been avoiding Kelen.

For the first three days, he called me dozens of times and sent me a myriad of texts. I didn't respond to any of them. I had a good excuse: with Malphas, Sean, and a few Tracker colleagues, I was clearing out my grandfather's house, packing his belongings into boxes, and loading his furniture into trucks to be taken to an auction house. I inherited this house and everything in it, but I don't want to keep anything except a few photos of my father and me. A real estate agent came to make an estimate. According to him, I wouldn't have any trouble selling it and could even get a good price. But I don't care about the money. I want to get rid of it as soon as possible because I can't stand this old place anymore.

I got another blow to my morale when I discovered that Amon's basement had been set up to house Owen for the past three years. There was an underground studio where my ex-fiancé lived, and I had no idea. Photos of the victims, information sheets, and crime plans were pinned to a wall, just like in police movies. And the *pièce de résistance*: in a hidden compartment behind a painting… I came face-to-face with his collection of morbid trophies. Aydan's feather, John's heart floating in a jar of formaldehyde, Gabriel's horns.

There were also other photos of me sleeping in my bed. Super creepy.

The pieces of evidence were taken to the CIT to be added to the evidence room, and the organic trophies were destroyed by me in Lexi's lab.

I'm doing my best to hold on to the image of Owen before his first death, when he was the human love of my life, but now my happy memories are polluted by nightmarish visions of him as the Virtuous Hybresang, mutilating and murdering his victims. As for Amon… even though he's dead, all I feel for him now is hatred and repulsion. To think he was ready to kill me just to complete his absurd revenge… To think he ordered Owen's murder…

Killing my ex-fiancé was undoubtedly the hardest thing I've ever had to do. This will haunt me for the rest of my life.

I went back to work the day before yesterday. I was starting to go crazy brooding alone in my apartment; even the purring of Putrid and binge-watching shows couldn't comfort me. I would burst into tears over the slightest thing… and because it frustrated me to cry when I was supposed to face the situation like a warrior, I would sob even more. A vicious cycle. Thank god, no one saw me in this tear-stained mess except my cat.

Yesterday, I intervened with Malphas in an armed bank robbery. Since the Sinner criminals slit the throats of two hostages and shot at us, we had to kill them all. It felt good, in the moment, to feel useful again and save some innocent demons. Well, innocent… so to speak. No one is truly innocent in Infernum.

Nevertheless, I feel a bit better now that I'm back at work. Action is undoubtedly my best medicine.

After three days of incessant calls mostly consisting of *My little cat, call me back, I'm worried about you* Wills gave up. I expected him to teleport to my place in Hybresang mode to force the issue, but surprisingly, he respected my wish to keep some distance between us. I suppose he must be super busy, too, and for good reason…

Today is a big day for Infernum. It's the first round of the Federator elections. The media are all over this event. Many demons have gone to vote at the administrative offices of our world.

Not me.

Exhausted, I get home from the CIT around five PM after conducting a grueling interrogation of an Envyfiend smuggler.

And I find Kelen, sitting in the middle of my couch, with Putrid sprawled across his lap.

I'm shocked, not by his presence, but by the fact that he's petting my cat, who he couldn't stand before. And the big black tomcat is rubbing against his tanned hand, delighted by the demonic pampering. You have to understand, my Putrid hates strangers, especially men, and he *never* lets anyone scratch his belly, not even Ondine or me. In other words, this scene is surreal.

"How did you manage this feat, Wills? Are you capable of hypnotizing animals, too?"

"No, I just brought him some food," the Magistrate answers calmly.

My gaze flies to a tuna can lying on the floor near the couch. Great, he's corrupting my cat, too. My shoulders slump.

"Your obese nutria smells a bit less awful than last time," Kelen notes, staring at me. "Or maybe I'm just getting used to his stench."

"What are you doing here, Wills?"

"In three hours, they're going to announce the election results."

"Exactly. I repeat: what are you doing *here*?"

He gestures with his chin toward something on my table. A large, elegant, white box adorned with a black bow.

"What's in there, several kilos of tuna?" I suggest with a sarcastic grin.

"Open it and see," he encourages, displacing Putrid from his lap so he can stand.

I untie the bow and lift the lid of the box.

Oh, okay.

The guy brings a can of tuna for my cat and a stunning evening gown worth thousands of Forks for me to bribe us both. Everything's just perfect!

I close the lid, exhaling to keep my cool while my guest vigorously brushes off the dark cat hair from his clothes.

"Wills, out with it. What do you want?"

"For you to put this dress on your lovely body and accompany me to the Magistrates' Palace for the gala tonight to celebrate my majestic victory as Federator, Myrina," he states in a penetrating voice.

"First, don't count your chickens before they hatch: you haven't won the election yet; there will be a second round. Second, I didn't vote for you, just so you know. Third, no."

He stuffs his hands in his pockets and leans his fine backside against the edge of my table. Oh, dear lord. His. Fine. Butt. On. My. Table. I close my eyes for a second to forget my sudden urge to bite his divine ass.

"After the results are announced, revealing my name and Beliale's, my rival will publicly withdraw in my favor. I will be elected Federator of the Sinners tonight, Myrina." He flashes a charming smile. "Even if you didn't vote for me."

"You're very confident, Mr. Unicorn. Why is that?"

His smile fades, as I hoped. He growls at the sarcastic nickname I just gave him, teasing him about his new handicap.

"I made an arrangement with Beliale."

"Arrangement, right! You blackmailed her by threatening to expose that she presided over the tribunal that condemned my parents to death."

"Blackmail is a form of arrangement."

My intuition was correct. The initial involvement of the Lustspawn Magistrate was kept quiet when the investigation's outcome was revealed to journalists at a press conference at the CIT five days ago. Zagam didn't want to give me any explanations and ordered me to keep my mouth shut about it. I made my own deductions; the witch covered her tracks. This isn't the first time a Magistrate has funded the CIT, in my opinion. I didn't press the issue at the time because I could be fired for opposing this hierarchical decision—and because I have other demons to deal with—but I don't forget anything. Karma, Beliale…

"Would you have preferred the judge who ordered Arthur and Lysippé Holmes's death to become Federator of Infernum, Myrina?"

"Of course not. But you're no better than her in politics. The proof is that you're blackmailing her like the scum you are."

"A small evil in service of a greater good. I'm going to reform our government and elevate our society, my little cat. Believe in me."

"I don't believe in you. Neither of you should be Federator. This so-called democracy is a farce."

"That's your opinion, not mine. Nor that of the millions of demon voters."

"This debate is as pointless as it is boring, Wills. Take your gift and go back to Infernum to rehearse your dishonest thank-you speech. I'm not coming to this ball of pompous jerks."

"Even if I promise to remove your mark after the ball, Myrina?"

A disillusioned smile spreads across my lips. More blackmail. The sly bastard had planned this.

"You'll remove it anyway. I'll make sure of it."

"But you know me, my little cat, I intended to drag it out as long as possible to drive you mad," he says, drawling. "If you agree to come tonight, you'll be freed from my seal sooner than expected. Unless you're not in such a hurry to break the bond after all? That would explain why you've been avoiding me for a week."

Pffft. What a two-bit trick. He's usually more subtle than this.

"I'm not avoiding you, Wills," I lie, frowning. "In case you haven't noticed, I've had more important matters to deal with than your Hybresang navel-gazing after everything that happened at the factory. Wrapping up the investigation, dealing with my grandfa— Amon's inheritance, fighting with my sister because of your advances. Why do you want me to be your official date? I bet you have tons of demonesses lined up outside your office, eager to play arm candy and giggle for the cameras. I don't belong among the high society people you mingle with, and you know it. We're not from the same world. I'd despise them, and they'd despise me right back. The idea of setting foot at this social event horrifies me."

Kelen removes a hand from his pocket and, with two fingers, begins to caress my bare arm with a voluptuous delicacy. Goose bumps rise on my skin.

"I want to share my victory with *you*, Myrina. You alone. Not with them. They mean nothing to me," he states, his tone heavy with implication.

I bite the inside of my cheeks, my heart beating faster at his words. My skin burns where he touches me. And beneath my pants, the mark on my thigh tingles.

"*I* don't want to share anything with you, Wills. You've messed up my relationship with my sister," I retort through clenched teeth, pulling my arm away.

"That wasn't my intention."

"Bullshit. You did everything you could to make me give in to temptation, even when you were with her."

"But you didn't give in. You repeatedly denied me the one thing I desire more than anything."

Damn, he's been so serious and intense these last few minutes, it's unsettling.

"I was wrong about you."

What, Kelen Wills admitting he was wrong? Did I hear that right? Did his tongue slip? Is he being sincere?

"When I invited myself into your dream after our first meeting, I told you that you wanted to submit to my authority. I misjudged you. We talked about domination and submission. Now, I can assure you, you don't need a master to flourish. In truth, you're far too strong to be dominated by anyone."

He stares at me while I stare at the wall. "You need an equal. I've realized that's what I've been searching for, too, for centuries. I have no desire for another submissive woman for a night; I hope to find my equal someday. That's why I marked you, Myrina. To not lose the one who could be my life partner."

I stiffen with nervousness and turn my head toward him, stunned by his last words. I stammer, "Y-your life partner? But Wills, that's utterly ridiculous! I only have about fifteen years left to live, at best!"

"The honor of spending those next fifteen years by your side would be a wonderful gift to me, Myrina. Its fleeting nature is precisely what makes it so precious and intense." His pupils dilate, his voice softens. "I swear to you, I won't waste a second of that time."

My breathing quickens. I'm on the verge of a breakdown. I step back to clear my head.

He's crazy. His neurons must have taken a vacation last week when Owen tore off his horn.

"You should go. I have things to do."

"It's up to you if you want to keep my mark or not, Myrina. But if you want me to remove it, consider my proposition. Oh, and if you change your mind about tonight's event, know that I've added your name to the guest list and authorized access to the Magistrates' Palace on your badge. The dress is yours regardless of your decision; I never return items I personally purchase from luxury stores."

Personally? Yeah right, he probably delegated that task to a subordinate!

"Wills, damn it, I'm not going to that eve—"

He teleports before I finish my sentence.

CHAPTER 39

THE TASTE OF RISK

"We have two lives, and the second begins when we realize we only have one."
~Confucius

KELEN

She's coming tonight.

She hesitates. She's afraid. She's filled with doubts.

Yet, she will do it.

I feel it through our bond. I know it deep within my being.

She's not ready yet to accept being my partner, I'm aware of that. However, she's dying to take the next step in our relationship, to evolve it, and to demolish the barriers she has erected between us. It's a considerable risk for a woman like her, with the emotional baggage she carries, composed of her fears, pains, uncertainties, mistrust, and independence.

But I am intimately convinced that tonight, she will take the leap for me.

Because Myrina Holmes is a hybrid Tracker.

Because she has a taste for risk.

Because she lives for danger.

And because, in her busy mind, I embody both the most dangerous risk she could ever take in her life…

… and the comforting hope of finally connecting with someone who truly understands and accepts her as she is.

She has a double nature. Like me. I recognized it. She hasn't yet. That will come in due time.

Standing in front of the mirror in my office at the Magistrates' Palace, I skillfully finish tying my black- and white-striped silk tie around my shirt collar. This dark Federator suit was already impressive in my wardrobe, but on my sculpted body, it's a thousand times better. If I were impressed easily, I'd impress myself. All the demons of Infernum will have their eyes on me tonight, whether they're at home behind their TV screens or in the hall of the Palace. While getting dressed, I played my favorite retro music on my phone: "Johnny B. Goode," performed by Chuck Berry. It perfectly matches my mood. I discovered this rocking gem with its lively rhythm when I heard it in the movie *Back to the Future*. I hum along to the catchy tune, swaying lightly.

There's a knock on my office door.

"Come in, Sam."

In the mirror's reflection, I see my lieutenant open the door, wearing full armor. He's in charge of the security that has been reinforced for the occasion. All the Ragebeasts of my legion have been mobilized. Major officers with telepathic powers have verified their identities beforehand because I won't allow a repeat of the Rebels' attack during the Horn of Plenty ceremony to tarnish my political ascent.

"It's almost time, Kel."

No delays this time. I must set an example. "How do I look?" I ask, turning to him with a smirk

"Arrogant, tyrannical, rugged, lazy—"

"In this suit, idiot!"

"You look stunning, Kel." Sam sighs, sounding bored. As always.

He's not buttering me up; he genuinely thinks I look hot. If he weren't in my service, he'd have tried to get me into his bed. He admitted it to me last century, one tipsy night. I teased him about it for ages to make him uncomfortable. I enjoy arousing desire in both women and men, even though I'm a pure-blooded heterosexual.

However, my sin of pride was shaken by the loss of my horn. Except for Myrina, the Virtuous jury member who was imprisoned in the abandoned factory, and Sam, to whom I confided this secret, no one knows I'm an amputee in my demonic form. I resumed my human appearance before the Trackers arrived and made sure not to shapeshift this week, as this new mutilation could have discredited me with some of my Sinners voters. But I'm realistic; it will inevitably come out. I won't be able to hide something like this forever, even with tricks. I'll deal with it when the time comes. And if any demon dares to mock my disability… I'll slaughter them.

Except my Tracker, of course.

Mister Unicorn.

By the way, is this childish nickname amusing or annoying?

I haven't decided yet.

MYRINA

Don't turn on the TV, Myri.

Don't turn on that bitch of a TV.

Too late, my finger is already on the remote button.

I immediately see Magistrate Hybresang on screen, cheered on by his Sinners supporters. On the podium, he's fully savoring his glory; thousands of black confetti swirl around him. I read the banner at the bottom of the screen: *Kelen Wills, Federator of the Sinners!*

Well, there it is. It's official. He's climbed to the top. I missed the election results announcement and Beliale's declaration of stepping back in favor of her rival.

The Lustspawn Magistrate in a tight black dress looks like she's swallowed a lemon, while he flashes a radiant smile, arms raised in triumph. Ugh, they look like a damn Hollywood couple at the Cannes Film Festival…

The camera zooms in on Wills. Oh my god, that insane suit! I swallow hard as saliva gathers at the corner of my lips. The supreme bastard is devastatingly handsome, it's infuriating. This impeccable outfit triggers an outrageously violent fantasy in me: I imagine shredding his pants with my claws, ripping off his shirt, and strangling him with his tie, I don't know in what order.

I sneak a sidelong glance at the box containing the haute couture dress he brought me earlier. I should have hidden it under my bed, or maybe thrown it out the window. But I didn't.

Anyway, it doesn't matter, I'm not going to that party. I have nothing to do there. I've already messed up my relationship with my sister because of him. I'm not going to fall into that trap again and get fooled!

"The honor of spending those next fifteen years by your side would be a wonderful gift to me, Myrina. Its fleeting nature is precisely what makes it so precious and intense. I won't waste a second of this time, I swear to you."

Hot air. Wills is just a smooth talker, that's all.

On screen, he scans the noisy crowd with his golden eyes while receiving obsequious congratulations from his Sinners rivals. He shakes hands and exchanges hugs, a slightly forced smile on his lips, never looking his various interlocutors in the eye. He seems to be searching for someone among the spectators.

He's looking for me.

At that moment, I feel all his disappointment at not seeing me like a slap in the face.

At that moment, I start to hesitate.

KELEN

It's been almost an hour now since I became the Federator of the Sinners of Infernum.

An hour of tedious and insipid discussions with these people, most of whom I despise. An hour of emptying glasses of Dragon's Bile and Ambrosia Nectar while mingling with guests, shadowed by Sam, who serves as my bodyguard. An hour of longing for the only person I really want to see and with whom I would have liked to share my joy, which diminishes minute by minute due to her absence.

I'm not enjoying myself. I'm no longer forcing a smile. There's a bitter taste on my tongue that not even alcohol can dull.

Only one person is missing, and the whole world seems depopulated.

That damn quote keeps running through my head.

I want to go home and be alone with my piano. I'd like to play Beethoven's *Moonlight Sonata* to externalize and soothe my emotions through music. Except I can't afford to leave so early. I have obligations, responsibilities, duties, a reputation. It royally sucks to be here right now, but that's how it is.

In fact, when yet another Sinners demon comes to congratulate me, I rudely brush him off. The idiot retreats, surprised by my hostility.

"Kel, chill. Make a little effort," advises my lieutenant quietly.

"I've been making efforts non-stop, Sam," I snap back sharply before downing the contents of my glass. "Get me another."

"No, you've had enough to drink tonight."

"It's not for you to judge, don't challenge my orders!"

"You're acting like a spoiled brat craving affection, Kel. Not like a Federator. You need to get yourself together."

"Fuck off, asshole," I growl, not knowing what else to say to him.

"Turn the page, Kel. She's not coming."

If we weren't in public, I'd punch him in the face.

"If you hadn't *accidentally* told Ondine that I marked her, Myrina would have come."

"I didn't do it on purpose, and I've already apologized to you about it. Besides, she would have found out sooner or later. It's just an excuse and—"

He keeps blabbering, but I stop listening.

A surge of static electricity runs through my skin under my suit. *She's here. She came.*

I forcefully shove my empty glass into Sam's hands, who has stopped talking.

My impatient, feverish gaze scans the crowd, sweeping past all these smiling faces that I couldn't care less about, searching for a bichromatic mane crowning the most beautiful pair of amethysts in the world.

After a few endless moments, finally, I spot her.

She's at the back of the room, perched on the first step of the staircase, a hand on the stone railing. Alone, inaccessible, ethereal. The timeless statue of a sublime creature, part goddess, part demon. My gaze collides with hers, instantly setting fire to my dick, my loins, my lungs, and my stomach. And she smiles at me, completing my internal combustion by burning the organ beating in my chest.

I. Am. Screwed.

I vaguely aware of this in this moment, but I'm too stunned to fully integrate what it implies. I attribute this bewildering, irrational sensation to my mark and our connection. Her irresistible violet gems framed by smoky makeup ensnare me in their sparkling nets, engulfing me in their mystical depths. And here I am, willingly imprisoned by those deep eyes and that gentle smile. A consenting castaway, a masochistic victim of her sadistic charms, a suicidal Sinner, unable to surface at the moment.

Only reluctantly do I tear my gaze away from hers to run it over her body. I harden even more at the sight.

I had a keen eye in the store. I immediately knew the dress would be perfect for her, and I was not mistaken.

A long iridescent satin gown in the same color as her scales, both refined and sensual. It seems tailor-made to accentuate every curve of her slender figure. With thin straps and an indecent V-neckline, the shimmering dress drapes fluidly down to the floor. Slit mid-thigh on one side, it highlights her chest, waist, and hips.

Her hair is styled in a neat bun, adorned with a dark feather above her right ear. This is the epitome of sexy and glamorous.

I'm not the only man admiring her, by the way. Several male Sinners in the crowd undress this dazzling half-succubus with their eyes, accentuating the exotic femininity she exudes.

But she didn't come for them.

She didn't come for me to remove the mark either.

She didn't come to dance, drink, eat, laugh, chat with these snob demons, or to show off on my arm in front of cameras and photographers.

No, she came solely for me.

Not for the Hybresang.

Not for the Magistrate.

Not for the Federator.

Just for Kelen.

And to give a real chance for our relationship to evolve.

To give *us* a chance.

I lift my eyes to hers. Knowing she can read my lips, I silently form these words that hover between us above the others, "Tonight,

Myrina Holmes, I'm going to fuck you."

She raises an eyebrow before slowly articulating in turn, tapping herself between the breasts, "No, asshole, I'm going to fuck you."

I quickly loosen my tie. Suddenly, I'm short of breath.

Yes, I'm definitely screwed, I think as I watch her turn on the stairs.

But this downfall has a wonderful taste.

She ascends the steps with a swaying gait, her ample buttocks hugged by her dress, and gives me a mischievous glance over her shoulder, as if inviting me to follow.

Game on, Wills.

CHAPTER 40

SUCCUMBING TO TEMPTATION

"The only way to get rid of temptation is to yield to it." ~Oscar Wilde, *The Picture of Dorian Gray*

MYRINA

I step into the new office of the Federator Sinner, as spacious and luxurious as a presidential cabinet. First, I notice a leather L-shape sofa positioned in front of a monumental stone fireplace where a few embers glow, but it's the view of the sprawling city behind the large bay window that then captures my attention.

Under the two moons of Infernum, countless lights cluster along the slender columns of Neethoraa's skyscrapers, like golden witnesses to the demonic life teeming behind the gray and black facades. The ancient Palace of the Magistrates perched on its rocky hill proudly overlooks the entire valley and the bustling capital of the Ragebeasts.

I could spend hours gazing at this view, but I didn't come here to swoon over the nighttime landscape.

I'm not one hundred percent sure about this. I even wonder if I'm making a mistake. Oh, I'm dying to, that's for sure… but a small part of me still remains wary of him. I don't know if I'll manage to forget my reservations and completely let go. I'd say that, in a way, I'm testing myself as much as I'm testing him.

Kelen teleports behind me.

His presence warms the seal under my dress like an invisible ember just pressed against my thigh.

His arms around me, I don't turn around. If I dare to bathe in the darkness-gold of his eyes, I'll lose all control. My poor heart is already beating at a crazy pace.

His palms mold around the curve of my bare shoulders. My muscles contract and tremble under his light touch.

"I've missed you."

These words whispered into my ear are both a caress, a confession, a promise, intimacy. My mind swims in the mist saturated with sensual electricity that floats around us, and my body is more sensitive than ever.

"We saw each other four hours ago."

His lips brush against my earlobe as he murmurs, "Those four hours could have been four centuries. I thought you wouldn't come."

So did I.

He starts pecking my neck with fleeting kisses while his hands run up and down my arms, raising the fine hairs that dot my skin. I feel like tendrils of velvety warmth are wrapping around me without suffocating me. I close my eyes and take a deep breath.

"What should I call you now? Mister Federator?" I inquire with a hint of cynicism.

I never called him by his name so far; I've never been that familiar with him.

"Just call me Kel, Myrina. Although, don't expect me to use the diminutive of your name, I find it ridiculous," he remarks, his breath tickling my neck.

"I prefer calling you *asshole*. It suits you better."

As a gentle punishment, he abruptly bites my ear. Opening my eyes, I curse as I elbow him in the stomach in retaliation. It's futile; his abs are so firm he feels nothing. An amused and carefree laugh escapes him.

I'm a fan of his husky laugh. I wish I could lock it in a music box to savor that melody whenever I'm feeling down.

"Do you want me to remove the mark tonight, my little cat?"

The million-Fork question…

"I'm not sure yet. We're on a trial period for a permanent

position, aren't we?"

Kelen smiles against my skin without answering my question.

Then he starts removing the feather and pins holding my hair while continuing to kiss my neck, throat, and shoulder. I melt a little more with each kiss. Every gesture exudes wild eroticism. The languid tenderness he displays is almost unsettling; he deliberately prolongs the anticipation.

"There's another advantage to this seal," he points out casually, tucking the pins into his pants pocket as he removes them from my hair.

"What's that?"

"It will intensify your orgasm and mine."

"Hmm. We'd need to have one in the first place," I note as my long mane, freed from its bun, cascades down my back.

His fingers slide under the straps of my dress, lazily tracing the ends of my collarbones. My breathing becomes shallow. Goddamn, my nipples are as hard as rocks, and in my thong, it's like Niagara Falls.

"You won't have just *one*, Myrina," he replies in a husky whisper, slowly descending the zipper of my dress.

"Braggart," I mutter as his index nail trails down the curve of my spine to my tailbone.

The back of my dress fully open, I take three steps forward to evade his hands.

I pivot toward him, keeping my distance. A half-smile on his seductive lips, Kel anchors his gleaming, greedy gaze in mine.

His irises have adopted a deep red hue.

Without breaking eye contact, I lower my straps along my arms and gently slide the satin dress down my body until it falls around my feet.

✳✳✳

KELEN

My Virtuous Sinner stands before me, enhanced by semi-darkness of the room, clad only in a black lace thong. She wears no bra. Her eyes, becoming heterochromatic, shine like a pair of gemstones: one ruby and one diamond. Her milk and chocolate strands cascade over her shoulders, her swollen breasts rise and fall irregularly, her long slender legs press together. My gaze lingers on the beauty mark near her areola, and even longer on my seal at the top of her thigh. I savor every detail of this enticing sight. My dick's hungering desire for her is increasingly painful. I'm glad I didn't wear boxers.

Tonight, she will be mine. Finally.

"You're a work of art in your own right, Myrina Holmes."

"Another one in your collection," she murmurs softly with a hint of bitterness.

Her words briefly catch me off guard. How could she suggest such a thing?

"You know better than that, my little cat. You don't compare a masterpiece to the preliminary sketches that came before."

She shoots me her dark, probing Tracker's gaze, as if assessing my sincerity. Despite the strength of our bond, she still harbors doubts about my intentions toward her.

She won't have any doubts once I'm deeply buried within her.

Unable to wait any longer, I decide to join her, but she beats me to it.

Almost naked, she walks toward me with determination, hooks her neck around mine to tilt my head toward hers, and passionately captures my mouth.

Her tongue slips between my parted lips, plays vigorously with mine, ignites me like a wildfire. I try to grab her mass of hair, but she forcefully pushes my arms aside and hastily unbuttons my suit jacket, tearing off two buttons in the process. While nibbling and licking my lips like a panther famished beyond measure, she pulls down my jacket, slides it down my arms, and throws it to the floor, all in less than five seconds. I growl into her mouth, breath increasingly short, loins on fire. Damn, she's already unleashed; I feel like the foreplay won't last long.

Myrina fumbles at my collar and loosens my tie further. She backs away from my lips, panting, to pull it over my head and loop it around hers. As she swiftly undoes the buttons of my shirt, I smile at the sexy sight of my tie hanging provocatively between her ample breasts. But she barely gives me time to enjoy the view before she dives back into my mouth with a passionate kiss, ripping my shirt halfway open with her claws. Good god, she's as hot as Vésave's lava. I love it, but I can't afford to stay on the sidelines for another second in our race toward a monumental orgasm. *Wake up, Wills! Take control of the situation; your reputation as a fiery and beastly incubus is on the line!*

Without waiting for her to strip me of my shirt and while continuing to kiss her passionately, I grab her by the thighs and swiftly lift her off the ground. Her firm legs clamp tightly around my hips, her hands gripping my tense shoulders, her supple chest pressing against my already sweaty torso. The erect peaks of her breasts burn my skin, and her pussy presses against my erection. Her sweet womanly scent and musky succubus pheromones permeate me. I seize the exquisite curves of her ass to forcefully rub her wet pussy against my stiff cock. Myrina arches against me, rolling her hips, moaning plaintively into my mouth, and it drives me wild.

If I were to listen to my instincts, I'd unzip my pants and fuck her right here, standing, still dressed, holding her against me. I can keep the rhythm in any position, and I'm sure she can, too. But for our first time, I don't want to skip the foreplay; it's essential for building up desire and pleasure.

I teleport us right in front of the bay window and push her roughly against the glass. I devour her luscious lips, nibble on her jawline, and lap at her throat like a wild animal. Each of my kisses draws a sigh of delight from her, each lick a low moan. The delicious sounds she makes electrify me like never before. This is the music that makes me intensely vibrate, the music I want to hear every day, every night.

She throws her head back, clutching at the collar of my shirt. I slide my hand between our burning bodies to brush against her mark on her thigh, making her shudder. She caresses my chest and claws at my stomach. We're both sweaty and panting, and we haven't even started yet.

"Tell me, my little cat," I whisper against her lips, pulling aside the edge of her thong to insert my thumb into her mound. "Tell me how much you want me."

"I want you, Kel. I want you…"

I press fiercely on her clit.

"Ah! So much!"

Oh, she's going to have me. She's going to feel me, every inch. Many times.

As I stroke her bud with the tip of my thumb, she presses her palm against my shaft through my pants and massages it with energetic sensuality. She makes me lose control.

I set her down to rip off her lingerie; she lets out a small cry of surprise that makes my cock throb under her hand. She shoots me a sharp look as I toss the lace to the floor, but I don't care. I spread my fingers between her legs and plunge my index and middle finger into her drenched pussy as far as I can. With her ear caught between my sharp teeth, she mewls and writhes under my wild thrusts. I aim to coax every note her vocal cords can produce, from the lowest to the highest pitch, and to make every part of her feline body tremble.

Suddenly, she grabs my shirt and pushes me back, forcing me to pull my fingers from her. I scowl with a growl of protest, but when I see her drop to her knees in front of me, my displeasure turns into undisguised delight. She unzips me in no time, pulls down my pants, and wraps her slender fingers around the base of my dick to give it the attention it deserves.

The sight of her beautiful face right in front of my stiff cock is exhilarating. I've dreamed of this a thousand times. With one hand resting under her chin, I stroke her jaw with my thumb.

"Myrina…"

She looks up at me with fevered eyes. A mischievous smile spreads across her lips. She wants to kill me.

"Wills?" she says innocently, lightly scratching my skin.

"If you can't take it all in your mouth, I won't hold it against you. I know I'm very well endowed."

She laughs joyfully. I'm not joking, though. My throat dry, I swallow hard as she runs the tip of her pink tongue over her lips, reddened by our kisses.

"Who says I'm going to blow you, asshole?" she purrs, sliding her free hand between her thighs.

Unable to stop myself, I watch her touch herself without a shred of modesty. Her still fist remains around my blood-engorged cock, her half-closed eyes locked onto my face. This is a form of torture far worse than what she put me through at the 1001 Nights of Lust. If she had done this during our bondage session, I would have answered all her questions without hesitation.

"And who says I won't just leave you hanging after I get myself off?" she taunts cruelly, Sinner to the tip of her claws at this moment.

"You wouldn't do that," I protest, tense in every sense of the word.

"Are you sure about that?"

Continuing her erotic self-touching, she runs my swollen tip along her sealed lips, spreading my pre-cum on her mouth, making it glisten. She's provoking me, leaving me breathless. I apply a little pressure on her mouth by thrusting with my hips, but she doesn't open up. She's still denying me access. I've never been this sexually frustrated in my life. I almost regret insisting on foreplay. I usually love playing around, but this is too much for me, damn it!

The little vixen flicks her tongue over the tip of my cock for a split second. I wrap around my hand the tie that is around her neck and yank it sharply, trying to urge her head forward to give me a blowjob. But she pulls back with a mischievous laugh, licking her lips, which finishes me off. The deadly swish of a guillotine echoes in my mind. Furious, I slam my palm against the damn window in front of me, shouting.

She's even more wicked in bed than I am, it's unbelievable!

"If you could see the look on your face, Kel… I'm tempted to take a picture and send it to the press," she says with a caustic tone that still carries a hint of tenderness.

"I bet you'd be a lot less cocky and make a funny face, *too*, if I jerked off in front of you and finished with a facial, kitten."

This time, she freezes, eyes wide, mouth agape… and I take the opportunity to slip gently into her open mouth.

Thank Satan, Myrina doesn't resist or make me wait any longer. She eagerly takes in my tip, then greedily swallows the rest like a starved female Gluttonfiend who has been fasting for days. Her teeth graze my skin as she deep-throats me and sucks powerfully. A moment later, her head pulls back. She twirls her skilled tongue around my length before plunging back down, taking me in between her warm lips. Pressing my forearm against the glass, I bury my other hand in her silky hair at the back of her head, no longer holding back my grunts of pleasure. Meanwhile, my lover continues to pleasure herself while giving me the most exquisite blowjob… It doesn't take long before I lean forward, resting my forehead against the glass and clenching my fist tightly.

This blowjob is devilishly divine: I'm in heaven.

*****

MYRINA

"Stand up, my little cat," he murmurs, gently placing his fingers around my throat.

I comply without hesitation. Perfect timing; I can't take it anymore, I need to feel him inside me.

"Are you on the pill?" he asks, brushing my cheek with the back of his hand.

It's the only birth control demons use since we're immune to STDs.

"Of course."

His fiery gaze locked onto mine, Hybresang lifts my right leg for me to wrap around his hip and presses me against the bay window. Breathing heavily, he closes his hand over mine around the base of his dripping cock. Together, we guide him to his destination between my thighs.

He finally plunges into the depths of my feminine flesh, imposing his presence, both burning and massive. Slowly, gently halfway… then with a violent urgency to the hilt. The powerful jolt of his penetration tears an endless groan from me, which Kelen muffles with a new, fervent kiss. I wrap my trembling arms around his neck, entwining my tongue with his. My lover withdraws slowly, leaving only his tip inside, then thrusts back in with such brutal frenzy that he pins me to the glass with his movement. I moan to my heart's content. My claws dig into his neck and shoulder blades. He kisses me even more intensely. No, correction, he doesn't kiss me: he ravages my mouth like a madman to *claim* me.

It's not just good; it's fantastic. And I know he feels exactly the same, I can sense it through our bond. I can't believe he's finally inside me. He sets me ablaze from the tips of my toes to the top of my head. Filaments of light flutter before my eyes. Honestly, it feels like

I'm living the hottest fantasy of my life. No doubt it's because of the mark enhancing our physical sensations, but I've never experienced such pleasure with a man. And we're just getting started…

"God, you feel amazing, Myrina," he growls in a rough voice against my lips.

Thrusting into me harder, he unclasps my arms from around his neck, roughly grabbing my wrists and pinning my arms against the window on either side of my head. The coldness of the glass forms a striking contrast to the fiery heat of his body deliciously colliding with mine. Several crystal elements of the chandelier hanging from the ceiling rattle. I blink.

"Kel… The chandelier. Your telekinesis…"

"Don't give a damn about the furniture," he growls, thrusting even harder, making me moan louder.

So hard, in fact, that the glass behind me starts to crack. Oh Lord, the Hybresang isn't holding back! If he doesn't moderate his fervor, we're going to shatter the window and fall!

"Teleport us elsewhere, you idiot of a Sinner!"

Another thrust, another crack in the glass, another tremor of the chandelier. But finally, Kelen realizes he's putting us in danger. In the blink of an eye, he teleports us in front of the couch. Okay, time to switch positions.

I push him back, and he collapses onto the seat. I immediately straddle him, he grips my hips, and we're back together. Perfect, now I can set my own pace. I undulate above him, my hands in his tousled hair. His piercing, depraved gaze locks onto mine as his fingers sensually caress my buttocks. His masculine dimpled chin draws my eyes, and without thinking, I tilt his head back to give him a treat. While impaling myself on him up and down, I suck on his chin until he lets out an annoyed cry. He grabs my throat to push me away and rubs his lower face. Oops, a bruise is already darkening his skin.

"Damn, Myrina! You gave me a hickey, I bet!"

I flash him an apologetic smile. "Yep, so what?"

"On my chin! How am I supposed to hide that?"

"It'll be gone in half an hour, stop whining. Worst case, I'll put some foundation on it."

He glares at me as if I called him Virtuous. Laughing, I intensify

my thrusts to make him forget about the little cosmetic mishap…
and it works for a few seconds. But without warning, he decides to
get revenge by leaning toward my breast. That lunatic actually bites
my nipple. The pain makes me scream on the spot. Despite him
licking to soothe the bite, I'm fired up. So, in retaliation, I scratch his
chest until it bleeds over a seven-inch span.

Yes, things are starting to get out of hand. It's rare for sex to stay
soft and gentle between demons. In fact, between Kelen and me,
I'd say this was inevitable. Knowing us, fighting and fucking were
always going to be closely linked. Good thing, it adds a double dose
of spice to our interactions. Wrath and lust, an explosive mix of sins!

Five minutes later, the leather couch is marred with multiple
scratch marks, and we are both covered in bloody bites and
lacerations, bruises, and hickeys.

Struggling, we tumble and collapse onto the floor, with him on
top of me. I roll him onto his back to straddle him again, but he
shoves me off and regains the upper hand, cursing. I let him take
charge for a moment, just long enough to regain my strength. With
a sigh of contentment, I close my eyes, arching against him, my legs
wrapped around his hips. When I open my eyes again, the demon
has teleported us to the floor in front of the bay window to cool his
sweat- and blood-soaked skin, because Mr. Federator is *starting to get
too damn hot*, as he put it. Such a wimp.

The crystal chandelier, constantly bouncing and swinging due to
the uncontrollable waves of his telekinesis, detaches from the ceiling
and plummets to the floor six feet away from us with a thunderous
crash. Well, there go the first major material damages.

About a minute later, as our pleasure escalates exponentially, a
mirror to our right shatters, and a rolling chair flies into my field of
vision over his shoulder, crashing into a wall.

"KEL!" I remind him, pinching his nipple.

He squints at me in annoyance, and somehow, I find myself lying
flat on my stomach on his desk, with him behind me. Everything on
the desk flies off abruptly, swept away by an invisible hand: computer,
papers, pens, lamp. Without a word, my hot-blooded lover spreads
my thighs, lifts one leg onto the desk, and enters me doggy style,
unleashing all his demonic ferocity in his final thrusts. My god, that
rhythm! He grabs my hair *and* my tie to force me to arch backward.

My hands grip the edge of the desk, which cracks and trembles with each deep thrust from Kelen, and I climax spectacularly, my mouth wide open in an unending cry of ecstasy. When he joins me a second later in rapture, roaring like a lion, a myriad of multicolored stars dance before my eyes, my body shakes with an exhilarating quake, and every fiber of my being ignites.

The Hybresang lies down on top of me, nestling his burning face into my neck. Inside his heaving chest that's pressed against my back, his heart beats as fast as mine. Is it enjoyable? That's an understatement. I'm in fantastic shape, thanks to our energetic exchanges of Lustspawn and the hormonal torrent coursing through my body. I could compete in a triathlon.

"Mm, that was amazing," he whispers, planting a kiss on the frantic pulse throbbing in my throat. "And you didn't do too bad yourself."

I burst out laughing and smack his butt with a loud slap. What a jerk!

"We've half-destroyed your workspace."

"There's still the other half to destroy," he murmurs in my ear. "Ready for round two, my wild little cat?"

Hell yes. He promised me multiple orgasms, and I haven't forgotten.

Oh, did I not mention?

Incubus don't lose their erection between rounds and can ejaculate multiple times in a row without any issue.

Two hours later, we have to interrupt our volcanic romp because Sam is banging insistently on the door, reminding Kelen that many people are waiting for him downstairs. The hickey on his chin is nothing but a bad memory now, and I made sure not to leave any visible marks on the exposed parts of his body, so he's presentable.

Lounging naked on the battered sofa, I watch him thoughtfully as he gets dressed. Pants, shoes, a new shirt (yes, the man even has a backup wardrobe in his office), and an impeccably tailored suit jacket.

I sigh in dismay. Presentable? No, Kel is even more radiant than before our tryst. I'm melting and falling apart at the same time. This guy could fuck me another ten times, and I still wouldn't be satisfied. I desperately want him again, but I'll have to be patient.

"Why don't you get your little butt off that couch and come downstairs with me?" he asks, trying—and I mean trying—to tame his dark hair with his fingers.

"No. I told you, galas aren't my thing. How long do you think you'll be, Wills?"

A mischievous smile stretches his lips, which are swollen from our bold kisses. My question clearly delights him.

"An additional hour among the pack of hypocrites should be enough. Why do you ask, Holmes?"

I shrug, deciding it's best to keep quiet. Kelen approaches the sofa and crouches down next to me.

"Would you like us to spend the *whole* night together?" he interprets in a velvety voice, cupping my breast in his large, tanned hand and squeezing it sensually.

I shrug again, trying not to commit too much.

He gently takes my chin, still smiling, and plants a soft kiss on my lips. "There's an Arcadus in the adjoining meeting room to this office, Myrina," he reveals, taking something out of his pocket and balancing it on the swell of my breast. "I'll join you at my place later; we'll make love on my piano."

It's his personal badge.

My surprised gaze meets his. I shiver, but not because of the object. Make love? A strange phrase coming from him. It's the first time I've heard him say that.

"I didn't say yes," I point out, eyeing the card that wobbles with each of my breaths.

"But you didn't say no, my little cat."

He winks confidently and sexily, then teleports downstairs among his many guests.

"Go fuck yourself, asshole," I mutter, grabbing the badge between two fingers.

✷✷✷

As I finish getting dressed, my phone rings. I open my evening purse to take out my smartphone. Unknown number.

"Myrina Holmes speaking."

"Good evening, Miss Holmes," a deep woman's voice greets me. "I hope I'm not disturbing you, my child? We haven't met yet, but I hope to remedy that as soon as possible."

This voice sounds familiar. I've heard it somewhere before. *On TV, perhaps…?*

"May I ask who's calling?"

"I'm Beliale, Magistrate of the Lustspawn Legion."

My whole body tenses. One of the individuals responsible for my parents' execution.

"What do you want from me?" I question coldly.

"I saw you earlier in the reception hall. Nice dress, by the way. Kelen came back downstairs just two minutes ago with the satisfied look of an incubus, so I assumed you two finished whatever you were doing together."

A nosy one. Figures.

"Ahem. You should also assume it's best for you to mind your scaly ass if you don't want trouble with me."

I refrain from adding the insult *blonde bimbo*, which would probably be in bad taste.

"Miss Holmes, I seek to make amends with you regarding… you know what."

Sure, I believe you, bleach blonde.

"It was a lapse in judgment and direction that I regret. At some point, I'd like to explain myself to you so that there's no lingering animosity between us. In the meantime, allow me to warn you about this shameless womanizer and the undignified way he regards you."

A jealous and possessive ex. Great, just what I was missing! And since he blackmailed her to eliminate her from the second round of elections, she must be even more embittered.

"You can shove your warning where the sun doesn't shine."

"Charming… For centuries, Kelen has kept a red-covered notebook that he keeps in the top drawer of his home office desk. He's extremely proud of it and only shows it to his closest friends. He reveres it like the Holy Grail."

"So what?"

"It's his trophy list, Miss Holmes. If I were you, I'd check if my name is listed in that book to understand his intentions toward you in the short, medium, or long term."

"But you're not me, Beliale."

"Indeed. Only you can decide what to do with this little piece of information. Have a good evening, Miss Holmes," she says calmly before hanging up.

I bite my tongue, torn with doubt. My clouded eyes drift toward Kel's badge.

Lord, I hope with all my soul that this Lustspawn bitch is wrong or lying to me.

***

I open the first drawer of his desk.

A notebook with a red leather cover, just as she said.

My heart skips a beat. A frozen weight lodges itself in my stomach.

Damn it all.

I pick up the thick notebook. I flip through it. Some kind of record.

Hundreds of women's names. Strangers. Celebrities. I flip through the pages, growing paler with each turn. No, I correct myself, *thousands* of names. Alphabetically arranged.

I go to the letter H. What, Halle Berry? He can't be serious!

My name isn't on this page, but… the letters match the first names, it seems.

I reach the letter M, taking a deep breath.

Dozens more names.

And I see my name at the bottom of the page.

Can't be true.

I stare at it, incredulous.

"Myrina Holmes."

One name.

One name among thousands.

A masterpiece, he said.

I was just a challenge, nothing more.

I tear the page out mechanically. Crumple it in my trembling fist.

I close my eyes.

Open them again, jaw clenched.

Trust. What a monumental mistake.

Amon, Owen, Ondine… and now Kelen.

I should have never let my guard down with such a player. I should have realized he was lying and manipulating me from the start. He only wanted my body and to corrupt my moral principles in the process.

I feel so foolish for believing his fake story about an exclusive contract. In reality, he never saw me as anything more than an addition to his collection.

This is exactly why I avoid getting attached to the men I sleep with. To protect myself from pain, disillusionment, and abandonment. But this one deceived me with his actions and words.

I make my decision in less than ten seconds.

First thing, I light a fire in Wills's fireplace and toss the notebook in to burn.

Second thing, I grab a pen.

Third thing, I smooth out the list of names and, beneath mine, hastily write a few lines.

Fourth thing, I spread the sheet on his desk, prominently displayed so he won't miss it.

Fifth thing, I leave.

***

KELEN

I don't understand why she's not at my place when I return from the party. If she were there, I would sense her presence through our link. Could she have had an urgent matter, something come up? If so, why didn't she text me to let me know?

I felt something was wrong at some point. Intense pain. Deep disappointment. At that moment, I thought maybe she was remembering her parents' death, her grandfather's betrayal, or

Owen's murder, perhaps even all three at once. I resolved to do everything in my power tonight to erase her painful memories and her bout of sadness.

The open door to my office catches my attention.

Filled with a sense of foreboding, I teleport inside the room.

An odor of burnt leather and paper freezes me in place.

I find the torn sheet from my notebook on my desk. I pick it up to read, feeling as stressed as a young demon about to take flight for the first time in his life.

Damn. No. Not this.

Her name has been crossed out. And beneath it is written:

You just wanted to fuck me from the beginning. Mission accomplished, congratulations. Next time we meet, you'll remove that damn mark. And then, don't ever try to contact me again or I'll really kill you.

I'm furious with myself.

Intense pain. Deep disappointment.

They're not just hers anymore.

I crumple the paper in my reddening fist. My Ragebeast power slips beyond my control.

The sheet ignites in my hand. A moment later, it's reduced to dust crumbling between my clenched fingers.

Much like my fleeting story with Myrina Holmes.

EPILOGUE

"Strong souls, after failing, rise again and grow from their fall." ~Jules Sandeau, Marianna

ONE MONTH LATER

MYRINA

A beautiful night to die.

I turn off the engine of my bike, parked on the narrow sidewalk of the bridge spanning the four-lane highway.

After unbuckling my strap, I lift my helmet up to place it on the motorcycle seat. I shake my head briskly to tidy up my tousled hair. Two seconds later, a gust of warm wind blows it back onto my face. I curse. It's better to tie my hair back to avoid being bothered during the fall.

I check the time. Eleven-thirty-seven PM. I'm good on timing. I pull out a hair tie from my leather jacket pocket, twist my mane, and fashion a quick messy bun. There, much better.

I swing my leg over the railing overlooking the road and sit on it, legs dangling. Winged demons have a significant advantage over humans: they never get vertigo. But tonight, I have no plans to mutate or fly.

I light up one last menthol cigarette before taking the plunge. Inhaling slowly with the first puff, I gaze dreamily up at the Earth's sky. That's the drawback of the city compared to the countryside: you see far fewer stars here. On the other hand, the pearly moonlight is stunningly beautiful.

Moonlight…

My thoughts drift to *him* for a second. The echo of a sonata, both sweet and melancholy, escapes from a memory, resonating in my ears as if the tiny electronic parts had automatically memorized every note. Shaking my head, I banish his face, the piano, and the music from my mind. This isn't the time; I need to keep a clear head. I have something important to do.

Eleven-forty PM. Just one more minute.

Crushing the half-smoked cigarette on the guardrail, I flick it onto the highway below. Then, I rise to my perch, stretching out to loosen my muscles. Looking down at my boots, I realize they're dirty. Damn it. If I had noticed before leaving the apartment, I would have cleaned them, of course.

Eleven-forty-one PM. It's time.

Time for the leap of faith.

I lower my gaze to the noisy road where various vehicles with headlights on are passing by. One hundred feet of freefall without wings, Myrina Holmes.

It's going to be okay.

Stepping forward to the edge of the parapet, my phone vibrates in my leather jacket pocket, signaling it's time. Sean is on it; he's placed a tracker on the tanker truck to pinpoint its location.

There it is, right on cue. It passes beneath my bridge.

I spread my arms, inhale, and throw myself into the void.

A fall like that, I can tell you, really wakes up every pore!

I land crouched on the long black box truck speeding at sixty-two miles per hour. *Nicely calculated, Myri.* My claws extend from my fingers, embedding into the metal to stabilize my balance, buffeted by wind, mobility, and the speed of my new temporary means of transportation.

I stand up. No time to waste. I run along the truck toward the cabin. With momentum, I leap from the trailer to the cabin, over the elements connecting them.

The first salvo of silver bullets strikes beneath my feet. Holes appear in the bodywork. A bullet grazes the tip of my dirty boot.

I'm spotted. I need to act fast.

I drop flat onto the cabin, lean up to the windshield, and press my palm against it. Within five seconds, the glass is covered in a layer of black ice. The driver brakes and slows down, unable to see anything. I literally break the ice with my fist, dodge a silver bullet with my demon speed, then violently grab the passenger, who's still in human form, by the throat, propelling him backward onto the road. The guy tumbles and rolls on the concrete, screaming in pain before being hit by a car bumper that screeches to a stop. As the Gluttonfiend begins to transform, he passes under the wheels of another tanker truck, which conclusively settles his fate. Not very appetizing, this Gluttonfiend.

Jumping inside the cabin to the passenger seat, I deal with the driver, who points his revolver at me with one hand while gripping the wheel with the other. I disarm him with a vicious heel kick to his wrist and catch his firearm in mid-air, earning myself a racist insult. *"Fucking half-breed?"* Not very nice! I swiftly turn the gun around and put a silver bullet through the Sinner's temple.

Immediately, I throw the corpse out of its seat, sending it tumbling onto the road like his buddy the Gluttonfiend, and take his place just as the truck dangerously veers toward the central guardrail. Just before the tanker hits it, I hurry to turn the wheel to avoid a highway disaster. The massive vehicle straightens out just in time.

Three minutes later, I take an exit and soon park on the shoulder near a sunflower field. I step down from the cabin, walk around the van, open the rear doors, and draw my trusty Feather.

An unruly Envyfiend demon leaps out of the shadows roaring. I dodge a sharp tail swipe by spinning around, then swiftly behead it with a sword. One down!

I whistle to lure the others out. None of them join me. How rude. Am I not good enough for them or something?

"Come on, guys, don't be shy! I'm not going to bite, just decapitate!"

No response.

Fine, then. Since it's like that…

I summon an ice shield to protect myself from silver bullet impacts and climb into the van, brandishing Feather. They're about to meet their match.

Less than five minutes later, I emerge from the trailer, my jacket sticky with Sinner blood. No big deal, black on black works. Now, I just have to wait for the other Trackers to clean up after my mess.

I'm pleased with myself because I managed to save four human girls who were prisoners of those fucking traffickers who planned to sell them to sadistic demons. They're in zombie mode in the van since they were hypnotized by their captors. The girls are slightly injured, a few bruises here and there, but considering their situation, they're not doing too badly. My CIT colleagues will take care of them and erase their memories.

Leaning against the truck's bodywork with my ankles crossed, I light up another cigarette. Oh, I'll quit smoking one of these days… But not tonight. Right now, I'm savoring the famous smoke that symbolizes my small satisfaction of a job well done.

Taking a drag, I glance at the decapitated Envyfiend corpse on the ground. Then, I raise my head to the starry sky and exhale a long puff of smoke.

Truly, a beautiful night to die.

End of Book 1

Myrina and Kelen will return in Book 2, Myrina Holmes: Exquisite Corpses.

PLAYLIST

Chapter 2

Highway to Hell, AC/DC

Chapter 8

Would You Sleep with Me Tonight, Lady Marmelade
Naughty Girl, Beyoncé

Chapter 10

Baby Boy, Beyoncé

Chapter 23

Moonlight Sonata, Beethoven

Chapter 32

Rocky Road to Dublin, The Dubliners

Chapter 39

Johnny B. Goode, Chuck Berry

BONUS CHAPTER
SIN OF GLUTTONY

ROBYN

Wiping the glass I just washed behind my bar, I glare at the last two customers inside O'Brien's with exasperation. All the other idiots cleared out ages ago, but this couple is having a private after-hours affair just as closing time looms. And they've only ordered one drink, of course! Paid for by the lady with the white-streaked hair, to boot; I saw her slip two bills above the bill. The discount Casanova who hit on me in front of her is a miser—I could have bet on it. I can smell them from ten miles away.

What a jerk, seriously. *The customer is always right*, my ass!

I really should have hung a sign on the pub door that read, *Zero Tolerance for Assholes.*

Well, I should have known. Notice how it's always the loudmouth machos who can't zip up after coming back from the john. There should be a study on that. Maybe I'll write to a scientific journal with the idea.

I don't get what a gal like her is doing with a guy like that. Judging by her biker chick look, she seems to have just as much fire as I do. Don't judge a book by its cover, I guess.

They seem deeply engrossed in their conversation. They're speaking some bizarre language I've never heard in my life. At first, I thought it was Chinese, then it seemed like German, and now it sounds like Spanish. It makes no sense at all.

Truth be told, I've encountered a fair share of oddballs and shady characters in my life, but these two take the cake. They honestly give me the creeps. They're almost too good-looking to be real. Maybe they're aliens. Or androids? I don't trust them at all; they look like a villainous couple straight out of a cartoon where the evil princess plots a grand Machiavellian scheme like, *We will dominate the world and exterminate you filthy parasites!* The guy could be Gaston from *Beauty and the Beast*. The girl, a young and sexy Cruella de Vil from *101*

Dalmatians.

Anyway, I need to stop fantasizing and kick them out.

"Come on, lovebirds, closing time's approaching, so hit the road!" I shout from behind my bar, eager to see them leave.

The cocky brown-haired dude, thinking he's some kind of stud past his prime, gives me a smug look, which I shoot right back at him. The tall hot chick with purple eyes obediently gets up from her seat.

"All right, let's go. Thanks, miss, good night." She nods toward the discount Casanova. "Come on, Wills, move it."

The guy takes his sweet time getting up, shooting me a challenging look. Damn it, I should've spit in his Irish coffee. I resist the urge to stick my tongue out like my daughter would; admittedly, it would be a bit immature for a twenty-five-year-old barmaid.

I hope they never come back here!

Once the door closes behind them, I peek out the window to make sure they're gone.

On the pub parking lot, the guy named Wills—even his name screams jerk!—leers at the girl's butt as she walks ahead of him toward her motorcycle. What a loser. Oh well, the bike looks pretty good though, it looks like Val's bike.

The girl puts a cigarette to her mouth, and I see the guy raise his hand to light it. Huh, I didn't see him grab a lighter. I squint at his fingers. It's strange, it looks like a flame is coming directly from his—

My phone starts vibrating, drawing my attention to the pocket of my apron. I turn away from the window, answering with a big smile. Just seeing the wonderful name on my screen is enough to forget the hassle at work and lift my spirits.

"Hey, you."

"Just showered and waiting for you to come to bed, *cuore mio,*" purrs a warm, husky voice on the phone, sending shivers down to my core.

Did you catch that? My super-hot Italian boyfriend, who recently earned his degree in cunnilingus with a minor in languages, with honors, is missing me.

"Closing up and heading over, Val. Had a couple of duds lingering at the pub. Are you like lay down naked in bed, huh?"

"I'm not just *like* naked, Rob. I'm naked," he corrects matter-of-factly.

Mm. My eyelids grow heavy with desire. I moisten my lips as I walk toward the table of the two goofballs. I can picture him perfectly. I better hurry up; tonight, I plan on pursuing a doctorate in applied blow job techniques.

"I'm on my way, macaroni. Take the whipped cream out of the fridge in exactly ten minutes," I declare, tucking the girl's bills into my apron pocket.

"I don't have any whipped cream at home, Rob."

What? No whipped cream? I furrowed my brow, freezing in the middle of the room, dismayed by this unforeseen complication. I don't like it when things don't go as I've imagined. I have a very clear image in my head, and I absolutely must make it happen. It's a matter of my mental integrity; all my inner voices are adamant about this.

"In that case, I'll have to swing back home to grab a can of whipped cream before showing up at your place," I state firmly.

He sighs. Yep, I'm quite stubborn. It's only been two weeks since we officially got together, but my expired macaroni is starting to realize my character a bit more every day. He better not complain; I never hid from him what he was getting into by dating me.

The other day at the zoo, Anya told him, "Mom's like a pink, sweet, cotton candy. Once you've eaten it all, all that's left is the sticky stick. And when the stick hits your arm, it really hurts and even pulls out the hairs." You don't get the metaphor? Neither did I. Val looked as perplexed as I did at the time. Kids...

"Forget the whipped cream, *tesoro*, we don't need it to have fun."

"Don't mess with me, Val. I'm not giving up on the whipped cream. I want to gobble whipped cream off your dick, and I'm going to, damn it!"

I hear a little laugh on the phone. "Okay, what do I say to that? Deal, *piccola golosa.*"

I hang up, laughing myself. After putting the cash in the register and clearing the table, I return to the window. While I was on the phone with Valentin, the two customers vanished—the girl's motorcycle is gone. Instead, there's another guy, even weirder than them, sniffing the girl's cigarette butt. Probably a bum... Gross, what he's doing? I head to the pub's door, and when I open it three seconds later, the homeless guy is gone. I scan the parking lot with eyebrows raised in surprise, but I don't see him anywhere. Looks like he disappeared into thin air.

Super weird night!

I shrug, closing and locking the O'Brien's door. I quicken my pace, untie my apron, and turn off the lights.

After all, who cares about dumb customers and ghost bums? When you've got a double date with an Italian hottie and a can of whipped cream, you don't dwell on these kinds of details.

ACKNOWLEDGMENTS

Here we are, at the end of the first book of the *Myrina Holmes* saga. Soon, we'll meet our provocative demons again in a tumultuous second volume, *Exquisite Corpses*.

Since Kel stirred passions even before this novel was published, I'll start my acknowledgments by thanking two dear friends, Marie and Farah, who fiercely claimed him as their lover and left their Sinful marks on him. To thank and reconcile them, I've decided to compromise with this pact between us: I *split* my hero for them. I offer my lovely Marie the human form of Kel (which she can share with her co-lover Max if she wishes), and I give my wonderful Farah his demonic form, knowing their respective preferences. Anyway, what fun we had with our fantasies; Kelen Wills is a real pro at causing mischief! But jokes aside, your support and enthusiasm have deeply touched me. A huge thank you, girls!

And because it's obvious to me, I dedicate *Demons and Wonders* to both of you.

A heartfelt thanks also goes to my editor and accomplice, Sarah, who once again supports me in a new genre with her eternal kindness. The trust we've shared since *Prince Charming Exists! (He's Italian and a Hitman)* is so precious that sometimes I still can't believe it. *Demons and Wonders* is my fourth baby published in less than a year with Black Ink Editions, and the other two books of the *Myrina Holmes* saga will soon join it. It's pure joy to be part of this absolutely fantastic publishing house! As always, I'd like to thank the entire Black Ink team, with affectionate thoughts for Shelby, Noémie, and Max, who are all loves. A big thanks to Isabelle for her stylish trailer. I also applaud the cover art killer, Layla, who once again nailed it with this book's cover.

I also want to thank my husband, my son, my family, my in-laws, and my girlfriends. I'd like to send a special shout-out to my parents, who have been closely following my publishing adventures from the beginning. Thank you for always supporting me no matter what choices I've made in life. And thank you for teaching me that believing in your dreams can sometimes make them come true... It's still surreal to see my novels on your huge bookshelf, among those I've known since I was little. When I look at them, I think incredulously, "Wow, I wrote these?" Thanks to my dad for passing down his cheesy humor that seems to make a lot of readers laugh, and to my mom for always being there when I need her (which happens often). In short, thank you for being you. Not only do I love you, but you're the best parents in the world. (Mom, don't cry, okay!)

I also want to express my gratitude to the amazing women I've met in the publishing world these past few months. Nathalie, the talented creator of stunning video editing and fan art that amaze me every time. Aly, the Black Ink reviewer and ambassador, as wild and passionate as my Robyn. Gaëlle, my reader and reviewer friend with a heart of gold. My dear Eloïse, whom I adore. A shout-out to the most active members of my Facebook group, Anna Triss & Contes, as loyal as they are witty. I can't name you all, but you know who you are.

Thank you to my Wattpad followers who show up for every release and have flooded each chapter of *Myrina Holmes* with comments, votes, and compliments on the platform. I dove into the urban fantasy genre with both joy and hesitation, something I've wanted to explore for a while. It's your unwavering support that has fueled my writing.

And of course, thank you to all my readers, both longtime and new.

If you want to keep up with me on social media, I have a Facebook page, Anna Triss Author, and an Instagram account, anna.triss. I'm eager to hear your thoughts and comments on *Demons and Wonders*.

See you soon in *Exquisite Corpses*, and until then… behave, my little demons ;-)

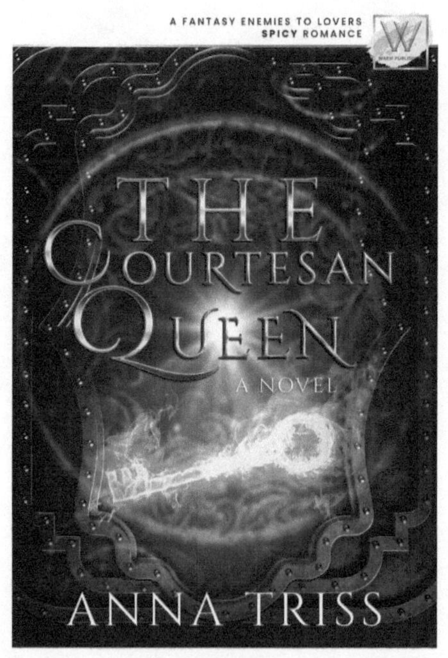
A FANTASY ENEMIES TO LOVERS
SPICY ROMANCE
THE COURTESAN QUEEN
A NOVEL
ANNA TRISS

Other novels from
WARM PUBLISHING

Scan to easily acess all of Warm Publishing books:

Join also our Facebook Group, Book Warmers, to get the lastedt updates and talk about books and more!

Falling for the Voice
by *Mag Maury*

The sexiest of surprises... and the most unbearable!

My plan was simple: Find a job quickly in order to make rent. And I found one. A waitressing job at the hottest pub in town!

Everything was going smoothly until he arrived: Matt. Sexy. Arrogant. Six feet three of muscles that drive women into a hysterical frenzy at every single one of his concerts.

This guy is really comfortable on stage and oh, so enticing. We girls can try to put him out of our minds but we end up wanting him anyway. And he knows it.

Except me, Charlotte. I say no!

Well... Maybe! After all, I have never really been good at resisting temptation...

My Hipster Next Door
by *Mag Maury*

In Liverpool, the barbershop Hipster Maniac is an institution. Run by three bearded, tattooed friends, it is the place to listen to great rock, get a trim, and have a drink.

But for Line, it also spelled trouble. For starters, when she first got to the neighborhood, she rear-ended Jordan's car, who turned out to be one of the three barbers. Then she discovered that they were neighbors in business and residence! So no way can she escape this muscle-flaunting, smoldering man who is covered in tattoos and... completely insufferable!

He draws her near only to push her away. He toys with her shamelessly. But worst of all he hates Christmas whereas that is Line's very favorite time of year!

Beneath a backdrop of festive fairy lights, intoxicatingly passionate kisses, and blistering banter... It's on!

The Cocky Heir
by *Ana K. Anderson*

She is about to get married. But not to him.

Quinn MacFayden, an accomplished expat businessman in New York, is set to return to Scotland in extremis to protect the precious family legacy. His 91-year-old grandfather is about to marry a perfect stranger sixty-six years his junior... And that is out of the question! Quinn swears it. Over his dead body will Dawn Fleming ever be part of the family!

But Dawn is not a future bride like the others. She is nowhere near the gold digger he imagined and, above all, she knows just how to stand up to him. And so a game of cat and mouse begins between them. A war with no holds barred and where surrender has never been so tempting...

My Stepbrother: A Sexual Revelation
by *Sophie S. Pierucci*

Cassie is a highly intelligent young woman... Too much so for her own good!

And she is as daunting as she is intriguing. Carl, the son of his father's second wife, would hardly say otherwise!

Carl is the exact opposite of his steady father. He is a player and a slayer. Afraid of nothing and no one. Except for Cassie when she asks him to introduce her to the pleasures of the flesh.

And when the situation gets out of control, it is too late to turn back, and the two lovers find themselves ensnared in forbidden passion. Forbidden by everyone: society, their parents, their friends.

But how to resist the desire that consumes them?

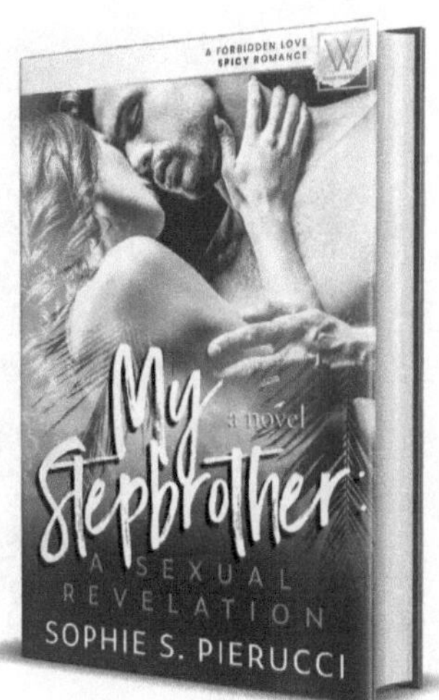

Roommate with my Boss
by *Erin Graham*

Boss, roommate, fake fiancé... real lover?

Étienne is cold, charismatic, and he never shies away from a challenge.

He masters everything down to the smallest detail... until a little accountant with an unlikely look and flowers in her hair inserts herself into his daily life.

She is whimsical, full of life, laughs at the rules and gets around them, talks all the time except about her past... and she drives him crazy. Yet, it's impossible to fire her.

She needs a job and a roof over her head; he needs a fake fiancée...
Is it a deal?

Your Power Over me
by *Missy Heart*

A family home heavy with secrets, a dangerously charismatic owner.

Will her arrival at Iron House be the end of her?

Ever since she was a teenager, Lovisa has known it: at Iron House, anything can happen, especially the worst.

However, when she is forced to return to the family home for her stepfather's funeral, her heart races: she is going to see him again, this "brother" who she never wanted and who yet turned her whole world upside down.

Now at the head of a drug cartel, authoritarian and brutal, Niklas is nothing like the teenager she knew nine years ago. At his side, Lovisa finds herself immersed in a harsh, ruthless—but fascinating—world.

Irremediably attracted to this man who wants her as much harm as good, will Lovisa manage to fight her unmentionable desires? Or will she give in to Niklas' magnetic darkness?

Touchdown
by *Sonia Birdy*

She's a runner, but the campus star quaterback runs faster than she does!

Rocky has had a chaotic life from which she concluded three fundamental things: life is a succession of problems to be solved, men are assholes to be avoided and promises are only binding on fools who want to believe in them. So, unlike the other girls on campus, boys are not a priority for her. Worse, she sees them as an obstacle to her success!

But during a student party, she meets Jude. Freshly transferred from Harvard to play on Brown's soccer team, Jude is the new star on campus. Handsome and inaccessible, he is the type not to get attached: the perfect candidate for a one-night stand.

But the chemistry is too strong. And though Rocky is determined to run away from him, he is determined to conquer her heart.

Kalliopee: A Princess's Sacrifice
by *Koko Nhan*

After years of violent battles, Kalliopee agrees to sacrifice her freedom by marrying the prince of the enemy kingdom in order to bring peace.

In a world where women are treated as slaves rather than wives, she is still delighted to be reunited with her first love, Karel.

However, life is unpredictable, and the horrors of war have transformed Karel into a tough and ruthless heir to the throne, who despises the Viridians more than anything. While he has no qualms about mistreating Kalliopee, his determination wavers when confronted with her striking eyes. In the midst of desire and animosity, schemes and plots, dreams and disillusionment, will the princess's heart endure the price of her liberty?

The Private Garden
by *Oly TL*

The most disturbing and transgressive of contracts...

Tiger Sexton seems to have it all. Charisma. Respect. Relentless business acumen. More fortune than he could spend in a life and a sublime wife, Sophia.

When Oceane is invited by Mrs. Sexton for a job interview in one of the restaurants that her husband gave her, the young French tourist knows nothing about this couple. Their name means

nothing to her, people are not her thing. She just wants a job, a place to live and to move on with her life... Sophia's proposal comes at the right time: the Sextons are looking for an *au pair.*

But by opening their doors to her, many other locks are likely to open. Is Oceane ready for this? And what about Sophia, and especially the Tiger lurking in this Secret Garden?

About the Author

Anna Triss devoured her first fantasy novel as a teenager and fell in love with this literary genre. This event marked the beginning of an unconditional passion: writing.

Enclosed in her little bubble, she escapes into her own universe thanks to her pen, guided by her imagination and madness. Publishing is a long-time dream come true.

With a degree in art history and archaeology, married and mother of a little boy, this passionate author lives in La Rochelle, France, where she writes intense stories populated by atypical heroes, always charismatic, often badass, with developed psychology. She writes in a variety of genres (fantasy, contemporary romance, urban fantasy, dark romance) and has several bestsellers to her credit, including The Courtesan Queen, an enemies-to-lovers fantasy romance tinged with magic and secrets. In addition to reading, Anna loves art, travel, TV shows, movies, and... dragons!